MW00893293

Legally Wedded

Legally Wedded

The Legally in Love Series

Jennifer Griffith

© 2016 by Jennifer Griffith

All Rights Reserved. No part of this book may be reproduced or transmitted in any form or by any means, electronic or mechanical, including photocopying, recording, or by any information storage and retrieval system without the written permission of the author, except in the case of brief passages embodied in critical reviews and articles.

ISBN: 1523271701
Published by Jennifer Griffith, Arizona, USA
http://authorjennifergriffith.com
ASIN: B01AIN936U
First Edition

This is a work of fiction. Names, characters, places and events are creations of the author's imagination or are used fictitiously. Any resemblance to actual persons, living or dead, events or locations is purely coincidental.

Cover art by Laura Lynn Tolman from a photo via Shutterstock.com

For Donna

You have a Heart of Romance

Chapter One

Morgan's mouth turned to cotton. "What? What do you mean I'm not getting the financial aid? I've had it the past three years." The walls of the office expanded and contracted. Morgan had to grip the desk. This was the absolute worst case scenario—especially since her grades tanked last spring and she lost her scholarship.

The financial aid clerk kept looking at her computer screen and adjusted her polo shirt with the embroidered Clarendon College logo. It barely stretched over her buxom frame. "I'm sorry, Miss Clark. The rules are the rules. Income limits apply. The tax records set the boundaries."

"I'm an accounting major. I know all about taxes." *Don't lecture me on taxes.* That was for her professors, not this dead-eyed clerk.

"Then you obviously understand that the student's ability to qualify for federal grants and loans depends wholly on the parents' previous year's income." This came at Morgan in a patronizing tone. "And you obviously know that the rules apply, even to you." The clerk smirked and then looked over Morgan's shoulder at the next person in line. "Next."

Shock and despair created a desperation in her.

"Wait. Wai-wai-wait." Morgan put on a fake smile. "Yes, I know there are rules. But the thing is, see, my mother had a major financial departure last year. After a lifetime of basically no income, she made a mint on her poetry book sales. *Frogs in the Sand.* Maybe you've heard of it?"

1

The clerk raised a ten-percent-interested eyebrow. "Everyone in the state of Oregon's had *Frogs in the Sand* shoved down their throats for the past eighteen months." She lifted one side of her upper lip, like the book was a piece of junk. Which it was.

"You see what I mean, then. That's never going to sell another copy again. Ever! That book was a total fluke." Morgan loved her mother, but the truth was, that book was lame. She had no idea why the TV talk show host ever mentioned it, let alone got a half a million people to buy it. "No one knows that fact more than you and I do, uh, Resistencia." Perfect name for a financial aid clerk. Resistance! "But what no one else knows is that my mother used the whole *Frogs* fortune to pay back rent, to fix her old car, and to pay bills my father left that have been dogging her for years. All that money is gone."

"Like a frog in the sand." The clerk smirked, still looking at her computer screen. No sympathy. Not even a drop. "Next."

There was nothing more to say. As she left, dejection turned Morgan's legs to cement and the marble floor of the Student Life Center to tar. In fact, she couldn't even trudge. It was more of a slog-through-sludge as she walked out into the overcast day to the parking garage and her old pickup.

Summer term kept the parking lot mostly empty, just like that financial aid office mostly emptied Morgan's hope of ever finishing her senior year. And if she never finished, she'd never get a job that paid well enough to put her sister Tory through school. And Tory had already been waiting a full two years to start classes. And even though by next year, Mom's bad finances would allow Tory to qualify for a grant, both girls would have to be working to cover rent, and two part-time jobs and two grants would never cover both rent *and* tuition at Clarendon for both of them.

It was hopeless. Hope drained from her, like oil from

her truck's leaky engine.

She started the engine—on the third try—and then gripped the steering wheel and slammed her hand against the side of the wheel in an angry rhythm. "Stupid, stupid, stupid!" Stupid time-sucking job, stupid lost scholarship, stupid financial aid rules.

She pulled out into the winding roads of campus, through the beech trees and oaks and pines that on most days made Clarendon College so charming. Charm and prestige: it's what had drawn her here. Well, that and the scholarship—which she no longer had.

Honestly, it wasn't like she'd had any choice about the stupid part-time job last year. She'd had to take that ridiculous job last semester to pay for housing when rent prices close to campus skyrocketed. Working at Veg-Out escalated quickly from part time, and then it had taken all her evenings which meant her study time. Her scores suffered. Her scholarship evaporated when her grades dropped. And still she only made enough money to afford rent in the worst apartment complex on the wrong side of the tracks in Starry Point.

Not that Starry Point necessarily had a wrong side. It was a pretty posh town, with the narrow exception of Estrella Court, where she lived.

She pointed her truck toward there now, hating how naïve she'd been—thinking the letter she'd gotten denying her financial aid application had been in error. What a fool! What a ditz! Because she, Morgan Clark, the accounting department's once-favorite daughter, of all people should have known.

For the zillionth time, she cursed all those stupid frogs and their sand.

She jammed the truck into park and sat in the parking lot of Estrella Court for a moment. She'd have to calm down before going inside. She didn't want Tory to see her upset because then she'd have to tell her sister about this setback, and she'd rather not until after she'd figured out a solution. Because this affected Tory as much as it affected Morgan. Maybe more.

She rested her chin on her elbow, which was leaning on the dusty window ledge of the old yellow Dodge that swilled gasoline like a Kentucky wino drank bourbon. That's where the other half of her paycheck last year had gone—to feed this truck's drinking habit. Ah, yet another no-win situation: she had to have the truck to get to work, but she had to work to keep the truck running. But if she'd lived closer to campus, she could have just walked, or ridden a bike, like the rest of the environmentally-conscious Oregonians did.

Man, money troubles just sucked.

She got out of the truck and slammed the door so hard that dust rose from beneath the crack around the hood.

"Whoa, there. You'll make it fall to pieces," a guy's voice joked. "It looks like it's vintage. Might be worth something someday."

Morgan shook her head and tried to see who was talking to her from over by the collective mailboxes. It wasn't Mr. Reeves, the cranky old maintenance guy she loved, or any of the other usual suspects at Estrella Court. He was tall—she could see that—and held a laundry basket. Did he live here?

"Not with the miles it's got. It's worth about half what it'll cost to have it towed to the wrecking yard." She got close enough to see him at last, and the cotton mouth she suffered at financial aid came back. He was about a hundred times better looking than any of the guys she'd ever seen roaming the weedy sidewalks of Estrella Court. Okay, maybe a thousand times better looking. She'd never been remotely good at talking to guys, especially gorgeous ones. If she'd seen him before she spoke to him, she probably wouldn't have said anything.

"Hi. I'm Josh. Just moving in." He patted the laundry

basket, which appeared to be full of kitchen and bathroom supplies instead of laundry stuff. "You live here?"

"Since January." Boom! She'd eked out two words. This was a miracle. Maybe she'd try for a few more. "You going to school at Clarendon?"

"Re-enrolling this fall. Took a couple of gap years. Well, assuming everything comes together I'll start up. You in school, too?"

This was a complex question. It dumbfounded her. *Yes, for three years, but not this year, unless everything in the universe turns on its ear and I get the funds to continue?* How could she explain when she didn't even know herself?

She probably stood there too long looking stupid because finally Josh nodded. "Uh, okay. I'm just going to head up to my apartment. See you around."

And he was gone.

And Morgan was a dimwit. Couldn't even answer a simple question. She wanted to do one of those face-palm things, but there was a chance he'd still be at his door and see her, so she resisted. A moment later, she was at her own door shoving the key into the lock.

The apartment smelled like cherry candles and home perm solution. Not a great combo. Tory must be home. Morgan went in the kitchen and saw her sister there, squirting chemicals from a clear plastic bottle onto curlers in an elderly woman's hair. She caught the drips with a wash cloth.

"You get things straightened out on campus?" Tory asked. "It's okay. Mrs. Reeves took out her hearing aids while I put on the solution. You can speak freely."

Mrs. Reeves was reading a Hollywood gossip magazine. Morgan waved to her, and then went to the fridge for an apple from their tree back home.

"Not yet. But I'm close. The bureaucrats want to work against people."

"It's to protect their kingdom."

"Precisely." Morgan bit the apple. She had to change the subject. "Did you see the new guy?"

"I've already nicknamed him—James Bond in Jeans."

"He doesn't have a British accent."

"He doesn't? Wait. You talked to him? Shut the front door!" Tory dropped the plastic clamp she was using to enclose the woman's curlers in a plastic bag for catching the fumes. "You're not serious."

"I talk to guys." Morgan tried to sound defensive, but she knew Tory knew the truth. "When they're related to me or way out of my age range."

"Exactly." Tory shook her head. "So what did he say? Was he as dreamy to talk to as he is to look at?"

"Dreamy? Uh, totally." Morgan had gone into a dream-like trance, that was for sure. "More like coma-inducing."

"Oh, no. Not the Conversation Coma." Tory sighed. It was legendary, Morgan's inability to talk to men.

"Sad but true." Morgan dropped onto a kitchen chair and took another bite of the apple. "But I at least managed a couple of sentences before its onslaught. And he seemed pretty nice." She shrugged. "I'm sure he has a girlfriend. Any guy that good-looking has a girlfriend."

"Don't go all sour grapes. You don't even know—unless you asked. Did you ask?"

Morgan shook her head. "Be serious."

"Okay, okay. But did you at least get his name?"

"Joshua Hyatt." He hadn't said his full name, but she'd seen it on his mailbox—and taken note, of course.

Tory set the timer on the stove and then pantomimed twenty minutes to Mrs. Reeves before saying, "Josh Hyatt. Why have I heard that name before?" She looked at the ceiling. "Oh, I don't know. But if he's half as nice on the inside as he looks on the outside, you're in trouble."

"Me? Why not you?" Morgan knew this guy would never take an interest in her. Not now, after that neon

Vacancy sign had lit up her eyes when he asked her a simple question.

"Because I met someone, too." Tory looked smug. She met someone new all the time. It baffled Morgan. "He's at the theater. I'm making a Hamlet, Prince of Denmark, costume for him."

"You can sew now?"

"How hard can it be? I'm up to the challenge. Especially if it means spending time with this guy getting his measurements."

"Does this guy have a name?" Morgan raised an eyebrow of interest. The truth was, she was kind of glad Tory relinquished her I-saw-him-first rights to Josh Hyatt. Not that it mattered.

"Let's just call him Hamlet for now. Until things get more serious."

In her bedroom, Morgan let out a long breath she didn't know she'd been holding. She didn't have time to think about good-looking guys. She had a huge problem to solve—with only days until school started. Her copy of *Frogs in the Sand* ribbitted at her from the bookshelf, mocking her pain. When in the history of Oregon had a book of poetry been a runaway bestseller?

Never. Not until this stupid book ruined her life.

She flipped through its pages. If her mom hadn't dedicated the book to Morgan and Tory, Morgan would have dropped it in the garbage and set the contents of the can on fire.

Such. A. Killer.

And now she had to go to work—at a job where she was required to wear roller skates.

Oh, heart. She'd been so close, so very close to finishing her accounting degree. And now unless she could figure out how to come up with the remaining five thousand dollars she needed by the end of September, which was the last day tuition could be paid, that chance was basically everlastingly lost, as was Tory's chance at ever starting college and moving on from sewing costumes and doing home perms.

Stupid frogs.

Morgan kicked imaginary sand on her bedroom carpet and grabbed her hot pink uniform for Veg-Out, the vegan drive-in where she worked—probably for the rest of forever. Or until her ankles gave out.

Chapter Two

Josh chucked his mail key and laundry basket on the ratty couch. Again? Still nothing from the government? He'd changed his address with them as soon as he knew he'd be moving here weeks ago, and he was still waiting for word. There should have been an approval. His appeal was airtight. They had to give him the grant this time.

Because he absolutely had to start school this semester.

And, *ugh*. What was that smell? Was it here when he signed the rental agreement? It smelled like thousand-year-old cooking oil and burnt popcorn. He opened three windows, hoping to air the place out.

It was a far cry from the college brochure's depiction of the lush living quarters at Clarendon College. But it was what he could afford: a time warp of brown shag carpet and brass and glass decor that looked like it had come straight out of a K-Mart in the 1980s.

If the whole concatenation of Hyatt family millionaires could see him now…

Well, they weren't millionaires—yet. They'd have to wait for old Bronco Hyatt to finally kick the bucket to get their share of his inherited fortune. Not that Bronco was anywhere close to letting the Grim Reaper take him as harvest. And probably none of the other family members were looking forward to it fondly, like Josh was. Okay, fine. Truthfully, he wasn't wishing for his father's early demise—just the demise of a few of his more tightly held preconceived notions about how Josh ought to be living his life.

As a plumber.

Did Josh strike anyone as a plumber?

No. Especially not himself.

The fresh air did wonders for the burnt popcorn smell, but that oil was probably here for the duration. At least when he set up his hobby in the second bedroom no one would notice the smell of the compost barrel he was planning to use. That was a plus to living in this dive, as was the price of rent, and the proximity to the ocean—if not campus. And the girls at the mailbox weren't bad. Not that he was noticing.

His phone chimed a text.

Brielle: *Hey. You get moved in? I'm about ready to go to the airport. I can meet you at the curb in front of my apartment in ninety minutes.*

Josh clenched his jaw. Ninety minutes to Brielle's place outside Portland, and then to the airport. And then, it was over. For a year. Or maybe forever. A year was a long time. Too long. Unless he could convince her—

Josh: *I'll come upstairs and help you bring down your luggage.*

Brielle: *Always the gentleman. xox*

The x and o made him think of Brielle's kiss, her embrace. And how fleeting they were.

***

"Joshua Hyatt, I'm going to miss you." Brielle's words flowed through him, the sweetest honey. "But this year is going to fly, and then we'll be together." She placed a soft kiss on his lips, and an ache erupted in his chest, one that he knew wouldn't stop until she came back to him.

The bustle of Portland International faded to a din as he looked at her freckles and spiral curls. "Don't overpay for a leather jacket while you're there." He tweaked her nose. It might not be romantic words for a farewell, but everything else had been said—including when he'd asked her to stay and she'd said no. It had been half-hearted—for both of them.

"Germany isn't exactly known for its leather."

"Okay. Cuckoo clock, then."

"That's never been my weakness. Wooden birds on springs."

That was another thing he liked about Brielle. She was so practical, never awed by the trivial things of life. She looked at the big picture, which was probably why she was leaving him here to spend the next year off eating bratwurst and schnitzel and saving the world from extremists while he tried, again, to get himself back into school.

Meanwhile, Brielle was done. Just graduated, and off starting a real-life, big time job. In an embassy. In Europe.

The gap between them widened yet another span.

"You're going to have a lot of amazing experiences." He spun it to a positive.

"So are you."

Right. At home. In Oregon. While she was living the diplomat's life, meeting with foreign leaders, making decisions, and maybe going to Wagnerian operas on the weekends if she had time in her packed professional schedule.

"No, I'm being serious. You'll be in school, which is amazing after all you've been through. You're going to be so amazing that Clarendon College is going to put your picture on their next recruiting brochure. You're going to be living in Starry Point, which is—just amazing."

"Three amazings."

"Probably more like three hundred. Trust me."

He did. "I do."

She threw her arms around his neck and pressed herself against him. She felt amazing. "So you trust me now, eh? Including when I say that when old Bronco Hyatt sees the incredible success his son is having at one of the most exclusive, top-ranked programs in the nation, that he'll roll over and relent? Bring you back into the Hyatt fold?"

Josh smirked at that. "Bronco Hyatt isn't the type to relent."

"Neither are you. I think that's what I admire about you most, Josh." Her words sent a tingle through him. "You set your mind on what you want, and no matter what the naysayers throw at you, you stand your ground. You're finishing your degree—in the major you chose: foreign policy. You pretty much told everyone else where they could put their complaints about your choice, even when your dad cut you off. You stood firm." She pressed her mouth to his and let it linger in a kiss of passion—finally. Josh returned it until she pulled away and with half-lidded eyes said, "What a man."

"No overpaying for Toblerone." He murmured this in her ear. He kissed her again, just as they were calling her flight. She hadn't even been through security yet. He'd detained her as long as possible now.

"I have to go."

"I know." He took her hand and looked into her anxious face. "Should I wait for you?"

"You mean to watch the plane take off? That'd be nice. Sometimes there are mechanical problems, and passengers get sent home."

"No, no." It wasn't coming out right. He wasn't prepared to say all this, even though the weight of the issue had pressed on him ever since she signed papers to go work at the embassy two months ago. "Should I *wait* for you?" Something in him refused to be plainer in speech. She had to understand his meaning. His face, he was sure, was pleading with her.

Brielle was the most incredible woman he'd ever met. Sharp as nails, gorgeous—serious and driven and real. She made him want to be more, do more. Most of all, she'd stuck by him through thick and thin.

She was looking up at him with her softest face. "It's only a year. And by then you'll be a year closer to your degree. We're young. There's no huge rush. We have forever, and I want you—the best version of you, when we're both ready to be who we are for each other. I'm going to grow a lot, and so will you, and we're just getting ourselves all settled and set. I want you to be satisfied with me. Things will be calmed, and everything will smooth out." She gave a wan smile. "It feels like a long time, though. I know." She patted his hand that was clutching hers as if she were dropping from a cliff and only he could keep her aloft.

"I swear, I'll make progress while you're gone." This wasn't the vow he'd wanted to be making to her, exactly, but he wanted something for them both to hang onto while they were apart. "I've been accepted to the program. They're holding my spot."

She gave him a reassuring look. "And it's the best program in the country, hands down. I know I wasn't accepted there." Now she was flattering him, but he couldn't fault her. Her fading away from him gave her a filtered perfection, and she could do no wrong. "It's a major step in the right direction for us."

If Bronco hadn't been such a blazing jerk, they wouldn't be in this situation right now, and Josh might even be done with school and boarding the plane with Brielle to Germany instead of getting left behind, missing the adventure that he and Brielle had outlined for their lives together. In some ways, he couldn't believe she'd stuck by him through all that family drama, through the fight and the estrangement and the threats from his dad that ended in Josh finally being disowned. Josh had dated a hundred girls at least, and none of them would have touched the chaos of his family with a ten-foot pole.

13

Brielle's commitment to him through it all proved many things—that she did love him, was willing to sacrifice for him, and that she was unlike any other girl he'd ever dated, in that she didn't care whether he was the son of Bronco Hyatt or not, and didn't give a rip whether he was going to inherit a cent from his dad.

This was the woman for him. Now he just needed to turn himself into the man for her.

"I'll call you."

"Maybe you shouldn't. I'll be sequestered. It's not going to be a place where I can have a lot of outside communication."

What? She hadn't told him that. Sure, he knew that she'd been hired to work at the embassy, but it wasn't like she was going into the CIA, or anything. Undercover, deep silence, whatever.

Or was it?

"Don't look so alarmed. I'll find a way to keep in touch. Actually, snail mail is probably the most secure way these days. Watch for letters from me." She glanced over her shoulder at the line at security. She really did have to go.

"Can I write to you?" Or was her address there some kind of secret? Why hadn't they discussed this before? She should have told him. He might not have taken it well, of course.

"I really don't know yet. Wait to hear from me."

He nodded. She kissed him one last time. It was a good kiss, the kind that went all the way to his toes. It reassured him more than all her words or lack of them. She did love him, and what she'd implied was right: she wanted the best, mature version of him, the one ready to be her match when their time came.

Determination poured through him like wet cement that insta-dried, solidifying his resolve. *I'm going to be that man for her, no matter what it takes.*

She bustled through security. He stood watching until she went through the X-ray, put her shoes back on, and disappeared around the corner to the international flights concourses, on her way to her direct flight to Munich. Or München, as she called it. German. He'd never learn it.

Or maybe he would. Because he was going to finish his degree in foreign policy faster than any student at Clarendon College had ever matriculated. He'd double up on credits, skip sleep, go nights and summers. Because the sooner he finished, the sooner he'd have his job, and Brielle would finally give him the yes he craved.

***

"So, that's what I'm going to do." Josh plunked down his glass, sitting back and folding his arms over his chest. Noise from the garlic-infused Italian restaurant made it so he'd had to yell his grand scheme to his brother over the din. It sounded a little less grand when yelled.

Chip frowned and nodded, chewing the last bite of his pizza. "Well, it's a great idea ..."

"But? I hear a but." Josh pulled his own frown. He came to the one brother who was still talking to him — the only one who dared to defy old Bronco's edict of shunning the black sheep of the family — for positive reinforcement. "I'm covering all the bases."

"Financial, too? Clarendon isn't exactly — well, you remember from when you were there before, it was no cheaper-chicken school. Maybe start back at the community college and get some generals out of the way since Bronco won't back you. You could get back into the study mode. It's been a few years since you were in school."

Josh heard the implied *What if you flunk out?* but sent it packing. "How do you think I got into the Department of Foreign Policy at Clarendon? There were exams for even applying." And they weren't for the academic slouch.

15

Chip took a deep breath and wadded up a napkin. "Well, there's no question you're up to it intellectually. Of all us brothers, you're the one who won at chess."

"And Scrabble. And Monopoly. And Risk."

"And shut up." Chip jarred the table, making the ice in Josh's glass rattle. "I was probably the most shocked of all of us when Dad went on his wild tear about your becoming a journeyman plumber. Ha! After forcing Rocky to go to medical school? And Wyatt through the bar exam?"

It killed Josh even now to think about his dad's volatile decision, insisting Josh quit school after his sophomore year when he decided to change majors from bio-tech engineering. Getting so upset when he met Brielle and changed his major to foreign policy that he demanded Josh change back to his old major or quit school and go off to become a plumber or suffer the wrath. What a despot.

"And you into veterinary school." Josh wasn't the only one who'd suffered their dad's tyrannical whims.

"All of us, way out of our elements."

"But you're happy." Josh shrugged. "So that's what matters."

"Yeah." Chip drained his glass and refilled it. "I've got a great wife, anyway, and that's where the real happiness lies." Chip did have a great wife. Heather made his world go round, and everyone knew it, just like Brielle made Josh's spin. "So, if going back to school and studying foreign policy is what it takes to get this girl, then go for it. Make it happen. If you're sure of her, and this is what you've got to do, then I'm here for you. I'll back you up."

Josh relaxed. "Thanks, bro." For the first time in months, maybe years, it was nice to have someone in his family say they were on his side. "How's Heather holding up under the pressure?"

"Like a champ. She doesn't even see the photographers anymore. It's like they're part of the landscape."

Being a Hyatt, marrying into the family, had its pros

and its cons — that was for sure. Josh would be asking a lot of Brielle when they finally made things official. Whether they were the estranged members of the dynasty or the favorite son and daughter-in-law duo, they'd get their share of the harsh glare of the spotlight.

"Brielle will handle it well. Like a boss."

Chip toasted to that, and then it was time to go back to that '80s dive in Starry Point, which, when he thought about it, was another upside to his new digs: no Hyatt-hunting paparazzi would ever think to look for him there, even if they got wind he'd enrolled at Clarendon College.

If, that is, his financial aid ever came through and he could actually officially enroll.

Chip's face clouded. "Hate to point out the elephant in the room, but how are you going to pay for this scheme?"

That was the kicker. "I'm in the process of working it out. Eventually the government grant should come through. I've appealed. I should hear from them any day now. They're going to see reason, I'm sure." First they denied based on Bronco Hyatt's earnings. So Josh appealed, saying he was not living with Bronco and was financially independent of him. They said it didn't matter and denied him again. Next, he'd gone into his dad's financials and verified that Bronco didn't claim Josh on his taxes as a dependent. Josh rolled his eyes. At least the man had the integrity to drop that ruse. If he wasn't going to pay a cent for Josh's maintenance or education, or even invite him for dinner once a year, he shouldn't get a tax break based on him. Armed with that argument he'd appealed.

The grant people should see that. It was common sense.

Now if the letter would just come. He'd check the mailbox again as soon as he got home.

Chapter Three

Morgan's anxiety didn't let her relax, even on the sand of Cannon Bay with its regular, soothing waves and view of the eternal Haystack Rock.

"I think I'm getting a sunburn." She couldn't just sit here, frying her skin while all these worries nudged at her. She needed to do something about them.

"This is Oregon. It's cloudy. No sunburns." Tory leaned back on the sand and closed her eyes. They always repeated this fallacy to each other—usually right before they hit lobster red.

Summer was almost over now, and they'd decided to come for one last warm day to Starry Point's closest beach, Cannon Bay. Morgan needed the waves to calm her stress, and it had been totally working—until she made the mistake of looking at her phone to check on the books she'd need for her classes in a moment of false hope that she'd somehow get this problem solved.

Stupid book prices! Why did the college allow the professors to get away with that? Selling their own authored books for prices like that. If she were in charge...

She'd never be in charge. They didn't put college drop-outs in charge of universities. It just wasn't done. And with every passing day, that status seemed more and more likely to be her destiny.

Dang it. Yeah, the waves were now stirring her up. "I'm done here. Let's go home." She dragged her sister up.

"What? But I still have twenty minutes on this side. I'm going to have a sunburn on the backs of my legs and not on the fronts. I'll be like some kind of warped candy cane." Tory followed along, dangling her sandals in her hand, still complaining. "The rejected kind they sell for five cents at the factory seconds store." They crossed the rocky part of the beach, pausing to put on shoes, then the headed over the driftwood area.

Morgan took one last glance at the beach over her shoulder. "Summer's over. You can play like it's camouflage for the Christmas decorations they're already putting out for sale at ThrifteeMart."

"Exactly. So, hey. What are you in such a rush about?"

"I think the mail is here now. I want to see if the college sent me anything." Financial aid decision reversal, scholarship decision reversal, tuition waiver for being awesome—any of those would do.

"Oh, the mail." Tory hung on the vowel. "Or do you mean the m-a-l-e?"

It took Morgan a second to follow the insinuation. "Oh. Well, if you're hinting at Joshua Hyatt, I haven't thought about him." Much. Maybe only six or seven times. The smile he'd given her when she talked about her truck—just the memory of it sent a jolt of high voltage through her.

"Sure you haven't." Tory plopped down in the truck. "I know you noticed his very good smile."

"I did not." How did Tory know? Morgan pumped the gas pedal twice before turning the key. "Okay, fine. Maybe his smile did cross my mind. You're right. It's a very good smile."

"Truth." Then Tory took a phone call from someone in the Hamlet cast, and Morgan was alone with her thoughts and the exhaust fumes of the truck until they got home. She did not let her mind stray to Josh's smile, or his teeth, or his other attractions, at least not for more than half of the drive. She limited herself.

And dang it. Why did Tory have to even bring up Josh? It was so pointless. After the Conversation Coma

19

she'd slipped into, he was never going to give her a second thought, let alone the seventh, or seventeenth, she was giving him. She'd just look like a spot of white-out to him, like she did to every other guy she might see as interesting.

Usually her comfort in these situations was that she probably wouldn't see the guy again. But in this case, he lived a few doors down. It was almost inevitable she'd run into him sooner or later, and her brain would go blank, and he'd think of her as just that—a blank.

They hit a pothole, and the nonexistent shocks on the truck magnified it. Tory dropped her phone for a second, and then she picked it up, still talking, not even missing a beat. Tory could talk to anyone. She just said whatever she was thinking.

How would that be? Morgan might never know.

Well, except there was that one time. It was her sophomore year, and she'd just gotten a test back in her Business Practices 465 class, and there was a whole section graded unfairly, and she was furious. On the way out of class that good-looking senior guy had said, "How'd you do on the test?" and Morgan had just launched into a tirade. For once in her life, she didn't think about what she was saying in front of a guy, she just went on a roll. "Glad I asked," he'd said, kind of laughing. "You want to talk about it more over dinner?"

Morgan went to dinner with him. And while there, she'd clammed up again. Disaster. He never called for another date.

That pretty much described most of her social experiences in college. She knew she was pretty. Guys hit on her often enough. Her quietness just seemed to shut them down after a few minutes.

Josh Hyatt was no exception.

They pulled into Estrella Court, and Tory stayed put in the truck, still talking to Hamlet, but she made an aside to Morgan. "Go get your m-a-l-e."

Morgan rolled her eyes and hoisted her beach bag out of the truck bed. Sand silted off the tote. In her rush, she'd driven home in her swimsuit, not bothering to throw on a wrap. With the beach less than a mile from her place, what was the point?

At the mailbox, she found nothing but a pizza coupon and their utilities bill—which made her choke. "What in the—"

"Got your highest offer ever from the modeling agency?" Up walked Josh Hyatt, swagger and charm emanating from him like the sun's rays. "Because if not, they should be pounding on your door."

Despite the charm, that was the lamest pickup line ever. Somehow it disarmed her. She could answer, for once.

"Ha, ha." She waved the electric bill in his face. "Just the diametric opposite of that. Someone wants to charge me for my hairdryer usage, not pay me for it."

Josh was looking her up and down. "Their mistake."

Suddenly, Morgan became conscious that she wore very little clothing, and this James Bond in Jeans was taking stock of her figure, sunburn and all. At least he wouldn't see the blush blazing on her face for the sunburn.

She had to go on the offense or she'd clam up again. "You must like your mailbox." She shoved her pizza coupon in her tote. "Mine never does anything but make me irritated."

Josh blinked, as though it took effort to stop looking at her, and started filtering through his key ring. "I'm waiting for some paperwork. You know, school stuff."

"Don't remind me. I'm about ready to take a bulldozer to the financial aid office."

"You, too?" He stopped messing with his keys.

"They're my chief persecutors." She sighed. She was exaggerating about the bulldozer, but not much.

"Right?" He looked at her like they'd just forged some kind of bond. The light in his face drew her full attention. "I mean, who do they think they are, playing God with our futures?" He took a step toward her, energy filling his frame. She could feel the indignation of injustice coming off him. He must feel as strongly about this as she did.

"A lot of it seems so arbitrary and, frankly, dissing the economically downtrodden."

"Exactly!" He took another step toward her. "It's almost like you have to figure out a way to cheat the system to get what ought to be fair."

She sighed, and it felt heavy. "Do you know, if your parent makes over a certain amount of money, you can't get financial aid—even if you've never taken a cent from her to pay for college? Does that seem right?"

"Preach, sister." He wagged his head back and forth. "I mean, if we're over eighteen, aren't we allowed to declare ourselves adults and financially emancipated? When does it end?"

"Twenty-four." While baking on the beach today, Morgan researched the rules the financial aid clerk foisted on her yesterday. Every new one she read was a kick in the gut.

"Precisely." Josh shook his head. "I was trying to wait it out, myself. Couldn't stand the delay any longer."

So, that meant he was still under twenty-four—and dealing with parents and finances and a strong desire to finish school, too. He looked pretty frustrated at the situation. Maybe they did have something in common.

"You wait long?"

"Just since I was nineteen, when my dad decided to disown me for not wanting to be a plumber."

Morgan choked a little. "You're not being serious."

"Dead serious." He shook his head. "And speaking of dead, don't suggest an untimely death. I've already mentioned it to him, and I'd be imprisoned immediately as the only suspect with motive."

She laughed a half laugh. Poor guy. It sounded like

maybe his dad was his chief antagonist—and that would be far worse than Resistencia and her army of automatons at the financial aid office. Her heart went out to him.

"I'm racking my brain to figure out some way around it—besides the bulldozer." She kind of couldn't believe she was sharing this personal stress with a total stranger. Might not be prudent. But tuition was almost due, and it sounded like he might be in the same soup as she was. Maybe he'd have some insight.

"I've been the rounds on this. Believe me. It seems like, short of petitioning Congress, the only solution is either to get married or resort to identity theft." He half-punched the brick wall, looking frustrated. "See, the way I figure it, if I could find an illegal alien whose fake ID shows he's been orphaned..."

Morgan lowered her voice and looked back and forth surreptitiously. "Shhh. I might know a guy. After all, I've been living at Estrella Court a while now. Good place for contacts."

At this, Josh gave a hearty laugh. "I'm half-serious."

"So am I."

"You might come in handy." He raised an eyebrow and looked her up and down once again. This sent her spinning wildly into a self-conscious shell. She tugged a towel from her bag and wrapped it around herself. He looked slightly disappointed. He opened up his mailbox, took out some pieces of mail, and wadded up the pizza coupon. They were done here, and he started walking toward the apartments.

"But seriously." She hoisted her tote bag up onto her shoulder and started walking toward her apartment. "Why go the route with a felony when you could just qualify for grants by proposing to your girlfriend?" They strolled through the courtyard portion of Estrella Court, past the dead landscaping plants and live weeds. "That seems like the better route, and ends with a kiss and a big fat check."

23

Tory would be astonished that Morgan had mustered the nerve to ask about his girlfriend, even in this oblique way.

"Not really feasible."

Vagueness. Not satisfying at all. With all the courage her soul could dredge up she asked the follow up question, even though her cheeks burned as the words came out. "Why not?"

Josh stopped beside Morgan at her door. "Well, she's out of the country—for a year." This seemed to make him sober. "And she's the academic type, wants to wait until we're both done with all our schooling before we make any big decisions."

Right. Morgan's heart deflated. The heart which she'd foolishly allowed to expand in the last five minutes of talking—actually talking!—with Josh Hyatt and seeing his smile and the way his eyes had lingered on her face. He had a girlfriend. A serious one. They'd talked marriage. She'd postponed it, but he'd been in deep enough that he'd brought up the subject. It was stupid of Morgan to even let a cubic centimeter of helium float her balloon of hope.

She'd better not show how bummed she was. "Well, then, you'll just have to find some girl as financially desperate as you are who's willing to fake a sham marriage for the next year, or else you're basically stuck with either patricide or ID theft." She gave her most nonchalant shrug, hoping he wouldn't put two and two together that she was in a financially desperate bind as well and realize she was throwing herself at him.

Meanwhile, the outrageous electricity bill she'd picked up at the mailbox was burning a hole in her hand, and she hoped he didn't see it, or hear the distant sound of frogs in the sand, mocking her with their empty croaks.

"Well, if you run across any desperate friends, introduce me." He smirked, and she went into her apartment, flooded with a mixture of relief and disappointment—and fighting the instinct to be hurt.

Chapter Four

Josh splashed cold water on his face. He wished it were ice water. And he needed a full shower of it after standing there next to that swimsuit model, with all her sympathy and good humor about his dilemma, looking like she'd stepped right off the cover of a magazine to stare into the depths of his soul.

But it was weird. When the conversation ended, and he'd had such a rush from it and how funny and sharp she was while looking so gorgeous, she'd looked a little sad. He didn't know why. Women—what man ever understood them? *If you have any desperate friends, introduce me.* That's what he'd said. How could that bug her?

Well…

He shook himself. He was over-thinking it. Better not allow himself to notice her too much. She was way too fresh, and his wounds were pretty raw from saying goodbye to Brielle. If he wasn't careful, he'd be tempted to go on some kind of secretive, behind-Brielle's-back rebound and possibly hurt the girl.

Ha. As if. As if a girl like that *could* be hurt by Josh. She surely had stadiums full of men lining up to get a chance at her. He was just flattering his own ego.

The truth was, he used to have to worry about things like that—back when he was Joshua Hyatt, heir to Hyatt Holdings. Now he was a penniless guy at the bottom of nobody's totem pole yet. The kind of guy girls should see a *play at your own risk* label affixed to.

Not that he was a total loser. After his dad pretty much kicked him to the curb, forcing him to drop out of

Clarendon, Josh hadn't just sat around playing video games for the next three years. He'd had a full-time job, even though minions from Hyatt Holdings had been working against him when he was first trying to find one, poisoning the well at any job interview Josh had set up—until he finally got his current position as the biologist's assistant at the water treatment plant, counting bacteria through a microscope all day.

When Bronco Hyatt went on a search and destroy mission, he didn't mess around. It wasn't entirely impossible that Bronco was behind this whole financial aid roadblock Josh kept running into—and would keep running into until the government didn't let Bronco use that same tactic anymore.

Man! Twenty-four! Like the girl at the mailbox said, he had to be twenty-freaking-four to not be tied to those apron strings anymore. Boggled the mind. That was still two whole years off. Brielle wouldn't seriously wait another two full years for him to even start on the foreign policy credits he needed. He'd already postponed classes for three, and she was not exactly the most patient person he'd ever met, not that she was chomping at the bit to move their relationship forward in the way Josh wanted to, but she did want them to be together—working side by side. And that was close to the same thing, close enough for Josh for now.

Two more years. He punched the wall.

Worse, that letter from the mailbox was waiting for him. He couldn't open it while he'd been standing there talking to the hot girl. A man should be happy to do any number of things while a girl in a swimsuit was standing there watching him, but opening bad news from the federal government was not one of them.

Because in his heart, he knew the letter held nothing but bad news.

Josh eyed the brown government envelope on the ugly

brass and glass table. He could almost hear it singing a funeral dirge at him, mocking his struggle.

He went to the fridge and popped open a Coke. Then he sat down at the table across from it, staring at the letter while he sipped the cold drink and thought about the consequences of either outcome.

If it had good news, he'd be paying tuition, starting classes, moving — ultimately — toward life with Brielle. Along with that, he'd be showing his dad and all his fear-riddled satellites that Josh Hyatt didn't need them. He could make his way in life just fine without Hyatt money.

And without becoming a plumber.

Not that he had a huge problem with plumbing. But he'd tried it. He'd done some in his last apartment for the landlady when pipes burst in a freak winter freeze. He sort of had a gift for it. But it sure wasn't the thing that made his heart go pitter-pat — not like it did for a girl standing in front of him in a swimsuit, with her funny lines and her willingness to conspire to help him solve his problem. Ha. What a good sport. She must be fighting off the hordes daily, which was why her truck looked like a battering ram. *Were those curves all natural?*

Never mind that. He shoved himself back from the table and went into the spare bedroom where he had the stuff he was working on.

Into the big composting barrel he poured the dregs of his Coke. There. The acid of that would eat a hole in every old newspaper and potato peel he'd thrown in.

Then he went to his workbench. It wasn't a hobby he talked much about, not lately at least. He'd mentioned it to Brielle offhand a couple of times when she'd seen his setup in the garage of his last apartment while she was visiting from Portland.

"What are you, a moonshiner?" she'd asked half-jokingly.

Ha, ha. He'd brushed it off. Not every guy had a hobby

of what basically amounted to modern day alchemy—developing bacteria that turns kitchen compost into crude oil. Brielle was pure Oregonian, and the only acceptable fuel besides wind or solar for a lot of his state-mates was used french fry oil. He never knew when somebody was going to freak out on him for doing genetic engineering, a taboo word these days.

A glance through his microscope showed the bacteria had mutated slightly. Just not enough yet. He'd need more testing.

An hour later, Josh wiped his hands off and washed up. That letter almost hummed at him from the table. For a guy who checked the mailbox obsessively for that particular piece of mail, he sure was being a chicken about opening it.

Finally, he ratcheted up his manhood and opened the letter.

And then dropped it in the trash in utter dejection.

Chapter Five

Morgan went to her fridge and took out another apple from the tree at home and bit hard. She shouldn't be hurt. It wasn't a rejection of her. He didn't know she was desperate—maybe more desperate than he was himself. He was just being polite. What if he'd said, *Sweetheart, you look desperate*? That would've been worse.

She was being irrational.

She should focus on the fact he didn't see through her awkward joke that could have been construed as a come-on, think of that instead, and be relieved he didn't say something like, "Oh? Are you offering?"

Heavens. That would have been mortifying. This route—rejection—was far less embarrassing than being transparent. Because, if she was truthful with herself, she sort of meant it.

An agonized groan rose in her throat. Geez, he was gorgeous. So, so, so handsome. And that smile, it went arrow-straight to her heart.

And he had a girlfriend. Boom! End of story. End of crush. It had to be.

One crunch into the apple, Morgan heard the front door slam. In a second, Tory was at her side, panting.

"Are you kidding me?"

"What?"

"You, Morgan Clark, just stood talking to the best-looking guy in a hundred-mile radius for almost ten minutes. You! This is a record."

"Please. Let's not exaggerate. It couldn't have been

30

more than three minutes."

"It was ten. Believe me. I was hanging back, waiting it out in the truck because I didn't want to interrupt, so I know. But seriously? If it was ten seconds instead of ten minutes, that's still a record."

Sigh. Probably true. "We were just talking about financial aid stuff."

"You told him about losing your scholarship?"

What? Tory knew? Morgan nearly dropped her apple. She'd been as vague as possible when talking to her sister about the situation, not wanting to worry her or to let her know how bad things had gotten. But she still didn't know about the loan denial. Or the grant denial. Morgan could keep up appearances—at least until she figured out some kind of solution.

"Don't worry. Mom told me."

Mom. Great.

"Forget that. What did Josh Hyatt say? He's luscious."

It didn't matter how luscious Josh Hyatt was or wasn't. It was irrelevant to Morgan's life. "He has a girlfriend." And he'd pretty much told Morgan she wasn't good enough to be considered on his search-list of desperate women.

Tory deflated. "No."

"It's serious." Morgan nodded, resigned to the sad truth. She tossed Tory an apple from the fridge and they both crunched a bite of sorrow in concert.

But in a second, Tory perked up. "Wait. You asked him about his girlfriend?" She shook herself. "What has this guy done to you? You're talking—to a guy."

Morgan shrugged one shoulder and kicked off her flip-flops. "Probably my soul instinctively knew he was unavailable and therefore zero threat." She told Tory what Josh had said about his girlfriend.

"Oh, please. If he wanted to seal the deal with her, he would have. She'd have a ring on her finger. If they were serious, she wouldn't be leaving him — for a year." Tory huffed. "She's an idiot. And she deserves to have her man stolen if she's stupid enough to leave a guy as mind-blowingly gorgeous as that up for grabs. Don't hesitate for a second, Morgan. He's not committed. Snag him."

Morgan turned her back and looked out the sliding door onto the sad excuse for a deck off the kitchen. Tory answered her phone.

It figured. The one guy in the world she didn't completely clam up around, and more attractive than a French Silk Chocolate pie with real whipped cream, and he wasn't available. At least not available to someone as non-predatory as Morgan was. Ha! The very thought of Morgan stealing some other girl's boyfriend. As if.

***

Morgan headed across town in her truck, hoping the engine wouldn't cut out and strand her, making her late for her appointment with Professor Wyeth to see if she could work out some arrangement where she could borrow a copy of his textbook from him or someone else. She was determined to make this work somehow.

Her phone rang.

"Sweetums!" It was Morgan's mother. "I'm just so glad you finally picked up."

"I've been at work, Mom. Sorry." Morgan had the ankle bruises to prove it. "Everything all right?" Mom usually only called when things were not all right. On good days, she waited for her daughters to make the call.

"Oh, dearie. I wish I had better news."

"What is it?" Morgan pulled into the parking lot near the Van Cleef Accounting Building and heard a sad little *woof* in the background. The dog. "Nothing wrong with Nixie, is there?" Mom loved that dog more than life itself.

"I'm afraid so. They've found a cancer in her. It's either

operate or let her go."

Morgan closed her eyes and leaned up against the railing to the building's front steps. "There's no other choice?" How was Mom going to pay for dog surgery? Sell her own organs?

"I'm afraid not, but the vet says Nixie has a very good shot if she gets the surgery now. If we wait even a week, things don't look so good."

She asked the golden question. "Will the vet take a credit card?"

"You know I don't have one." Mom sounded scared. Morgan hadn't known, but now that she thought about it, Mom's credit probably was shot, since those numbers took seven years to repair. "I'm not sure how I'm going to do it." Her voice trembled. "I don't know how I can live without Nixie."

Morgan swallowed hard. She ran a hand through her hair and sat down on the cement steps. "Mom, I know how important Nixie is to you. And you wouldn't be calling if you had any other choice."

"So you'll help?" Mom's voice came like a tiny breath.

"I saved all my tips from this summer. You can have any of them you need."

A little sob echoed through the phone. "I'm so sorry, Morgan. I'd never ask in any other circumstances. But—it's Nixie." Next came a full-on hiccupping sob. "Thank you so much."

Morgan leaned her head against the metal railing. No sense going up to see the professor now. No reason. She'd be dropping not only his class but all of her classes.

She climbed in her truck and headed back to her apartment without even a glance in the rearview mirror at the dream that was almost hers.

Chapter Six

"Chip, forget about it." Josh paced back and forth in his front room, the shag carpet only tripping him once. "I'm not lowering myself to asking Bronco for cash. You know he won't give it to me."

"You don't know that, Josh. Sometimes he's in an unexpectedly generous and forgiving mood. That's the thing about volatile people. You never know—you might catch them on an upswing."

Josh rolled his eyes. "Bronco is a jerk ninety percent of the time, and a happy, self-centered philanthropist ten percent of the time—but never to disowned sons. You know that as well as I do."

"Well, it's worth a shot."

"I'm glad you think so." Wait, had Chip made a laying-the-groundwork phone call to Dad already? Because that's what it was starting to sound like. "But I can't imagine a universe where he and I are ever going to see eye to eye. Not until he has a personality transplant and stops trying to tell me what to do with my life. I don't do anything like that to him. Golden Rule applies."

"He who has the gold makes the rules."

"Luckily for him, I don't need or want his gold." That wasn't precisely true. Josh very much needed his dad's money. But he refused to pay what it would cost him to get it: his dignity, his future career, and the girl of his dreams. The price was astronomically too high.

"Then how are you going to pay tuition? Commit bank robbery?"

"I almost would if I thought I could get away with it."

Josh loved Chip, but he was done with this conversation. "I'll figure it out. But thanks for being interested." It was, actually, nice to have someone in the family who cared. "Maybe I'll win the lottery."

"You can't win if you don't play."

"Oh, yeah." He hung up.

Josh needed some air. He locked up the apartment and went out into the courtyard. It was going to rain. Like always. He liked the coast, but couldn't the universe send him just a little sunshine? Please?

As he unlocked his old Ford Explorer, a monstrous sound roared up behind him, and gravel spewed everywhere, pelting the side of his vintage red paint job on his truck.

"Hey!" he yelled, but then he twisted around and saw the source of the rocks and noise. The swimsuit girl in her old Dodge truck. She'd jammed it into park and her head was on the steering wheel. She wasn't moving. Was she dead? No, but something definitely wasn't right.

Josh jogged over to her and knocked on the window. She jarred upright, looking at him in fright. Her eyes were red.

"You okay?" He motioned for her to roll down the window. She swiped at her eyes and shook her head. "Come on, what's wrong?" He shouldn't be prying, but she was clearly in distress. He opened the door so he could talk to her.

"Did someone die?"

"Not yet." She slid off the truck's bench seat and stood with her back against the yellow door panel. Her eyes closed. She looked almost as good in her jeans and t-shirt as she'd looked in the swimsuit. Not that he was noticing.

"But they're gonna? I get the sense you're ready to kill."

She opened her eyes. "It's my stupid mom's dog."

"Wait. Your mom is stupid, or the dog is?"

"Yes." A little sob hiccupped from her throat when she drew a deep, shuddering breath. He watched her chest rise and fall.

"Okay." Josh definitely understood stupid parents, if anyone did. One more breath and the girl opened her eyes again. Wow. They were really blue. He hadn't noticed before.

"Oh, I love my mom. She's got troubles, but I love her. And the dog—whatever. I love it, too."

"But they're stupid."

"The dog is her life." She tilted her head to the side, making her blond ponytail swing a little. It was bewitching. He had to make a fist to keep himself from thinking about burying his face in it. It probably smelled like honeysuckle or something. He waited until she continued—and when she did, it flowed out in a torrent of information. "She loves the dog more than I love chocolate, and she just called to say it's sick and needs surgery and will die without it, but the surgery costs a mint, but it will almost guarantee the dog's life will be saved."

"Well, that's good news, right?" Josh didn't get it. What he did get was how her eyes sparkled through the tears as they looked upward at him, all forlorn. It tugged at his heart in a way he'd never experienced before. Suddenly, he had to help make everything right for this girl—whose name he didn't even know. "It's not every dog that can be cured. I lost my dog last year. It about ruined me."

"I'm sorry." She snapped to life, as if suddenly realizing she was talking to him, and not just lost in her own world of thoughts. "That's so sad."

It had been sad, and it was kind of cool that she cared enough to notice him and his old wound when she clearly had a hill of problems of her own. He nodded. "So, why are you so upset?" He wanted to place his arm around her shoulders, to comfort her or something.

She swallowed hard. "Because my mom just called to

36

ask for help. She doesn't have money for the surgery."

Josh pushed his eyebrows together. "Wait. Weren't you just telling me about school financial aid problems?" He hated to bring up a sore point, but it seemed salient.

She nodded, and a big, round tear spilled out of her eye and down her cheek. He saw things pretty clearly, he thought. "Don't do it. Don't give her the money you've saved up for school, or rent, or books, or whatever."

"But it's Nixie. Her dog. Her life."

Josh recoiled at this. "Oh, come on. That's just not right of her to ask you. She's the mom, not you."

"You don't know how it works in our situation." The girl started walking. "I have to do this."

"But you have a part-time job, right?" He followed after her on the gravel, listening to the cute slap of her flip-flops.

"Waitressing at Veg-Out."

"The place with the roller skates?"

"That's the one. Also known as The Weedeater. Or Lettuce Feed You. Or Miso Sorry. Or Wholly Frijoles. My sister has a million names for it." She sounded resigned to her fate. "And I'll have a lot more time this fall to be earning tips. Maybe I can go to college next year. Maybe they'll hold my slot in the accounting department."

That wasn't how things worked at Clarendon College. Josh knew. He'd personally dropped out and tried to get back in, and it wasn't simple like that. "You can't just drop out. People don't just drop out of Clarendon College." Well, he had, but that was different.

"I don't really have a choice, now, do I?"

"You absolutely do. Don't give your mom money for her dog. Dogs—they die. All pets do. Every dog you ever own will die. Until the last one—which will outlive you." He was getting tripped up. "That's just the deal with pets. We love them, and then they die. It's the way life is."

"Try telling that to my mother. I dare you." The girl

sounded desperate, hopeless. "Look, I appreciate your interest. Really. But I'm just done fighting against fate. A bachelor's degree just isn't in the cards for me, apparently. The job at Veg-Out isn't that bad, really. I might work my way up to management someday. And I'd be off the roller skates then. Don't tell me I haven't got dreams." She stopped and was looking up at him.

"Big dreams." What she had was big, beautiful blue eyes.

The side of her mouth twitched, and the tears welled again.

"What?" He stepped closer to her. "Is there something else?" He couldn't help it. He rested a hand on her shoulder. His pinkie finger brushed the skin just where her sleeve met the soft brown of her arm.

"It's just—I told my younger sister as soon as I finished my degree, I'd put her through school."

Realization dawned on him. This girl was a really good person. She had goals, and they weren't just for herself. "And if you quit, she can't go?"

The girl closed her eyes and shook her head in the slightest movement.

"Well, for that reason alone you shouldn't quit. Not now. What year are you?"

"Starting my senior year."

Oh, she was close. No wonder it seemed so tragic to her. Nearly grasping the brass ring, only to have it snatched away.

"Look, is there anything I can do?" He asked this, knowing full well he was just as broke as she was, but that he might have access to something that might be useful—if Chip would go for it. "I know somebody. My brother is a vet. Maybe he'd help you out."

She looked up at him with a glint of hope. "Really? You think he'd do that?"

Josh tugged his phone from his jeans pocket and

redialed Chip. "Hey, Chip. Remember when you said you wished there was some way you could help me out? You got time to do a pro bono dog surgery?" A few moments later, he snapped the phone closed. "Done."

The girl flung her arms around his neck, and then she pressed a kiss to his cheek. Maybe lack of Brielle had made him ultra-sensitive, but this woman's body pressed against him revved his engine more than he expected.

"Thank you! Josh, you're amazing! I can't wait to tell my mom."

He couldn't help smiling. It felt really good to be able to help this girl. She seemed like such a good person—and she really rocked a swimsuit and did blue eyes better than anyone else. Ever.

Suddenly, though, she let go of him and started walking away looking dejected.

"What is it now? Does she have a sick cat, too? Because my brother Chip owes me a few more favors."

The girl shook her head. "It's no use. Even if I don't have to give my mom all my savings for Nixie's surgery, I still come up way short for tuition for this fall. I don't know why I even let myself rejoice. It doesn't matter if the money goes for the dog or not. I'm still never going to be able to afford to start school."

This came as a slap in Josh's face, reminding him he couldn't pay tuition either. He slumped down on one of the graffiti-covered boulders Estrella Court used for landscaping.

"Same." He shrugged one shoulder.

The girl came over and plopped down beside him.

"Do you actually know a guy willing to get me a false identity?"

"I wish. I'd get one myself." She pulled her legs up to her chest and hugged her knees. Estrella Court, for all its shortcomings, was close to the ocean, and a slice of it was visible past the parking lot. She was staring out at it, he

39

could tell. "I'm desperate."

The word sparked a memory in him from their earlier conversation. "Desperate guy seeks equally desperate girl to fake sham marriage to apply for government student financial aid."

Without missing a breath, she said, "I'm your girl."

Josh's head jerked toward where she sat, unblinking, looking at the sliver of ocean visible over the trees. "You're kidding."

"I wish I were."

Josh was so stunned he couldn't move, could only sit staring at this very pretty girl who just, sort of, agreed to sacrifice herself so he could go to school. Well, and so she could, too.

"You're being serious," he finally managed. "You'd do that for me?"

"For myself, too." She looked up at him. "I'm that desperate."

The words had a tiny sting to them. All his life he'd considered himself pretty much a good catch. Well, lately, he'd been the play-at-your-own-risk guy, but he still wasn't the kind of guy a girl had to be desperate to accept, was he?

Oh, stop it. He was being ridiculous. She wasn't any more or less emotionally invested in this idea than he was. "It's like a business arrangement, then."

She looked up at him. "Exactly." With a shrug she said, "Once the check for the financial aid comes in, we can just get the marriage annulled. Done. Over. Problem solved." Her blue eyes looked up at him, a spark of hope in them, energizing at the option lying open to them.

"Problem solved." Josh's heart started to beat again. In fact, it started to race. This gorgeous wisp of a blonde just agreed to pull him out of disaster and fix everything. Tuition—paid. "Problem solved," he echoed. "Wow." Josh got up and started pacing back and forth in front of her, progressively faster. "Wow. So, you really mean it?"

She shrugged one shoulder, a little smile breaking near the corners of those pretty blue eyes.

Josh stepped toward her. "Have I told you how beautiful you are?" He swept her into his arms, picking her up. "Thank you!" He swung her around, and she was lightness and gloriousness in his arms, this gorgeous girl who just made all his problems go away. He pressed a kiss to the side of her blonde hair.

She let out a sweet laugh. "Stop! You're making me dizzy."

"Let's get down to the courthouse and make this happen." He carried her to the passenger side of his Ford Explorer and set her inside.

"Deal." Her eyes, sad a few minutes ago, now sparkled with excitement and relief. "I'm Morgan Clark, by the way."

"Nice to meet you. Now, let's go get married."

Chapter Seven

Well, here goes a mockery of something sacred.

Morgan didn't even pause to let Josh get the door for her. She was about ten feet ahead of him going into the courthouse, and he'd stopped to tie his shoe. It was an inauspicious beginning to something that shouldn't even be starting in the first place.

If this many butterflies were at war in her stomach on her fake wedding day, she'd probably be vomiting all the way to the altar on the day she really got married.

If that ever happened.

Especially after her *future* husband found out someday what a cavalier attitude she was taking toward something that really, truly ought to mean something.

Maybe that was the source of the butterfly wars in her gut. And maybe it was her own nature, not the winged insects of nature.

Either way, she couldn't see any other solution to her situation. Tory absolutely should not wait another year to start school after this one. And there was no guarantee that Morgan would be getting financial aid next year, either. Somehow the gods of fate would snatch it all away from her again. She had to take the reins and make her own fate.

Even if it meant roping Josh Hyatt into this mess with her.

She looked up at him. Dang, he had nice teeth. Morgan had always been a sucker for a good smile. It was doubly terrible, this thing she was doing — faking a vow — being as she wouldn't actually mind exploring a future with this guy sometime. He seemed like a really nice person, and he did help her mother with Nixie without asking anything in return. Wow. He'd carved out a spot in her heart forever for that deed alone.

Nevertheless, together they were perpetrating something wrong. And that made neither of them nice people.

"Hi," Josh was saying to the Clatsop County Clerk. "We'd like a marriage license."

The clerk handed them some paperwork, and Morgan began filling it out. "I have better handwriting, hon. I'll do it. But you have to make sure I spell everything right." She winked at the clerk. "I'm an awful speller." Then at Josh she said, "Isn't that right, Josher?"

Josher. She'd just called Joshua Hyatt *Josher*. She'd hit rock bottom.

Or so she thought.

"Hyatt has a *y*, not an *i*." Josher pointed a fingertip at where she'd misspelled his last name. He laughed. "You'll need to know that soon, sweets."

Sweets. Hearing him call her sweets, she shouldn't have been so taken aback. After all, she'd just called him Josher, but it made her drop the pen.

They bent down simultaneously to pick it up, and they bumped heads. He laughed, and then whispered, "You're handling this like a dream."

Morgan nodded. This kind of felt like a nightmare. Heart pounding, she finished filling out her portion of the paperwork. "I can never quite remember the exact date, hon." She pointed a finger to where he needed a birth date.

"January sixth."

She dropped her pen again. Her mouth went totally dry. After a second he looked at her, and she oh-so-casually pointed at her own birth date. January sixth. He wrote in the year. He was exactly two years older than she.

"Oh, how cute, y'all. Matching birth dates. What'd you do this year to celebrate? One cake or two?"

43

"Uh, no cakes. We hadn't met yet."

"Ooh, a whirlwind romance." The clerk gave a little shiver of happiness. "You're such a gorgeous couple. When's the big day?"

Josh answered immediately. "Today, if possible."

"Oh, you're talking really whirlwind stuff." The clerk laughed. "Well, when it's right, it's right. Let me just check with Judge Byron to see if he's got a time available this afternoon." She scooted out and left them together at the desk.

Josh turned to her. "Josher?"

"Sweets?" was Morgan's weak retort.

"I thought it'd be the perfect balance for when you called me *hon*."

"Touché."

He took the pen from her hand, and in a flash he'd filled out all the remaining lines on his portion of the paperwork. To think, they'd been eating cake on the same day every year of their lives up to now. Weird. Morgan peeked and saw his father's name was Bronco. Bronco? He'd never been married before, and neither had she. He verified they weren't first cousins.

"Look," Josh said with a lowered voice. "I know we honestly haven't discussed all the implications of this, but if we're going through with it, we need to make sure no one ever finds out it's not for real. We could get in a lot of trouble."

Morgan just nodded. She never thought about the fraud implications of what they were doing. She'd had the moral implications running through her brain on a loop, but now were they lawbreakers, too?

This was just getting worse.

"I mean it. Don't tell anyone."

"But isn't that the point? We're supposed to tell everyone, so it seems like we truly mean it."

"Well, yeah." Josh hesitated. "Of course. But I mean we

don't tell anyone it's temporary, or that it's just for, uh, you know, money." It sounded so bad when he put it that way. Morgan's stomach turned over.

"That's fine. Fine. But I have to tell Tory. I live with her. She'll figure it out, anyway."

"She's your roommate?"

"Sister."

He chewed on this a second. "Fine, but no one else. And I'm telling no one."

Morgan wondered if that included his girlfriend, wherever she was. That could be problematic at some point, for sure.

"Maybe we should just forget it." She closed her eyes and chucked a little prayer toward heaven, but it hit the ceiling of the Clatsop County Clerk's office and bounced back and hit her in the face.

"Do you see any other option?" Josh's mouth made a grim, straight line.

Morgan let it all tumble through her brain. At last she whispered, "No."

Josh took her hand. It sent more electricity through her than she would ever admit. "Then are you with me?"

She nodded.

In walked the county clerk. "Wedding day jitters, eh? I see it all the time." She laughed. "I'm happy to tell you the judge has an opening for the next few minutes. Do you have friends or family waiting outside?"

Family. Wow. Morgan always thought her family would be beside her when she did something as momentous as this. But then she remembered it wasn't momentous. It was just a moment. A means to an end.

"We're being spontaneous." Josh took Morgan's hand again. "Gotta strike while the iron's hot. Before she has a chance to change her mind."

If only the county clerk had any idea how literal that statement was.

"Okay, young lovers. Follow me." She led them past a labyrinth of cubicles to the judge's chambers, where there was a large mahogany desk littered with papers and paper cone-cups from the water cooler. "He's a bit of a neat freak. Can you tell?" She said this under her breath, just as the judge entered.

Judge Byron came in. He was younger than Morgan expected, with messy curly hair and hipster glasses.

"Hello, folks. You'd like to get married, eh?" He added a Canadian lilt to his *eh* at the question's end. "Marlene, would you round up a couple of my clerks? I'll use them as witnesses, since these two lovebirds came here to elope."

Elope. That's what they were doing. It had always sounded like running away to Morgan, with the root word *lope*. Which didn't that mean run? In a way, she was running away from her financial problems, she guessed.

"We're eloping," Josh whispered. "That's one way to put it."

"Uh-huh."

In a minute, the judge's staff came in—two women. One had a bouquet of silk flowers she handed Morgan. The silk Gerbera daisies in it looked a little tired. Dusty.

"Now, do you want the short version or the long version?"

"Short," Josh and Morgan said simultaneously. Then their eyes shot toward each other.

"Oh, anxious, eh?" The judge chuckled. "Gotcha. I have an extremely short one. You want that?" They did.

Judge Byron proceeded. Extremely short it was. "Do you, Joshua John Hyatt agree to marry Morgan Elise Clark?"

"Yes."

"Do you Morgan Elise Clark agree to marry Joshua John Hyatt?"

This was the moment of truth. It was all happening so fast. And she hadn't even had time to listen to the implications of the vow she was making. It was so short. Could it possibly be real? Could it be of any legal force? Her ears roared with the blood racing through her veins, but not so loud that she couldn't hear herself say, "Yes."

"Then by the laws of the State of Oregon and my authority as a judge in Clatsop County, I declare you married. Congratulations."

Morgan should have felt something. Instead, a cocoon of wool encased her, and she went emotionally numb, her mind a blank. She stared at Judge Byron, who looked back and forth between her and Josh, her husband, expectantly, but she couldn't move.

Finally, the judge spoke. "Well, what are you waiting for, eh? Kiss the bride." He jostled Josh's shoulder, and it bumped Morgan back to life a little.

Kiss? She hadn't even thought about the inevitable kiss. Her mouth went dry. It had been a long, long time since she'd been in a position to be kissed. Blame the Conversation Coma if she must, but she'd had a kissing dry spell of many months. Or more.

Apparently Josh had the same misgivings—and he was probably thinking of that girlfriend he'd sent off to wherever, of what she would think of his kissing—let alone marrying—some random girl he met. He spluttered an answer to the judge. "Oh, uh. Right. We'll save it. I'm sure you people get a little weary of wedding PDA."

PDA. Public Display of Affection. Relief washed through Morgan at not having to be subjected to the humiliation of having her first kiss in, oh, however long, be in court.

But the judge was too jolly for that. "No way. I love weddings. It's a new family unit bonding together. New life. New joy. Don't hesitate on our accounts. We love it."

Morgan braced herself. The pressure was pretty strong, and she realized they'd have to cave to it, if they wanted to sell their story to anyone. She turned to face him. "It's okay,

Josh. They're rooting for our success."

Josh had a worried, slightly sick look on his face, and she could see he was thinking of someone else. Which, of course, made this whole experience all the worse. But she knew this was part of the deal, and he had to pay the price, too.

The room went into slow motion. Josh cupped Morgan's jaw with his hand. Her heart sped at his touch—it had been so long since a guy had looked at her this way. And there was definitely a look coming at her from Josh Hyatt. It looked to be part guilt, part resignation, part desire. She'd have to focus on the desire part, or else she couldn't even get through this one-second-long kiss.

She tilted her chin upward, and slightly parted her lips. His eyes closed, and she closed hers. And then his mouth brushed her lips, pressing them softly, like a mere caress.

A thousand needles of tingling pierced the wool cocoon that had encased her, and her every nerve sprang to life.

Kissing her fake husband should not feel this good. It should feel as fake as this marriage. But instead it felt as real as anything she'd ever experienced.

Dang it.

He pulled away, and their eyes met. He blinked a couple of times, and his eyes looked just a little afraid—yet another thing to add to the guilt and desire already visible there.

"Thank you," he said softly.

Morgan nodded. "I should be thanking you."

The clerks clapped. The judge pressed a hand on each of their shoulders. "Congratulations."

Morgan took Josh's hand. "That's it, I guess."

One of the court staff said just loud enough for Morgan to hear, "That kiss was serious stuff." The other one said back, "Electric. Now after work I won't need to watch my soaps I recorded."

Oh, brother. If they only knew how hollow the whole thing was, they'd probably throw rotten fruit at Josh and Morgan.

As she and Josh weaved their way out of the cubicle maze, the county clerk saw them pass. "Oh, look-a there. You two really did it. Wonderful. So, where are you going to honeymoon?"

Morgan gave her a mind-your-own-business giggle, but outside the doors of the county building, she answered the question for Josh to hear. "Right here in Starry Point. Filling out paperwork."

Chapter Eight

"Well, uh." Morgan fidgeted in her seat beside him. "I've got work in a little while. Gotta change into my uniform." She seemed really awkward—and it pretty much mirrored how Josh squirmed inside. They weren't going to go out to eat to celebrate. They weren't going to even tap two Coke bottles together as a victory party for moving themselves a giant step closer to their goals. They were just going to say, *thanks, bye, see ya.*

Weird. This whole thing was weird. But necessary. He kept telling himself that. It was a means to an end.

Josh dropped Morgan off at her apartment and went back to his place, where he exhaled for the first time all afternoon.

Talk about conflicting feelings. Man, that girl had a kiss on her. It was a good thing that was the only time they'd be required to lock lips or else he could actually be in danger of losing focus on Brielle—which was stupid. The whole point of all this was to get himself in a place where he and Brielle could really be together.

Wasn't it?

Dang. That blonde could potentially throw off his groove. He'd better minimize contact, just to be safe. Maybe he should move. Then he wouldn't be seeing her in her swimsuit walking around the complex at any given moment. Because that? *That* made him want to maximize contact.

His mouth went a little dry.

He went to grab a Coke from the fridge. It hissed a

satisfying release when he twisted the cap. Ah, yes. The cool tang of the liquid hit the back of his throat, and his body knew the caffeine hit was coming. It responded with a *yesssss*, and the tension flowed from the muscles in his neck and shoulders.

All right. Now he could think. And frankly, he'd done it. He'd taken a giant step toward getting what he wanted. Best of all, now Bronco couldn't stop him. Josh could pay tuition; he was getting that foreign policy degree and making his life happen—despite any and all naysayers, including his wacko dad.

He set down his Coke bottle, satisfied.

Well, no time like the present. Josh did an online search for the grant forms to fill out for married students. Married. Weird, again. There were a lot of pages. Morgan wasn't lying when she said they'd spend their honeymoon filling out paperwork.

And worst, it wasn't even fillable forms. It all had to be printed out. Government—so slow to get with the times. They probably wanted everyone to jump through as many hoops as possible to qualify for the funding. Oh, well. He was always pretty good at jumping. He did hurdles and the high jump back in his track and field days in high school, and during his first go-round at Clarendon he'd been on their varsity team.

That seemed like a long time ago.

He hit print for the forms and waited for his printer to spit them out. Oh, no. Not again. This stupid piece of junk never worked on the first try. He fiddled with the cords, looked at the settings on the screen, and sent it again.

Whoosh, whir. There it went. Finally. At least this time he didn't have to either kick it or swear at it to get it to work. That was a good thing. And a rare one.

When it kept printing and printing though, Josh smirked. Man, there were a lot of pages. He pulled the stack-ola of them off the feed and started thumbing through the sheets. Oh, great. It printed two sets. Fabulous.

Just as he started to drop them in the trash, something stopped him. Morgan, his wife, would need these, too. He might as well be the nice guy and take them over to her. Not that he wanted to see her again, necessarily, even though she wasn't bad to look at. The blue eyes really did have something to them, and even though Brielle had auburn hair, Josh had always been a sucker for a blonde. Going over there with these would just be the right thing to do—for the environment. Otherwise, waste of trees. And the disinherited heir of Hyatt Holdings, former logging conglomerate, should know better than anyone else about the importance of trees.

"Hi," he said when she opened her door. He held out the half-ream of printed paper. "You were right. There's enough to keep us busy filling out paperwork for at least the duration of the normal couple's honeymoon."

After he said it, some kind of heat rushed to his face. He didn't know why. And suddenly, looking at the way she stared up at him with those deep blues, he had a blast of shyness he'd never really felt before. What the heck?

"Thanks. My printer is down, so I was going to have to print stuff out at the library. This helps." Her voice was really soft—a lot calmer than earlier, when she was telling him about all the struggles she was having. "Oh, and tell your brother thanks. My mother already made an appointment, and he's taking care of Nixie this afternoon for her." She pressed the pile of papers to her chest. "I can't thank you enough."

He stood looking at her for a moment, not sure what to say, but almost like his eyes had been glued to hers, he couldn't look away from them. This girl was too amazing. *And he was married to her.*

Which was why he was going to have to move. Far away from Estrella Court.

"I don't know what all is on the forms, but text me if

52

you have questions." He gave her his number and got hers—he'd probably have questions, too—attaching it to a picture he snapped of her, with a lock of her blonde hair falling across her right eye.

So much for putting more distance between himself and this distracting woman. He now had her number in his phone. *Morgan Clark Hyatt.*

If only Brielle hadn't put the kibosh on his making calls to her. He could really use a dose of normality right now to set his brain back in its rightful rut. Not that his relationship with Brielle was like being in a rut. Oh, whatever. Morgan was still looking up at him, hugging the paperwork.

"Well, I'll see you, I guess." She bit her lower lip, which reminded him of how it felt when he'd kissed it—like he was running satin across his mouth. Satin that tasted like raspberries.

Brielle used Mentholatum. Completely different.

"Right." Josh took another second. "Thanks again." Then he couldn't help himself. He leaned over and kissed her on her forehead. Yeah, her hair smelled like honeysuckle from his mom's garden a long time ago. He'd been right. "Uh. See you."

He walked away, tripping a little on the stray vine of a weed that had grown across the sidewalk. He didn't look back, but he flattered himself that Morgan was watching him walk away. Even if he'd stumbled, she probably thought he was charming. And a good kisser. And had a nice rear view.

Right.

And that he'd just used her. For money. And to get another girl.

He was a jerk.

***

Morgan shut the door behind her and leaned her back against it, glad beyond words that Tory wasn't home right now to cross examine her about the disaster she'd just made of her life. She pounded the back of her head three times against the door. "Lame, lame, lame."

Josh Hyatt was even cute when his flip-flops tripped him on the sidewalk. And when he blushed, she could have just died of how much charm came off him, like a faint-inducing pheromone.

As much as that you-may-kiss-the-bride moment had been a mind-blowing pleasure at the time, the memory of it was going to haunt her, mix up all her emotions forever. Every time she saw him she'd be remembering how it sent all her systems past the red line. That was going to be awkward. All manner of awkward.

Worse, why did he have to just now kiss her head? What was that? Fatherly? Or friendly? It felt to her like a weird mix of condescension and affection. Misplaced affection—just like he'd misplaced where he should put his mouth. Lips, dude. Lips meet lips. Not forehead.

Still, she felt the phantom memory of that kiss on her forehead almost as much as the one that he'd placed on her lips earlier. Josh Hyatt not only had great teeth and a great smile, the kiss from them was exceptional, too. In which case, she was in quite a bit of trouble—because she'd just married him.

And she could probably never kiss him again.

The door behind her jostled, and she scrambled out of the way, not sure what to do with the stack of papers in her hands.

"Hey," Tory said as she came in, bearing an armload of green velvet and gold lamé fabric. "What'cha been up to?"

Uh—great. How should Morgan answer? *I just got married. How was your day?*

"Looks like a lot of papers. Already doing homework for some overzealous prof?" Tory came over and peeked at the papers. "Or did you just borrow that one jerk's book and go get it photocopied? Serves him right."

"Naw. Just a grant application."

"What? You're still dealing with financial aid? I thought you said you had that handled."

"I did. I mean, I do. Now." Morgan's heart beat a frantic pace. She was going to have to tell someone first. It might as well be Tory. Eventually, it was going to have to be public knowledge—and in order for the whole thing to work, she was going to have to admit it—to everyone. Including Tory, who was dropping her yards of fabric on the sofa.

"You sewing?" She chickened out. "Is it for Hamlet?"

"Hamlet it is. He's not bad, for an actor. Kinda seems to have his head on straight."

"That's unusual."

"I know, right?" Tory threw the fabric on the coffee table beside the sewing machine, which had taken up residence in front of the TV. "And he doesn't even do weird things like refuse to bathe for months at a time, so I'm counting that in the win column."

"Frequent, regular bathing is always a win." Morgan realized she had no idea whether her husband was a frequent bather. He might be anti-bath. Oh, what had she done?

"You look kind of sick. Is everything all right? I mean, if you want, I can help you with the paperwork for the grant. I like putting numbers and letters in little individual boxes. It's a weird thing of mine." She got up and took the paperwork out of Morgan's grip.

Morgan held them tightly for a second, then she allowed them to go. She watched Tory's face as Tory started digesting the gist of the papers' requirements.

"Married student grant application?" She flipped through the tall stack. "Looks like you accidentally printed the wrong stuff. Wait, our printer is down. Did you pick up someone else's papers at the library copy center? You should take them back."

Morgan just shook her head. Her stomach's temperature rose about ten degrees.

"Uh, Morg. It's not like you can just lie and say you're married when you're not. They don't run the grants that way. I mean, I'm not a student, and I haven't ever done one of these applications, but I'm not exactly dumb. And neither are you. So, go get the right papers."

"I did get the right papers, weeks ago, and they turned me down."

"What?" Tory cocked her head. "I thought you just had that scholarship problem. Are you saying they shut you down on grant money, too?"

Morgan nodded.

"Oh, man. That stinks. Can you get a loan?" Tory was all into this conversation now. In a way it felt good to unburden herself of the truth, but Morgan hated letting her sister know the depth of the problems she'd been facing — especially because it affected Tory so dramatically.

"No loans except unsecured. Because of *Frogs in the Sand*'s income, I don't qualify."

"That book! I can't express how much I hate that book. The fire of a thousand suns doesn't even describe the magnitude of my hatred for that book." Tory got her theater friends' air going. "We should never have let Mom do that."

"Mom didn't need our permission. And besides, it got her out from under Dad's leftover debts." Morgan had to view it this way or she'd launch into orbit at her own hatred of the book and all the troubles it continued to cause her.

"Dad's. Debts. Even when they're paid off, they continue to dog us." Tory sat down on the sofa and pulled a pillow to her chest to punch. "I mean, geez. He might have been a nice guy, from what Mom says, but such a bad credit risk never existed in all time. I'm so sad for Mom. Don't you think she saw that coming when she married him? Don't you think young women should be taught to look a generation ahead when they're choosing a husband?"

This was all well-trodden ground. Dad's exit from their lives when Morgan was six, Mom's never asking for a divorce, Dad's debts slamming Mom when he died. Morgan thought about her own choice, the one she'd made without looking a generation ahead — or even about her own generation, *herself.*

"Never mind all that, Morgan. Just take those papers back up to the school and get your stuff. I'll make us some fabulous apple pie, since we still have about forty pounds of apples from that tree — the one good thing Dad left us — and then we can have a filling-out-forms party. It'll be awesome. Paperwork à la mode."

It was time. Morgan had to come clean. "Uh, actually..." She inhaled sharply and then just spit it out. "These are the right papers. I got married this afternoon. It was the only way I could qualify for federal grants. I tried to think of every single other solution in the world, both legal and illegal, and this was the only way I could make it work so I could finish school this year and get that job so you can start school next fall, and finally get into that design program you've been waiting two whole years for already. I know it was probably a rash thing to do, but I had you in mind, and I hope you'll understand that I meant to do it mostly for you."

When she finished, Morgan felt like she'd been a machine gun and had run through a whole belt of ammunition, and now it was all empty. She plopped on the sofa beside Tory and lay her head on Tory's shoulder. "Forgive me?"

Tory's jaw dropped to her chin. She blinked six times. She shut her mouth. It fell open again. Finally she spoke.

"Forgive?" She shook her head. "Forgive! I mean—what on earth were you thinking?"

"I told you. I was thinking I had to finish so you could start, and this was the only way."

Tory spluttered, "Well, who did you marry? I mean, did you just grab some homeless druggie off the streets and drag him to the nearest preacher-man? Or have you got some kind of secret boyfriend you never told me about? Are you really working at Eat-n-Leaf, or have you been on clandestine dates with your new husband?" Tory was on a tear. "Wait a minute. You got married today. Why aren't you on a honeymoon? Are you insane? You've been saving yourself all these years. You should be somewhere else right now, don't you think? Like heading for a beach cottage?"

Morgan couldn't answer the questions all at once. And she intended to never answer the honeymoon question. What went on between a husband and wife—even if it was nothing—was nobody else's business.

"Come on, Morgan. Don't go into the Conversation Coma on me." Tory's voice then softened. "I'm not upset. I'm just in shock. I mean—seriously. I never saw this coming."

"Neither did I." Truthfully, she was in shock herself.

"Then what happened?"

Morgan gave a skeleton outline of the sequence of events.

"So, I was desperate, see? And this guy I met was desperate, too. Neither of us had a prayer of getting into school this semester without a drastic change in our eligibility status, and we struck a deal. Yeah, it was basically, 'Hi, I'm Morgan.' 'Hi, Morgan, let's get married.' And we drove down to the county building and signed the papers, and the judge said, 'You're husband and wife.' Boom. Eligible for funding. Took about half an hour was all." She strategically omitted how the electricity sparked through her at you-may-now-kiss-the-bride. "So now I can fill out these married student forms and I'll be paying my tuition in full before the college drops all my classes for me at the end of September. It's perfect."

Tory paused. "It's fraud."

"It's not. We have a real marriage certificate and everything. We're legally and lawfully married."

Clearly, Tory wasn't convinced, but she looked like she bit back several sentences, because she opened her mouth and shut it three times before finally saying, "Look. I don't know about this. You don't even know this guy. Do you have any idea what could happen to you? This stranger could steal your good name, ruin your credit history, demand some kind of marital rights—you don't know." Tory's voice had risen in pitch, and it scared Morgan a little. "This is really risky. Did you even think through the implications?"

Morgan had no response. She couldn't even start to say what had possessed her at the time, other than sheer panic about her future in one, tunnel-vision aspect.

"Come on, sister. Let's just hustle you down to the courthouse. We can get this annulled. It's only been, what? An hour? And I'm assuming you haven't consummated the marriage. Or have you? Was this some ploy on his part to get you to—"

"No. No!" Morgan's jaw hinge finally un-rusted and she could speak. "It's not like that. I mean, I told you when I first met him that he said he has a girlfriend. He's in the same financial aid bind I've been in. This is a business arrangement, pure and simple. And your plan for annulment? We've already discussed it. As soon as our grant checks arrive, boom. We're back down at the courthouse to sign the paperwork. I'm not as dumb as I look right now through your eyes." Well, that might only be half true. Morgan knew she didn't deserve genius-status going through with this harebrained scheme.

But what choice did she have?

Tory exhaled. "This, Morgan, is just...it's out of character. You're measured. You don't jump into big things without thought. I don't get it." She lifted her head from where she'd tilted it back against the couch and looked at Morgan. "What happened? Did you develop some horrendous crush on some guy in the past few days and figure this was a way to snare him? Because it won't work."

"No. I did not develop a horrendous crush on him in the last few days." Uh, maybe in the last two hours, maybe since she'd experienced his incredible kiss, but not in the last few days.

"Okay, so is this some kind of brain tumor? A fog you've entered?"

"Enough. Tory, I made this choice. It's going to help me. It's going to help Josh Hyatt. It's going to help you."

"Wait. Wai-ai-ai-ait. You married Josh Hyatt?"

"Yeah. Didn't I say that up front?"

"Uh, no. You most certainly did not. You said it was someone you saw in the parking lot, but I figured it was Leonard or Mr. Reeves, I guess."

Morgan must've omitted that detail.

Tory looked like she'd just swallowed a Christmas tree. "Josh Hyatt. *The* Josh Hyatt? James Bond in Jeans, the guy from apartment six?" Her face was all sparkly as she gushed about him. "He's gorgeous. To die for. Geez, Morg. Why didn't you say so?"

"What's with the sudden about-face? You can't be basing all that on his looks."

"Of course not. Come on. I mean, yeah, I like a pretty face as much as the next girl. But, no. I internet-stalked him after you talked to him and I saw him hauling trash out to the dumpster." She raised an eyebrow. "I may have also daydreamed about the days when he'd be hauling trash out for the two of you someday, so it's kind of a dream come true."

"What do you mean? You already had us married in your mind?"

"Of course. We're women. It's what we do—plan marriages, extrapolate seconds-long conversations into eternal relationships. Come on. You've done it, too, I know. Anyway," her face lit up, "I figured out where I'd heard of him."

"Where?" All this changing of reactions from Tory was giving Morgan a bit of emotional whiplash. Tory did have a point—Morgan had no idea what kind of risks she was taking by marrying him, basically sight unseen. It was a stupid move, but it was done, and she was all in—no matter what kind of criminal past he may have had.

"You hit the jackpot, Morgan. He's part of that Hyatt family that made all the money in logging back in the day. Now they have the construction company in Portland. Pretty much Portland royalty, if there is such a thing. Huge family fundage."

"Hyatt Holdings?" The corporation name had come up more than once in her accounting and business classes. That was some serious assets column they had, since their great-grandfather had basically been the super granddaddy of all logging in Oregon back in Oregon's logging and paper mill days. Now it still swam in cash, but they did construction projects for other corporate interests, and a million other things.

Tory sniffed. "What's a rich boy like that doing at Estrella Court?" She cackled a little. "Maybe we've moved up in the world and didn't notice."

Not when the rich boy wasn't rich anymore—because he refused to be bullied into becoming a plumber.

Tory hugged Morgan. "Look, I appreciate that you sacrificed for me. I'm sorry I gave you a hard time. He's a good guy—we said that at first. And the way he helped get Nixie's surgery arranged? That says something about him. I'm going to give him a chance. Maybe you should, too."

61

She cocked an eyebrow at Morgan, shooting worry and hope through her simultaneously.

"He really is pretty nice." *And a lot of other things.* But she should stop thinking—because he was not actually available, weird as that was, as her husband. "But like I said, he's got that girlfriend. So the point is moot."

"Then what in the *H* is he doing marrying you?"

"I told you. The financial aid deal." Suddenly, Morgan remembered—she wasn't supposed to tell a living soul about their real situation. And she could see why, based on some of the things Tory had said. "But listen. Tor. I'm not in this for reals, but I'm definitely in this. I can't have anyone know that Josh and I didn't do this with sincerity."

Tory thought about it for a second then nodded. "Oh. Okay. I see." She took a deep breath. "You're asking me to keep your secret...a secret. I get it."

"Thanks. I really appreciate it. We can't tell anyone it's a sham. Not a single soul. Not even Mom." Mom. The thought of Mom finding out that Morgan got married without her permission or knowledge—that was just sickening, for a lot of reasons, several that Morgan didn't want to think about right now.

"Mom's not going to take this well."

"I know." Morgan's heart filled with dread. "I'll figure something out. I promise." She tried to make it sound like it would be all right.

"Okay, Morgan." Tory sat up. "I'll keep your secret. I'll tell people you and Josh Hyatt are happily married. That you fell in love over the summer here at Estrella Court, that you couldn't help your beautiful selves. That everything is great."

"Oh, Tor! Thanks—"

"But," Tory interrupted, "my silence comes at a price."

"Oh, really?"

"Yes. You are never allowed to think of that so-called girlfriend of his as your competition. Ever. Not once."

"Uh, it's his *girlfriend.*"

"And you're his *wife.* Whatever. You have the certificate to prove it. Besides, she's on the other side of the world. If he'd wanted to be married to her before now, and she wanted him, too, Josh wouldn't be getting married to you for grant money instead of her. Just keep that in mind." Tory looked satisfied. "Or I'm telling everyone."

Seemed like a fair price to ask — not that Morgan could begin to dream of keeping the promise.

Chapter Nine

Josh bounced between texting and calling. There was no way he could fill out even this first section on his application without asking Morgan about sixteen questions. This was ridiculous. So many questions! What were they going to ask for next, his firstborn?

Uh, not that he and Morgan would be having any firstborn or second-born or any other kids, but it seemed like this form should have been named Rumpelstiltskin. Guess what I need or I'll take everything you dream of.

Joshua: *Hey, Morgan. I need some details for the forms.*

She texted back almost immediately. Morgan: *Me, too. This is a crazy amount of personal information. How am I supposed to know this about me, let alone you?*

Joshua: *So should we text it back and forth?* He, of all people, with a girlfriend in, what had she called it? Sequester? Josh should know better than to be sending all his personal details through the cell towers. The problem was, getting together had some level of danger for him. He was a man committed to his woman, and hanging out with Morgan Clark (make that Morgan *Hyatt*) didn't smack of committed boyfriend. Not a bombshell like that. At least Brielle wouldn't see it that way.

Morgan: *It's already taking forever to write it all in.*

That was for certain. He'd almost gotten a cramp in his pen hand. She was right.

Josh: *I'll call you.* He was throwing caution to the wind, he knew. Someone somewhere could be listening in. In fact, it could be Brielle. But he'd rather undergo that minuscule risk than put himself in a situation where he might lose control and kiss Morgan on the forehead again and maybe take an even longer whiff of her floral shampoo. Or her raspberry lip gloss.

Uh, now he had to wait a few minutes to call her, just to clear his head of those details.

When he finally dialed, he could hear music and voices in the background of wherever she was.

"Hi, Morgan. It's Josher."

"Josher!" She sounded a little weary. "Hey, I'm super sorry about that. I don't know what made me say it."

"You're forgiven, if —" he let the if hang for a moment, "if you tell me what county and state you were born in." Since he already knew her birthday. As if that weren't weird enough.

"I was born in Portland."

"Me, too." So that meant he and she both knew the county: Multnomah. Now they both paused as they filled in their blanks.

"That's cool. What hospital? Wouldn't that be something, same birthday, same hospital?"

But they were born in different hospitals. That was a relief. Things were getting too spooky.

After that, they exchanged information about high school graduations, college entrance dates, the amount of money each of them made at their jobs last year. It brought up little asides. Not that Josh minded. It was kind of fun.

"I can't believe you went to that high school. They had the worst football team."

"Legendarily bad football team. If they could have scored negative points, they would have."

"I remember that one game, I was a freshman —"

"Oh, yeah. My junior year…"

It went on. She was pretty funny. At least he hadn't married some drippy, boring chick. Or a shrew. Good for him. His family wouldn't mind when they met her.

Whoa. What did he just say?

But that was going to happen. Unless the checks came immediately and they could race down for their annulment, there would be a family meeting.

Geez. What had he gotten her into?

***

Morgan hung up the phone and then kind of danced to the kitchen. She shouldn't have such a spring in her step over this. It was paperwork, for heaven's sake. But it was a Paperwork Honeymoon, so she let herself do a mini-celebration for ten seconds as she crossed the room to get a mailing envelope for the sheaf of papers she and Josh had just managed to fill out, and which had cost her about eighty-five minutes on her pre-paid phone plan—most of which minutes were spent on talking about funny stuff that happened to him when he was enrolled at Clarendon a few years ago and making fun of high school memories.

Besides, she should celebrate, even if only because it meant she was definitely qualified for the funding for her classes. She did a toe twirl—and it wasn't based solely on the little bubble of excitement that ping-ponged inside her after talking to the very charming Josh Hyatt.

Her legal husband. Whom she could never date.

Whatever. Today was a good day. And now, she would seal the deal—by affixing postage to the envelope and dropping it in the mail slot down at the post office near the beach.

She did, and then she celebrated by going for a brisk, early fall swim.

Yes, everything was going to work out just peachy.

***

Josh was back in his obsessive mailbox-checking routine again.

For one, he still hadn't heard from Brielle. Weeks, and no word. This was getting ridiculous. What, exactly, was she doing in Germany that meant she couldn't Skype, FaceTime, send or receive an email, or do any social media with him? Come on. He'd started a couple of snail mail letters to her, telling her that he'd be starting classes, that he had things really rolling, but without a mailing address, he had nowhere to send them and stuck them in his desk to send later. Maybe.

And, if he were honest, he felt a pang or two of guilt because he couldn't tell her everything. Certainly he couldn't tell her about his marriage to Morgan Clark. And that was, as they said, the elephant in the room of his life at this point. *I married her so I could pay for school and finish it so I could marry you.* Uh, pretty weak, and she might not get it. If he were to switch places with Brielle, and she pulled this shenanigan, no way would Josh be Sensitive New-Age Understanding Guy about it. Safer to omit the major detail until after things had ironed themselves out. For sure.

Which they would. For sure.

But meanwhile, there was the other reason he was obsessively checking the mail — watching for the check from the federal student aid people with the grant. Why they couldn't just do automatic deposit like every other entity in America at this point, he didn't know. Even the IRS could do an automatic deposit. And they'd basically asked for every other detail about his life — why not a bank account number, too? And a credit card number while they were at it? And his blood type? And whether he liked milk chocolate or dark chocolate?

Criminy.

He inserted the key in the bronze box. Nothing. Nothing! Again. He swore under his breath.

"Josh! Josh!" Morgan's voice lilted through the corridor to where he stood. "I'm so glad you finally got home. I've been texting you for an hour. The mail is here!" She bounced toward him, this time wearing workout clothes, which accentuated the bounce. Blast! He looked straight at her face. Her blue eyes sparkled. "It came to my box—both letters."

There were two letters? Oh, no. The one from Brielle got accidentally put in Morgan's box? That was not cool, Mr. Postman. Not cool.

Morgan extended a hand with a yellow-brown envelope. "I opened mine immediately. It's back inside my apartment. But here's yours."

Oh, the two letters were both checks. Yes! Josh tore his open. There, in all its shining, digitally printed glory was the six thousand dollars he'd gone to extraordinary measures to obtain. Finally! It was his.

He kissed the check and threw his hands to the sky. "Woo-hoo!" He grabbed Morgan up in his arms and swung her in a circle, planting an impromptu kiss on her mouth. "This is awesome!" When he set her down, she looked at him, a little dazed, and it suddenly dawned on him what he'd done. The spontaneous kissing—it was going to have to stop. Instinctively, he stuck out his tongue to taste his lips. Yep, raspberry lip gloss. Again.

"Uh." Great. *Caveman brain strikes again.* "Sorry."

"No, this is an awesome day." The blonde came back to her senses. Man, she was gorgeous. If he could clone himself, he'd have one Josh take Brielle, and the other Josh could take this raspberry chick who had just made his day. His year.

Yeah, he'd take this chick and her raspberry lip gloss and her swimsuit model body and, since he was married to her... *Stop.* He'd better reel in that hook and bait right now. Josh might be good at the bio-tech stuff he was working on in his spare time with compost, but he was nowhere near perfecting cloning yet. And the real Josh wanted Brielle. Right?

Morgan was talking. "I think they must have sent both

of them to my address, since we're married. They must have just inputted the one apartment number. Maybe they thought yours was an error."

The words hit Josh like a punch in the gut. Same address. The two of them had to have the same physical address if they were going to pull off the ruse that they were actually married. They could be found out. Separate apartments would be a dead giveaway. So would separate bank accounts, although not as much. And the fact she hadn't changed her name officially. Sure, this was the so-called modern age, and some women didn't take their husband's names, but they needed to cover as many bases as possible. He ran a hand through his hair, pulling the front of it to a peak.

Morgan was looking at him with those deadly blue eyes. He needed to think this over.

She spoke. "I guess, now that we have the checks, we can go get the marriage annulled." Instead of sounding business-like, she sounded a little hesitant. It made him look up.

"Oh. Right." Maybe she was right. Maybe they didn't have to worry about any of the trappings. They had the money. Time to annul.

"Smart. Okay. Well, I've got to go deposit this, get the tuition paid, and then I'll text you. We can meet back at the county building?"

Her nose wrinkled. "My truck is down. Needs spark plugs. Maybe tomorrow, but after I head to my bank?"

Josh spoke before he thought. "I could give you a ride."

"Thanks. That's awesome. I'll sleep a lot better tonight."

"It's a date." Josh lifted his hand to give her a fist bump, then lowered it. Too ironic—he was high-fiving a girl over a date to get their marriage annulled. Something about that couldn't be right.

"Just a sec. Let me get my purse and my check." She accented the word check with glee. Oh, so she wasn't going to make him wait while she changed out of the workout clothes. Excellent. Gorgeous, hot, raspberry-flavored, *and* considerate. Maybe he shouldn't be dumping her. She didn't even seem crazy, and that was almost impossible for a girl to be as hot as Morgan was and *not* crazy. He scruffed his hand up and down his cheek. *Hold the horses, boy. You're a man with a woman already.*

Then it hit him—she said she was going to sleep better tonight. Was that because her tuition was going to be paid in full? Or was it because she wasn't going to be his wife anymore?

It turned out they used the same bank. Convenient. That saved time.

Next, he drove up the hill to campus so they could go pay tuition. Late payers had to go in person with money orders or credit cards, Clarendon College rules.

"Looks like we're not the only people who got their grant money today." Morgan pointed to the line for financial aid and the cashier's office. It stretched long. "They all look mad. Turns out maybe misery doesn't love company."

They walked over to the back of the line. Ugh. It could be an hour. "Too bad I didn't bring cards. We could play poker while we wait." Strip poker. That'd make this whole place a lot more interesting.

"I'd clean you out."

"Oh, you think so, huh?"

"I know so." Morgan lifted a shoulder. "Try me sometime."

"I will." Josh would so beat her.

A heavy hand clapped down on Josh's shoulder. "Well, I'll be. If it isn't Joshua Hyatt. Back at Clarendon, eh?"

Josh looked up and saw a familiar face. It took him a second, but, "Wow. Rick Van Zandt. Hey." Great. Rick Van

Zandt. A giant blast from the past—but more like a blast of stench.

Rick roared. "Well, how about that? You are a sight for sore eyes. Remember all the good times we had—bonfires on Cannon Beach? But it looks like you've got a beach bunny of your own. Is that where you've been all this time? Hunting bunnies?"

"Ah, Rick. You always were so funny." Better to change the subject to Rick's favorite topic. "What you up to these days?"

"Me? Got my bachelor's degree a while back. Just working my way through grad school now. Did an internship with Agri-Gen this summer." Agri-Gen. That was where all Josh's pals during his first go-round at college were dying to work. How did Rick get in that door? "So, where'd you get off to anyway, after you quit school? Last I heard, you had a couple of patents in the works."

"Yeah, still doing my thing. Hey, you probably have stuff to do. Good to see you. I'll probably run into you again."

"No way. You can't give me the old brush-off. Not before you've introduced me to this one." He reached out and ran a hand down Morgan's arm. "Please say you're Josh's hot cousin."

Josh recoiled at seeing that caress. He almost lashed out at the guy, but he got it together fast. "This is Morgan, my wife."

Wife, wife, wife, wife. The echo bounced from the marble floor to the cathedral ceilings of the hallway. The first time he'd said the word out loud, and it hit him like a thunderclap.

"Wife!" Rick roared again, now like a second boom of thunder. "Well, good on ya, man." He looked Morgan up and down. "Really, really good on ya."

Rick's eyes slithered up and down Morgan, and Josh turned to see that Morgan had gone red from collarbone to scalp. Poor thing.

"She's awesome. I'm lucky I found her." Josh put an arm around Morgan's shoulder and jostled her. Holy crap. This was not the way he ever saw this going, his announcement to planet Earth that he'd gotten married. Rick Van Zandt was never at the top of his announcement list.

"Well, hey. Gotta go." Thank heaven Rick suddenly lost interest. That was so like him. When he had nothing to gain, he was gone.

Josh let his arm slide off Morgan's shoulders. "Sorry about that guy. He was always a jerk."

"It's fine," she said, but she didn't look fine. He watched her face until she finally said. "It's just—it's weird that you announced that, and then in half an hour we're headed off to do that other errand. You know. I guess it just seemed...weird."

"Well, I couldn't stand here and let Rick Van Zandt hit on you. He's a jackwagon of the highest order."

"There's an order for jackwagons?"

"Yes. And he's their Grand Poobah."

"I see. I could sense the poo part of that."

Josh laughed a little. The line had moved forward quite a bit. He checked his phone. Morgan was reading some paperwork from her purse. She was funny. He liked funny. Brielle was pretty intense all the time, and she didn't really get some of his jokes. That or she didn't think his jokes were funny. That sucked when it happened, but whatever. She had other charms, like the fact she knew he was penniless and loved him anyway, both before and after the blowup with Bronco. She'd been tested in the fires of trial, and she came out pure. Josh couldn't say that for certain about any other woman alive.

It took a couple of minutes, but the adrenaline from the Rick Van Zandt encounter subsided. Speaking of weird, he'd liked and hated how Rick's eyes crawled up and down

Morgan. Made him want to punch Rick and protect Morgan at the same time.

"You probably get that all the time, huh?" he asked.

"What?"

"Getting hit on by big creeps."

Morgan just rolled her eyes. "It's...whatever." She went back to her reading, turning another page of the big, stapled stack.

So she did. So why didn't she have a boyfriend? There were a lot of things about her he didn't know. Morgan was pretty quiet—until she was upset—although they'd talked kind of a lot on the phone when they were filling out the applications. It wasn't like she was all silent with nothing to say. That kind of woman drove him up a wall.

Which was why he liked Brielle. Brielle never lacked for things to say—with certainty or drama or animation. *Geez. Back to reality, dude.* Brielle Dupree had information on almost every conversational topic. Legitimately. She'd given serious reflection to history and politics and foreign relations. She had a mind. A memory of their dating floated back to him—not their trip to Acapulco when she'd been practicing her Spanish and got a killer bargain on a woven blanket for Josh at a street vendor's then found out it was half price at the next booth—but after the break with Bronco. Too poor then to do much of anything else, they'd gone to a board game tournament and entered the Trivial Pursuit bracket. With Brielle's knowledge on history and current events plus Josh's answers for the science questions, the two of them had cleaned every other team's clocks. They came out fifty bucks richer and blew the whole wad on dinner and a movie.

Brielle was a cool chick, and he smiled just remembering. Josh started to text her, but then he stopped himself. If she hadn't contacted him, a text from him might actually put her in danger. That was how she'd made it sound, anyway, when she left. She'd made it pretty clear.

73

But still, he and Morgan were almost at the front of this line. In the next ten minutes, Josh was paying his tuition, putting himself one step closer to getting that foreign policy degree, and then Brielle was his forever.

"Uh, Josh?" Morgan rested a hand on his arm and talked so low he almost didn't hear her. "I think you'd better look at this." She held out the paperwork she'd been reviewing, and her finger ran back and forth, underlining a section of a long paragraph a few pages into the stack.

"What is it?"

"It's the grant requirements." She sounded a little sick, and Josh took the papers from her, his eyes running along the sentences—sentences that spelled their plan's doom. Morgan's blue eyes were pools of worry. "It looks like we won't be going to the county building this afternoon."

"Next!" the lady in the Clarendon College embroidered polo shirt called.

Josh stepped forward, sick to his stomach. "Mr. and Mrs. Josh Hyatt. Here to pay our tuition."

Chapter Ten

I can't believe they'd charge interest—on top of requiring us to pay it back," which they couldn't now, anyway, because she and Josh had just forked over the whole amount to Resistencia and her greedy tuition-devouring fingers. Morgan and Josh stood together at the deepest back corner of the Clarendon College bookstore, next to the theoretical physics textbooks and the laptop keyboard cleaner spray. "Man. What have we accrued in interest already, just by standing in that horrendous line?"

"Wait. I can calculate that." Morgan let her mind reel through the interest formula from her Mortgages and Amortization 395 course. "Probably over thirty dollars, just since the mail arrived." Her stomach hurt. She started pacing back and forth. "What are we going to do, Josh?"

Josh came toward her, taking both her arms in his hands and steadied her. She looked up into his face while he answered her slowly and calmly. "We're going to stay married."

They were? This was *so* not in the plan. Not that she had anything against Joshua Hyatt, but he was totally not into her, and— "But it's for a whole year."

"Yeah, so?" He didn't sound like he minded too much. Of course, his girlfriend was gone for this whole year. *Promise you won't allow her to be your competition.* Tory's hush-money demand echoed in Morgan's brain.

Did he even know how long a year was? It was like…five percent of her life at this point. Well, a little less, but still. "So it's just not what we had discussed." Of course, there were way worse things in the world than having to keep up a fake marriage to the handsome son of a millionaire. Like root canals. Fifty mile hikes with shoes that didn't fit. Being stuck with her old Dodge truck broken down. "Aren't you upset? I would have thought..." She pictured him hand in hand with his faceless, globetrotting girlfriend, but then Tory's voice in her head shouted that image away.

Josh shook his head. "It is what it is." He pulled a textbook called *Ectoplasm and You* off the shelf and then put it back. "We should have read the fine print. We were dumb. But it doesn't change much of anything."

Why not? It changed her marital status. That seemed like a lot. "Look," she said, "if we can't just annul, there's a lot we are going to have to do." Being at the bank earlier reminded her that married people generally have joint bank accounts. And when he was at the cashier's desk, Josh had given his address to good old Resistencia, who gave him an appreciative look in return. He really was that good-looking. "You saw what happened when I went to use my debit card to buy that stupid textbook. They asked for ID, and whether it was up to date. This is going to keep happening."

"I've already been thinking about that." Josh's voice reassured her. "You're absolutely right. We're in this, and it's pretty much go big or go home."

"If go home means the go to the big house for fraud, you mean," Morgan hissed.

Josh opened his mouth to argue but shut it. He took a deep breath then spoke again in calming tones. "It's going to be fine. So we have some hoops to jump through. So the annulment takes longer than we planned. You seem like a patient person. You graduate in a year, anyway, and all this goes away. I go away. You won't ever have to think about me again."

Yeah, right. Chances were he'd occupy her mind as fully as now for years to come. Those teeth. That kiss.

And that other kiss—the one by the mailbox earlier. Why on earth did he have to do that to her? If he wanted her to be his fake wife, he was going to have to keep that kiss far away. Very far away.

"Since you're not arguing, I take it you're game." Josh reached for her elbow. Great. If it wasn't the kiss, it was the touch. She suddenly wished for a lot more layers of clothing right now between her skin and his electric touch. "It's details, but they have to be done."

"Right. Like at the very least, we have to get a post office box together. Address change, my name change at Social Security, renewing my driver's license." She'd thought some of this through, and her accounting background demanded to know what were they were going to do, come tax season. File jointly? Geez. This was such a mess.

"Bank accounts, everything. Frankly, we have to sell this—everywhere."

"So you're game." Morgan felt sick all over again. "If you're in, so am I." What other choice did she have? She'd drunk the Kool-Aid, and there was no stomach pump for this.

Josh nodded. "Look. It's not going to be that bad. After this initial bunch of details, you'll probably just forget it's even happening. Like somebody with a pacemaker. A few days after the surgery, they forget it's even in there."

Right.

"We can start this afternoon, head to Social Security, change your name. I still have the marriage certificate in my truck. It'll take two seconds."

Okay. She was feeling a little better about this, a *little*. He made things sound simple, not terrifying. And when he was around, something loosened her jaw, like the oil can for the Tin Man.

"And then we can go to the DMV and get you a new driver's license printed."

But her hair wasn't done. She lifted her hand to feel how much of it was a matted mess. She'd just been working out. Her face must have shown the terror because Josh waved his hand and said, "Come on. You look totally hot today. That ponytail is…" He trailed off. He thought she looked hot? She glanced down. She was in Spandex. Geez. She'd barely noticed, but apparently Josh had taken note.

Suddenly, a guy came around the corner. He caught sight of Morgan and smiled. She'd seen him before. "Hey, Morgan. How's it going? Chad from Business Stats spring semester? We talked?"

It was vague. She pulled a smile. "Hi, Chad."

"You look fantastic." He gave her that eye crawl, and she tried not to let her wince show too much. "I was wanting to ask you — do you want to go surfing with me sometime? The water's getting kind of cold now, September, so we'd have to go soon. You up for some waves this weekend?"

She didn't surf. And this was all manner of awkward. "Sorry, Chad. Hey, have you met Josh? This is Chad from my major. Chad, this is my husband — Josh."

Chad's face went from sunshine and surfing to cloudy and waterlogged faster than a coastal storm could roll in from the beach. "Husband. You're married?"

This was so weird. Every millimeter of it. She took a deep breath. "Yep."

"But you don't even have a ring."

***

Out at the truck, Morgan dug through her purse for a Tylenol, but she wished she had something stronger — like something to knock her out completely. Why was all this going on?

Not that she was interested in Chad, but it just hit her that she wouldn't be able to date anyone this year. She couldn't even begin to look for a relationship. She was putting herself in cold storage, basically, for the remainder of her college days.

Dang it. And something inside her always kind of thought she'd meet her husband in college.

Of course, not this way.

Not through defrauding the government.

Josh, though, had gotten her door. That was sweet. She didn't mind Josh at all. He wasn't exactly fulfilling all the roles of husband she'd always dreamed of, but he wasn't screwing it up so badly she'd end up deciding never to get married again in the future. After this marriage ended next year.

A year. She sighed. A whole year.

That was long enough for her left ring finger to get a little indentation around where the ring would sit. If she ended up wearing one, that is. Just because Chad from Business Stats suggested a ring didn't mean Josh was going to get her one. He'd just spent all his cash on tuition, anyway. It was dumb of her to even be thinking about it. Then again, Morgan did like rings, just like pretty much all girls did, but more for proving she was taken than for flashing a bauble.

Josh got in on the driver's side and pulled out of the parking garage. It was a little more full than the last time she'd faced down the stonewalling bureaucrats in their kingdom at financial aid. Yes! They'd done it! She could take classes. She didn't have to drop out!

"You okay?" he asked, eyeing her Tylenol packet.

"It's stressful, Josh. But it's not nearly as stressful as thinking I was going to have to drop out of school, so thank you." She smiled at him then dipped her eyes. He swerved a little in traffic, and she had to grip the armrest. "Where are we going first?"

79

"Let's hit the DMV, then Social Security for the name change before they close. Then the bank. Then...I have something in mind." He made it sound enticing, whatever it was. It sent a little zing of excitement through her. Maybe it was only going to be the post office to rent a joint box, but it made her secretly happy to get to spend the afternoon with Josh. He was kind of fun, even if this whole thing was just a business arrangement.

She could get used to him.

Even though she really, really shouldn't.

Chapter Eleven

Nobody ever called the DMV a party. Or the Social Security office either, which was full of cranky old men in white sneakers with thick soles. Or even yet the bank, which did not give away free Tootsie Pops when a customer opened a new account, which they should, according to Morgan Clark.

Make that Morgan Hyatt, now that they'd stood in line with the cranky white sneakers for an hour to change her name.

Morgan Hyatt. Josh watched as she signed it officially on the forms for her new driver's license and at the post office for their joint mailbox. She crossed each *t* separately. Who did that?

"Is that it for today?" she asked when he helped her into the passenger side of the Explorer after their exciting time without lollipops at the bank. "I need to do some laundry and get my uniform clean before work tomorrow."

"At the Tofu Palace?" He started the engine.

"My sister calls it The Weedeater. I prefer Leaf Me Alone."

"I don't know how you do it."

"What? Roller skate and carry a tray full of deep fried, pesticide-free okra? Believe me, it's no picnic. My ankles are going to need replacement surgery by the time I'm thirty."

"No, work all those hours and keep your grades up." In Josh's first two years at Clarendon he'd never had to worry about working part-time. School was his full-time job. Well, that and hanging out on Cannon Beach with the likes of Rick Van Zandt. Waste of time. His grades hadn't been stellar.

"Oh, that? I don't. I mean, I didn't. That's why I *had* to get this grant in the first place. My grades took a nosedive last spring, starting when I first tied the laces on the hot pink skates. Lost my scholarship when they cranked up my hours."

"Why not quit?"

"Same reason. Needed the money."

"So, it's kind of like your truck. You needed the truck to get to work, but you had to work to keep the truck fueled." He turned toward Starry Point's quaint shops along old Main Street. "You had to work part-time to pay for school, but working part-time made it so your grades tanked and you couldn't stay in school."

"Catch-22."

That was kind of sad. "But if you had a scholarship for the years prior, why take the job partway through your junior year?" It only made sense that if something wasn't broken, why fix it with tofu?

Morgan leaned her head against the window, her voice resigned. "I didn't have a choice. Rent went up near campus. I couldn't pay."

"But Estrella Court?" That place was a hole. It was the cheapest place in all of Starry Point, which was what Josh was doing there.

"Was all I could afford, and then only if I split rent with my sister."

Man, that was harsh. "It's not so bad there. Some of the people are nice." He tried flashing her a charming smile, and he kind of tweaked her elbow, forgetting for a second that he wasn't supposed to be touching her bare skin, per his own rules.

That skin was soft. He probably let his hand linger there a second too long. Was that a little sigh Morgan let out?

Ignore. Ignore. Ignore.

"Here we are." He swung into a parking spot in front of Rothwell's. "I'm stupid about these things, but you can help me figure it out."

"It's a jewelry store." Morgan looked a mixture of shocked and terrified.

"Yeah?"

"What are we doing here? I mean, we just blew all our cash on tuition. This isn't some dime store." She turned those blue eyes at him, obviously worried. That was sweet of her — to care about his cash liquidity.

"I know." He was doing this all wrong. "I just want you to come in and point out which styles you like. Don't worry about it. The ring has to be your style though, or your friends won't buy the scenario." He would work out the details later of how to do this. Meanwhile, they had to do this.

"And we have to sell it convincingly. You're right. Okay. I'm game. But I do wish I were wearing something a little less...elastic for this outing."

"You look amazing." He wasn't just saying that. She looked like she could be the aerobics instructor chick in the window of the fitness club, the girl the gym owners use as bait to trap lonely guys into year-long memberships. "It shows off your tan."

"My sunburn, you mean."

"It's a tan now. That burn was a few weeks ago." Not that he'd noticed. Not that he'd been staring her up and down when she came all red and talked to him by the mailboxes in just her swimsuit. Not that he'd been thinking about it against his will fifty times an hour ever since. It sucked to be living next door to the hottest chick in Starry Point, or maybe anywhere else, while his girlfriend was six thousand miles away. And not tan.

Remembering Brielle threw cold water on the serious flame Morgan was starting to fan. Okay, that was a lot of mixed metaphors, but he was back now, ready to do business in Rothwell's.

The salesman turned around, and Josh saw Manny. "Hey, Josh. What are you doing in here?" He came over to shake Josh's hand. "Oh, I see. Hell-o." Manny apparently noticed Morgan.

"Manny, this is Morgan. My wife."

Manny did that eye-slither thing that the other men they'd met today had done. Morgan—she was probably sick of that. If she noticed. "Congratulations. So why come in here? Need the ring sized or something?"

"I guess we kind of put the cart before the horse." Josh had been hanging out with the white sneakers crowd too long today. His metaphors had gone from mixed to old-man-style.

"We eloped," Morgan clarified.

"Oh, right. Morgan, is it?" Manny slipped into sales mode. "Let's see what would look perfect on your lovely finger."

Josh stood half-watching as Manny and Morgan went past a dozen ring cases. She refused to try any on, which he didn't understand. But eventually, after about fifteen minutes of Manny pushing bigger and bigger rings on her, she put her foot down.

"I'm just not a zillion-diamond girl." She looked at Josh for help. "All these styles are too...I don't know. Ornate."

He walked over to her, and a glance in the case told him exactly what she meant. Huge diamonds surrounded by a bunch of other diamonds. Josh didn't like them either.

The bell hanging on the door of the shop jingled. More customers walked in. Manny smiled at Morgan. "I'll let the two of you talk this over."

"Good," Morgan whispered. "Now we can get out of here." She looked relieved. He'd never imagined a woman looking relieved to exit a jewelry store. He figured their very souls resonated to gemstones and that they'd be happier here than among a million pairs of shoes. Even Brielle, serious about everything on earth, got goggle-eyed about diamonds. Morgan was different from other girls—and not in bad ways. Not at all.

"Josh? Josh Hyatt?" A shrill voice pierced his ear. "I can't believe it. It's been months. How have you been?" There, beside the door stood his worst nightmare—the last person on earth he wanted to see right now.

"Claire. Oh, hey." Of all the jewelry shops in all of Oregon, she walks into this one. He swallowed his bile. "Just heading out." He gave a dramatic glance at his wrist, even though he wasn't wearing a watch. "Late for a reservation."

"Oh, stop it," she growled playfully. "Come here. Don't tell me you don't have time for Brielle's best friend in the whole world." Claire tugged Josh's arm, pulling him into an awkward hug. "I want you to meet Buster, my fiancé. He's from Starry Point. We're planning a Christmas wedding at the Chapel in the Pines, and since I can do my publishing business from anywhere, I've relocated here while I plan our wedding. Isn't it great? We can run into each other while Brielle is out of the country and..."

Yeah, just *great*. If he kept the topic on Claire, he could maybe weasel out of here before—

Manny spoke up. "Isn't that nice? Your friend just eloped."

All the air whooshed out of Josh's lungs, and the word hung heavy in it, floating like a flashing neon sign. *Eloped. Eloped. Eloped.*

Fabulous. That dun-dun-dun music from movies hung in the air. Claire knew. Even if Brielle couldn't be reached for now, there were other serious implications of this moment which hit Josh in fast succession, like the fact that in about thirty seconds, or as long as it would take for her to send a text, every single one of Brielle's fifty other Best

Friends in the Whole World would know that Josh had married another girl less than a month after Brielle left the country. He'd become the biggest villain in the Portland twenty-something singles crowd, maligned and vilified all over social media, and shoot to *persona non grata* status among all of her friends, maybe forever — even after he and Morgan eventually accomplished the annulment. Brielle's friends might hate him so much that they could potentially talk Brielle out of her relationship with Josh.

This. Was. Not. Good.

"Eloped." Claire snagged the reverberating word from the air.

"Yeah. Heh-heh." He felt like such a jackwagon right now. "Claire, I want you to meet my wife, Morgan." There was no stopping the runaway train now. He might as well ride it to its inevitable fiery, crashing end.

Morgan smiled, but she didn't say anything.

Claire progressively turned as red as the cherry Kool-Aid color of her hair. First her neck, then the lower half of her face, then the red crawled to her scalp. "Brielle didn't tell me you broke up."

We didn't. How stupid would that sound? Beyond stupid.

Morgan slid her hand into his. On her tiptoes she reached up and gave him a gentle kiss on the cheek. "We're late, Josher. Everyone will be waiting for us." She gave his arm a soft tug, pulling him toward the door. He went willingly.

"Wait just a minute there, Josh Hyatt." Rage bubbled in Claire's voice. "I don't even know if I believe that you're married. A breakup is something Brielle wouldn't have kept from me." Her voice was starting to fade as Josh and Morgan left the store. "I'm serious. Come back here, Josh. I have more to say to you. If you're so married, what are you doing in the ring store after the fact? Come back here, you two-timing jerk!"

At this, Josh picked up speed. Morgan shouldn't be subjected to those insults. She hadn't done anything wrong. He put her into the Explorer and started the engine. "What do you say to some music?" He adjusted the radio to the rock station, hoping to drown out Claire's voice from his head. But the anger of the music only amplified it. Morgan reached over, placed her hand on his, removing it from the dial, and shut off the radio.

"It's okay, Josh. People are going to be mad at us. I think we just have to plan on that from here on out."

Mad. That was pretty apropos. Josh was boiling at Claire. It was none of her business in the first place, and...

He'd jammed the car into gear and was driving too fast down historic Main Street. Morgan was on her phone, typing something.

"There."

"What?" He had to slam the brake when the light turned red, reminding him of Claire's awful head.

"Smile for a selfie of us."

What? Was she kidding? But he could smell the honeysuckle that was Morgan when she leaned over the gear box toward him. It must have softened his anger because the pic of them, which she held up, didn't look as strained as he felt.

"I need a shave."

"Yeah? I need a shower." She started tapping on her phone. "There. I just took the bull by the horns."

"How so?"

"I just made our marriage social-media-official. Bring on the avalanche—because it is coming."

Chapter Twelve

Morgan dried her hair, wishing her one picture with Josh on social media didn't have her looking like she'd been at CrossFit all afternoon. What a way to foist the news on the world.

The front door slammed, hard enough that Morgan could hear it over the hairdryer. In stormed Tory.

"What on earth do you think you're doing?"

"Fixing my hair so I don't look like a yeti?" Morgan shut off the hairdryer, done with the process.

"You never look like a yeti. Abominable snowman, yes. But not a yeti."

"What's the difference, even? And how would you know?"

Tory just rolled her eyes. "Irrelevant. I'm probably going to kill you so it won't matter anyway."

"It will totally matter. You'll have to put it in the funeral program as one or the other. Don't forget to sing 'Amazing Grace,' though. That's my favorite. I like that one version—"

"Stop changing the subject. How could you do that to Mom? She is a blubbering mess. What with Nixie's surgery and all, she can barely function, and you chuck her to the wolves?"

"What are you talking about?"

Tory pulled out her phone and held up the icky picture of Morgan and Josh. It was taken at the worst angle, from under their chins, and Morgan seriously looked like The Great Unwashed next to Josh whose nostrils were flaring. He'd been pretty mad at that shrew Claire when Morgan snapped the photo. But what choice had she had at the moment?

Well, probably a lot of choice. Still, what was done was done.

"Since when is Mom on social media?" Morgan tried to tamp down her guilt with this lame excuse. "I never dreamed—"

"Mom is as social media-obsessed as anyone ever."

"No way. She hasn't posted to her page in months. Just a couple of pics of Nixie here and there."

"She doesn't post, but she lurks, like, hours a day. She watches everybody's stuff, comments on it when she sees them in person. Haven't you noticed?"

Now that Tory mentioned it, Mom did seem pretty up on their lives, even when Morgan hadn't called her in a while.

"Check your phone." Tory left the bathroom, shaking her head. "And think about how other people feel once in a while, why don't you?"

Where was that coming from? Morgan wasn't exactly the callous brat Tory was insinuating she was. She threw her clean hair up into the required Meatless in Seattle twist-bun and found her phone. She'd had it shut off.

Whoa! Eighty-six missed calls? What was that all about? She scrolled through them. It appeared about fifty were from her mom. The other thirty-plus were from friends, probably freaking out that she hadn't told them she was married. She'd deal with them later.

There was also a voice mail. Mom was the only person in Morgan's world who still left voice mail messages.

Morgan, honey. I love a prank as much as the next person, but the least you could do is let your old mother in on it ahead of time so she doesn't lose her head with worry. Sweetheart? I always thought we'd planned...well, never mind. You should know, Nixie is going to be just fine.

Her voice sounded hurt. Morgan would drop

everything right this second and go straight to Portland, even this late in the day, and explain everything in person, if only she didn't have to work in a few minutes. It seemed like a better way to atone for her mistake than just explaining over the phone, but thanks to Veg-Out, a call was the best she could do. She dialed.

"Mom? Hey, it's Morgan."

"Morgan Elise Clark." Oh, boy. The full-name treatment. This could be bad. "Or is it some other last name now?" The words were coming through clenched teeth, all hissy.

"It's Hyatt, actually."

"What? You married the veterinarian?" Mom sounded genuinely confused.

"His younger brother, Josh."

"And you've never, ever said anything about him. Not once. And now, poof! You're a married woman."

Basically. That was basically it. How could she explain to her mom? Especially when the whole thing was what it was? For one thing, Mom wouldn't understand the deep necessity for it. She was a firm believer in the sanctity of marriage—not that Morgan wasn't, but somehow this was different. Anyway, for another thing, Mom would feel horrible for not being able to remedy Morgan's situation herself—especially when she was the main cause of it, she and her *Frogs in the Sand* catastrophe. And for another, she couldn't actually be trusted to keep the secret.

If Morgan wanted everyone to know something, she told Mom and said it was a secret.

"Point of fact. It's not actually okay to let your mother find out about your marriage via social networking." Anger seethed through the airwaves.

Morgan's insides writhed. She had to find something true to tell her mom. "He's a really nice person. He's the one who came up with the way to save Nixie's life. He called his brother and asked the favor."

Over the phone, Morgan could hear her mother expel a loud breath, as if she'd been holding it a long time, waiting to explode but had simply deflated instead.

"Well, that is fine of him." Mom's voice came out small. When Desiree Clark felt gratitude, she was apt to forgive quickly. That was a good quality Morgan had always admired in her. "I hope he's not as freakish as he looks in that picture of the two of you."

Morgan couldn't stifle a laugh. If that was Mom's big worry— "He's really good-looking, Mom. That isn't the main reason I eloped with him, but it doesn't hurt."

Mom gasped a little.

"What? Is something wrong, Mom? Is Nixie okay?"

"You're not pregnant, are you? That's not the reason for the elopement, is it? Because, I mean, if it is, I'm glad he had the honor to marry you, which makes me like him all the more, but Morgan! You were always the girl who was saving herself for marriage, and the last thing I thought—"

"Mom! No. I'm not pregnant." Jehoshaphat. Morgan had never considered this would be the perception of her family. Her friends probably thought so, too. Great. Just marvelous. "I'm still the good girl I always was."

Mom did that exhale again. "Well, at least there's that."

This whole conversation was awful. "Mom, I'm really sorry I didn't manage this better. I should have called you first."

"You should have introduced him to me first."

There was that, too. "I'm sure you'll love him when you meet him."

"Well, if he's anything like his brother the veterinarian, I'm sure I will, but any young man who doesn't do his due diligence and at least ask the girl's parent before ripping her from her mother's bosom is someone I instinctively distrust. He's going to have to do more than get me a doctor appointment to win that."

"He did save Nixie's life."

"Okay. I'll give you that." She harrumphed a little. "It's just that, Morgan, I thought we always had this big wedding planned for you. Bunting, the white dress, the organ playing as you walk down the aisle, lots of flowers and a big cake."

"I know, Mom." She could feel her mother's sadness through it all, the disappointment with the change from her expectations. Morgan didn't know how to be honest and comfort her and keep her secret at the same time. She couldn't just say, *It's all right. We can probably still do that when I get married for real.* Nor did she want to admit to the hint of relief inside herself—at escaping all that pomp. Especially the walking down the aisle part.

"Because if this was about your old hang-up—if you only eloped to get out of what you were forever saying you wanted to avoid—I told you I'd get Uncle Boswell to walk you down the aisle. Lots of girls still get married and walk down the aisle without a dad beside them. They work it out."

Yeah, but Morgan hadn't wanted to work it out. She'd wanted a dad. And without one, that whole fairy tale wedding thing would always be a broken fairy tale, as far as Morgan was concerned. So this trial run elopement might not be such bad practice for when she really did get married. No bunting, no bridal procession, no ring on a velvet cushion. And no glaring void where her dad should be standing beside her to give her away.

"I've never even met Uncle Boswell, and none of us have two dimes to rub together right now, let alone plan a big wedding. It's ridiculous to be discussing this." Which was part of why she had eloped. Er, sort of. "But that's not the point, Mom. I'll bring Josh up sometime to meet you." It was small consolation for the dream she'd just apparently ripped away from Mom's life. Still, she had another daughter whose wedding she could dream about. And, who knew? Morgan might actually meet Mr. Right one of these days, after her annulment, and then she could make it up to her mom somehow, just not with the walking down the aisle part.

"Oh, no need. As soon as Nixie is feeling better, we're planning a trip to come see you and Tory anyway. I'll have to see the apartment of Mr. and Mrs. Joshua Hyatt."

Uh, what? She hadn't thought of that. Having to keep up appearances for her mom? Create a phony cohabitation?

Great. Josh was going to love this.

***

Josh's Explorer was almost out of gas, but he was near Chip's house. The two-hour drive had drained the tank, but he was going to have to risk it since it was getting so late. He dialed the phone.

"You and Heather still up?"

"It's ten-thirty, Josh. What are you calling about? Another hot blonde's mom have a dog disaster? Because I'm off the clock until tomorrow."

"Thanks for taking care of that, bro." Josh maneuvered around a double-parked car on Chip's street. This Portland suburb had more of that...wait. "How did you know it was a hot blonde's mom?"

"That woman didn't stop talking. Even showed me the picture of the girl."

Heather's voice hollered from the distance. Apparently he was on speaker phone. "Plus, there's that whole firestorm her photo of the two of you set aflame online. What were you thinking, Josh?"

"Yeah, Bronco is not amused." Chip huffed. "Probably no one is."

"Didn't think he would be. Which is why I'm coming by." Josh pulled into the driveway of Chip and Heather's duplex. "Do you still have that box of stuff from Mom?" He jumped out of his Explorer and rang their doorbell, hoping the three minutes on the phone had given them time to prep for his arrival.

Luckily, they were still up and dressed. "What is going on with you?" Heather let him in. "And what happened to Brielle? Didn't she just leave a month ago? I didn't even know you'd dumped her."

"I didn't dump her." At least that was true.

"Oh." Heather didn't press for details, just got a little sad look on her face. She brought him a Coke with ice. "And this Morgan girl is okay with being a rebound? You told her about Brielle?"

"I told her." There was no way to elucidate further. "She's a good sport."

Heather half-laughed. "She'd have to be, to marry into this family." She kicked back on the couch across from Josh and put her feet on the coffee table. Heather was so normal, so good for Chip. "Now, while Chip looks for that box in the attic, as I assume that's why you came and sent him up there, tell me all about your latest progress in the lab. Any luck securing the patent yet?"

"One patent applied for, two pending, and the big one awaiting a breakthrough." Josh gave Heather details about the research he was doing with the compost barrel. "I'm about three mutations from actually making it work, I think."

Heather pushed her head against the sofa's back. "I can't believe you. The bio-tech companies are going to be pounding down your door to get hold of it. You're going to change the world."

Josh still hadn't seen the full result, so he didn't let himself get his hopes up yet.

"By the way, what does, uh, Morgan—that's her name, right?—think of sharing a house with an open barrel of compost day and night? She must have a strong stomach. Stronger than Brielle's."

Brielle shared only a little enthusiasm for Josh's

94

research. *You should concentrate on learning Russian and Chinese instead of playing with all this, uh,....* She'd omitted the word *garbage*, but he'd heard it loud and clear. Instead, she'd bought him study books and they'd read online articles in Al Jazeera at night together so he could bone up on foreign happenings. That wasn't exactly a barrel of monkeys, but the nights they stayed up late watching German language tutorials on YouTube, and laughing so hard when trying to copy the throat-clearing sounds to perfection were good times. Brielle knew so much about the real threats facing all different areas of the globe and cared so much about the welfare of her fellow earthlings, he couldn't help but get caught up in it. She was the one who was going to change the world, make it a safer place. And as soon as Josh finished school, he was going to be right at her side. By then, she'd know people, the right people, and he'd be able to use her contacts to get the right job.

They had plans.

"Like I said, Morgan's a good sport." He did wonder if he'd ever have to tell her about the compost barrel. Probably not.

Chip came in, holding a familiar-looking box. "What did you want this for? And so late at night?" He sat down and plopped the box in Josh's lap. It was heavier than he expected. "What kind of old perfume and jewelry emergency could there be at this time of night?" Chip's voice caught. "Oh. Ohhhhh."

Josh rolled his eyes. "Glad you figured it out."

He slid the lid off the box and peered inside. The smell of Mom's perfume wafted out, just faintly, and her smiling face flashed before Josh's eyes for a second. She'd been a good mom.

"I just need the ruby ring. And it's not forever. I'll bring it back when I'm done with it." Chip dug through the stacks of papers, photos, trinkets of thimbles Mom used to collect and tugged out a little velvet bag. From inside he extracted a gold ring with a ruby solitaire.

"What do you mean, bring it back? Mom would want you to have it, especially after how Bronco has treated you. She'd want to make up for it somehow. You know that." Chip sounded final.

"No, I'll bring it back. I don't need it forever." But he caught himself—he didn't want to let on that anything between Morgan and him was temporary. He had to watch that he didn't leave any clues—anywhere. "It's just until I can get her something of her own."

"She'll want an heirloom, especially this one. It's a real ruby." Heather came over and sat on Chip's lap, entwining her arms around his neck. "Every woman wants a ruby."

"I'll get you a ruby someday, Heath."

"I know you will." She kissed Chip. "I tried that ring on a while back, and it won't even fit my pinkie or I would've pilfered it a long time ago."

That, at least, made Josh feel better about taking the ring that had been Mom's engagement present from Bronco. He pocketed it.

"I should tell you no." Chip closed the box and set it on the table. He punched Josh in the arm. "What do you mean, not telling me you were getting married? From the pictures her mom showed me, she's gorgeous, but I'm your brother. I thought we were close."

"It was kind of spontaneous."

"So she's pregnant."

"No." Josh rolled his eyes. "Come on, man." The suggestion made Josh's thoughts slide where they shouldn't go.

"Not that I could blame you. From the pic we saw, she's Hollywood. Makes Brielle look like a potato with—"

"Hey. No trash-talking Brielle."

"Fine. I'll just say you picked your rebound very well."

Heather gave Chip a visible arm pinch. "Josh made sure they went into it with their eyes wide open. They're going to be fine."

Good for Heather, coming to his defense. "I think you'll like her. But, hey. It's getting late. I'm heading back tonight. Is that gas station still open down on the corner?"

"You can't drive back at this hour," Chip said. "It's a bad, winding road between here and Starry Point. And it's supposed to rain."

"This is the Oregon coast. It's always supposed to rain. But thanks for this." He patted his pocket. "I'm sure Morgan will love it." He hoped that was true. Even if it was a fake-out, he needed her to have something she liked. It was the least he could do for the sacrifice she was making. Geez. She was taking herself off the market for a whole year for him, not dating any of the dozens of guys who'd be asking her out. Sure, she got the monetary benefit from it same as Josh did, but Josh had someone, a sure thing after this was over. Morgan might not, so the incredible ruby ring was a weak consolation prize for that. But it was all he could do at this point.

Chip opened his mouth to protest Josh's leaving—he had his jacket on—but Heather stopped him. "Chip, hon. He's a newly married man. He has reasons for wanting to get back." Heather gave Chip a pointed look and then a wink, and then Chip nodded like he knew a dirty secret.

Good thing they didn't know how wrong they were about that.

Chapter Thirteen

There came a tapping on Morgan's window, the one facing the Estrella Court courtyard. She peeled open an eye. It was still dark. She pushed aside the curtains and saw a figure of a man, silhouetted by the light behind him. She stifled a scream and shut the curtain, pulling the covers up over her chest, clutching them.

Just then, her phone beeped a text. She grabbed it, trying not to hyperventilate.

Josh: *Can you come outside?*

Morgan: *Josh. Geez. Don't scare a girl like that.*

Josh: *Sorry. Sorry so late. Or early. Or whatever.*

Morgan: *Give me a couple of minutes.*

She hurried, and soon she was out under the stars—which were exceptionally bright tonight. No clouds. Josh was pacing back and forth in the courtyard, between the decrepit bench and the dead hydrangea bush, when Morgan came outside in her fuzzy slippers, teeth brushed but nothing much else done. He looked crazed.

"You all right? You don't look all right." A stab of fear pained her. "Did someone find out?" They were going to jail. They had to flee in the night. Phony, marriage-fraud fugitives! Her heart raced.

"No. It's fine. I'm fine. Just had way too much caffeine in the last couple of hours." No wonder he looked hopped-up. "I have to work really early tomorrow, er, today, in the lab," he checked his watch, "in about forty-five minutes, and I didn't want to wait another day. I've been getting questions, and I think you have, too."

That was an understatement. She hadn't bothered to return any of the thirty-five missed phone calls or the fifty that had accumulated since then. Her heart slowed to a normal pace.

"Maybe this will make it easier to change the subject." He reached into his pocket and pulled out something small. It was hard to see in the poorly lit courtyard, but Morgan did catch a little glint as Josh held it toward her. "What? You look kind of disappointed. Don't you like it?"

She loved it—what she could see of it here in the dark of Estrella Court's dilapidated courtyard. "No. I mean, I'm sure I'll like it. It's just—"

"What?"

"I just kind of told a couple of people you proposed on the beach."

"Beach it is! Nice we have one so handy." He grabbed her hand and tugged her toward the parking lot. In a second, she was seated on the rough seat cover of his Explorer, at which point she realized just how short her nightgown and robe were. The backs of her legs noted the worn parts of the seat. When was she ever going to be dressed appropriately for any activity she and Josh did together?

By the light of the dash, she could see he'd noted her bare legs as well. "Need a blanket? I've got one in the back." His eyes might have lingered on her legs a little long.

"It's okay." She tugged her robe around her shoulders, wishing for at least a sports bra. This was ridiculous. But, she thought, looking out at the night, the moon was sure pretty tonight, or, this morning, or whatever time it was. "The heater is working." Indeed, it was blowing down on her ankles and warming her just fine for the three minute ride to the beach, which was ending already.

"Do you want to be down by the waves, or is the rocky shore close enough?" Josh asked as he pulled into the parking lot at the beach. He came around and let Morgan out.

There was a fifty-yard walk from the parking lot down to the water. In her fuzzy slippers, she'd rather stay up here. Plus, here by the light of the parking lot's streetlamp she could see the ring, and Josh's very nice teeth. The air smelled of salt and pine, the Oregon coast smell.

"Here is good." A tremor of a chill shook her stomach muscles.

They stood together on the gravelly asphalt. He was so jumpy. She didn't mind. It was kind of cute to see him all excited. "It's all out of order," he said, "but we need a story to tell, and we might as well be telling the same one. Beach proposal it is."

"We don't have to include all the details."

"Like the bats swooping for mosquitoes above us."

"Exactly. But this works." Morgan shivered. "We might have to hurry." Her stomach and kneecaps were trembling from the chill of the night.

Then Josh seemed to come to himself, and he slid to one knee. He pulled out the ring again. Morgan stepped toward him. The waves sloshed in the distance below, and Josh looked up at her with expectancy in his face as she inched closer.

He didn't say anything, didn't ask anything. It was super awkward.

Finally, Morgan said, "Thank you?" What was she supposed to say? Was this a proposal? If so, he needed to phrase it right.

He stood up and placed the ring on her finger. "Thanks for marrying me, Morgan."

She held the ring up, and then Josh extracted his keychain from his pocket and shone a little flashlight on the ring. "There," he said, and Morgan could see it at last.

It took her breath. "It's beautiful!" It was red, not a diamond. Wow. She loved red stones, real or fake. "It even

100

looks real. Oh, I hope you didn't spend money on me."

"It's a ruby."

"Ruby! Those are more expensive than diamonds. Especially for one this size." Morgan felt sick. Here was a guy who'd gone to extraordinary lengths to pay tuition. He should not be blowing any cash on his fake wife's vanity.

"It was my mother's."

His mother's! Warm tingles flushed through her, followed by a cold shower of guilt. How could she accept such a thing?

Josh towered over her, and at this moment, Morgan realized he still had hold of her other hand. "She's been gone a few years. She won't miss it."

As if that made it any better! "I can't wear your mother's special ring." Because this ring had to be special. It was too gorgeous not to be.

"Well, I can't afford anything else right now. Can you just humor me?" Josh looked down, pleading with her. Morgan's eyes had adjusted to the night's dimness to see as much as that of his expression. "My mom would be the one person who'd see all the humor in this situation. Honestly, she wouldn't mind. In fact, she'd probably give you her heirloom china just to perpetuate the story so everyone else would believe it."

Morgan had relaxed, a little, and looked at the ring. "It's so pretty. I feel guilty."

"Don't. Honest."

Morgan tugged her nightgown around her tighter, suddenly conscious again of her bare legs and the chill of the autumn night.

"Thanks, Josh. I'll wear it. And I'll tell people you gave it to me on the beach. Under the stars."

"Good. That'll make me look good." He looked relieved, and some of his caffeine energy seemed to relax for a moment, until a wicked grin crossed his face. "And now I've seen how you look right when you wake up in the morning."

Morgan winced. "What's that got to do with anything?" They walked back over to the Explorer and got in.

"It's what guys think about. That lunkhead Rick Van Zandt is bound to ask me. I don't want to have to *lie*." He raised an eyebrow at the irony of it. Josh started the engine and drove them toward their apartments again. The heater was a blessed relief, and her stomach stopped quivering after a minute.

"Oh, really." That was new. She'd thought lying was their new full-time hobby. "And what are you going to tell him when he asks?" No way did guys ask that kind of thing. She didn't believe it for a second.

"That your hair sticks straight up."

"Thanks."

"But that your legs are amazing."

Cold prickles ran up her bare legs. Great. She really should start sleeping in sweats, or she should've at least pulled some on before she came outside and stood half-naked with a strange man, even if he was her husband.

They got back to Estrella Court. Josh shut off the engine. He came around and opened her door for her, and they walked toward the courtyard again.

Fine. If was going to be like that, he'd have to take some of his own medicine.

"Well, if that's what guys ask each other, and I seriously doubt it, here's what girls really ask." Morgan batted her eyelashes and affected a girly voice. "Ooh, Morgan, when he proposed to you on the beach, how was his proposal kiss? Did it blow your mind?"

Josh cleared his throat. "And what are you going to tell them?"

"The truth." She shrugged. "That I didn't even feel it." She might have said this with a challenging air, but he'd put her up to it. "It was lighter than a breeze."

"Oh, no you won't." Josh reached for her and yanked her to him by her waist. In half a second, his mouth was on hers, pressing firmly, and in another half second he was giving her a kiss so imbued with passion, she succumbed and was kissing him, too. His hand slid up and down her back, and she was pressed up against his warm chest. After she didn't know how long—ten seconds? A full minute?—Morgan had to pull back just to catch her breath.

"Whoa there, cowboy." Holy cannoli. If this was how he faked true love's kiss, she gulped to think what a sincere one was. "Hold those horses."

Josh's grin pulled to one side. "You can tell them about that one." And he stalked off, with a serious swagger, leaving Morgan twirling the ruby ring on her finger, and forgetting all about the cold of the night air.

***

A week later, Tory came into the room, squealing. "You got it! You got the interview!"

Morgan looked up from her cost accounting assignment. Her brain hurt, trying to make everything balance with all the variables and rate changes. Tory was hopping from foot to foot and rubbing her hands together.

"What interview? The last thing I need is another part-time job." Veg-Out was demanding her time again in just a few minutes—and she'd barely started these accounting problems. If she flunked out of this semester, after everything she'd been through to enroll, it would be a tragedy on the scale of the Hamlet play Tory was immersed in every day.

"Amen to that. The Weedeater is enough. Is your skinned knee doing better today?"

"Yeah. Thanks for the antibiotic ointment. I don't think it will get infected, after all." She'd biffed it on the roller skates last night—in front of three cars. Murgatroyd, she'd

103

love to quit that job.

"Look. This interview could make it so you don't have to strap on skates and bring someone a deep-fried tofu patty *ever again*."

Now, that was something worth looking into. Morgan snatched the paper from Tory's hands.

"I hope you're not too mad I nominated you." Tory was biting her nails. She didn't have many to start with. They could bleed.

Morgan looked over the letter.

Congratulations, Victoria Clark. Your nomination of your sister Morgan and her husband Josh Hyatt for the Seagram Scholarship has been reviewed. Mr. Seagram will see them on Friday at noon at his home, 5466 Big Piney Way. Please inform them of this wonderful news. Mr. Seagram looks forward to meeting them.

"What is this for?"

"It's a scholarship—the Seagram Scholarship. And I had no idea the interview would be so quick. He must be itching to give it out."

Whatever amount the scholarship was, Morgan needed it. Especially if it was enough to let her quit that job at the drive-in. "That's great, Tory. I'm in!"

"Good, because I have to go meet Hamlet right now and let him know I'm nothing more than Banquo's ghost as far as he's concerned. I'll tell you all the details when I get back—I mean about the breakup, not the scholarship. You know as much as I do about that."

Morgan had to leave for work right now, and she had classes all morning tomorrow, but she'd wear her best suit and meet Josh there at noon, if he was available. *Please be available.*

She grabbed her phone and texted Josh.

Morgan: *What are you doing at noon tomorrow?*

***

104

Tory didn't tell Morgan any details when she got back after *Hamlet* practice because Morgan was gone, stuck in a homework spiral at the Belliston Library on the third floor among the statistics textbooks. How could so many assignments be due this early in the semester? Clarendon College was known for being rigorous, but the senior projects were almost as mind-blowing as Josh's engagement kiss. Or whatever that occasion was. Did they get married first or engaged first?

So screwed up.

Morgan had crawled into bed at two, her mind swirling with numbers and formulas. And then at five-thirty her phone rang.

"Morgan, it's Carl." Her manager from Veg-Out. How could he? At this hour? When she'd worked forty-five hours this week already? "Can you get down here? Javier called in sick, and I don't have anyone to run the meals for the breakfast crowd."

"Carl, I've got an early class. Eight o'clock."

"I can get someone in by then. Can you just come in?"

"You'll pay me overtime." It was an empty threat.

"You know I can't do that." The franchise rules forbade it.

"Make sure I get good tips, then." As if. For some reason, the morning crowd never tipped. This was so depressing. There was only time to shower, but not do her hair. She had to stick it in a messy, wet bun and get in there before the doors opened at six.

What if she'd said no? She should have said no. Her truck started with a snort, and then it lurched out of the gravel parking lot toward the beach.

Dang it. She forgot her skates. Well, Carl would have to deal with that.

Two hours, sixty-eight cups of organic coffee and nineteen veggie-sausage muffins later, Javier rolled in.

"You look rested." Morgan had to get in the jab. Javier hated the early shift.

"You look like fertilizer."

"Thanks." This job. If she didn't have to have it to survive, she'd tell them all where they could stuff it—right in their stuffed bell peppers. "I have class. Here's the order list." She stuffed everything in Javier's hands and untied her white pinafore apron.

"Who's that guy checking you out at the door?" Javier aimed a thumb over his shoulder. "Not that most of the customers don't check you out, but he looks like a meat-eater to me." Javier was a True Believer and claimed he could determine a non-vegan on sight.

Morgan was in a hurry to get to class (and redo her hair in the truck), but she shot a glance the guy's way.

"Josh," she semi-gasped.

"So you know him?"

"Yeah, that's my, uh. Yeah." She wasn't sure Javier deserved to know, and it would take forever to explain, time she didn't have this morning. She went over to where Josh stood at the door.

"I wanted to see what this place was." He gave the place a cursory once-over. "And ask what's going on today."

"It's not much, but it pays the bills." Sort of. "I don't actually know about today. My sister nominated me for a scholarship, and I guess you're supposed to be there."

Josh nodded. "Okay. And this scholarship is called…?"

"Seagram? Have you heard of that?"

Josh cocked his head to the side.

"Me, neither. I never had any scholarship but my academic one before, but dang, honestly, I need one." She pulled him outside into the morning air. There was a general cloud-up, like most mornings on the coast. "This place is killing my grades. It won't matter that we paid our tuition if I flunk out."

Josh nodded gravely. "Actually, I have heard of Seagram, if it's Sigmund Seagram. He might be a media guy with a lot of other company spinoffs. I've heard Bronco mention him, but not with praise."

"Okay." Something about the situation was bothering him, it seemed. "What else do you know?"

"That Bronco's non-endorsement of a man means very little to me. Wait a sec. I'm looking this Seagram guy up." His mind went down the rabbit hole of his phone while Morgan tugged her hair out of the bun, trying to fix it before class. Seeing Josh research the scholarship made Morgan feel guilty for not doing so herself. If she was going to ask a guy for money, the least she could have done was find out a little about the scholarship, or the man who was offering it.

"And?"

"And, Morgan? It's for a hundred thousand dollars."

Chapter Fourteen

Morgan looked like she was going to need something to hold onto, so Josh grabbed her elbow and steadied her. She looked up at him with those blue eyes full of...something. He wasn't sure what. It might have been fear. But it might also have been relief or hope or something. This waitressing job was weighing her down, he could tell. She looked almost haggard this morning, her eyes a little dark beneath, worry lines around her mouth.

"A hundred thousand dollars?" She gulped. He nodded back. "And what, exactly, is it for? Who? How did I, or we, qualify for an interview?"

Josh might as well spill the news to her, good or not. "If it's the scholarship I think it is, it's specifically for newlywed couples who are both in school and within one or two years of finishing their programs."

"But, Josh. Do we really qualify? That's just getting us in deeper and deeper, isn't it?" Morgan sounded nervous. "Isn't it?"

Josh closed his eyes. "We got the interview. If we don't show up for it, there'd be reason for suspicion later when we annul. Maybe it's better that we go." It was a weak argument, but he had to make it—and in no uncertain terms. It was for her own good, no doubt in his mind. One glance toward the doors of Veg-Out, and a near brush with a roller skating waiter with a huge, curly afro of light brown hair, compelled him to it. Morgan could *not* keep working here, not for as many hours as they apparently demanded. She was too close to her goal to throw it away for a portobello mushroom burger and sweet potato fries with vegan ketchup.

Morgan sighed. "Look, I'll be honest. I'm exhausted. I'm not doing my most spectacular thinking right now. If you say we have to go, I'm just going to trust you. But if this goes south, remember, you're the one who dragged me into it."

"There's very little chance of our getting it. There are many more-deserving couples, I'm sure." As he said this, he considered — the trend for marrying during undergrad was on a severe downturn. Sure, some guys he knew had gotten married during their junior or senior years, but most had waited, or were still playing the field, or were living with their girlfriends. There might not actually be that many applicants for Seagram's scholarship.

It was a risk. He looked down at Morgan, at how tired she looked. "Should we meet there, or should I pick you up?"

"Pick me up, I guess. It will look better if we arrive together. And I'll bring you my father's wedding band so you look as married as I do."

"Right." He agreed. She wasn't completely brain dead, no matter how tired this place had obviously made her.

***

Just before noon, Josh and Morgan rolled through the enormous iron-gated driveway of Siggy Seagram's mansion on the highest hill of Starry Point. It overlooked the evergreen forests and had a view of the big, solitary Haystack Rock landmark down on the beach. At low tide, there was a causeway to it, and Josh had walked out there a few times during his earlier enrollment at Clarendon. What a great view.

Morgan must have thought so, too, because she tugged at his arm, not letting him get out of the car. "Wait just a sec." From inside her purse she pulled something small and pressed it into Josh's hand. "It was my dad's."

Her dad's? So her dad wasn't alive? Josh gulped. He couldn't take this. "Morgan, I—" He stopped himself and slid the ring on his finger. If she wore his mother's ring, he could wear her dad's.

"Nice view, eh?" A man's voice came bellowing, interrupting their moment. "You should see it in December. If I get my binoculars out, I can see the whales as they migrate past. I'll invite you up here to see them if you'd like."

Josh turned to shake his hand.

"Sigmund Seagram." The guy's voice matched his size. He was a jolly giant. A bearded guy who looked like he should be holding a big beer stein and singing a drinking song in German. Germany. Josh's thoughts shot to Brielle. He hadn't thought about her once today. And now, here she loomed up, almost scary in his mind—scary because Josh suspected how much she would disapprove of what he was doing here at Seagram's place today. He needed a drink from a stein himself.

"Nice to meet you." Morgan at least had some presence of mind. She extended her hand and smiled at him. Seagram looked taken with the sweetness of that smile.

"Come in. Come in! I have a lunch prepared. I hope you like salmon."

Josh loved salmon. It looked like Morgan did, too. Her blue eyes had lit up. Brielle hated all seafood. But—he wasn't going to start comparing or contrasting Brielle and Morgan. It wasn't fair to either of them. And it definitely wasn't healthy for him.

Focus. He needed to focus. And not get caught. Seagram most likely knew Bronco. Big company presidents were few, and the pond of them was small, at least in Oregon. Word could go like wildfire back to Josh's dad and

110

whole family if there was any kind of hint that this marriage was not in earnest. Bronco, Josh had no doubt, wouldn't hesitate to notify the authorities and have Josh prosecuted for fraud.

Seagram's house loomed large, almost as large as Hyatt Place, which was what Bronco had named the house Josh had lived in as a teenager. He'd built it for Mom, but Mom only lived a few months in it. And it was against her will. She'd wanted to die in the little three-bedroom tract house Josh grew up in. Bronco would have none of it. His wife deserved a mansion—even if what she wanted was a cottage home.

Josh didn't know whether Seagram knew he was Bronco Hyatt's son. It was tricky, though. He didn't want to tell Seagram, for fear of looking like some pathetic name-dropper, or for fear that Seagram disliked Bronco personally. But he didn't want to conceal it, either. That would probably be worse.

They all sat down at the lunch table, and Seagram was talking to Morgan. "I read your mother's book."

"You did?" She looked stricken. "I'm afraid to ask for your opinion."

"My opinion is she was very brave to have it published." Seagram passed Josh a little bowl of lemons, and Josh squeezed a section onto his salmon. He hadn't eaten anything this good in a while—but had consumed more frozen burritos than he'd like to admit, instead.

"Well, there's that." Morgan didn't look proud of her mom's literary efforts. Josh didn't know about the book. If her mom had a book that was well-known enough to have been read by Seagram, what was Morgan doing working at that Salad Shooter place? Now was not a good time to ask about it, though. That was the kind of thing a real-life husband would already know about.

After taking a bite of her lunch, Morgan went on. "I wish she'd never written it."

"A lot of people share that opinion. But why do you?"

Morgan pressed her lips together. "Oh, it just derailed things for my sister and me."

"Her fame?" Seagram looked concerned. "Because I can see how having a mom famous for *Frogs in the Sand* might adversely affect a young lady."

What! Morgan's mother wrote that awful book? Oh, that poor girl! It was like the "Achy Breaky Heart" of poetry books. Everyone had heard about it so much they were sick to death of it. Frog fatigue, it had come to be known. To begin with it hadn't been so bad, maybe, but— well, yeah. It was. Never mind. He tried to make his face a mask of complacency, but Morgan looked at him, and she'd seen the surprise in his eyes. She looked weary of the whole thing.

"If I'm going to be honest, it was the fortune that tripped us up, not the fame."

Seagram looked interested. "It seems like it sold well. Exceptionally well, for a poetry book. In fact, I'd love a signed copy, if you could get me one."

Morgan looked like she was having a hard time swallowing some bile. But she answered civilly. Good for her. "Yeah. Look, I don't know why I'm telling you this. I shouldn't. It's personal."

"Go ahead. Think of me as a kindly uncle. I'll keep it all in confidence."

Morgan looked worried a second, and then she plunged in. "She made so much money last year, and only last year, that she was able to finally pay off my dad's debts that were transferred to her after his death. Which great, don't get me wrong. It cut the rope of a huge millstone around her neck. But then, after that, she was penniless again."

"Penniless before, penniless after. I don't see the big derailment." He led them to a sofa. They'd finished their lunch. He sat on the coffee table in front of them, the wooden legs creaking a little under his weight.

"Right? It shouldn't have been that way. That's what I told the financial aid people a thousand times, trying to get them to approve my applications, but they only see raw numbers, not people, not situations. My mother paid too much in taxes. End of argument."

No wonder! Josh chewed on this for a second — until he realized just how dangerously close Morgan's story was to outing them — and the fact they'd married hastily. If the wedding had been long-planned, then Morgan wouldn't have needed to include her mother's earnings on her taxes.

This was not good.

Luckily, it didn't seem like Mr. Seagram was digesting all those details and connecting those dots. Josh prayed he never would put that stuff together. Seagram nodded gravely. "So your mother can't help you out in any way."

"She can't."

"And your father won't." Seagram turned to Josh, and Josh knew he'd been vetted somehow. Maybe it was on the interview application Morgan's sister had turned in. Whatever the source, Seagram knew who Josh was, and that Bronco was not helping him financially.

"Exactly."

Seagram took a deep sigh. "I know Bronco Hyatt. Have known him since he married your mother, heaven rest her soul."

Wow. Seagram knew his mother — and that there was no question she was in heaven. "Then you know what he can be like." Bitterness may have crept into Josh's tone.

"I do."

This whole interview had gotten a lot more personal than Josh had expected. Morgan had bared her heart and problems to this guy about things Josh had never bothered to ask — things he should have asked, even as a friend, let alone as a husband, and Seagram had bombarded Josh with memories, sending him tripping through old feelings he'd kept buried deep.

Seagram put his hands on his knees and leaned forward, considering. Josh shot Morgan a look. She was staring at her hands. They were pretty, delicate hands, small enough to be wearing the ruby ring of his mother's. They should not be washing dishes at that McMushrooms place. Josh had to get this scholarship for them—for her sake. She deserved it, even if he didn't.

"Morgan's been working full-time this past six months. She's seen her grades take a hit. I admire her for not giving up." Josh admired her, yes, and he admired her legs for a second as well, stemming down from her light blue skirt. Then he refocused.

"Where are you working, Morgan?"

"I'm a waitress at a vegan diner."

"Veg-Out?" Seagram frowned. "Don't look so surprised. It's the only one in town. I'm too much of a carnivore myself, but my valet eats there regularly."

Seagram had a valet. Who had a valet these days? It sounded so old-timey. Even Bronco didn't have a valet, but Josh bet he would if he heard Seagram or some other self-made businessman had one.

"Josh, would you go pour me a glass of water and bring it to me?" Seagram waved him off. "I need to talk to Morgan."

Josh obeyed. But if Seagram wanted to speak privately, he'd have to send Josh all the way down to the beach because the guy's voice carried everywhere in the house. Josh didn't intend to eavesdrop, but there wasn't any way around it.

"Morgan, I knew Josh's mom before she married that knucklehead. I would have given anything if she'd loved me instead, but I guess the heart wants what the heart wants. Eventually I married my Nellie, though. Do you know why Josh's dad cut him off?"

There was a pause. Then Seagram went on.

114

"If Martha knew what Bronco Hyatt was doing to her son, she'd be rolling over in her grave so often it'd be like she was on a rotisserie. Thanks for leveling with me. I'm going to do something for Joshua for Martha's sake. Don't tell him I said so, of course. I don't want him to think anything he receives isn't for his own merit." There was another pause, but then Seagram finished, "I have to say, your openness is refreshing."

Pangs of guilt at the word openness almost made Josh drop the water glass he was holding. It bobbled in his hand, sloshing a bit out onto the marble floor, but he recovered. "Here, sir. You did want ice, right?"

Seagram took it. "Thanks, Josh. Tell your father hello."

"I probably won't see him."

"That's what I thought. Thanks for coming by, kids. It's been a pleasure." Seagram shook their hands. "Winners will be notified by mail."

Out in the Explorer, Josh exhaled for the first time in an hour. "Glad that's over. What did you think?" He was trying to decide whether to tell her how close she had come to screwing things up.

Morgan chewed her nail for a minute. "I thought he seemed lonesome."

Lonesome! Leave it to a woman to interpret it that way. "I meant about how the interview went. I hope we came across as needy but not needy enough to get the scholarship. I'd hate to be fake for a guy that nice." And as Josh said the words, he realized he meant them. Seagram was a stand-up guy who almost reminded Josh of an extra-loud Santa Claus. He didn't need fakers trying to take his kindness. Josh let his ire toward Morgan's willingness to blab so much personal information about him die down. It didn't really matter, since Seagram seemed to know most of it before meeting them anyway. Besides, worst case scenario, if Seagram did put two and two together about their hasty marriage, he just wouldn't give them the scholarship. End of story. Morgan would keep working at the diner until Josh could figure out some other way to get her out of there.

***

The next day, right after work, Josh checked his mail. Still nothing from Brielle; instead, there, in a long green envelope was a letter with Seagram's return address.

"Morgan?" Josh broke into a jog toward her apartment. "Morgan!" He pounded on her door.

She came and answered it. "Josh. You look upset. Is everything all right?" She let him in, and sent him to the couch, where he plopped down in fear. In a second she'd reappeared with a cold bottle of Coke in her hand. The bubbles and fumes off the top of its rim calmed him a bit.

"It's from Seagram." Did his nerves show as much as they rattled him?

Morgan wobbled a little, and he pulled her down beside him. She smelled like flowers again. She must not have gone to work yet today. Good. He wished she'd never have to go. But then, he wished this envelope didn't say what he thought it probably said.

"Do we have to open it?" Morgan's blue eyes met his. "I don't want either answer."

"We have to. We have to accept or reject it if it's an offer."

"I'm so mad at Tory I could scratch her. She put us in this situation."

Where was that sister? This was the first time Josh had been in Morgan's apartment with her alone, and he'd only met the sister once or twice in passing. Huh, it smelled like cherry candles and, well, Morgan in here. Every time he smelled her, his stomach did a flop. He was going to have to start wearing nose plugs around her.

That'd be easy to explain.

116

Why are you wearing nose plugs?

Because every time I smell you I forget I have a girlfriend.

Morgan lifted the green envelope from his hand. "I'm opening it."

Her finger slid under the lip, and she extracted the paper. Josh leaned across, closer to her waves of honeysuckle blonde hair to see it, too. But he only needed to see the first word: *Congratulations.*

His stomach did more than a flop. It did one of the moves those gymnasts did in the Olympics—round-off back handspring—but it didn't stick the landing.

This was not good.

Morgan let the paper flutter to her lap. "How can we tell him no?"

"We can't."

"We have to."

"If we do, it will be even more suspicious when we annul next spring." Josh picked up the letter and read further. Maybe the scholarship wasn't as drastic as he feared. Maybe it was only five or ten thousand. "Maybe we can take it now, and then we can repay him later."

"A hundred thousand bucks?" Morgan looked stricken. "That's more than my mother's house cost."

The back of Josh's throat collapsed. It was more than Josh's mother's house had cost—by twice. Her original house, anyway. Before Hyatt Place. He scanned the letter. Worst fears realized. The disbursement was for the full hundred thou'. Payable by check or direct deposit. In a lump sum. To be delivered at five p.m. on Monday.

Josh closed his eyes. This was so bad.

"How are we going to have all those cameras come?"

Cameras? "What cameras?"

"Didn't you read the whole thing?" She shoved the letter at him, pointing out a paragraph near the bottom of the letter. The fine print of all these letters was killing him.

I'm expanding this scholarship's reach this year. Because the

117

two of you are such an attractive couple, I'm making a big to-do out of the presentation of the scholarship. Frankly, I'd like more young couples to get married while they're still on campus. You two are the flagship couple, in my eyes.

For that reason, I'll be over on Monday to deliver the check to you at your apartment.

At that time, I'll have another surprise for you.

Another surprise? Oh, geez. What next?

Morgan didn't look like she'd like the surprise, either. "Film crew?" Her lips had gone white.

"Yeah. Seagram's a media mogul, among other things. He made a lot of his money in TV reality shows."

Morgan looked like she was going to throw up. He didn't blame her. He might, too, later, when this horror sank in. "Hey, Morgan. Look on the bright side. You can quit your job now, eh?"

"Look on the not-so-bright side, Josh. We have to move in together and fake a record of our courtship and completely invent a married couple's apartment. Before Monday."

Chapter Fifteen

J ust when I thought things couldn't be worse." Morgan dropped her head onto her arms, her nose hitting the sand. It was too cold to be down here beside the ocean in her swimsuit, but Tory had insisted. Morgan had looked too stressed. She needed the beach, her sister had said, but even the waves weren't helping right now.

Why, oh, why had she been such a blabberhead when she was at Mr. Seagram's place? Maybe being around Josh had suddenly primed the pump of her talkative nature. Then again, she'd always been able to talk to men way out of her age category. And something about Sigmund Seagram had just put her at ease. Josh had called him Santa Claus with brown hair.

But that was no excuse. In fact, she'd been so loose-lipped she could have sunk her and Josh's ship—because what was she thinking telling him about her mother's tax status screwing up her financial aid? Josh would probably call that a trail of breadcrumbs for someone to figure out their game.

She had to be more careful.

She and Josh had to make the apartment visit as convincing as possible—barring actually moving in with him.

Cohabitation was definitely not in her premarital game plan.

Even if she was sort of married.

Tory listed a few things they'd have to do. "You'll need dishes, a frame for your marriage certificate..."

119

"People don't do that. That's overkill."

"Okay, maybe so. But you'll have to have some kind of framed item. Do you even know what his apartment looks like? Does he have decoration? It has to have a woman's touch."

The fact she'd never been inside the apartment of the man she was married to hit her like a truck. She was such a phony right now. She sent an apologetic silent prayer to the heavens and to Sigmund Seagram.

"What am I going to do? I don't even have a picture of us besides the selfie I took where we both look pretty nasty."

"I can take your pictures. We'll get them developed at the drugstore, the one hour place. They even do eight-by-tens, and larger prints. The pictures are doable. We can shoot them here on the beach. You'll look gorgeous. Call him up and get him down here."

Morgan wasn't ready to deal with Josh yet. She was too mad at him for not putting the kibosh on this whole ruse. He was older, and he should be more responsible than she was, be the smarter head.

Poor Mr. Seagram.

"What about everything else? Where are we even going to stage this fake apartment?"

"His place, of course. We can just relocate your clothes and things over there, a few toiletries, and you're good. Mr. Seagram isn't going to do a big exploratory surgery of the whole apartment."

"Who knows? He's an eccentric millionaire. I have a creeping feeling we'll be scrutinized."

"It's the price you pay for being a gorgeous couple. Millionaires automatically like you."

"But that's it! We're not a couple! We're neighbors."

"You're legally wed."

"We're not really married, though. Not in his heart. He's still going to the mailbox every single day looking for letters from that girl he loves who's out of the country."

"Why don't they just Skype?"

"I don't know. Maybe they do." Morgan didn't want to think about Josh's girlfriend. It was getting harder and harder not to think about Josh as only hers as time went by. Especially every time she snagged the prongs of the ruby solitaire on something and remembered his kiss. It squeezed her heart to think he wasn't hers and he could make her feel like that.

It wasn't fair.

"Hey, you promised not to think of her as competition. Besides, it's like I told you a hundred times, Morgan, you're the one who's here. You're the one who is wearing his mother's ring. Think about that. It doesn't matter who or where she is. Possession is…"

"I know, I know. Nine-tenths of the law." But Brielle possessed Josh's heart. And that was all that really mattered in this situation. She was such a fool for letting her feelings actually get sucked into this situation.

If he just wasn't so danged full of swagger. Sometimes when he walked into the room, smelling like that spicy cologne, she thought her hormones were probably glowing neon. And she was married to him, which made it twenty times tougher to keep from throwing herself at him, especially after those kisses.

And now, heaven help her, she was going to have to move in with him?

Wait, no. No, she wasn't. All she had to do was make it *look* like she'd moved in with him.

Tory turned over and pulled the floppy hat's brim over her face. "How did Carl take it when you turned in your skates?"

"Not well. He promised me a raise."

"Really? How much?"

"Ten cents an hour."

"Tempting."

121

"Yeah." Morgan probably shouldn't have burned that bridge already, but Josh had insisted, and she found herself irresistibly compelled to follow his advice. It was like she was under his spell. Plus, she had a serious test for her senior project on Monday morning, and Carl had scheduled her to work two sixteen-hour shifts this weekend. There was no other choice. But when Carl had flipped his lid and warned her to never come back begging him for a job again, she'd promised she wouldn't.

"When does Josh get off work? We should start redecorating over there tonight." Tory sat up and reached in her beach tote. "I have my camera with me. Are you going to want wide-angle or narrow-angle lens for the pictures?"

"Narrow-angle. Close-ups." Josh's voice sounded as he crossed the sand toward them. "And wearing just what you are."

Morgan sat bolt upright. What was he doing here? "I'm in my swimsuit."

"All the better." He raised his eyebrow. He was in his trunks. And shirtless. Morgan had to avert her eyes so she wouldn't gawk. He apparently had time to work out.

"But nobody takes engagement photos in their swimsuits." The thought!

Josh had a retort, though. "Everybody knows we eloped. So we naturally wouldn't have engagement photos."

"Right. Just fun dating ones." Tory scrambled to her feet. "Perfect. Thanks for coming down here, Josh." Then to Morgan she said, "Sorry. I swiped his number from you and texted him about this. It had to get done as soon as possible. We'll get some shots of you in the waves."

Morgan shook her head. "Those waves are freezing!"

"I know, but you'll have to pretend they're warm from the summer, when you met and fell in love." Tory pointed to the icy water, and Morgan groaned but obeyed, stifling a squeal as the polar-chilled wave covered the tops of her feet.

"Oh, that is cold!" Josh shuddered as a wave sloshed against his legs. "Snap fast, sister."

The moniker brought Morgan up short. Josh was calling Tory his sister—which she was, at least legally. It hadn't struck Morgan that way before.

"Okay, I need some fun, playful shots. And then I need some shots of...togetherness."

Nice word for it.

Josh had no hesitation with the playful shots. In two seconds he'd splashed Morgan three times with cold salt water.

"Hey!" She splashed back. "You'll pay for that!" The water fight lasted until she couldn't stop her teeth from chattering, and until he came over and scooped her up in his arms.

"Ooh, you're cold." He hugged her to his warm chest. "Time for the togetherness shots, I guess."

Morgan just nodded dumbly. She'd never felt so secure while being held aloft. The wide world narrowed around just the two of them.

"There! That's just it." Tory came closer, aiming in on them. "I like that. Morgan, good. You're really into him. Josh—keep your eyes on hers. Just like that. Oh, I like that energy surging between you two. Electric. It might short out my camera's batteries. Yes. Nice. Now kiss her, Josh. We have to have a kiss shot."

All during Tory's photography commentary, Morgan had barely heard it, like a voice from way down in a chasm. Instead, she'd been shivering against Josh's strong chest, her arms wrapped around his neck, his arms holding her as if he were carrying her over the threshold. Their eyes met, just like that faraway Tory voice said, *Energy! Electricity!* Her heart was already going like a jackrabbit to keep herself warm against the chilly wind, but when Josh looked into her eyes, the rate spiked—and sparkles of longing spread through her whole body.

"Kiss her," the distant voice commanded, and instantly, he obeyed. Morgan fell into the ecstasy of kissing Josh Hyatt—again. This time it wasn't as zealous as when he gave her the ring and she had challenged him to prove his passion, but it was something new. It was tender and fun at the same time.

How could one man kiss so many different ways?

"That's it. I think we got it, folks. You want to get out of the water now?" Tory yoo-hooed to get their attention again.

Morgan had to catch her breath, but she got it together.

Josh was smiling wickedly. "What are you going to tell your friends about that one?"

Nothing. She was never telling. "We'd better get back and get started on redecorating Josh's apartment," she called to Tory.

"What?" Josh stopped in his tracks. He set Morgan down on the sand. "What do you mean, redecorating?"

"Come on. We have to make this as real as possible. I'm moving my stuff into your place. Making it look homey—in case it doesn't already."

"It doesn't. Can't we just use your place? I was in there. It looks about as homey as a college apartment at Estrella Court is going to get."

"Uh, seriously? There are two bedrooms—both with pink curtains. You can't be supposedly living with two women. That's so *Three's Company*." She'd seen the reruns. She didn't know if he had.

"Come and knock on my door," he murmur-sang. "We've been waiting for you." So he had seen the sit-com. And his singing voice wasn't too bad. "Okay, fine. I'll come move any heavy stuff after I get off work."

***

Josh sat at his desk, looking through the lenses of the microscope. "Hey, George. I think the bacteria count is a lot lower today. The chemists must be doing something right."

George came over and took a look for himself. "Lookee there. First good bacterial count all week." He pulled away from the instrument. "You taking off early today?"

"I have some stuff to do." Josh's head hurt. Putting his apartment in the equivalent of a Halloween costume version of itself was not his idea of a great Friday night, even if he'd be doing it with two gorgeous women.

Worse, there was no way to disguise his spare room and the compost barrel in it. When Brielle first (and last) saw his hobby, it hadn't been good. Morgan and her sister were bound to see it—and react.

"School got you down? You not liking your classes? I never figured you for a political science type."

"Classes are fine." He was keeping afloat in Statistics and Research Methods, which he'd been familiar with in his bio-tech major when he'd attended school before, albeit not with the social science aspect of them, so they were a challenge. However, International Political Economy, Cold War Relations, and Politics of Developing Countries had him struggling to keep his head above water. "I guess I found my niche late."

"I guess you are barking up the wrong tree. Look at your patents, kid. All that bio-tech research being relegated to a hobby? Are you sure you want to do that?"

Josh thought about Brielle, their future together. He might not love poli-sci, but he loved Brielle. "I'm sure." What George said was true, but in reverse for Josh's case. If he were to take foreign policy as his career, then he could always love bio-tech research, and his hobby would then never become a chore. It would always be the excitement in his life. If he went after biological research as a career, sooner or later he would come to hate it. Everyone hated their job, right?

Besides, a job with a foreign embassy would get him away from Bronco long-term, which was what Bronco apparently wanted.

"Any word on your patents coming through? Because when that happens, I'm sure Oregon's Environmental and Energy Commission is going to be interested."

"Nothing yet." He'd waited months now, but the U.S. Patent Office still hadn't ruled on his applications.

"Okay. Well, have a good weekend." George went to hang up his lab coat. This place wasn't bad for a part-time job. Nice people. Interesting work, important to public safety. Even if that whole Seagram Scholarship came through, Josh probably wouldn't quit his job.

Unlike Morgan. He'd insisted she quit that Green and Lean place—and even if he had to double his hours here, she was never strapping on roller skates again. That was an order.

Order. Ha. As if he had any right to tell her what to do. The relationship lines between them were blurry, but he knew he didn't have that right. He also knew that if he intended to keep the lines drawn between him and that blue-eyed blonde at all, he'd have to stop kissing her, especially when she was wearing only a swimsuit and dangling her long legs over his arm. He muttered a curse at that raspberry lip gloss. When she wasn't looking he'd search her purse and throw it in the trash.

Of course, after she saw the barrel of rotting kitchen trash in his spare room, she might not allow him near her ever again. That'd clarify things. So this exercise tonight might work out fine.

Meanwhile, no more kissing that raspberry lip gloss.

Even if raspberry was his favorite flavor.

Josh hung up his lab coat and went home to face the compost and the decorating team.

Chapter Sixteen

Josh's phone rang. He opened his eye and saw it was already past six a.m. Then he opened his eyes further and saw the pink and white curtains at his window, the cleared-off counter of his dresser, the piles of women's shoes at the bottom of his closet, and wondered if he'd been teleported to another dimension, a pink one. Huh. It smelled like cherry candles in here. Oh, right. His apartment had been wife-ified.

The phone rang again. He answered, trying not to sound too groggy.

"Josh Hyatt? This is Siggy." A big, jolly voice boomed through the receiver.

Siggy? Who was Siggy? He didn't know anyone—

"I hate to wake a newlywed, but I've had a sudden change of schedule. Have to go see some assets in Chile all of a sudden." Siggy. Sigmund Seagram. So they were on a first name basis now?

Josh sat up and rubbed the sleep from his eyes, seeing for the first time the enormous kissing picture of him and Morgan in swimsuits looming over his bed. She looked amazing, with that long leg and pointed toe draped over his arm. He looked away fast. Good thing it was coming down Monday or he might let himself drift into a fantasy about that long leg.

"If you and Morgan aren't busy this morning, I'd like to come and deliver the check today instead of Monday. How's fifteen minutes?"

Fifteen minutes!

"You can let Morgan know, right? Hi, Morgan!" Siggy

127

hollered as though Morgan were nearby and could hear him over the phone.

"Uh, how's half an hour? Can you give us half an hour?"

Josh shot out of bed, pulling on some jeans and a t-shirt. The house was miraculously clean. Those girls had worked him late. But the place shone, and when Morgan saw the bio lab he had set up in his spare room, she'd said, "Cool."

Josh had balked, not sure what she meant by it, whether she was being facetious, but then Morgan had asked, "Are you working on something important?" and he hadn't known quite how to answer. But she was in earnest, and he'd finally replied, "I hope so."

"Cool." She'd said *cool*.

He dialed Morgan. "Hey. Seagram just called. You home? Can you be here looking like my wife in less than thirty minutes? He's coming with the check in half an hour."

She gave a little shriek and hung up.

She'd be here.

And she was—about five minutes early. She smelled like lavender, and her hair shone. She even had makeup on. Maybe she was a morning person and Josh's call hadn't awakened her. Chalk it up to yet another thing he didn't know about his wife. So-called wife. Pretend wife. Wife that made him able to go to school—and marry the girl he actually loved.

Morgan was a good sport if ever there was one.

"We should put something on the coffee table." Morgan's eyes shot around the room, assessing. "School books?"

"It should be some of yours and some of mine, if we do."

"Right." Morgan had brought her backpack with her, and she took out a huge textbook, *Advanced Accounting*, and set it next to Josh's laptop. "Do you like how the walls turned out?"

Josh hadn't even looked, but he did now. All across one wall were small photos from their shoot yesterday, followed by a wooden plank that read, *The Josh and Morgan Hyatt Family.* Then, smaller, below it were the words, *Families are Forever.*

Right. Or at least until the annulment comes through.

They were such heels.

"I don't know if we should go through with it." Josh shook his head, and then he caught a glimpse of Morgan setting a box of cereal on the table and two bowls, neatly placing them on placemats. It was definitely not a bachelor apartment look.

"We've been over this, I thought. We have to make it look right. If we don't spend any of the money, then we can always just give it back to Mr. Seagram when all this is over. We'll put it in an escrow account, so neither of us can touch it. Something like that would safeguard it."

After a little thought, Josh knew she was right. They could do this without taking advantage of Mr. Seagram — even if he had intended to do something to help Josh for Josh's mom's sake.

"What are all these books on the political history of Europe doing here? I thought you were a biologist."

"Nope. Foreign policy is my major."

"What? Why? Then what's with the awesome biology lab in the back room and your job at the water treatment plant? It's a non sequitur."

"Be that as it may, it's what I'm doing." Why was he getting all this backlash against his major from people who shouldn't care about his decision? Was Bronco infiltrating his friends and coworkers now? His wife, even?

That was another thing. Bronco didn't know about Morgan yet, at least Josh didn't think so. Chip and Heather wouldn't have said anything, as Josh was a taboo subject in the family, and Bronco wasn't exactly up on social media. There'd been no word of approval or disapproval from that front, but this TV interview might be the death knell of Josh's peace of mind. Everyone was going to know after this segment aired. *Maybe even Brielle.*

"How do I look?" Morgan grabbed his attention, and she spun. She was wearing a casual dress and high heels that showed off calf muscles she must have earned on roller skates.

"You look great." He'd better understate it. "Lots better than in that pink uniform they make you wear at Tomato Tornado."

"Tell me about it. I hate hot pink. So glad I quit."

"You quit?" She'd listened to him? Obeyed his orders? "That's great." He could hug her for it.

"I tried to give them notice, but the manager was so ticked off he just told me to never come in again. I don't know what I'm going to do for cash now, but I can't say I'll miss the place."

"If you're dying to add stress to your life now that you just jettisoned some, you could find a campus job, one that would work with your schedule."

"This late into the semester?" She had a point. Josh knew how tough it was to find work in Starry Point, and even tougher on campus. The slots were filled before classes began.

"Something will come up." Now he felt bad for telling her to walk away from a paying job. He'd told himself he was urging her best interest, and in a way it shocked him that she'd actually been persuaded by his influence. That fact did do a little to make his shoulders square up. *She listened to me.* But now…

"There's one more thing." Morgan interrupted his thoughts. "And I'm really sorry I have to say it, especially after what happened on the beach yesterday."

"What? What happened on the beach?" They'd made

out in the waves. What was to apologize for? Unless she knew her raspberry lip gloss was a lethal weapon against his willpower and had used it on purpose.

"You know. Tory—in the name of togetherness—forcing us to..." She faltered.

"Kiss? For the picture. You and I both know it was just a formality—for the pictures. We needed some *togetherness* shots."

Morgan opened her mouth to say something, but then she colored and stopped.

"The pictures turned out great, by the way. The one in the bedroom is almost professionally good."

"Tory must have put that up while I was at work. Well, quitting work. Can I see how it looks?"

Josh took her to the bedroom, and she hesitated before stepping in. Was she nervous—about being in his bedroom? His innards twisted. She couldn't be thinking what he'd been thinking—against his will, against Brielle's confidence and trust. This was a business arrangement for Morgan. That was all.

"Wow." She stared up at the photo, almost wandering in, and sat down on the bed. "It looks fantastic. How did she get that shot?" Morgan tilted her head, her blonde curls spilling over her shoulder, her leg trailing off his bed.

Josh tore his eyes from the leg. He tried to look at the photo over the bed, but that wasn't much better. This girl was here—in his bedroom, on his bed. His girlfriend was thousands of miles away and hadn't contacted him in over a month. What was stopping him?

The doorbell rang, snapping him back to reality.

"Seagram's here." Morgan jumped up. "Well, this totally looks like our bedroom. Except that it's a twin-sized bed." She winced and headed for the door.

A twin bed! How had he not thought about that? "If anyone asks, tell them we couldn't afford a bigger one yet. Or better, that we like togetherness."

***

Morgan swung the door open, and there stood Mr. Seagram, jolly giant that he was, his beard trimmed and in a nice, light gray suit. The thing that made Morgan almost lose her breakfast, though, was that he wasn't alone—he had an entourage.

"Mrs. Hyatt! Good morning. Don't you look fresh as daisies. This is Walt and Ernesto. They're my film crew. And this is Darshelle. She'll be interviewing you for the video we'll be posting on the Seagram Foundation's website, and which we'll use to bait the local TV stations into doing more publicity." Mr. Seagram pushed his way into the apartment, and Morgan realized she should have expected other people to be with Seagram. Mr. Seagram wouldn't be interviewing, running the camera, the sound, the grip, or whatever. "Not to hurt your feelings, but I didn't realize Starry Point had a ghetto quite as bad as this apartment complex. I hope you're not paying more than fifty bucks a month for it."

Morgan stepped aside as the film crew bustled in and began setting up a tripod and pulling black boxes and wires out of bags. Film! Morgan couldn't be on film. Not speaking, anyhow.

"You've been wired before for an interview, right?" Darshelle had a roll of duct tape and a microphone. "We'll just tape this apparatus to your back, and then no one will see the mics. Easy peasy lemon cheesy."

Morgan always thought it was lemon sneezy. Or was it squeezy? Anyway, putting on a microphone wasn't lemon or easy peasy anything, it turned out. The tape might give her welts.

"I'm not sure about this…"

"Oh, you'll be beautiful. I promise." Darshelle gave her a reassuring smile with her dazzling white teeth against her dark skin. "You look like a dream this morning."

Mr. Seagram wasn't idle, meanwhile. "Josh! Here you are. Nice place. Oh, look. Somebody's working on something big." Seagram had swung wide the door to Josh's spare room, the one with the big plastic barrel of trash in it. Josh had said it was for biology research. He probably didn't want Seagram snooping around in it. Morgan snapped into action, leaving some cords dangling against her legs.

"Mr. Seagram, would you like to see some of our engagement photos?" She took him by the arm and steered him toward the living room wall to the series of pictures Tory had taken. She wished not so many of them were of that inflammatory kiss, and that she'd been wearing something more, and that Josh hadn't made her feel so at home in his arms. She was sinking deeper, and the only way to stop herself once this ordeal of today was over was to stop seeing him—and absolutely to never kiss him again. Each time he kissed her, it was like adding another layer of adhesive on her feelings, gluing them into place. She was really in danger of getting addicted to that smile.

Morgan held her hand out for Mr. Seagram to see. "Josh gave me this ring on the beach. We really like living so close to the water. Some nights you can hear the waves from here."

"Well, I guess that'd be the only perk." Mr. Seagram didn't look impressed. Granted, Estrella Court was a dump. No one was arguing that point.

"Yeah, it's a little far from campus." She shrugged. "But we're starting out. It's our little home." Something pinched inside her as she perpetrated this lie. The apartment complex was her home, though. She justified it that way—but it made her dizzy, all this deception. She wanted to fly away for a thousand reasons, not the least being that someone would be interviewing her on camera any second now.

"Can you please come right over here beside your husband, Mrs. Hyatt? We'd like a tight shot of the two of you. Mr. Hyatt, please stand behind her and plant your hands on her hips. Yes, like that."

The pressure of Josh's hands on her hips, pressing her down, grounded Morgan. If they stood together they could get through this.

"Nice. Now, I'm Darshelle. I'll be asking you a few questions." The grilling began. "How did you feel when you first found out you'd been selected for the Seagram Scholarship?"

Morgan couldn't answer that one. If she had, the adjectives would have been terrified, guilt-ridden, worried to death, and so forth. Luckily, Josh picked it up.

"Morgan has been working herself to the bone as a waitress to put herself through school. This scholarship will allow her to focus on her studies in the Accounting Department, and work, she hopes, toward her CPA certification."

Well, that was half-true. It didn't actually help her focus on her studies, as she was going to have to find another job, but she was actually dreaming of her CPA certification. How did Josh know that? Lucky guesser.

Darshelle smiled. "That's great. I'm sure she'll be great. Next question. Tell us about your courtship. That's what all the viewers want to know about. Morgan, you start. Girls always tell it best."

Not in this case. "It was short," was all Morgan could manage to eke out.

Darshelle laughed. "How short?"

Morgan couldn't respond. The time ticked by. Josh nudged her, and when she didn't say anything, he wrapped his arms around her waist and picked up her dropped ball. "Blessedly short. I mean, I saw her across the parking lot one day this summer, all tan and gorgeous and amazing, and I don't know. Next thing I knew, we were these spontaneous kids, eloping and getting married in front of Judge Byron downtown." He gave a little shrug and then kissed Morgan on her neck. Tingles went all over her skin.

Ooh, when this was over, they were going to have to have a talk about physical boundaries.

Unless, when this was over, they never had to see each other again until the next trip to the Clatsop County Building, spontaneous kids in front of Judge Byron for their annulment.

The thought stopped the tingles.

"Tell the world about how he proposed, Morgan. If you can."

That one she could answer, at least. "He took me to the beach. The moon was sailing high. The waves crashed in their dreamy rhythm. Josh said, 'Will you wear this ring?' and placed it on my finger." She held out her hand, and one camera did a close-up on her hand, while the other camera held steady on her face.

"Tell them what I did next, Morg." Josh squeezed her.

Fine. If he insisted. "He gave me a kiss that turned me into his slave forever." There. That served him right. She glanced at him sideways, and he wore a look of both shock and new interest. Ha. Ha, ha.

"Wow. Can we get an instant replay of that for the cameras?"

Morgan snapped back to earth. "Uh, I don't know. It might not be safe for prime time."

"Oh, I'm sure our cameramen can make it work for the audience." Darshelle insisted, Morgan resisted, and Josh balked, until Mr. Seagram walked up and put his foot down.

"A kiss for the cameras, kids. Let's quit being coy. Man, I've never seen two newlyweds so shy about public displays of affection. Usually it's too much. In your case, you have to be commanded." His boisterous laugh filled the room, and Morgan looked up at Josh with a little trepidation. What if he refused? But the look in his eye said otherwise.

As he came in for the kiss, Josh nuzzled her ear, and he said, "Love slave, huh?"

"Slave for life was the verbiage, not love slave." Morgan whispered this back just as Josh attacked her lips with a totally Hollywood-style kiss that made her need to grip the fronts of her shoes with her toes just to remain standing. It went on for possibly too long because eventually Mr. Seagram started clearing his throat.

"Uh, that'll do. It's a wrap. You can wind that up now." The three reminders finally got Josh to pull away from Morgan's mouth, and at last loosen the hold he had on the back of her neck, where he'd been stroking her skin and sending her even deeper into lifelong slavery.

She gulped and touched her collarbone, her face, doubtless, flaming red.

"So after that, I imagine you said yes." Darshelle was fanning herself.

"I think he knew I was already his." Morgan whispered after coming back to the now, knowing she had to obfuscate but still be accurate at the same time, and it killed her. Lies were not her thing. At this moment she ached for this to be a true story, to be her real story—a moonlight proposal on the beach with a kiss so explosive it made television news.

But it wasn't.

She suddenly clenched. "Are we done yet?"

"Almost." Seagram bustled over to them, one of Tory's snapshots in his hand. It was a smiling shot, just sweet. "I like this one. Can I have it for my files?"

Morgan nodded, and Mr. Seagram got one of the cameramen to swing toward himself. "I have to say, the delicious decrepitude of this apartment complex makes what I have to say next all the more satisfying. What's that I

136

saw in there? A twin-sized bed?"

The camera swung back at them, and Morgan's nails dug into Josh's forearm. She pulled them back as soon as she noticed what she'd done.

"We like togetherness," Josh stammered. One of the cameramen hit his forehead with the heel of his hand before swinging back to Seagram.

"Young people. Young, poor people." He tsked.

With the camera aimed at Mr. Seagram, Morgan could relax a little. It seemed like the questions were done, thank heavens. She'd made it through without complete embarrassment, maybe, thanks to Josh. He really came through for her when she couldn't respond.

Nice guy. He made her look good, or at least not bad.

"First, I'd like to say, as the media-feature couple for my newlywed scholarship, the two of you are the ideal. Smart, driven, facing up to your challenges."

"Not to mention drop dead gorgeous," Darshelle added. "Doesn't hurt the publicity."

Morgan colored. She wasn't drop dead gorgeous, but Josh totally was. That smile? It could make her drop dead with bliss.

"I hope this scholarship will be a light in the wilderness. I have an agenda with it, you know. I think the trends are troubling, people waiting longer and longer to get married. I say, if I'd waited late into my twenties to marry, I never would have had my few short years with Nellie. She left me too young."

Oh! So he was widowed. Morgan's heart stretched out to him—and her hunch had been right: Seagram was lonely.

"For that reason, you two are just the right example." When he smiled on them beatifically, Morgan writhed inside. She was such a liar. "And now for my surprise. Drum roll, please."

One of the camera guys did a slapping drum roll on his

137

thigh. Seagram's eyes twinkled. One camera trained itself on Seagram while the other swung around to aim at Morgan and Josh again. She instantly tensed up, but she forced a pleasant, eager look to her face. She probably looked like a sea turtle struggling up the shore.

"This wasn't my original intention, but after meeting Mr. and Mrs. Hyatt last week, I decided it was the right thing to do."

Oh, dear. Morgan reached down and gripped Josh's hand, which was gripping her hip tightly. Just when she thought things couldn't get any worse.

"For the next year, or until both of you graduate, I'm giving you the sole use of my campus house."

From behind the camera, Darshelle gasped—loudly. "Sir!"

"Shh. Darshelle. I know what I'm doing. The two of you will live rent free in one of my local properties, the one nearest to Clarendon College where you're both enrolled. It's not as nice as my home, but it's a darn sight better than this place." He guffawed, then continued. "Bigger, too. Room for a baby, if you want."

Baby! Holy moly.

Mr. Seagram's eyes crinkled at the corner. "Just kidding. No pressure. But seriously, you can move in as soon as you like. Today, if you ask me." Seagram gave a disgusted last glance around the room. "I hope you like your surprise. You looked more stunned than surprised."

Morgan's throat had closed over. The camera moved even closer toward her face. No way could she speak now.

Leave it to Josh. "Thank you so much, Mr. Seagram. This is beyond anything we'd ever dared dream."

"Oh, believe me, that is so true," muttered Darshelle. Then aloud she said, "That's a wrap. Good work, Mr. Seagram." She patted his shoulder and bustled him outside. As the crew packed up she turned back and spoke to Morgan. "Just a word of warning. I wasn't kidding when

I said the place was too much. Keep the place as tidy as possible. The current PR plan is to do frequent check-ins on the two of you."

"On camera?"

"On camera. So nothing too wild or kinky."

Kinky! Morgan shuddered. "Of course."

This was too much. She almost slammed the door behind them after they paraded out, but she restrained herself. Then, in a fury, she swooped down on Josh.

"How could you? How could you tell them we'd go there? This is so far beyond ridiculous."

"What's wrong?" Josh looked puzzled, as if he didn't realize that their lives had just turned to dust. "We're only touring the place. We're not moving in. We can go look at it and politely decline."

"Ha. Like we declined the hundred thousand dollars?"

"That's different. We can give that back later. Like we said, we won't touch it. We'll put it in a fund and then give it back at the end of all this. We can't repay back rent, so we just decline the offer."

Morgan exhaled. Relieved, she said, "Okay. I'll go with you to tour it. But that is all."

***

Josh watched Morgan leave. He shouldn't have been watching her hips sway, but the high heels she had on created such a great horizontal motion he couldn't help himself.

She was right. They could not even contemplate a move in together.

He shut his door and then went to his room and took down that huge photo of the two of them en flagrante above his bed. He turned it to face the wall, and then pulled out his phone and found Brielle's number. Her photo smiled out at him, the pretty one, where she'd just opened her letter notifying her of the position in Germany. She was so happy her eyes sparkled. Not blue, like aqua depths of a clear lake in Switzerland, but a sparkling green like life and springtime.

He should not be comparing Brielle's eyes to Morgan's. Blue eyes versus green eyes. It was like apples and oranges. A person could like eating apples *and* like eating oranges. There wasn't one or the other in a higher moral echelon, or even an attractiveness echelon, for that matter. It was a matter of preference. *I can't help that I've always preferred blue over green.*

He dialed Chip. "Hey, man. Thanks for helping me out with that ring."

"Did she like it?"

"Of course. Women like jewelry." And it had fit Morgan, first try. Huh. He just realized that.

They talked about Chip's vet practice for a minute and Heather's new job as his office manager. Then Chip asked, "So how are things with you? I never asked about your breakup with Brielle. You okay with that?"

It wasn't something he'd expected his brother to ask. Josh looked around for a reason to hang up, but the conversation would have to come up sometime. "I'm fine, actually."

"Really? Because—" Chip sounded worried.

"Really."

Chip waited a moment, and then he said something else Josh didn't expect. "It's just that—I thought you told me she was going to be incommunicado for a few weeks. So, how did the breakup even happen? Sorry, you know I'm a puzzle guy." That was true, and Josh should have seen this question coming, but he didn't, and he didn't have a ready answer. So he punted.

"It was something at the airport. I didn't want to talk about it then, so I didn't. We just agreed to date other people while we were apart, and so I did. And boom.

140

Things were right with Morgan. It was our time."

"Huh." Chip chewed on this. He didn't seem convinced, but he let it drop. "How's school then? You changed your major back to biology then, I assume, since Brielle was the only impetus for the switch to foreign policy."

Another piece of the puzzle! Dang it. "I'm still doing foreign policy." Josh scratched his head as guilt at the deception started to make him itch.

"Huh," Chip said again.

That *huh* bugged Josh. "Look, Chip. I know Bronco kicked my trash right out of the family when I changed my major, for whatever prejudiced reason. And yes, it was for Brielle. Pure and simple. I still love biology, and I probably always will. But even if it was for a woman, an incredible woman, that doesn't mean it was the wrong thing to do, so I'm sticking to it."

"It doesn't sound like you're totally over her." Chip's voice came low. "Is Morgan okay with that?"

"She has to be." Josh seethed. He never should have called Chip. There was no way he could make him understand, not without jeopardizing everything by telling his brother exactly what had gone down. He measured his breathing and continued. "Sorry. Maybe you're right. Brielle still occupies a big place in me, but Morgan honestly doesn't mind."

Chip gave his third *huh*, and the conversation was over.

Josh punched one of the new bright blue throw pillows on his bed, and then he chucked it across the room. It landed on a line of Morgan's shoes, toppling them in a domino effect. Sight of the shoes made his mind conjure an image of the backs of Morgan's legs standing in them.

"Bah!" Josh shouted. He couldn't see Brielle's face, hear her voice, even read a text from her. He growled in frustration. He should have pushed her harder to marry him before she'd left. Then he wouldn't have a closetful of another woman's shoes turning him into a cheating boyfriend who kissed blondes with stage fright and a soft spot for sick dogs. He swore.

Eventually he calmed down again.

Snail mail, she'd said. He could write her a letter.

Since she'd never come through with an address, he hadn't written anything more than a few half-baked lines. He wasn't much of a hand-written letter guy. Who was, anymore? Besides, if he couldn't send one, why write one, he'd told himself. But that wasn't good logic. Nothing should keep him from writing, even if she couldn't get the letter, or letters, yet. Maybe Josh could be one of those romantics. Not that Brielle was a romantic herself, but that didn't mean she wouldn't like to receive a stack of letters from him, written over time, as soon as things were safe for her to get mail. Wherever she was.

He found some paper and sat down. It would be so much easier for him to type the letter and print it out, but handwritten would be more personal. Women appreciated personal.

Dear Brielle…

Dearest Brielle? My darling Brielle? Or no endearment? Ugh. This was going to be harder than he thought. He pressed on, and after a long time, he had half of something acceptable. He folded it and stuffed it in an envelope. Then, remembering the promise he'd renewed in the letter, he opened his *Political History of Europe* textbook to chapter eleven: "The Hapsburg Dynasty." But his eyes landed on Morgan's *Advanced Accounting* book lying right beside his leg, and he pulled out another piece of paper and scrawled something that was really playing through his mind. He then tucked it into the desk drawer beside Brielle's letter.

Chapter Seventeen

They pulled up at the address Darshelle had given them yesterday. She'd said she'd meet them here after church—Seagram wanted to make sure they all had time for church first.

Morgan choked on her gum, which she'd swallowed involuntarily when she saw the house. "Are you sure this is the right place?" It had to be a mistake. She'd passed this house hundreds of times going and coming from class, and she thought maybe a wealthy retired couple lived in it, with its manicured gardens and the perfection of its colonial-style architecture. The columns! Were they marble?

"This is the address." Josh squinted at the numbers on the front of the house. "It's pretty nice."

"Pretty nice! It's a freaking palace!" Morgan's heart whipped into a frenzy of palpitations. "It's the kind of place they feature on TV shows with titles like *Lives of the Ridiculously Rich.*"

"It's not that nice. Come on." Josh shut off the engine. "That Darshelle person is going to be here soon." He was still in his suit and tie from church, and he looked like an executive. Morgan had always had a thing for a guy in a business suit. It was making Morgan's mind go places it shouldn't. She was going to have to say something to him—now.

"Just a second—before we go in. I just need to put something out there." How to say this and not reveal how much he was affecting her, she didn't know. But it had to be said. "We are going to have to put some boundaries up."

"Uh, Morgan. We said we're not moving in together. In

fact, we might not even have to see each other again after today."

Have to? She'd thought of it more as a *get to* see each other. That took some of the wind out of her sails, but she pressed on. "I mean, it just seems like every time we're meeting people, someone insists on seeing us make physical contact." Her voice trailed off, and she knew she was sounding completely stupid.

Especially when Josh got a wicked grin. "Oh, I see. My animal magnetism is getting to you."

She didn't have time to lie. "Frankly, yes. And if you're serious about this being a real marriage, we need to have that conversation, but until then, we are nothing but neighbors."

Josh frowned, and then it hit Morgan that she'd just opened the door to a serious conversation about their relationship. Which they did not have.

Stupid. She was completely stupid.

Luckily, Josh didn't seem hung up on that. "Fine. You're right. We need to probably at least scale back."

"Exactly." She started to calm down a little. She laughed, shaking her head. "Can you believe how many people out there think they have the right to dictate that we kiss each other? That's two in a twenty-four hour period. First Tory, and then Seagram's crew. Where do people get off?"

"Right?" Josh gave his own eye roll, and tension was broken.

Good. They could move forward, even if the film crew showed up.

Josh came around and opened her door. "We can just hold hands as we go through the house. That ought to be enough." He took her by the hand. This was not helping. Stupid shimmers of ecstasy that hit her every time they touched! Would she never just become immune to them?

A black sedan pulled up behind them, and out came

Darshelle. It looked like she'd been at church as well this morning, as she wore a suit and pumps. Seagram's people did church, it would seem. That was cool. Morgan did church. So did Josh—she'd seen him there at her local congregation most Sundays since they, uh, got married.

The phrase still made her wacko.

"Hello, Mr. and Mrs. Hyatt."

"This has to be a mistake. This place can't be right." Morgan walked toward the lady, and they shook hands.

Darshelle pulled out a key from a large envelope. "No mistake. This will be your key. It's for both of you. Don't make a copy." She handed it to Josh, who slid it onto his key-ring right away. He'd give it back later, right? For now, it seemed like he was playing along. "You can use the keypad to get in through the garage, if you need to. But I suspect you newlyweds will spend most of your time together. Am I right?" She winked.

The PR lady led them around the manicured grass via a cobblestone path. Every autumn flower imaginable bloomed in the flowerbeds. The canopy of tree branches made a shady bower for their entry into the spacious mansion that the massive wrought iron door revealed when it glided open.

"It's nice." Josh seemed less overawed than Morgan.

Was he kidding? This place was a glimpse into the eternities—if she made it to heaven in the afterlife, after living such a life of deception. It had flagstone floors, crown molding, ceiling medallions around the bases of the several crystal chandeliers. She didn't even dare look in the kitchen.

"I bet it costs a fortune to heat and cool the place. Look how high the ceilings are." Josh whispered this to Morgan, but apparently, Darshelle overheard.

"Your utilities will be covered. Don't worry about that. I'll be right back." Darshelle left them and went back outside to take a phone call.

145

Morgan turned to Josh, fear spewing from her. "This is too much."

"It's a lot." They walked through the grand arches into the living area of the house.

"It's not even in the same universe with Estrella Court."

"Thank heaven." Josh rolled his eyes. "Or Sigmund Seagram."

"We can't do it." But even as she said it, her soul stretched out to the baby grand piano that sat idle in the parlor, begging her to come play it. And her heart ached to cook—just once—on that six-burner gas stove. It was so pretty, all stainless steel and shiny. "I've never *dreamed* anywhere this nice, let alone lived in a place like this."

Josh plunked onto a barstool and slid one beside him at the quartz countertop for Morgan to sit beside him. "Don't get too starry-eyed about it. Pretty homes don't always house pretty people. It's the relationships that make the happiness, not the decorations."

Morgan traced a fingertip over the smooth rock surface. It was a gray-green with flecks of white and a streak of dark gray. "I think I could be sweet and kind to the world's vilest person if I was surrounded by this much beauty all the time."

"Maybe, but who's going to weed that flowerbed?"

"The gardener. Mr. Seagram said there would be one."

Josh clapped. "That changes everything. Get your stuff, babe. We're moving in!"

"Glad to hear it!" Darshelle's voice carried across the cavernous space. Her heels clicked as she entered the kitchen and opened the refrigerator, showing it to be full. "The pantry is stocked, too. I can't imagine what you have to worry about."

"This—it all just seems like too much," Morgan said, almost gasping.

"It *is* too much. I told Siggy that a hundred times, but

will he listen?" Darshelle frowned. "Look. He's generous to a fault. Don't hurt his feelings, or I'll have to hurt you." She made a fist, and Morgan winced inwardly, knowing how inevitable that was—for when she and Josh annulled their union, Seagram would no doubt be upset.

"You're really loyal to him," Josh said.

"I owe him everything."

Unless they declined everything he offered, Morgan would owe him everything, too. And she'd likely give nothing in return. Oh, this was not good. But what choice did she have at this point, when they were already in so deep she couldn't see the surface anymore? Walk away? Get in trouble? Go to jail for fraud? Never finish her degree, and have Tory keep floundering in life without schooling, dating different members of a community theater cast?

Crazy as it was, the responsible thing to do was go through with the deception. For now.

"Do you like the house?" Darshelle offered them drinks from the fridge, but they refused. "Did you go upstairs? I'll show you."

Five bedrooms, three bathrooms, and a master suite. The master looked like a designer had spent tens of thousands of dollars making it over just for Morgan's taste—if she'd even known what her taste was before this. But now she knew: it was exactly this room in every way. White linens and curtains, roses in a silver vase on the nightstand, natural light coming through the French doors that led to the balcony off the back of the room, and a sitting area. No wonder Seagram looked like he was holding his nose at Josh's apartment. The contrast was like going from a lean-to at the county landfill to the governor's mansion.

"Mr. Seagram sends this with his compliments." Darshelle produced a paper, handing it to Josh.

"There's a housekeeper, too?" Josh turned to Morgan. "Babe, you wouldn't have to do the cleaning."

147

"You mean *you* wouldn't have to do the cleaning."

"Neither of you has to clean. Not even dishes, if you don't want to." Darshelle led them back downstairs. "That card is Svetlana's number and schedule. Mr. Seagram wants to make your lives as simple as possible so you can focus on your studies." She showed them a large room with a fireplace and a wall of bookshelves stacked with books floor to ceiling. "He didn't have a TV installed during the remodel, but newlyweds don't watch television."

Josh put an arm around Morgan, and those infernal tingles hit again. She would have gone running away, but she knew they had to look affectionate.

Morgan staggered under the weight of the promise this life held. It was too good to be true. Far, far too good to be true. And if only it could be, if only she and Josh weren't horrendous frauds, she'd grab it and hug this life to herself so tightly they'd have to pry it from her cold, dead fingers to get it away.

"This is all unbelievably generous." Josh slid his arm down and took Morgan's hand. They stood in the soaring front entryway. "I can speak for Morgan, that we appreciate the offer more than we can say."

She nodded. Lots more than she could say.

"But—"

"No buts." Darshelle held up a hand. "Mr. Seagram isn't going to brook any arguments. I was instructed firmly."

Josh's hand stiffened in Morgan's. "I wish we could. It's just too much."

"I told you from the get-go. It is too much. Nobody's arguing that."

"Nevertheless, we have been too blessed by him already."

Morgan at last found her voice. "Couldn't he pick a runner-up couple in his newlywed search and give them this gift? He could spread out the generosity and bless more lives. The scholarship is already far more than we can hope to repay."

"Nobody wants repayment. And no. Mr. Seagram has made up his mind, and he's not one to back down. He's used to getting his way."

Morgan had seen that, even in their brief interactions. But Morgan didn't intend to be bullied into living with a man—because, frankly, that's what this situation would be. Her morals were on the line here. She was a good girl, and she intended to stay that way.

But you're married to him, a little voice at the back of her mind whispered. *How immoral is it for a woman to live with her husband? It's not.*

She shushed that voice.

"Our minds are made up." Josh fished his key-ring out of his pocket. He let go of Morgan's hand to unthread the key. Morgan's fingers felt the absence of his.

"Just a minute." Darshelle sent a text, and then shook her head. "I'm sorry. Mr. Seagram was afraid you'd be too modest to accept, so he made me build in some contingencies."

Morgan narrowed her eyes at this, and she felt Josh's spine stiffen at the word.

"I just sent the text to the owner of your apartment complex, Estrella Court. Yesterday Mr. Seagram offered to purchase it from the owner for twice its value."

No. "Why would he do a thing like that?" Morgan almost spluttered this. Fear washed through her as she realized something very bad was about to happen.

"Don't worry. The owner didn't accept it—he needs it for an investment."

Whatever. This couldn't make any difference to Morgan and Josh's decision.

"However, he did agree to take Seagram on as a partner, and beginning today, to raise rents. To quadruple them monthly—at first. And then to raise them by tenfold soon thereafter."

"Raise rents! By that immoral amount? Why would he do that? He'd lose all his tenants." Josh stepped a little in front of Morgan, as if shielding her from this arrow, but Morgan knew everyone in Estrella Court was on a month-to-month contract and at the mercy of a sudden rent change. They were the working poor, the elderly on fixed incomes, the otherwise homeless. There was nothing that could shield her, or them, from that danger.

"Maybe. But Mr. Seagram offered to pay the monthly installment for any unfilled apartment until things had worked out to his satisfaction. And at that point, he offered the landlord a lump sum."

Morgan's mouth went dry. Through clenched teeth she asked the burning question. "What exactly are the terms of Mr. Seagram's satisfaction?"

"I think you know, Mrs. Hyatt." Darshelle nodded slowly. "So, if you'd like for all your Estrella Court neighbors to have a nice, safe place to live over the winter—and not the freeway underpass—I'd say the two of you should give the offer some serious thought."

That was blackmail!

"Chuh." Josh grabbed Morgan's hand. "There aren't any freeways running through Starry Point."

"Think how even more unsheltered that will make all those low-rent tenants." Darshelle lifted a challenging eyebrow. "Look, I know. It's drastic. It's cruel."

"It's blackmail." Morgan pinged with the bizarreness of it all.

"It's Mr. Seagram. Like I said, when he gets an idea in his mind, he's going to stop at nothing to get his way, so I advise you, young people, to take the gift graciously. I'll have a moving truck arranged to meet you at Estrella Court for your clothing and personal items tomorrow afternoon when Josh gets done with his work at the water treatment plant." She pulled a tight smile, gave a sorry bow, and left, the big iron door making a clanging thud behind her.

Morgan staggered, and she had to grab onto Josh for support. "It's so mean! How can he be so nice and so mean at the same time?"

Josh's mouth formed a flat line. His face was red, but there was a white area around his lips. "I've been around men like this all my life. If I knew how to deal with them, neither of us would be in this situation right now."

So even Josh couldn't fix this. Morgan felt a tear spring to her eye. She did want to live here—so much! More than anywhere she'd ever seen in her life. Circumstance kept throwing Josh and Morgan together, and every time she was with him, he did something funny or charming or kind. How could she help liking him? More and more, she found herself wanting to be with Josh Hyatt.

But not this way.

It was all wrong. All her dreams had come true, but in a warped, fractured fairy tale version. It was like looking at a gorgeous banquet, spread all across a long table, with succulent vegetables and meats and fruits and sparkling drinks on pristine china, and then going up to partake and finding it was all just plastic.

"Don't cry. Morgan, don't." Josh looked anguished. He lifted a hand and brushed away the tear rolling down her cheek. He gathered her in his arms and pressed her head to his chest. She didn't resist. "It's going to be okay. We'll think of something."

His touch did soothe her, but it didn't change facts. "If I left, Tory's salary at the community theater wouldn't pay the rent, even at Estrella Court. Now that I quit my job at Veg-Out, I don't know how I expected us to pay it anyway." She'd been so shortsighted! It wasn't like she could touch the scholarship money from Seagram anyway. "I'm such an idiot."

Josh took her hand and sat down on the staircase, pulling Morgan down next to him.

Distraught, Morgan's mind reeled under another blow. "And if Seagram manages to force a rent hike, then where will Tory and I be? It was the only place in Starry Point we could afford. Seriously. And with my old truck, it's not like we could move up to Astoria and rent some dive there and commute. The gas cost would kill us if the truck even survived it."

There wasn't an answer.

"I have an answer." Josh started nodding slowly. "What if you and Tory move here? I'll stay at Estrella Court. I can afford the rent, and then the two of you get this posh place, rent free, and no one is the wiser. I'll just show up when the film crew does. You can text me."

"But it won't look like a man lives here."

"It will. I'll leave some clothes, shoes, an old electric razor..."

It might work. "You'd do that?"

"Sure. I mean, Estrella Court is a hole, but I don't mind it."

Josh was unbelievably nice. Morgan's heart stretched out toward him in a little gold thread. "I can't believe you'd trade all this for Estrella Court."

"I've lived in nice places. They don't faze me."

Huh. Maybe that was true. His dad was Bronco Hyatt of Hyatt Holdings, after all.

For the first time, Morgan started looking around with a little less fear. The soft carpet on the stairs felt like real wool. She pressed it between her fingers. So soft.

"So it's settled?" Josh put an arm around Morgan's shoulders in big-brother fashion. "You and Tory can relocate. I'll even help you load boxes in the U-Haul."

"Now that's a sacrifice." She leaned her head on his shoulder. It fit nicely there. He smelled like some kind of spiced cologne. Morgan closed her eyes and inhaled, savoring it.

Suddenly, though, Josh's arm dropped. "Uh—"

"What?"

"Did Darshelle say Seagram was going to be a business partner with the Estrella Court landlord?"

"Yeah. Why?"

"So he will have records of who the tenants are."

Morgan's heart dropped. "He'll know you're there. Paying rent."

Josh leaned back and rested his head on the stairs. Morgan twisted to see the pained look on his face. "Unless you find me your buddy who can do fake IDs for illegal immigrants, I'm going to have to stay on the rental agreement and the utilities for my apartment."

"I'm not sure I'm ready for us to compound our level of fraud, Josh. It's not worth it." Her heart was sinking lower and lower. It almost hit her toes. This complexity left her still in the pits with Tory's rent problem. It would make perfect sense to have Tory move in with them, but from the looks of Seagram's fantasy world he was forcing them into, Morgan didn't dare push that question. He'd know if Tory left Estrella Court, and he hadn't offered to let Morgan's sister join them. It would be rude to ask, after he'd already done so much.

"I got us into this," Josh said. "Tory shouldn't have to suffer. I'll contribute to her rent, since I'm still working at the water treatment plant, but I just don't think we have any choice."

Morgan winced as she responded. "I know. You're right. We have to move in together."

Chapter Eighteen

Morgan showed the movers where to put the box of her clothes, the stash she'd relocated to Josh's apartment on Friday night. She hadn't needed to bring anything else, as Seagram's Campus House was fully furnished, right down to dishes in the cupboard and food in the pantry. While she'd been at class, someone from Seagram's team had replaced all the wall art in the bedroom with the photos Tory had taken. Man, that kissing one in their swimsuits where Josh was holding her in the air, her legs dangling over his arm, and her arms around his neck was a little over the top. Especially since Tory had printed it out almost life-sized, and it hung right over the king-sized bed, torturing her.

Morgan couldn't sleep beneath that, no matter how much she loved the room. Josh would have to be the one who slept underneath it and wake up to it every morning. The sight of it probably didn't do to him what it did to her. Morgan was going to take the smaller room down at the far end of the hall. No arguments. End of story.

But the movers didn't need to know that.

"In the closet will be fine. Thank you so much, gentlemen." She didn't know if she was supposed to tip them. Having made her living by tips for the past year, she sympathized. But, then again, she didn't have any cash, and she certainly wasn't going to dip into the scholarship. She and Josh, first thing Monday morning, had deposited the check in a special account at First Federal Bank. No touchy.

It was the only way to salve her conscience.

But, still, she'd have to eat the food in the fridge. It would go bad. Growing up with barely enough, and all through college living mostly on apples from their tree back home, taught Morgan that wasting food was worse than taking money from strangers in the moral hierarchy her mind was constantly concocting and reshuffling these days. For instance, moving in with a man who didn't love her, but was married to her, versus forcing fifty elderly or indigent families onto the streets for not being able to pay their rent. That hierarchy, painful as it felt to choose, she'd been forced to determine.

And here she was. In the lap of luxury.

The doorbell rang. "Yoo-hoo!" A woman's voice rang up the stairs. Morgan had left the front door open for the movers to come in and out, and someone had taken advantage of it. Nosy neighbors?

"Oh, Mom. Hi." Morgan came down the stairs, and there stood Mom in a floral blouse, clutching Nixie to her chest. She looked lost in her surroundings.

"Morgan! This is just beautiful. I can't believe it." Mom wandered around with her head tilted back, her mouth agape, probably exactly how Morgan had looked when she first walked into the place. "When I saw the news clip Tory sent, I had to come and bring you a housewarming gift."

"That wasn't necessary, Mom." Morgan cringed. How would Mom feel if she knew what an elaborate ruse this all was? "But it was thoughtful."

Mom held out a gift bag with tissue poking out the top. "Open it right now. Go ahead."

Morgan lifted a ceramic frog from inside.

"I know, it's tacky. But I don't want you to forget your tacky roots."

"Never. I promise." Morgan set it in the center of the beautiful dining room table and could almost hear its *ribbit*.

"Where is that man of yours? I still haven't met him, you know."

155

"He's at class." Morgan didn't know that for certain. They hadn't exchanged schedules. She wasn't sure they ever would.

"Oh, fine. But soon, right? Good. Now, let's find somewhere we can sit and talk."

Morgan wasn't sure of the house enough yet to know where was best, but she led her to the book room. There, on a special easel on the central shelf, Seagram had had one of his people display a copy of *Frogs in the Sand*. She winced. How perfect a reminder of all Morgan's pain. But Mom was in raptures.

"Oh, look! I'm shocked!" She went and picked it up, fanned the pages. "Is this your personal copy? I thought I'd signed it."

"No, it's Seagram's, I think. Did I tell you Mr. Seagram would like his copy signed?" Morgan had better tell Mom before she forgot.

"I can do that right now!" She bustled to her purse and took out a pen, taking her time to make the capital D in Desiree Clark have that special flourish. "Now, for the real reason I'm here."

"It's not just a visit?" Morgan knew Mom never did much of anything without an agenda. She'd had to scratch for an existence too long.

"I feel cheated."

"Cheated?"

"Yes. You know I always looked forward to your wedding. A mother has dreams, too."

Morgan didn't like where this was going. "Mom —"

"Let me finish. Even though you and Joshua didn't start things traditionally, that doesn't mean we can't celebrate your union."

"Mom —"

"Wait. I'm still getting this out." She pressed her hands together on her lap. "I don't have a lot of expendable cash right now, as you know, but I'd still like to do something to launch you and Josh in your lives together. A reception."

"Mom! No, it's just not—"

"It just is. Now, listen. I've got a few ideas. We can make this really nice. You need some things. Every young couple does."

"Mom, look around. What could we possibly need? We have it all."

Her mom glanced around, taking it all in. "Okay, maybe so. But you won't be staying here forever."

"True, but by then, we'll both be done with school and can afford what we need." By then she'd be back in the single life and sharing the thrift store dishes and lumpy sofa with Tory again. No need for pasta makers or gilded picture frames she'd just have to keep in original packaging and return in a year when all this nonsense ended.

"Maybe, but will you really buy yourself a crock pot or a waffle iron? It's not about *need*, when it comes to a wedding reception. It's about the stuff you'd never buy for yourself."

Because no one needs it, Morgan thought. She had to put the kibosh on this. It would make the annulment so much worse later, when she had to mail all the gifts back to her mom's kind friends and their relatives—not to mention endure their sympathy. There had to be a silver bullet here for this plan. Or at least a postponement. "Let me think about it."

But Mom was not to be deterred. "You won't have to think about anything. I'll handle it all." She and Seagram ought to get together and teach a seminar called "How to Railroad People to Get Your Way in Any Circumstance."

"I'm not sure Josh will go for it. I mean, there's a reason he wanted to elope." Just not the reason anyone suspected, Morgan hoped. "Our relationship. It's a tender plant, Mom. We have to be gentle. You haven't met him. You don't know."

This at least, had some effect. "Oh." Mom scaled back

her enthusiasm. "I see. Well, then, I expect you to use your powers to convince him. I mean, you had enough wiles to snare him into marrying you after an extremely short time, so you must be the most powerful person any Hyatt man ever met."

"Uh-huh." Morgan reverted to her teen self, rolling her eyes. "Look, I'll talk to him. But you have to promise not to plan a single thing until I give you the green light that he's on board with it." There! Victory! It was kind of nice to have Josh as a scapegoat here. Maybe he'd come in handy in other situations in the future. "And I can't guarantee anything. He's a man with a mind of his own."

"I know all too well about men like that." Mom's face took on a cloud of bad memories, but it cleared quickly. "Okay. That's fair. But the second he relents, you're calling me."

"Agreed."

Mom got a sly look. "Ask him first thing in the morning, while he's still half asleep. Cuddle up to him and whisper it. That's when they're most pliable."

Morgan's face flushed at the image, and she forced it away. Besides, she would not be taking marriage relationship advice from her mom anytime soon. "Thanks. That might be an idea." Or it might not.

**

Josh wadded up his lab coat and tossed it on the back seat of the Explorer. He should have left it on its hanger in the plant, but he'd been thinking about the move and messed up three samples in a row at work. Finally George had just told him to go home.

"Newlyweds," he'd said, shaking his head. "I guess you'll be quitting now that you have the house."

"Nah." Josh's salary was still going to go toward Morgan's sister's rent. She shouldn't suffer just because he and Morgan came into good fortune. "Sorry. I'll be better tomorrow."

"No, you won't. But you will in a couple of months." George gave a knowing grin, and it sent Josh's thoughts to Morgan, and in an unwholesome direction. Months of living with her might weaken his resolve. Already it had been a full weekend and he'd barely recollected Brielle's name once.

Fifteen minutes later, he pulled up at Seagram's Campus House. Morgan had the key for the movers today, but they'd solved that dilemma this morning by finding the garage door opener. Josh could still get in the house.

Garage door opener? Far cry from the gravel parking lot at Estrella Court.

He eased the Explorer into the stall beside Morgan's truck. Side by side, truck and truck. How she ended up with that piece of junk, he had no idea. But she rocked it. Gorgeous girl in an old truck was a fantasy for a lot of guys.

Not that Josh necessarily started out in that club. He had Brielle, who still hadn't written, and who now only had an out-of-date mailing address for him. He needed to hit the post office later to leave a forwarding address. Missing her snail mail letter after all this time would suck.

"Honey, I'm home." It was a bad joke to call it into the air as he walked in the door. "Mm. You've been cooking?" The smell of a pot roast wafted to his nostrils. Morgan could cook? Score!

"I looked at the expiration date on the meat, and I couldn't let it go to waste." Morgan came around the corner, wearing jeans and a thin cotton t-shirt. Her legs looked so long and the shirt hugged her just right. Josh was a sucker for jeans and a t-shirt. "I hope I didn't ruin it."

"It smells good." He went over to the oven and propped it open. "Is it done?"

"Probably. Good timing, huh?" She searched through a few drawers and located some oven mitts, and then bent

159

over and pulled out the roast. Its aroma filled the room, and Josh's stomach growled. He hadn't been in a house that smelled like pot roast since Mom died.

"Did you make plans, invite other people?"

"No. I didn't even think of that. It's just us, I guess."

Their first dinner together. Or maybe their only. He didn't know if this was going to be a thing. Maybe he wouldn't mind coming home and having food all ready. That could be nice.

"So you're not a vegan?" He helped put plates on the table. Morgan had put together a salad and it was already waiting, next to a really ugly ceramic frog. Weird taste, if it was hers. "I mean, the pot roast isn't a Veg-Out staple."

"Nope. And I took a lot of flak for it working there, believe me. Some customers could be brutal. Not all of them, of course, but some were just so high and mighty. I finally started evading the question when they'd ask me how I decided to go vegan."

Josh had seen this. Not in food choices, but other things. "People need a way to feel self-righteous."

"I don't remember that on Maslow's hierarchy. Food, shelter, love, self-righteousness..."

"Put it on Hyatt's hierarchy, then." Josh had thought this through. "Yes, they need all the Maslow stuff, but once those are met, new needs come up. And a way to feel superior is one of them."

Morgan placed a pitcher of ice water on the table. "Huh. Maybe you're right." Then she sniff-laughed. "Besides religion, my superiority complex is probably the fact I'm carnivorous. Or at least it was while I was stuck on roller skates for nine months."

Josh could admire a woman who prioritized meat. "Didn't I tell you? I'm only willing to stay together in this house if you'll bring me my dinner wearing skates." Morgan was also one who could take being teased. Brielle was pretty intense all the time and brushed off his teasing, but Morgan's tugging smile showed she could take whatever he dished out.

"Is that so?" Morgan raised an eyebrow, and her blue eyes shone. "I'd like to see you try it yourself. These flagstone floors will not be your friend."

There was an awkward moment while Josh couldn't stop staring at that blue-eyed challenge, then he shook it off. "I'm the head of household here, and it would help my superiority complex if we say grace on this meal."

"And for the hands that provided it."

Josh initially misheard the phrase referring to Seagram's generosity, thinking instead she said the hands that prepared it, which made him look at her hands. Dainty and slender, sporting the ruby that declared she belonged to him and him alone.

He cursed himself—so far in the past seven minutes since he walked in the door, he'd ogled Morgan's t-shirt, her well-fitting jeans, the tug of her smile, her two locks of stray blonde hair, her blue eyes, and now her hands. What was next, the curve of her waist? Another curse at himself—and just when he was supposed to be saying grace.

***

Morgan hunched over her *Advanced Accounting* textbook. This part about federal income tax was so confusing, she'd had to read it three times. It didn't help that Josh was in the next room but still close enough that she could hear him cough every once in a while as he studied there, totally throwing her concentration out the window. It also didn't help that the clock was inching toward eleven p.m. Moving and classes and cooking and getting ready for her test tomorrow had exhausted her. She wasn't necessarily up to the argument she knew was coming.

She read the tax part a fourth time, and then she heard Josh's chair at the kitchen table scraping back across the stone floor.

"I'm headed to bed. Good night." How polite of him to say something. She kind of didn't expect it. "I'll take one of the spare rooms. You can have the master."

"No, I've got my stuff in the room at the end of the hall. You take the master."

Josh frowned. "I thought you loved that bedroom. I heard you sigh in ecstasy when we toured it with Darshelle."

Bah. "Ecstasy. Not even. When I sigh in ecstasy, you'll know it." Suddenly she realized how that might sound, and she colored. "You take it."

Josh shook his head. "I'm taking one of the other rooms. You sleep wherever makes you sigh in ecstasy, then." He half-laughed. "I'll be listening for that."

Oh, great. "You wish." A challenging retort was her only defense.

Well, that didn't go as badly as planned. He did eventually back down and not insist she take the master with its huge kissy picture of them to taunt her. Boundaries! They were her blessing and her curse.

She looked up, and he hadn't gone up to bed like she thought. He was still standing there, watching her. She hoped she hadn't made faces reflecting the variety of emotions her brain took her through in the last ten seconds.

***

"What are you studying?" Josh leaned against the archway between the kitchen and the book room. He should head for bed. It was late. He had to leave for work at five a.m., and he'd better be a little more focused than he was today. But something kept his feet planted here.

"Tax accounting. You?" Morgan's bare feet were

162

tucked under her on the couch, her toes sticking out beneath her hip.

"Cold War relations between East and West." Not his best subject. They kept wanting him to analyze the Russian mindset, as if that were even possible. Those people ate beet soup as a staple, for Pete's sake.

"Interesting."

"Sort of."

"What happened to your barrel of bacteria?" Morgan tossed his bacteria into the conversation. So she remembered it? He'd strategically stashed it in the workshop out back, thinking maybe she'd forget. "Somehow I guess instead of the shirt and tie of an intelligence analyst, I always pictured you in a lab coat."

"That's because I work at the water treatment plant in the lab, and you probably saw me come back to Estrella Court wearing it at some point." He came over and sat down beside her, probably pushing some of those boundaries they'd set up. But she smelled better up close. "My composting stuff is in the shed."

"Cool." She unfolded a leg, reached it out and shut her book with her foot. She must be done for the night. He relaxed. It was nice to have someone to talk to. "I'm horrible at science," she said, "but I'm fascinated by it. I had to go a different direction with my math skills. Accounting seemed like the right thing once I started college, but I always secretly wished I could do chemistry or biology."

"I bet you're not as horrible at it as you say." Josh looked her over, and no question in his mind, Morgan had chemistry and biology down. Chemistry just emanated from her at him, and her biology looked like it didn't need an iota of help. "I took a lot of those classes my first time through Claremont. There are some good professors. Maybe you should change majors." Wouldn't Morgan's hips sashaying into Bio 335 really shake up the major?

163

"Hah. Not at this point in the game." She stretched herself out on the sofa, her wavy hair spreading across the far armrest. "I'm surprised you were willing to change horses halfway through the ride."

This kicked him in the gut, being the point of contention that caused pretty much this whole debacle of his being twenty-two and still not done with his undergrad. He frowned. "It didn't make my family too happy, either." What did he go saying that for? It wasn't anyone's business, not even his faux-wife's.

"Don't tell me that's what the wedge is." Morgan said this sleepily.

"What wedge?"

"Between you and your dad."

His inner shell opened a crack. "Maybe," leaked out through the crack against his will. He never meant to admit to her or anyone this was the source of his conflict with old Bronco. If he could hit the rewind and erase his answer to her right now, he would. She was only a business partner (who he sometimes kissed on command of strangers), and he didn't have any obligation to go telling her all his issues, especially when he hadn't even confided them even in Brielle, the girl he planned to spend the rest of his life with. He couldn't tell Brielle she was the reason Bronco had sent him packing or he'd drive one of those wedges Morgan mentioned between his family and his future wife that could never be gouged out. Brielle didn't understand how volatile Bronco could be, and the one time he'd dropped a hint of his dad's displeasure at Josh's change of course after meeting her, Brielle had been so upset he decided to drop the subject, go ahead with his plans, and just let time eventually take care of the problem—which it hadn't, and now the rift between father and son, between father and future-daughter-in-law, was wider than ever.

He couldn't help but wonder if Bronco's non-acceptance of Brielle was part of the reason she'd jetted off to Germany, taking a part of Josh with her.

Josh had tensed up, and it looked like Morgan could sense it. "Hey. Sorry. I won't pry. Husband or not, you've got your stuff, and you have a right to keep some of it all to yourself. Just, if you ever want to talk about it, I'm willing to listen."

"Thanks. I just don't like talking about my dad. He's pretty hard to deal with sometimes. It's his way or the highway."

"Do what he says or be a plumber. I get it. Parents are great, but they can also be a pain in the neck. At least your dad isn't out appearing on national television spouting poetry about frogs and sand."

"At least there's that." Josh let a little laugh slip out. Morgan could be pretty cool and put things into perspective for him, but he loved that she didn't push him all the time to *discuss*. Nothing irritated him more about Brielle than when she insisted he tell her what was bugging him when he hadn't worked it all out yet mentally. Morgan, though? She was easy. It was nice. He reached over and patted her knee, leaving his hand there for maybe a moment too long. "Bronco Hyatt is definitely not a poet, but that's all I can stand to say about him tonight."

"Don't worry about it. Boundaries, right?" Morgan uncurled her legs out from under her and stretched them across his lap, her pink-painted toenails and smooth-skinned feet on his thigh, the pressure of them making him suddenly more aware of her than he should be this time of night.

"Yeah, boundaries." Boundaries. Some were crumbling. And he'd better rebuild them — fast.

Chapter Nineteen

Morgan rubbed the sleep out of her eyes. A ray of sunshine filtered in to her between the white cotton panels of the curtains. What a beautiful room! Even if it wasn't as lovely as the master bedroom down the hall, she couldn't help loving the soft cream of the walls and the white accents of wood and furniture everywhere. And it was so clean, just like these crisp sheets she'd slept in, her bare legs sliding against their thousand thread count.

How did she get so lucky?

With a yawn, she padded down the wood planks of the corridor to the master. Even if she couldn't bear to sleep in there, beneath that suggestive photograph, she wouldn't skip the luxury of the jetted tub or the long counter in front of the vanity to use for doing her hair and makeup. Josh was gone — probably early to work and class — and she could relax. For the first time in months, she could see well enough to put her mascara on, thanks to the perfect lighting around the large mirror.

Bliss.

After a ridiculously hot bath, she stood at the counter in her thin robe, putting the last touches on her lashes, just about to try to do something with her hair. The waves were a constant struggle. Maybe she should take the time to straighten it. She slid to the door to glance at the large wall clock on one of the bedroom walls, when —

"Oh, my goodness!" There stood Josh. He was in a lab coat. But his eyes weren't part of his head, they were climbing up and down her half-clad body. "I thought you were at class. Or work. Or—" Morgan clutched the folds of her robe together, re-tying its belt. "Sorry. I thought since you were gone I could use the master bathroom."

Josh's Adam's apple rose and fell. He was gulping. "Uh."

"I'll do my hair down the hall in the guest bathroom." She turned and bent over to the basket on the floor to collect her supplies, but he interrupted.

"No. Uh." He collected himself. "I—it's—I just got off work. I overslept this morning and couldn't shower before my five a.m. shift."

"Of course!" Morgan's arms were full of her makeup bag, her hair dryer, a straightening iron, her razor (which had been fantastic to use on her legs in that deep tub), and assorted other things. She clutched them to her chest, but that made her bereft of a hand to keep her robe closed. "You want to shower before your class." She hustled out of the bathroom, practically running, her feet making the wood floor in the hall sound hollow.

"Morgan. Wait!" Josh followed her, but she slid into her bedroom and dropped all her things on the bed.

"I'll just get dressed," she called to him down the hallway, taking off on a babbling rampage. "Then we should maybe discuss a schedule. Because even if neither of us sleeps on that incredible mattress in the master, we absolutely both need to be taking advantage of that jetted tub. It felt like a dozen heavenly angels were massaging my skin. I refuse to give it up, but I refuse to keep it all to myself. It's too perfect." She shut the door and pressed her back against it, sliding down to the floor.

Her heart pounded. Why have such mixed feelings about Josh's eyes on her bare knees and collarbone? He hadn't caught sight of her just now in anything more revealing than when she'd worn her wrap dress to sit beside him in church on Sunday, but somehow it felt more intimate—a lot more intimate—and it drew her to him in a

167

way she should resist, even though day by day she was finding him more and more irresistible.

Morgan grabbed a hair clip from her pile. Today was a ponytail day. Totally.

Then she looked around for the clothes she'd lain out to wear, and realized she'd left them on the floor of the master closet where the rest of her things were.

Great.

Pricking up her ears, she listened for the water to start running in Josh's bath, but the house was too well-insulated for plumbing sounds down the hall to carry this far. For a few minutes, she paced, deciding what to do, but one look at the alarm clock on the nightstand alarmed her—her Business Practices test in Professor Wyeth's class was in fifteen minutes, and it was a nine minute walk from here.

Man, she'd been in that tub a while.

This was not good. She could not miss that test—it was worth a huge percentage of her total grade. And she couldn't go to class in just her robe and her nothing-else, obviously, although it might get her extra credit in that old lecher's class. Not worth it.

Why! Why hadn't she grabbed her clothes out of the closet as she ran away from Josh in her towel?

Sigh. She had no choice: Morgan had to go back in the master bedroom, even if it meant risking seeing Josh again before she was dressed. Geez. When she'd agreed to this— well, agreed to be bullied into this by Mr. Seagram—she hadn't thought she was signing up for heart-pounding stress over the simple task of putting on her jeans and sweater in the morning.

She creaked the door open. The hallway was clear. With ears open, she listened for Josh (she hoped) downstairs in the kitchen rummaging for breakfast. No such luck. The water in the bath wasn't running, as far as she could hear. And his car would be parked in the garage, so she wouldn't be able to peek out a window and see if he'd left.

The minute hand on the clock on the bedroom wall ticked loudly. Ooh, another reason not to sleep in that room. With a trembling hand, she pressed the master bedroom door open. *Please don't see me, please.* No Josh. She tiptoed in as softly as possible, a cloud of steam from the open bathroom door moistening the air. Just ten steps to the closet...

There! Triumphant she stepped inside the closet, and she bent over to the floor where she'd lain her underthings, her jeans, sweater and shoes.

"Boo!"

Morgan jumped, her heart lurching into near cardiac arrest, and a little shriek escaped her mouth.

Josh loomed over her from deeper in the long corridor that served as their closet. Morgan's heart raced, and she colored and snatched at her gaping robe at the same time. Her eyes focused. His hair was wet, and he stood in just his jeans, with his t-shirt hanging at his neck, his arms not in it yet. Nice upper arms.

"Thought you could sneak in on me, eh?" He stepped a little closer to her. "Couldn't keep away?" He inched even closer, and Morgan's heart revved even more. He kind of glistened. Yikes—she'd better get away from him right now.

"Oh, stop." Morgan grabbed her things—again—and used them to cover herself as much as possible. "I just left my clothes in here and have a test in about ten minutes. You sure shower fast." Her mouth was running as fast as her heart did from the scare.

"Well, then you'd better hurry. Put those on right now." He arched a brow, as if waiting for her to obey while he watched.

"As if." She waved him away and darted back down the hall.

Moments later, she was dashing out the front door and jogging toward the Villers Building, face still aflame.

No question, Josh's attractiveness level was climbing every time she saw him. And it wasn't like she'd forgotten how good his kisses felt. They induced the same feeling as having him look at her the way he had a few minutes ago. If he had a girlfriend, he didn't act like he even remembered her name at that point.

Tory's words bounced through Morgan's head. *Absence doesn't make the heart grow fonder. That's bull. You're right beside him day and night. You're married to him, for heaven's sake. Make the guy know you're here.*

He'd better stop flirting with her, or she might just stomp down some boundaries and actually take Tory's advice.

Josh Hyatt probably didn't realize he was playing with fire.

***

Josh sat on the bottom step to tie his shoes. He'd had a huge appetite for breakfast when he walked in the door after work, but seeing Morgan sent his appetites shooting in another direction. That girl was beyond gorgeous. He'd watched out the window as she ran across their front lawn toward campus and liked every curve and bounce. It made him feel a little voyeuristic, even if she was his wife.

Wife. Moments like this morning in the closet made him consider turning Morgan into his wife for real, forgetting Brielle, and just charting a totally new course for his life. Not that he'd actually do that — to himself, or to Brielle. Or to Morgan, for that matter. She was a really nice girl. He liked her too much to drag her into the swirling cesspool that was the extended Hyatt family — with its dysfunction since Mom died, and with the cameras popping up to catch one Hyatt heir or another doing

170

something salacious.

Luckily, Josh had gone totally off the tabloid news radar as soon as Bronco disowned him. He'd become a regular guy. And he'd been way off radar at Estrella Court. Now, with the whole Seagram fiasco going on, there was a slim chance he'd be rediscovered by the press.

But only slim. Nobody cared about a poor, disinherited son, especially if his destiny according to the patriarch of the family was to become a plumber.

Meanwhile, he'd better take Morgan up on her offer to schedule bath time. No sense repeating today's accident. Because it could turn into more of an accident for him.

Focus. He had to focus. Maybe he should arrange to take a night shift at the water treatment plant instead? Truth was, this morning in the closet felt like just an extension of last night on the couch. Too close for comfort—and too far for other comfort at the same time.

Distance. Distance was key here.

The doorbell rang. Josh crossed the flagstone entryway to answer. It almost seemed like he should have a butler.

But instead, there stood a maid. "Hi. I'm Svetlana. I'll be cleaning today." She was a heavyset woman of around forty with an Eastern European accent. "Please, do not mind me." She bustled in, and Josh dodged her like he would a steamroller coming down new asphalt at him. In a moment, she'd disappeared into the upstairs, and he heard singing in another language. She might see that a couple of the rooms were being used, but Josh had made his bed this morning while trying to cool off after seeing Morgan, so the woman would probably never be the wiser that he and Morgan weren't sharing a bed.

Nice. Having a housekeeper was awesome. He'd almost forgotten. And it was great that Morgan wouldn't have to divide her attention from her studies, either. Because if he understood her personality like he thought he did, she was the type who'd feel guilty about dust or

171

crumbs and spend all Saturday blitzing the house when she had a test to study for. He liked that, in a way, because it reminded him of how his mom had kept things so orderly when he was growing up, but he also knew it would be defeating the purpose of all the stress they'd endured moving in here.

Morgan. How was her test going? He hoped she'd ace it. She'd studied late enough last night, putting in time on the books. Now that she didn't have to roller skate around The Grand Old Okra, she'd probably put his grades to shame.

Josh snagged an apple from the refrigerator to take to class. When his chemistry realigned after the Morgan-in-only-a-robe incident, he'd probably be hungry again and need this.

The doorbell rang again. Josh would catch it on his way out. Maybe it was the gardener.

In the doorway loomed the most unexpected person.

"Dad?" Josh dropped the apple, likely bruising it into oblivion, and putting it to waste, which Morgan would be sorry about. "What are you doing in here?"

If Svetlana had seemed like a steamroller, Bronco was a Sherman tank. He crashed through the entryway and stomped so hard across the flooring he might have cracked some of the flagstone.

"Joshua John Hyatt. What in the name of Sam Hill do you think you're doing?"

Chapter Twenty

Morgan's running endurance was pitiful. She'd barely covered the space between the mansion and the Student Life Center before she was out of breath. It'd been too long since she'd had time to exercise, like since summer break, what with waitressing taking up all her time. Maybe she'd be able to carve out time for a workout now.

Still panting at an embarrassing rate, she came to the Quad, and across it lay the Villers Building. The bells in the Old Main clock tower chimed. She was late, but she might still make it before Dr. Wyeth shut the door and wedged it closed against her with a stack of textbooks he'd authored himself and charged students hundreds of dollars per copy to purchase.

"You." Narrowed eyes of an already pinched face popped up just feet in front of Morgan. She'd seen this girl before, but she didn't know where.

"Hi. How's it going?" Morgan tried not to slow down. She could not miss this test. Averting her glance from the apparent stink-eye coming from this girl, she kept up her pace.

"Uh, I don't think so." The woman stepped directly into Morgan's path, and then she put out a hand and caught Morgan by the shoulder.

"Oh, hey. I'm so sorry. I'm really super late for my test, and I've got to run."

"Not a chance, girlfriend." She caught Morgan's sweater and snagged it between her fingers. Her grip was surprisingly firm. Morgan lurched backward, pulling to a halt. It was either that or lose her top, not really an option. "You're the girl who won't leave Josh Hyatt alone. I have a few words to say to you."

"Can we meet for a bagel later? I'm seriously late." Morgan started walking, but the girl still had her by the sweater and didn't appear to be letting go—of the sweater or of Morgan's attention. "Tell me your name and number, and I'll put it in my phone and give you a call after my test." That wasn't necessarily a lie—she'd at least consider calling the woman.

"I'm Claire Salazar, and you'll stay right here and hear me out, you home-wrecking interloper. My lifelong best friend Brielle Dupree said nothing to me about any breakup with Josh before she left for Germany, and she tells me absolutely everything. If there had been anything other than wedding bells chiming in their future, I would know, believe me. We are like that." She held up her index and tall fingers, crossing them. "When Josh dropped her off at the airport, just minutes before you usurped her, there were things understood between them, and there's no way she broke any of them, and no way Josh would dream of breaking a promise—not to the one and only Brielle Dupree. Do you have any idea how brilliant she is? She's a rising star in the State Department, a potential ambassador to almost any foreign nation, and a serious catch, even for Joshua Hyatt." She huffed and tugged at the sweater in a threat.

The heat of mixed anger and embarrassment crept up Morgan's neck. She didn't even know this woman Claire, other than seeing her the one time in the jewelry store and noting how unpleasant she was, and Josh hadn't dropped any details about his girlfriend Brielle or what kind of a person she was—or even really the nature of their relationship. He hadn't been engaged before, Morgan knew that at least, so where did this girl get off calling her a home-wrecker? It was a little much to take, and Morgan

174

had to bite her tongue to keep herself from taking the bait and getting in a huge argument with this stranger. What did she know? Morgan reached down and peeled the woman's fingers off her sweater, yanking it back into place.

"Look, I'm really sorry if you're upset, but I don't know why you think it's all right to come and accuse me of these things when Josh Hyatt and I are legally married." She couldn't say they were in love, or that they had a real future together, or any of the other arguments that could have shut down this barrage of attacks, unfortunately, so she turned on the heel of her boot and headed across the Quad again. Her window of time to get to class was sliding shut fast.

Claire didn't stop her this time, but she came around in front of her, walking backwards and facing Morgan. Her already sour face looked like it had been sprayed with a dose of citric acid. "Josh Hyatt was nothing before he started dating Brielle Dupree. He had no direction whatsoever. She took him, molded him, made him the man he is today. If you think you're going to be the beneficiary of all her hard work, you with your big fake boobs and your fake blond hair—"

Nothing about Morgan was fake. She was too poor to afford fake anything, and Tory refused to color Morgan's hair, saying she wouldn't mess with what God got perfect. And who was this woman to talk? Her hair was the color of a ripe strawberry. Nature didn't do that.

"Please, you're out of line, and I'm sure you know it, and if you end up feeling bad about it tomorrow or some other time, just know I forgive you. I'm sure you're only defending your friend." Morgan broke into a jog and dodged around this shrew before she could snare her again. "Sorry—gotta run." Then she really did run, thanking Eat and Leaf for the strong leg muscles it had bestowed on her. Just as the clock tower chimed the hour, she wedged herself through the swiftly shutting door of

Professor Wyeth's classroom and collapsed in her seat next to Isabel, a girl in her major, and pulled out her pencil for the test.

Yeah, the events of this morning were definitely not the best way to prepare for an exam. She'd better clear her head and focus on economic formulas — if at all possible.

***

"What in the Sam Hill do you think you're doing?"

Josh instantly went on guard, tensing every muscle in his body. "Good to see you, too, Dad," slid through clenched teeth. "I'm heading to class after pulling an all-nighter at the water treatment plant, if that's what you're asking." Josh knew what Bronco was really asking, and he decided to evade instead of make it easy on him to see how Bronco liked the tables turned. Because when in the past three years had Bronco made a single thing easy on Josh?

"Are you out of your mind?" A few curse words peppered every phrase falling from Dad's lips, words that had crept in after Mom went out of his life. "Do you have any idea what you're doing here?"

Josh had been in enough of these vaguely stated interrogations to know they could go on for hours. "Can we just skip to the tirade and the irate lecture part of this conversation now? Because I have a class that starts in a few minutes, and the professor calls roll." He didn't mention the name of the class, "Cold War Relations Between East and West," knowing the very topic and fact that it was obviously part of his foreign policy major would send Bronco Hyatt into the stratosphere and prolong the agony of the conversation by at least fifteen minutes.

"For a guy supposedly spending scores of hours every week studying power struggles and strategies, you sure put your foot right in a bear trap with all the naïveté of a complete twelve-year-old." Bronco snorted. "I'm more

176

ashamed than ever to see you on television parading around with that so-called wife of yours."

So-called wife? That got Josh's back up even more. His fingernails dug little half-moon cuts into his palms. "You haven't even met Morgan, and you're already declaring her worthless? I'm sorry, but that says a lot more about you than it does about her."

"No," Bronco huffed, pacing the flagstone, his cowboy boots clunking so hard the rock beneath them might chip. "What says something is the fact you and your shotgun bride are on the dole, holing up in this place owned by one of the most ridiculous characters in the entire universe of Oregon businessmen. Sigmund Seagram is nothing but a joke, and you're making yourself a joke by association."

"And you a joke by association with me, apparently," Josh said darkly. He didn't want to stand here listening to this, but he knew that if he went outside, the rant would not end; it would merely trail him across campus and embarrass him in front of the whole student body of Clarendon College. Then both he and his dad would be the campus jokes, no association necessary.

"Do you realize you and your 'neediness' has been splashed all over television by that vindictive scum, and that the story has been picked up by practically every news channel in the state? Our family's reputation is being tarnished by your faking being welfare needy. It's making us a laughingstock."

"A scholarship isn't the same thing as welfare, Dad." Josh tried not to sound condescending, but the tone crept in. "It's merit-based, not need-based."

Bronco just snorted. "Merit."

"For your information, I'm a good student. And at one point, Morgan was at the top of her accounting department." She'd said so, right? But she'd taken that job, her grades had fallen and her other scholarship had dried up. Josh had a sudden memory of the despair in Morgan's

177

tone when they'd discussed her situation a few weeks ago, before all the lunacy that now defined his life had started. The thought of her returning to that despair if Bronco busted this situation for Morgan turned Josh's insides to fire.

Luckily, Bronco returned to his attacks on Josh instead. "Good student. Ha! At what? Travel? Foreign governments? We Hyatts, my son, don't give a flying rat about foreign governments. We have all the government we can handle right here in the old U.S. of A., and the rest of the world can all go be hanged. Hyatt Holdings makes all the money it needs from its American-based factories, selling American-made products to Americans. And that's all there is to it. You think you were raised in a big house with everything money could buy based on the whims of crazy foreigners? No, sir."

"I never cared about the big house, Dad, and neither did Mom, for that matter. Now, are you going to make me late for class?"

"And that's another thing. Your mother would not approve of your going off and marrying some girl none of us Hyatts have ever met. I saw the pictures, and she looks like you stood at the end of some beauty pageant runway and yanked her down into your lap. Which, you know, good for you, but you can't keep wasting your life on these floozies."

Floozies! "Morgan is a nice girl." And so is Brielle, he wanted to argue, but now was not the time.

Bronco harrumphed. "At least she isn't that pinhead Brie Cheese Dupree you thought you were in love with." There was some muttering under Bronco's breath. "With her out of the picture, I'm sure you've seen the light, though, and jumped as far away from that stupid line of studying she brainwashed you into taking. You're being a good American scientist again, aren't you?" For the first time in the conversation Bronco looked a little softer, but

Josh's answer would cure that.

"Still a foreign policy major." It wouldn't matter to his dad that he'd filed three new patent claims in the last six months, or that one pending patent was highly likely to be approved within the week, or that this property of Seagram's had the perfect location for him to continue his alternative energy research on the compost in his spare time. Bronco was fixated on the one fact. "And Brielle was right—it's a bigger world out there. I'm planning on being a citizen of it."

"Citizen, schmitizen."

Bronco Hyatt. For a guy who did as much business with others as he did, Bronco Hyatt sure had a narrow view of the universe.

"Look, this has been real nice. Thanks for stopping by. I'll give Morgan your love."

"You'll do no such thing!" Bronco exploded again— and just when he'd seemed to be winding down. "And that's another thing. Chip spilled the beans that he let you have your mother's ruby ring to put on that gold-digging female's finger."

Gold digger. Ha. There had been a while when Josh wasn't even sure Morgan knew Josh was a Hyatt, had no idea what dynasty she'd married into. He hadn't minded keeping it a secret from her, because the Hyatts put the *nasty* in *dynasty*.

"What if I did?" No use denying it. "Mom always wanted it to go to one of her daughters-in-law." That may or may not have been true, but Bronco wouldn't have known the difference. This seemed to take the wind out of Dad's sails, and his chest deflated a little at the mention of Mom. "Look, I am now officially late for my class. Good chat, Dad. As always." Josh held the door for him, and Bronco uprooted his boots from the floor and headed toward the door.

"Joshua Hyatt, if you can't pull your head out of your

179

hindquarters long enough to see what a mistake you're making, then you're no son of mine."

"Which leaves us at the status quo. And I'm still late." He resisted the urge to shove his dad right out the door. He watched him go, emotions roiling in his gut and blood flow screaming in his ears.

But a few paces down the walk, Bronco turned back. "Next Friday there's dinner at the house."

Josh assumed there was dinner at the house every Friday. So what?

"It's Heather's birthday. She insists. You'll show up, and you'll bring your wife—"

"Her name is Morgan." Josh knew Bronco couldn't deny any request made by Heather.

"You'll bring her and the ruby, or I'll call the police and have you both arrested for stealing the ring."

"Nice way to extend a dinner invitation, Dad." He'd clearly spent the last six months in an intensive charm school course. This? *This* was why Josh had determined not to bring Morgan anywhere near his family.

But for now, it looked like he didn't have any choice. Poor girl. He hoped her silky, creamy skin was thicker than it looked.

***

At the end of class, Morgan set her exam on the professor's dais and trudged over to pick up her backpack. Isabel was leaving at the same time and went down the staircase beside her, saying, "That was brutal."

No kidding. "I never bombed a test so badly in my life." Morgan would have sat down and cried if she didn't have to be at her next class in eleven minutes clear across campus. "I'm wondering why I even left the house this morning." If this test sank her grade and kept her from graduating, she was going to hunt down that venomous

180

redhead and give her a swift kick.

"Ooh, tell me about the house. You're in Siggy Seagram's house now, right? You are so lucky you scored that. I want to know, are there fifteen bedrooms and a game room like I heard?"

Morgan gave her a few sketchy details of the house and then said, "No game room, exactly. Just a library with a nice sofa and more books than you could read in a lifetime—oh, and a fireplace."

Isabel gave a dreamy sigh and launched into a monologue that carried them across the whole Quad. "A fireplace. I bet you and Josh cozy up in front of it at night with Dean Martin songs playing—I read once that Josh Hyatt loves Dean Martin. How romantic. And so close to campus, luxury living, housekeeper, gardener—I saw it all on the news, and it made me look up the details of the scholarship, and when I told my boyfriend about it, he was like, 'Wow. We should get married just so we can apply for that. It'd be worth it.' And I about fell out of his car because I've been wishing he'd propose for about a year. We've been together for three years, ever since high school. You're so lucky you got Josh—Joshua Hyatt!—to up and propose to you at the bat of an eyelash. Of course, whoever you batted your eyelashes at would have chucked armloads of diamonds at you, you're so gorgeous. Oh, I haven't seen the ring. Show me the ring. I bet it's amazing."

Morgan had missed that whole excitement of gathering her girlfriends around her and squealing over the ring, and this was the first time anyone had asked to see it. It felt weird, but she showed Isabel her left hand. The ruby looked a lot bigger in the sunlight, covering almost half the width of her finger.

"Oh, sweet honeybees. That is one red mega-rock. Is it real? Oh, what am I saying, of course it's real. You're married to Joshua Hyatt, for heaven's sake." Isabel gawked and went on about it for a full minute while Morgan felt a little rush of warm pride. It really was a spectacular ring, and hearing someone say those nice things about Josh didn't hurt either.

"It was Josh's mother's." The tidbit came out before Morgan realized what she was sharing. A faint wisp of a wish it could really belong to her and mean what it ought to mean rose up in her heart. *Sorry, Mrs. Hyatt, wherever you are.* It was also possible that this was top secret information, and she'd better clarify with Josh before she told anyone else. Except she wouldn't need to tell anyone else—Isabel would broadcast it to anyone unlucky enough to be in listening range.

Isabel put a hand over her heart and tilted her head to the side, speechless. "His mother's? That is just so amazing. Aw." She sighed. "When he proposed, was it super romantic? How was the kiss?"

That, at least, she could answer with full truth. "The kiss sent my soul fleeing from my body. That guy can kiss."

Isabel's eyelids fluttered as she rolled her eyes heavenward, and then Morgan had to run, again, to her next class. This whole charade was tricky, in that it was starting to make even the actress believe her own stories.

***

"Tory?" Morgan hadn't even talked to her sister since the move. Things had been too hectic for anything but a couple of texts. "Want to meet me for lunch?"

"Sure. Anywhere but the Garden Grubs."

"Come up to my house. The fridge is so full of food I can't possibly hope to use it all, and it's going to go bad."

Tory gasped. She felt the same way about food going to waste as Morgan did—it was a crime. "I'll be there at one."

By a little after one, they were eating sandwiches and drinking chocolate milk at the quartz counter in the kitchen of Seagram's Campus House. Tory kept running her hand along the cool, smooth surface of the stone. "I can't believe you live here. It's a palace."

"I know. I can't either." Every time she walked in, it felt like she was entering a luxury hotel by accident and she had to remind herself to breathe.

"Can I get a tour of the place?" Tory asked. Morgan promised one later, after they talked a few things out. "Don't tell me there's trouble in paradise. Because this, my dearest, is paradise. Especially with the gorgeous Josh Hyatt floating in and out at all hours. Have you ever considered that you might just be the luckiest girl alive right now?"

Morgan hadn't. It was too stressful to feel happy-go-lucky in any way right now. "It's not all fresh peaches with half-and-half. There's a glitch." She steeled herself and told Tory about the run-in with Claire. "So now I don't know what to do. Should I tell Josh there's a screaming red banshee threatening to bite, or just let it ride?"

Tory set down her milk glass. "That is a dilemma." She looked thoughtful. "Because you don't want to give busybodies like that an inch or they'll take a mile. Don't give her the time of day. Josh is yours; the she-devil's friend left town and lost him—her own fault. Finders keepers, losers weepers, the end." Tory gulped down the final swig from her glass and set it down with finality.

Morgan shook her head. Tory's assessment definitely didn't jive with her own. "No, it's that I don't want Josh to have to worry about it, when in the long run it's basically meaningless when he and I get our annulment. The point will be moot. Scary Clairey's best friend can have him back untarnished, with only a few kisses here and there to complain about."

"There's been kissing?" Tory's eyes lit up. "Tell!"

Morgan rolled her eyes. "Only when I challenged him after the proposal." And when they said *I do*, and when he spontaneously kissed her when the check came in the mail, and a few times on the forehead. And for Seagram's cameras.

"I think you're forgetting the make-out in the waves. I have photographic evidence of that one." Tory got a wicked look in her eye. "What other kissing has there been? Late night on that sofa over there in front of the sultry firelight?" She pointed toward the reading room, and Morgan remembered how it had felt last night, stretched out on the couch with her legs over Josh's lap, more relaxed than she'd been in a man's presence ever in her life. "Maybe a little more for the newlyweds at bedtime?"

"Tory. Don't you know me at all?"

"I know you're a married woman, living with a really nice, drop-dead gorgeous, wealthy, sharp-minded man who happens to be your husband. What kind of nun wouldn't be taking full advantage of that situation?"

"Enough with the peer pressure, Tor. I'm not going there."

"We'll see."

Morgan gulped. "Wanna see the house?" She led Tory through the reading room, which Tory had already glanced at and mentioned in that kissing fantasy, the other rooms on the main level, and then took her upstairs to the sleeping quarters. "You have to see the jetted tub in the master. It's beyond luxury." They went through the master bedroom without Tory commenting on the huge swimsuit picture above the bed, and Morgan exhaled a little in relief. "See? Isn't it amazing? It has about forty jets, and the water can come up to my neck. You'll have to try it sometime."

Morgan got a text and sent Tory to explore the rest of the bedrooms while she answered it. Tory came back in a moment, confused. "None of the beds look slept in. Where do you and Mr. Hyatt sleep?"

That was strange. Morgan definitely hadn't had time to make her bed this morning, not with all the hoopla after her towel scene. Would Josh have gone around and made the beds? She and Tory made their way down the hall, with Morgan checking in each bedroom to find them all as neat as a pin, her own discarded robe hanging on a hook on the bedroom door. Josh Hyatt—what a surprise. He'd never struck her as the neat-freak type, and less as the type to spend a full morning turning a house into a showcase.

"It's like you have a housekeeper or something," Tory said, taking a peek inside a well-stocked linen closet.

Housekeeper. That was right. Mr. Seagram had said something about having someone come in a few days a week so Morgan could concentrate on her studies and not have to spend all her time looking after this enormous house. "Isn't that fantastic?" she breathed.

"Yeah—unless she's nosy and loyal to old Siggy Seagram and figures out Mr. and Mrs. Hyatt are sleeping in separate beds and runs off and tells her boss. Then you and your charade are up a creek." Tory's eyes crinkled. "Luckily, there's an easy fix for that—sleep in the same room. In the same bed."

Not. Nothing about that suggestion would be easy or a fix.

Chapter Twenty-One

Josh tugged back the door on the Student Center and stepped out of the wind. It was coming up salty from the ocean today. He'd better grab what he needed from the bookstore and get home to eat before work —

"Well, if it isn't Joshua Hyatt." A woman's voice stopped him before his eyes had adjusted to the indoors — and unpleasant voice.

Josh blinked and finally the face came into focus. "Claire. Hey. What are you doing in town?" She should be back in Portland.

"Oh, I brought my publishing job here, actually. I told you, remember? So Buster and I could spend more time together while we plan our wedding. I'm surprised we haven't run into each other more often."

Once was often enough. Claire had never been Josh's favorite of Brielle's friends. He didn't have a polite response handy other than, "Yeah. Hey, good to see you. Gotta run."

But she caught his sleeve. "Someone with your same name is parading around as the poster child for Starry Point's biggest showboat and his weird little agenda. I bet people confuse you with him all the time. So glad it's not you."

Josh frowned and cleared his throat. His collar was getting hot.

"Drop the ruse, Josh. I saw it all on TV: the big house, the money, the Barbie doll." Claire was standing too close to him, wearing far too much Chanel No. 5, and hissing her accusation. "You sold out Brielle Dupree for that?" The scoffing came next.

Josh's mind split in two. The first half lurched to Morgan's defense. She was innocent here, and a totally good person, and she didn't deserve to be distilled that way. She was a smart woman with drive and ingenuity and hardworking instincts who had problems of her own that Claire knew nothing about. Morgan wasn't some piece of plastic with Mattel stamped on her back.

But he bit all that back. The other half of him knew Claire was boiling mad, and there was no way she'd keep this information from Brielle.

"Have you talked to Brielle?" He tried to ask it casually, but it might have sounded strained. "Is she doing all right?"

Claire gripped Josh's sleeve even tighter. "As soon as I tell to her about this, she won't be."

Josh exhaled. So Claire hadn't spoken to her yet.

"Don't look so relieved, sonny boy. I've tried six times a day to get in touch with her since all this crap about you went on the news over the weekend, and she'll answer my texts or emails soon. And if she doesn't, believe me, I'm taking the first plane to Dresden to tell her the truth about you and your cheating."

"No. Don't do that." Josh's throat went tight. It would be so much easier if he could just tell Claire the truth, throw cold water on all this anger and revenge and prevent Brielle from getting hurt by the appearance of what he'd done, even if it was a complete fake-out. "Someone could get hurt."

"Yeah, you. Or are you more worried about that ditz you got hitched to? Because please say you're not. She won't have any problems worming her way into the favor of some other wealthy bachelor for her gold digging scams. What kills me is that you, of all people, are trotting out the trophy wife to get cash. A Hyatt, for mercy's sake!" She gave a mirthless laugh. "The richest family in the whole state of Oregon, and their youngest son is off begging for money on television. What a joke." Claire's eyes narrowed. "Unless this is a big joke after all. I get it. You're in cahoots with old Bronco Hyatt to torpedo Siggy Seagram by building him up, making him look like a hero, and then bam! You'll explode his whole fantasy by doing something horrendous and shaming him in front of the world. Good for you, Josh. Ruthless, but brilliant. Care if I leak it through the tabloids, just for a little more fodder for them? You could get a lot of mileage if it started looking like a scam. Bronco might even bring you back into his good graces. That's what this is all about, isn't it? A way to bring the family back together. I can see it all clearly."

"You know that's not what's going on here, Claire, and you know I'd never do anything to hurt Brielle. She's the love —" He nearly said *the love of my life* but stopped himself in time. A thousand memories of the first year of dating Brielle flashed into his mind: skiing in Tahoe, the family retreat in Aspen (where Bronco and Brielle got in a tiff, but Brielle stood up to him like no one else), the film festival in Austin. She'd been so in love with him then, and it had been mutual, but she didn't bail when Bronco incinerated Josh's finances, either, and that was when Josh knew she really loved him for himself. Brielle was one in a million, but no one, not anyone, could know this whole thing with Morgan wasn't a hundred percent sincere. His innards twisted. "She was my first love."

It came out weak and sad, and Claire loosed her grip on his sweater, her vitriol subsiding a little.

"You don't know how to love, Josh Hyatt. You're nothing but a spoiled, heartless pig. If you ever did have an ounce of caring in you, it's clearly dead, and you don't deserve Brielle. You never did, but now it's clear for the whole world to see. I'm glad she made that lucky escape from you, and I won't stop until she knows it, even if I have to tell the world about her and you and this whole rebound marriage drama. If I can't find her, the paparazzi will. That's guaranteed."

"Claire, really." Josh winced. One word from him, and Claire would take all the ammo out of her guns. This whole global crisis would be averted. The tabloids didn't need to know about Brielle's apparently getting jilted — and Josh had been off their radar for over a year as the un-favored son of the Hyatt fortune. No sense putting himself — or Brielle, or Morgan — in their crosshairs.

One word from him and this whole bomb could defuse.

He opened his mouth to speak — "The truth is —"

Claire interrupted him, sucking all the wind out of his sails. "The truth is when I saw your wife this morning, she played all nicey-nice, and she's definitely the type to pull the wool over a guy's eyes."

Claire and Morgan had spoken? Josh felt sick. Not that Morgan couldn't hold her own, but this was not her fight. She shouldn't have to be within the radius of its blows.

"I can see how you got sucked into her fakery, but there's no excuse for going to the extent of marrying her. I'll tell you what I didn't have time to tell her: I have Paulie Bumgartner's number on speed dial, and unless you get me a satisfactory explanation, in writing, for what's going on by the end of the week, I'm calling him and telling him all the permutations of my suspicions."

Paulie Bumgartner was the most notorious tabloid photographer in the Portland area. He'd harassed Josh's family within an inch of their lives over the past decade, nearly causing his mother a nervous breakdown. In fact, Josh wondered if all the pressure of the press was what put her in a weakened condition and sped her too-early death. Claire couldn't be that cruel or heartless.

"You wouldn't do that."

"Oh, wouldn't I? Brielle is like a sister to me. Closer.

And I'm not going to stand by and watch what's hers get co-opted by some brainless interloper with beauty salon eyelashes and dental veneers." With that threat lingering, Claire turned on her heel and walked away, leaving Josh boiling mad and worried for Morgan at the same time. Oh, right, and worried for Brielle. She could get hurt, too.

"A real friend would never do that to Brielle," he called after her, and she stopped and turned back.

"What do you know about being a real friend? Or boyfriend?" Her voice ticked upward in pitch. She was getting really mad now, and her neck matched the red of her hair.

A real boyfriend would never marry some other girl for money, even as a means to an end. Claire was right. But he still couldn't tell her anything about what was really going on, no matter how close he'd come to it a moment ago before she slapped him with a threat. He'd feel a lot worse about the situation if he weren't so flaming angry at this irrational woman. If there was one thing he'd learned by being a Hyatt, it was to never deal with blackmailers. He wasn't going to give Claire so much as an inch.

"Don't hold your breath for that written explanation." He measured his words. "You're Brielle's friend. You wouldn't do that to her."

"Oh, no?" She was coming at him again. He stood his ground. "I wouldn't push me if I were you."

"Stop this. Right now."

Claire got her cell phone out of her purse and brandished it like a weapon. "I'm not the type you want to push. The deadline just moved up. Explain now or face the consequences."

He set his jaw and refused to be bullied, much as he knew her demands were in his own best interest—and Brielle's, and their whole future together. But this crazy woman was pushing too hard.

"Trust me, you don't want to do that. There's nothing

to be gained by it, and no *reason* for it either, believe me." It was saying too much and betraying Morgan to even let that one sentence slip out, and he cursed himself for it. He couldn't endanger Morgan and expose her to the legal ramifications of being outed for fraud. "I married Morgan Clark, and that's all there is to it. None of your threats are going to change what's been done."

There. He'd finalized the conversation. Josh expected the brandished cell phone to slip quietly back into Claire's purse and for her to walk away with her tail between her legs. No such luck. The phone went to her ear instead.

"Dial Paulie Bumgartner."

"Stop, Claire. Just quit it. You'll be hurting Brielle much more than you'll be hurting me. I'm the one who married someone else."

"Paulie? I've got an inside line on a scandal in the Hyatt Holdings family. You want it all now, or you want to meet for dinner? Can you drive out to Starry Point? Great."

Josh's stomach collapsed like he'd been roundhouse kicked — by Chuck Norris.

191

Chapter Twenty-Two

Josh drove his Explorer into the garage with a bowling ball in the pit of his stomach. He may have just ruined Morgan's life, besides wrecking any future with Brielle. But Brielle was ten thousand miles and ten months away, and he would have to deal with the mess he caused Morgan first, especially because she was the most innocent victim in this war. Brielle was partly culpable here for hanging onto a sycophantic, vengeful friend like Claire.

When he stepped in the door, the smell of meat grilling hit his nose, and he almost forgot the weight of the bowling ball. "Morgan? You here?"

From the sitting room off the front entryway, Josh heard soft sounds of a piano playing and went toward it. Who could be—? He pressed the door open and saw Morgan sitting at the keys, plinking out an old standard, one he knew Dean Martin had sung—the one where Dino compares love to getting kicked in the head, and where he gets roped into an engagement to a girl who has picked out a king-sized bed and the guy would only be happier if he was sick. She sang on, not noticing him yet. She had a pretty good alto.

Somehow, it resembled his life. Except, was Josh unhappy? Having a gorgeous blonde with a not-bad voice and a pretty good sense of rhythm on the piano sitting in his living room singing—Josh couldn't exactly start complaining. So instead, he started singing along.

"Like the sailor said, quote, ain't that a hole in the boat?"

Morgan looked up as Josh walked over. She missed a beat, but only one, before she continued on about her head spinning and her mouth grinning. Josh joined in, and by the end, the two of them were singing harmony of the final line of the chorus about the kick in the head again.

Morgan plinked out a flourish on the final chord. Then she turned to him and started to laugh, and it was infectious, so Josh joined in. "Not bad, Morg. I didn't know you were so good on the piano." Somehow he'd figured she couldn't have afforded lessons as a kid. She said they struggled a lot financially.

"Oh, I try, mostly by ear."

By ear! Not bad — at all. "I love Dean Martin. Know any more?"

"When the moon hits your eye like a big pizza pie, that's amoré." Morgan played the chords for the song, and Josh sang the next line. Then the two of them sang the third line together, and Josh figured out the harmony. It was pretty fun. They finished this song, followed by Dino's version of "Blue Moon," easily the coolest version ever recorded.

"You know your Dean."

"I love me some Dean." Morgan looked like she meant it, and an irrational pang of jealousy toward the late Italian crooner surged in Josh. "We don't blend too badly, you and I."

"Not badly at all." Josh looked at Morgan's fingers, the ruby ring, the delicacy of her hands on the keys as she moved them up and down the ivory. Self-taught! She was kind of amazing. "We'll have to do this again sometime. Whatever's cooking in the kitchen, though, is making me ravenous."

"Oh, that. I almost forgot. This piano is so gorgeous, and I was waiting for you. I couldn't stand to let the hamburger in the fridge go bad, and there was no more room in the freezer. I usually wouldn't make straight up hamburgers. I'd turn this much meat into something that would make it go further like tacos or spaghetti sauce, but there was just so much of it." She said all this as they moved back to the kitchen, where she tied an apron around her narrow waist and pulled a cover off a tray of cooked burgers.

Josh drifted over to the stove and saw an array of spice jars on the counter—salt, pepper, onion powder, garlic salt, ginger, season salt... "It smells really good." His mouth watered. "You having friends over?"

"Just you," she said, and then her eyes snapped to his as though she'd said something amiss. Those blue eyes double-blinked, and he thought he could fall into them. "You're my friend, right?"

He cleared his throat. "Right." It'd been amazing to sit by her at the piano, *friends,* just singing together. He'd felt some friendly feelings—but also a few more than friendly feelings, if he were honest with himself. Several of them were distinctly *more than friends* type inclinations, especially when he considered what a difference his life would be if this whole Morgan-as-his-wife scenario were his reality and not just his pretense.

Then he remembered: he wasn't exactly her friend— not with the mess he'd created for her today with the tabloids. It was only a matter of time before they circled like piranhas ready to chew all the creamy skin off her lovely bones. But that wasn't the only bad thing that would be coming at her, thanks to him. She had other flesh-eaters lying in wait, and he'd have to tell her eventually. Might as well be now. "We had a visitor today, and I have something to ask you."

Morgan winced. "I saw her handiwork." She set down the knife she was using to butter the flat side of a hamburger bun. "We're more than lucky. But I'm going to have to be careful about where I leave my bathrobe and things."

It took Josh a second to process what she was saying, but then he remembered that there had been more than one visitor at the Campus House that day—Svetlana the maid being the first. Josh had been thinking about Claire, but there was also Bronco as well. What a parade of unwelcome faces.

Morgan went on. "Tory was here. She said the housekeeper will figure us out based on which beds she has to make."

Josh nodded. Morgan was right. "We'll have to be careful about more than just bathrobes. You should start sleeping in the master bedroom, and I'll just be really careful about making my bed. Hospital corners, and stuff. For now, she might just think we're checking out all the rooms like newlyweds would do. As long as we're careful it's going to be fine."

"I'm not sleeping in the master." Morgan gave a visible shudder. Huh, maybe that photograph was a little much for her, too. Interesting.

"Okay, then we'll both just be careful. Make the beds like pros. We can watch a YouTube video on how to do it exactly right." He was trying to make her feel less stressed about it, but she was right. There was reason for high caution. Speaking of caution, "My father came, too."

"Bronco? Was he upset? He won't be angry with Mr. Seagram, will he? I sense there is no love lost between them." Morgan looked worried, but also very beautiful at the same time. She had on a sweater that matched the color of her eyes perfectly, and an even better pair of jeans than yesterday hugged her hips. She was super hot, no question. He'd scored in his choice of fake wife. "I don't want to hurt Mr. Seagram. He's been so generous to us."

Hurt Seagram? The words came like a slap in the face. Josh hadn't considered that as a risk. Morgan was right, Seagram had been generous. "Right." Man, she was really a nice person to be thinking of that. He might as well broach

195

the far worse subject while things were bad, "I heard you ran into one of Brielle's friends." He might as well dive in. "I don't know what she said, but I apologize for it. I'm sure it wasn't pleasant."

Morgan put the bread on the grill. "How did you find out about that?"

"You weren't going to tell me, I guess."

"I couldn't think what good it would do. She can't do anything to us. It's not like she knows the truth."

No, but Josh cringed when he considered how close he'd been to spilling the truth to that viper. "I wish that were the case."

"She knows?" Morgan gasped. "You can't go around telling people about our arrangement, Josh, not even Brielle's friends. We agreed. We could get into so much trouble." Her body tensed, and Josh put a hand on her shoulder to calm her down.

"No, no. It's not that. She is convinced we're married and all that goes with it." Josh watched as Morgan visibly relaxed at this news. "But it's not as easy as that. She went all fangs and claws on me and threatened to call the tabloids."

"The tabloids? What are you talking about?" Morgan took this, by comparison, in stride. She went back to taking care of dinner. "They're hardly interested in me or you, poor college students just trying to finish school. What could be the least bit salacious about that?"

Exactly his point for years — if only it were that easy. "I wish. But remember, I'm a Hyatt."

Morgan put all the food on a plate and took it to a beautifully set table that already had lots of different foods on it — salad, fried potatoes, watermelon chunks. "I'm sure that's significant in some way, but I don't really see how. Forgive me."

The fried potatoes smelled like the fried potatoes his mom used to make — with lots of butter and pepper, and it almost distracted him from the big issue at hand as his mind went time traveling to family dinners when family was fun. They sat down, and he said grace, and she passed him the potatoes. Yep. They were soul food.

"This is great, Morgan. You're a good cook."

"Thanks. Having every single food on the planet to choose from and every kitchen tool imaginable does help."

"You don't have to cook for me every night, you know." It wasn't like he married her to turn her into his personal chef.

She looked up. "You don't want me to?"

"No, no. It's not that. I love it, seriously. I just don't want you to feel obligated."

"The only obligation I feel is to use up the food in the fridge before it spoils. But otherwise, I love cooking. I never do it because Tory's always on some diet, and cooking for one is lame. Besides, my fridge generally consists of three Cokes, a bottle of ketchup, and a bag of apples from the tree at my mom's house." She took a bite of her hamburger, and some ketchup dripped from it onto her plate.

"You're a ketchup person?" he asked, feeling much less guilty about being so spoiled by showing up at home to a hot meal two nights in a row.

"Sometimes I think of french fries as merely a vehicle for the ketchup." She had a pool of ketchup soaking down into her potatoes on her plate. She wasn't lying about her love for the red stuff. It looked like she was the only person he'd ever met who liked it even more than he did.

"Ketchup. It's the all-American version of sweet and sour sauce."

"I know, right? Vinegar, brown sugar, tomatoes. It's just spicy heaven." She took a bite of her potatoes, and Josh followed suit. Were they bonding? Over ketchup? Well, he'd be un-bonding them in two seconds when he told her the awful truth.

"About the tabloids. There's a good chance they'll be

bothering us."

"I seriously doubt it, Josh. Sorry. We're just boring students, like I said. I am a blonde with an old truck and a good GPA. Big whoop."

"You sell yourself short." Really, she did. "That's exactly the kind of thing the tabs go crazy for, but they will twist it."

"I love that you live in this fantasy land where I'm suddenly of interest to anyone. What should I wear for my three seconds of fame?"

Not that sweater, he was thinking. It accentuated her positives way too much. And there were a *lot* of positives, not all just about her gobsmacking looks. Morgan was pretty on the inside as well, and a hard worker, and smart and funny and could cook and play piano and sing—with him. They did blend pretty well. His mind wandered back to how free he'd felt sitting beside her, just letting the songs roll out of his soul. For the five minutes they sang, he was Dean Martin, and she was Doris Day, and they were in some kind of movie together, a romantic comedy where they lived together but not as man and wife, and all kinds of funny hijinks complicated their world—uh, like now. With the tabloid photographer Paulie Bumgartner being sicced on them.

Josh crash-landed in reality.

Man, Morgan really wasn't understanding how dangerous things were. He was going to have to lay it all out for her with clarity.

"Look, I know you think I'm overreacting, but there was a time when I had to deal with this on a daily basis. Back before my dad and I got into it over my change of careers, the press was following me a lot. I had to be really careful about everything I did, but if I even went out with a girl, her face was plastered all over the society pages in Portland, and gossipmongers labeled her a gold digger. I lost a lot of sincere girlfriends that way." He frowned and set down his fork. "Luckily, when I got cut off from the family's fortune so publicly by Bronco, I also fell out of favor with the tabs. It was the silver lining to the dark cloud of being kicked out of my family."

Morgan's eyes had grown wide, and a sheen glossed them where the tears welled, making them a deeper blue than ever, like the sea off the Amalfi Coast, where he'd spent a summer as a kid. "I'm so sorry you had to go through all that. I can't imagine having my family be in shards like that."

Shards. That was an apt description, actually, but she'd be seeing it for herself on Friday, if possible.

"Uh, speaking of my family. I know I haven't painted a rosy picture of them, but if you don't have plans for Friday night..."

"I'm free." Maybe he was mistaken, but she looked almost happy to answer this way.

"Great. My dad dropped by and invited us to dinner." Josh omitted the police threat about stealing the ring, hoping but not trusting it was the empty blustering of the blowhard. "What time is your last class? Bronco Hyatt demands that dinner is served promptly at six." They'd have to drive to Portland, over an hour trip.

"I'm done by noon."

"It's a date." Josh let these words fall casually from his mouth, but then they hung resonating in the air between them for a long moment until Morgan finally picked up her forkful of ketchuped potatoes and he could breathe again.

***

"So, what you're saying is you're going on your first official date with your husband." Tory bent down and picked up a rock and dropped it into her sand bucket, while Morgan tried again to concentrate on seeing the agates among the pebbles on the shore of Cannon Bay

Beach. "And it's to meet his family. He must be serious about you. Love at first sight."

The weight of Tory's assessment of tonight's plans settled on Morgan heavily. One, she loved that he'd asked her go with him, and when the words *it's a date* came from his mouth, they pierced her. Should he have had any idea how close they struck her heart, he might have taken them back. For the whole day, after the idiotic incident with that she-beast redhead, Morgan had been feeling stupid — sure, she had Josh's name, but she by no means had his heart, hadn't even been asked on a date by him at that point. So, when he threw it out there at dinner, she'd had to use all her restraint not to throw her arms around him and kiss his face in her excitement. That'd scare the guy off like nothing else.

"Love at first sight. Obviously." She found an agate, a clear stone with a baby blue hue. "Oh, look. I found one."

"Lucky." Tory came over and examined it. She took her key-chain flashlight out even though it was morning and shone it through the stone so they could see its translucence. "Nice one. Those are rare. Not as rare as the pink ones, but all I found is white."

"White are everywhere."

"What are you going to wear to this big Meet the Hyatts affair? Is it black tie and dinner gowns? Or jeans and sweaters?"

The question made Morgan jolt. She had no idea, and suddenly she realized how out of her depth she was going to be at this thing. The wealthy lived very differently from how she and Tory had been raised, with apples from their own tree and new clothing being something other people bought so she and Tory could get it second-hand later on.

"Josh didn't say. I guess I'll see what he's wearing and go from there."

"Dangerous. What if you're not prepared? Do you even have a nice dress?"

"Uh, sort of." Not really. She'd been asked to the Homecoming dance last year by that guy with the gap in his front teeth, who she could not for the life of her hold a conversation with, and she'd worn a heavy satin gown she borrowed from Gina, a classmate. Gina graduated last year, but Morgan might still have her number.

"No. You don't. Let me tell you—I went through your closet when we were packing to fake-move you into Josh's apartment before the cameras came to Estrella Court. You've got zilch."

"So what am I supposed to do?"

Tory stood up straight and shook the pebbles in her bucket, making them rattle in triumph. "Costume closet at the theater. I'll snag you something."

"What? They let you do that? No, that could get you in trouble."

"Nah. I'll just sign it out. I'm doing alterations for Rosencrantz and Guildenstern anyway."

"They're dead, you know."

"I know. And England is just a conspiracy of cartographers." Tory was a theater girl, and could quote old stage plays by the hour. "Look, let me see what I can bring you."

"Nothing too fancy. I mean, what if I dress posh, and it turns out to be an Oregon Ducks sweatshirts and flip-flop sandals event?" Morgan could end up being completely embarrassed. Meeting Josh's family, whether she was up for long-term approval or not, had her petrified. What if they hated her? What if she lapsed irretrievably deep into the Conversation Coma and they thought she was a huge loser or, worse, pitied Josh for his choice? Sure, she was the nervous type around men in her dating range, but she was in untested waters when it came to meeting a guy's family. Josh's rich, famous family's faces seemed a thousand times more intimidating than any potential date. She'd said something to Josh about it last night before he left for work, but he told her not to worry. Their opinion of her didn't matter.

He was right of course—she wasn't there for the long game, so why would it matter what they thought of her?

But she cared.

"Right. Not too posh, not too beachy. Something from the Goldilocks zone." Tory bent over and picked up a pebble. "Look how clear this one is. Oh! And it looks like there's water inside, with a little bubble! This might be our lucky day."

Or it might end up being Morgan's unluckiest night.

***

"Wow. You look really nice." Josh couldn't take his eyes off Morgan. Blouse, skirt, curves everywhere, right down to how great her legs stemmed down to the high heels that made her nearly his height. But her eyes were the star, set off by the top in the same color of blue as she'd been wearing the other night. "I, uh, think that's your color."

Did she blush? She did, and it made her even prettier for the seconds that it lasted. He wasn't going to have any excuses to make to the family about his wife. They'd take one look at her and no questions would be asked about his decision.

"So you think it's all right? You're in a suit, so this works?" Morgan seemed unsure of herself. In all the times he'd been around her, she'd been a reservoir of calm, even when things were obviously not going their way.

"You'll blow them away."

"But they're not going to be wearing formal gowns and tuxedos or anything, right?"

"With Bronco Hyatt? Hardly." Josh had to laugh at that thought. "He thinks tuxes are for frauds and Euro-trash wannabes, or so he says. Suit and tie at most over there."

And his dad would wear a bolo tie.

Morgan relaxed against the seat of the Explorer, and they headed into the mountains toward Portland from the coast. It had been a while since he'd seen any of the family besides Chip and Heather, and a lot longer since he'd had any good interactions with them. He was throwing Morgan into the tiger cage, and he knew it.

"Look, Morgan. I don't want to scare you, but these people are unpredictable. Do me a favor and take everything they say with a grain of salt." He glanced over and saw she was wringing her hands. He reached out and took one in his, just to calm her. It was icy cold. "It's going to be fine, I promise. You're not on trial. They are by how they treat you."

He kept hold of her hand, caressing it, warming it up as they ascended the canyon, and he congratulated himself when it came up to a good temperature and Morgan's tension seemed to subside as the miles passed. It was the least he could do for her considering the mess he was throwing her into tonight. He lifted it to his lips and kissed it.

"Stick beside me all night, and things will be fine," Josh said as he helped her from the car in the circular drive in front of Hyatt Place, with its Greek pillars and its towering double front doors. She grabbed something from the trunk, and they went inside, into the belly of the beast.

Before they got ten steps down the hall, a ping sounded from the general direction of the dining room: Bronco Hyatt tapping his dinner goblet with his spoon for attention.

"Come on. We're late!" He took the stuff out of Morgan's arms and hurried her down the hall. "What's in the box?"

"My mother said never go empty handed to a dinner party. But if it's gross, I hope no one notices it's even on the table."

Oh, they'd notice, all right. Something home-cooked would be so out of place at any recent Hyatt event that it would be the sore thumb of all sore thumbs. But Morgan could cook—so maybe it would be okay. Good, even, to show them what they and their catered dinners were missing out on. Still, he was nervous that she'd feel out of place by bringing something unusual. He'd hate for her to feel any more uncomfortable than absolutely necessary. And it would be necessary. Tremors of *the most awkward dinner ever* loomed.

"So glad you could join us, Joshua." Bronco didn't look glad. It was still ten minutes before six, so what was up with the time shift here? Leave it to Bronco to create a situation where Josh would be embarrassed. "So this is the Clarendon College woman you are using to get revenge on me by taking a handout from Siggy Seagram." He looked Morgan up and down, and Josh stepped in front of her to protect her from the ogling, not only from Bronco, but from all dozen pairs of eyes of those seated at the long formal table.

"This is my wife, Morgan." It came out through clenched teeth. Josh would like to clench Bronco by the throat for his comment, but he had to keep things neutral, at least until dinner was over. This was Heather's birthday, and he refused to ruin her day.

Morgan lifted a hand and waved just her fingers. She smiled a little, but not much, and he could tell she was not used to being around such toads as the Hyatt family were.

Bronco went on, now addressing the group. "Just so you know, Josh is officially living on someone else's dime. He's a kept man." He turned to Josh and said, "What all are you going to owe, loyalty-wise to Seagram when this is over? Your firstborn son?"

Then he laughed raucously, but alone. No one else thought he was funny. He must have already insulted all of them earlier.

"You're working it, Dad. Where would you like us to sit?" Josh tried to slide them through the gauntlet without further incident, but Bronco wasn't having any of it. As Josh and Morgan found places at the table, Bronco re-launched.

"Everyone here knows you've been a horrendous disappointment in the past years, starting with that ridiculous freckled thing you dragged home out of the gutter and claimed she'd changed your life and you wanted to be an international man of mystery all of a sudden. At least you dumped her where she belonged. Heh, heh. We none of us miss her one iota."

Josh bristled, but what could he say? He'd done nothing of the sort, and he didn't like the love of his life being insulted, but the last thing he could do was tip these people off to the scheme he and Morgan were up to. They'd probably be the first to throw him to the wolves of the IRS and the college funding grant police.

"But now you upgraded to some gorgeous supermodel, and what? Didn't she know you'd been cut off financially? Did you turn into one of those loud talking empty-suits who claims he's got something big in the works, and if she just waits long enough he'll come through? Because we all know full well that's not you, Joshua. You're nothing but a garbage-stirring hack who counts bacteria in human waste for a living."

"Dad, you're charming us to death here."

"Charm is not my ambition. Success is—for me and for my children. And if you think that digging in trash in Starry Point, Oregon, is the key to success, you're up a flipping tree."

"The U.S. Patent Office begs to differ."

"Oh, you and your patents. That's never coming through, and you know it."

Josh looked around at the faces of his siblings and their spouses, all eyes apologetic, as he stood there, begging one of them to defend him and his research passion and his choice of women and his career path. No one breathed a word. In fact, they all looked sort of sick, but not courageous. Rocky the doctor, Wyatt the CPA, their wives—all yellow-bellied cowards, kowtowing to the noise of Bronco. What was their big fear of him? Josh couldn't take it for another second—he was exploding with it all, and lashed out.

"You all are so scared of Bronco and losing his favor and his money that none of you will step up to defend yourselves, let alone your little brother's decisions. Shame on you all. You're ridiculous. All of you." Josh's cheeks stung as he accused them, anger pricking his skin. "Mom would be appalled."

The air, by rights, should have gone out of the room, and everyone should have reacted with shame, but not this family. This was their usual form of communication. They just eyed him for a moment and then looked back down at their plates of catered, cardboard food, saying nothing in his defense. Well, at least they weren't heckling him, or Morgan. Morgan was a nice girl. She shouldn't be subjected to this crap. Brielle would have handled it differently, giving back to Bronco just as good as he dished out—which was probably the reason Bronco hated her with such venom.

"Sit down, Joshua. You're already holding up the meal. And go put your things in the bedroom upstairs. Don't come traipsing into the dining room with luggage."

"This isn't luggage." They'd agreed to drive back that night, rather than stay at Hyatt mansion and go through the whole bed-sharing stress that would inevitably ensue. "It's our contribution to dinner." He slid the dish out of its protective container and set it on the table. Everyone eyed it. "Morgan is a good cook."

The words let him exhale. Morgan shot him a confused wince, but they sat down by each other. He reached over and took her hand under the table. He wouldn't let anything worse happen to her than already had, with Bronco's attacks and his siblings' cowardly non-defense of him. Ridiculous. Why did he agree to come and put himself and Morgan through this? Oh, yeah. Threats of siccing the police on him if he didn't. Ridiculous!

All manner of awkwardness ensued as the meal went forward. No one spoke directly to either him or to Morgan. They just spoke about them, near them. It was rude, and he knew he should never have brought her here. Obviously everyone, including Chip and Heather, had been warned to say nothing to them, and this was all an exercise in public humiliation. Nice. Dysfunction on so many levels abounded in this family.

Then, something happened, and Josh noticed a sudden thaw toward him and Morgan.

"This rice stuff is good. Where did it come from?"

"Josh's wife made it. He said she was a good cook, but this stuff is ambrosia."

Josh waited until the dish was passed to him, and he took a bite. They were right. "What's in this?"

Morgan answered sweetly, as if no one around her had been a colossal jerk. "Shiitake mushrooms, bacon, caramelized onions, other things."

"Love it." Josh took another bite, and his eyes rolled heavenward. It was delicious.

"This is incredible."

"It's part heaven, part butter, which is the same thing."

"It's what I want to drown in if I have to die by drowning."

"Where did it go? I need more of that amazing stuff."

The wall everyone had built between themselves and Josh and Morgan crumbled a little. Heather was the first to dispense with it.

"I taste ginger in here. Is there ginger, Morgan?" For the first time, someone else in the room besides Josh uttered her name.

"There was some fresh ginger in the cupboard, so I grated it. Is it too much?"

"No. It's just the right hint of it."

Someone else mentioned the allspice, and then it was all over. People were talking about food and the merits of melted butter.

"Does she cook like this for you every night, Josh? Because if so, you're the luckiest man alive. And you're going to be the fattest man alive in six months."

"You'll have matching big round bellies when she's got your baby in her. Haw!" Bronco guffawed. It was crass, but it was the first (mostly) non-confrontational thing Bronco had said to Josh in three years, or maybe longer.

The meal and the thaw continued. Somehow, Morgan's cooking had been a salve. Well, that and the way she'd asked about each family member's interests, background, dreams. She'd charmed Wyatt by being interested in how he managed to pass the very difficult CPA exam and asking for study tips, which he was anxious to give in far too great abundance, in Josh's opinion, but hey, he was being normal—and friendly. That was a new thing for when Josh brought a girl home.

Morgan got Rocky to warm up to her by asking him about what Josh was like as a kid. Rocky couldn't stop laughing when he told about the time he and Josh put three cases of soda in the freezer and they all exploded and made Orange Fanta stalactites everywhere inside it. Or the time Wyatt shut Josh up inside the hide-a-bed and then went for a bike ride and forgot him for two hours. Or the time... Josh thought Morgan would gag on the nostalgia, but she seemed entertained.

Chip and Heather already thought Morgan was awesome, and Rocky and Wyatt's wives were anxious to trade recipes as well as talk about some shopping trips they'd gone on and wanted to invite Morgan along for next time.

By the time it was over, Josh was the most charmed of all. How had she managed it? Even Bronco didn't look like he'd spent the meal drinking vinegar. Not that his behavior improved much — he still said the wrongest thing at the wrongest moment, like the fat belly comments — but he looked less caustic in the meantime, and that, for Bronco, was huge.

Josh looked sidelong at Morgan. She had pulled a small velvet bag from her purse and was handing it to Heather. Heather hugged her. The embrace was warmth and a giant step closer to Josh's imaginary Family Ideal that he'd conjured up in his mind watching TV as a kid or looking at Norman Rockwell paintings. He'd never seen it even approximated in his own life, not since Mom died, anyway.

Something had changed, thanks to Morgan and her allspice and ginger.

As they were leaving, walking down the sidewalk to where he'd parked the Explorer, Josh asked Morgan about the contents of the bag she'd given Heather. In response, she pulled a little handful of something from a side zipper in her purse and extended it to Josh.

Josh took her hand and slid it open, fingering the contents in her palm. "Agates? Where did you get them?" She looked up at him, saying nothing. "You collected them on the beach, didn't you?" It was like a handmade gift. "I bet she loves them. Heather likes blue." So did Josh, especially when it sparkled up at him in from those huge blue eyes. "You're kind of amazing, you know that?"

Morgan let her long eyelashes drop, and Josh touched her chin, lifting it to look at her better. The cold air of the night parted, leaving a little warm pocket around him and Morgan.

"Thank you." His heart had sped up, and touching the satin skin at her neck wasn't helping that at all.

"For what?" she whispered.

"For giving me back my family." He leaned in and kissed her on her forehead, even though he hungered for a taste of her raspberry lip gloss instead. He knew, however, that he wouldn't be stopping at a mere taste. Not tonight. Not after what this healing goddess had done for him. Her hair smelled so good. Her eyes looked at him with so much innocence, and—he stopped—*love*. Those eyes looked like love.

Josh took a step away. He cleared his throat. "We, uh, had better get driving back. It's late."

She blinked, collecting herself. "Yes. Late," she said and closed her fist around the agates, as he placed her in the car.

It was all Josh could do to not take that cool hand of hers and warm it on the drive home. But touching her was not on the list of safe behaviors, especially because of how his family was obviously feeling about her. They were enchanted. And Josh knew how important it remained that they have an easy-out from this marriage. For that, annulment was the obvious solution; and the only way to guarantee a simple process for that was for Josh to avoid at all cost (and the cost tonight felt really high) pushing things too far between him and Morgan physically.

What was his family going to say when that annulment ultimately took place, when Josh came back next time with Brielle instead?

Chapter Twenty-Three

Morgan twisted the ruby ring around and around her finger. The air was cold this morning in her bedroom, and the ring was loose. She couldn't stop feeling the ghost of Josh's hand on hers from last night when he'd held her hand, couldn't stop wishing he were here to warm it again, instead of all the way down the hall in his own bed, doubtless not wishing for the same physical touch from her she craved from him. She flopped back on the bed and stared at the ceiling.

What would have been different between them if he didn't have that girlfriend? Brielle Dupree, whoever she was, had never even met Morgan Clark Hyatt, but she was wrecking Morgan's life from seven thousand miles away, or however far away Germany was. She'd have to look that up.

The other events of last night smashed together in her mind. Bronco Hyatt was at least as bad as Josh made him out to be; possibly Josh had been generous about the guy's personality. No wonder they came to loggerheads over what Josh should do with his life. That dad needed a personality transplant—or maybe he was only hurting over the loss of his late wife. Who knew? Even though everyone else had seemed pretty much under his thumb when she and Josh first arrived, at least they warmed to her over time and turned out to be not half as bizarre as Josh had made them out to be. Bronco, however, Josh had nailed in his description.

Maybe Morgan could think of a way to make things better there. *Not that you can fix crazy...*

211

She hoped Heather had liked the agates and didn't think she was a total dork for giving her what seemed like stupid rocks she'd found, which in essence it was. Maybe she looked like a little kid bringing a favorite rock to his mother and feeling all excited about it, only later to learn that the mother didn't value it. Or maybe Heather was as nice as she seemed. Josh liked her, that was clear.

Morgan wasn't sure about any of the Hyatts—other than Josh, and it was horrible. Truth was, Morgan could see more and more clearly every passing day that Joshua Hyatt was the man of her dreams, that she was married to her dream guy, and that a wall separated them far thicker than the one between the two bedrooms they occupied.

Maybe she should tell him, just go marching into his room, demand that he listen, and lay it on him that she was falling in love with him and he should choose her—forget that absent girl in Germany who didn't have the good sense to reel him in when she had him on the hook, and take Morgan for his girl. They were so right for each other; couldn't he see that? On the way home last night, he'd hesitated to take her hand, avoiding her the first half of the drive. But then, he reached over and seized it, and the way his thumb caressed the back of her hand, Morgan had basked in the energy surging between them. She'd been sure he would kiss her good night, but when the car had been parked, he'd helped her out of it to the kitchen and then made a beeline for the upstairs, leaving her with tingling, un-kissed lips that longed for his.

She craved him so completely, and not just his touch— his conversation, his thoughts, his company, that smile with those incredible teeth. Okay, and his kiss. It felt like it had been so long since his kiss. Kisses on the forehead didn't count—not enough, anyway. At this moment, Josh Hyatt was just a few feet away, beyond the wall from her. She put the flat of her hand up against the wall, imagining his hand pressed against the other side—almost touching but always separated.

What, exactly, was this game they were playing? She was his wife, but only in name. Did that make her a Wife In Name Only? A WINO? Was that the way a marriage was supposed to be? Obviously not, and she'd known that from the get-go, but she hadn't realized that her heart would be so much on the line here. She didn't know how much it would be tugged toward him like a rope strung taut, wishing she dared to grip it and pull him closer to her in every way. If Morgan were a hundred percent honest with herself, she'd admit she wanted to be Mrs. Joshua Hyatt in every sense of the word—to have him and to hold him, to cherish him, and to call him her own.

And despite all evidence to the contrary, meaning their shared address, their shared last name, and the beautiful ruby ring on her finger, none of that could be hers.

Maybe not ever.

Tears started stinging her eyes, and she knew she had to stop thinking about this mockery of sacredness they were perpetrating, this farce of something eminently good, ordained of God in the Garden of Eden and meant for the blessing of two lives and the creation of a family—none of which she'd ever be able to enjoy with the man she had grown to love and ached for with every ounce of her flesh.

Quick, she sniffled, *think of something else.*

She cast a fleeting glance at her pile of textbooks. She'd have to get to work on those any minute now if she was going to be ready for her three tests next week. Midterms were almost upon her, and she had to pass every single class or this whole stressful semester would be a waste of time, and she might as well have left her skates strapped on.

But her stomach growled, demanding she head down to make breakfast. Maybe Josh would like some, too. She got the batter going for some waffles and found a restocked supply of fresh strawberries and a can of that good squirt-whipped-cream in the magic fridge that never ran low on anything Morgan could possibly dream of wanting to eat. *Thanks, Svetlana.*

In no time, the house smelled of baking waffles. That should wake him. He'd come stumbling down the staircase in his robe, hair all rumpled, looking like a well-rested god, but unable to resist what she offered him.

She placed the plates on the table, hoping for his appearance. Nothing.

She dug through the fridge and found orange juice. Still no Josh.

Finally, she went upstairs and knocked lightly on his bedroom door. "Josh? You awake?" Clearly he wasn't, but she wanted him to be, and she needed his company whether he wanted hers in the same way or not. "Josh, do you want some breakfast? There were fresh strawberries in the fridge and—" Morgan pressed the door open, and saw his bed was empty, un-rumpled. He hadn't slept here.

He was gone.

***

Josh carefully lifted the eyedropper of sulfuric acid and squeezed exactly three milligrams of it into the beaker. This time had to be the ticket. He'd been so close in the last few days that he could almost taste it. Well, not taste it, since it was garbage he was working with here. He didn't care what disparaging comments Bronco made about it, he knew he was onto something. Ha! Bronco Hyatt had flunked high school chemistry, and he hadn't gone to college. How could the old git understand any of it? He couldn't. Period.

Josh scrawled his measurements onto the notepad where he was keeping track of everything he'd tried. Last time it'd been two milligrams, and it hadn't reacted. The time before it was four, and there'd been a nasty, smoke-

214

filled result. It was a good thing he did all this out in the garage, away from the posh house. Morgan would be gagging at the smell, and she'd probably make him quit.

Morgan.

Would she make him quit if she came out and saw (and smelled) all this?

He let that question float out to the stars over Starry Point.

Maybe the stars were gone by now, though. He checked his watch. He'd been out here all night working on this. During the drive home, while he'd had his hand on Morgan's, the idea came to him to adjust the sulfuric acid in his formula—and to make another adjustment: double the amount of live culture super-bacteria. As soon as he changed from the business suit he'd worn to the party into his work clothes, he shot out here to the garage and made the adjustments. And then, as soon as he added the super-bacteria (which he'd procured on-line and not told a soul about because they'd call him some kind of bio-terrorist), the reaction began to take place. But he knew they'd falter unless the sulfuric acid went in next, so after putting together three separate dishes of the concoction, he mixed them and checked his timer.

This time it would work, he was sure. He took a photo of it to give himself documented proof, and he made more notes in his notebook. Hope buzzed in him.

Or was that hunger? He'd been out here all night, with nothing in his stomach but that cardboard food from his dad's dinner last night, plus a little of that fantastic rice Morgan had made that had turned everyone at Hyatt Place into putty in her hand. Miracle rice.

Maybe some was left in the fridge.

"Josh?" a woman's voice floated out to him. "Are you out here?" The door pressed open, and there stood Morgan, with the sunlight streaming in from behind her. Her hair was all backlit like an angel's halo. She had on a short

215

nightgown and a sweet smile on her face—not the grimace he'd expect based on the smell of the compost. "Oh, good. I found you. Ooh, what are you working on?" She came over and stood beside him, her hands behind her back. She leaned over the first dish, eyeing it closely. "Is this the project you've been working on for your patent? I heard you mention it to your father last night."

She tilted her head to look up at him, and her fresh face had a sheen and a blush. He had to swallow hard to bring himself back to what she'd asked.

"I'm, uh, yeah. This is what I'm working on."

"You never really told me what it is. It's so amazing you know what you're doing with all this." She looked around the room, her white nightgown tied at her waist, cinching it to accentuate her curves. He liked seeing her in the morning. "Sometimes I think you might be the smartest man I know."

Really? Her blue eyes looked so sincere as she said it.

"You need to get out more." He brushed off the compliment, but it made a place somewhere behind his ribcage glow warm. "Actually, I think I might have just figured out another step in my process. It took all night, but I finally made it work—I'll know in—" he checked the timer— "exactly twenty-eight minutes and fifteen seconds."

"That's amazing, Josh." She smiled at him. "How exciting!" She looked genuinely excited for him, which was something new. He hadn't ever met anyone willing to muster enthusiasm for his compost experiments. Morgan really was a cool chick—with sinuses of iron. The stench didn't seem to faze her one iota. "And, if you've got that long, do you want to come inside and eat? I just finished making a stack of waffles."

Josh loved waffles. "With strawberries?"

"Lots. And they're good, even though they're not in season."

216

He walked beside her into the house, only occasionally glancing at the gap where the two sides of her white robe wrapped together and wondering absently what lay beneath them.

"Breakfast looks great." And so did the cook.

"Before you eat, though, there's something I need to do." She bit her lower lip. They were standing next to the counter, beside the table. She looked sweet, but a little afraid. "I hope you'll take this the right way."

Oh, no. People always started criticism with that phrase. She'd say his clothes stunk of compost and sulfuric acid, or worse, that he needed to brush his teeth, or even worse, that she was done with all this now that she'd met his horrible family—she was ready to run for her life, which she probably should if she valued her sanity. A year in their sphere of influence could turn even Morgan into a raving lunatic.

"Morgan, about last night…"

But she didn't actually speak next. Instead, she leaned into him, stretched up on her tiptoes and pressed her lips against his mouth and her body against his torso. The messy waves of her blond hair were suddenly threaded between his fingers, and then his hands were on her back. She was kissing him—of her own volition, not prompted by a challenge or anything else. This was a first. And he liked it, a lot—probably a thousand times more than was wise. The pressure of her mouth, of her arms and body, sent his mind shooting like fireworks on the Fourth of July. Her raspberry lip gloss wasn't distracting him this morning, too early to have her makeup on, and he tasted her bare lips. How could they be even more delicious than berries? But they were, oh, they were.

"Morgan—" he whispered.

"I just wanted to thank you for taking care of me. You're a good husband." She was looking up at him in earnest, almost pleading with him, an emotion that didn't exactly match her words.

"Fake husband," he whispered, letting his arms drop from the smooth fabric on her back, in his own defense, knowing he'd like to keep them there all day.

This, for some reason, apparently broke her spell, and she blinked and backed away. He hadn't meant to do that to her. Not this morning, not when she'd been so incredibly sweet, making him waffles, making him feel like the smartest man in the world, after making his family talk to him last night again like a human and not some pariah.

She sat down at the table, and Josh said grace. A thorn rotated in his chest when he saw how hurt she looked, but there wasn't anything he could say to fix it, since he didn't know what was causing it.

Unless…unless she actually was starting to have a sincere interest in him.

Morgan? Interested in him? It wouldn't have been a stretch a few years ago, before Bronco pulled the rug out from under Josh's whole life. Girls were throwing themselves at him then. But since then, the only girl who gave him the time of day was Brielle. Besides, Morgan was this blonde bombshell with every guy in the universe ogling her; she could have her pick of any of them. She knew the terms of the contract, and she wasn't dumb— certainly not dumb enough to let Josh into her heart, bad risk that he was.

"These waffles are great." Not as great tasting as Morgan had been a minute ago, but he knew where those thoughts could lead, and they'd agreed not to go there. Business. This whole thing was a business. Even if she was kissing him thank-yous in her nightgown in the morning, it was business.

Good business. He'd like to have a little more of it. He started entertaining the idea of a little more Morgan every morning.

She was frowning, though.

"Morgan, is something wrong?" he finally let himself ask. He knew something he'd said had turned her cold after that heat. Was the heat only the last flash before the star went out, and she was going to tell him this whole thing was done?

She exhaled long and then spoke. "What I don't understand is why you'd ever walk away from bio-tech research when it's clearly your passion and your gift and trade it for something that clearly annoys you, like East West Cold War Relations, or whatever that was called. You obviously love what you're doing out in the shop, and you're amazing at it."

Josh looked at the stack of perfect Belgian waffles beside the bowl of perfect red strawberries Morgan had prepared for him. He couldn't talk about Brielle and her influence over his current career direction at a moment like this.

However, what Morgan said next made him think she'd figured it out on her own.

"Tell me what it is about her."

Josh cleared his throat, and he would have tugged at his collar if he'd been in a dress shirt. "Uh..."

"I've never met her, and you haven't said what it is that's so special. What could make a guy like you be so..." She didn't finish the sentence, and he didn't know if she was going to fill in the blank with *manipulated*, like Bronco would have said, or *in love*, like the direction he could imagine Morgan going, or *wrapped around someone's finger*, which was more to the point of where his own mind automatically went. Because he was—wrapped around Brielle's finger. For the past several years he'd been tied to her, wrapped up in her, and they'd spent a lot of time together, when she wasn't in school in Portland and he wasn't working here in Starry Point. His future was pretty wrapped up in hers. Wasn't it?

Finally he concocted an answer he thought might

219

answer any of the filled-in blanks. "She's tough. Smart. On fire about everything. Got all her ducks in a row."

Morgan nodded and set down her forkful of strawberries. She didn't say anything for a while.

"Look, Josh. There are things we do for the people we love. But giving up all our dreams shouldn't be one of them. The person you spend forever with should love you for the man you are, as well as the potential you have in the things you're passionate about, not try to remake you into some ideal or in her own image. Making man in His own image is God's job." She looked at him with an earnestness so intense he didn't know how to respond. The words were true, and yet, he couldn't say whether they applied to his situation or not.

Did they?

Morgan's eyes broke away from his, and she stood. He watched the flutter of the hem of her robe at her thigh while she cleared the dishes. God had done a killer job on Morgan's image. He knew there was wisdom in her words, and that she wasn't saying them with malice. Still, they didn't sit right. What she said was nothing he hadn't, in essence, heard before a dozen times from Chip and Heather, or in much cruder tones from Bronco. Everyone was against Brielle, but none of them knew her like Josh did.

Besides, he wasn't in the mood to talk about Brielle right now. He'd just broken through a major wall, and now he had a gorgeous woman with bare legs from here to eternity offering him fresh strawberries.

"Thanks, Morgan. I'll think about what you said." He came around the kitchen island and laid a hand on her arm.

Morgan stopped what she was doing and turned to face him. "Think about what it would mean to the world if you pursue what you really love. Your work could change everything, Josh."

A spot at the back of his chest sparked. *The confidence of a beautiful woman. In him.* His spine straightened.

Just then, his phone's timer sounded for the results of his experiment.

"Oh, I have to run. Thank you so much for breakfast." He looked right into her eyes. "It meant a lot to me." Including the way it started with her luscious kiss, but he didn't have time to explain that now. He pressed a quick kiss on her cheek and hustled out to the shop.

"*Yes!*" he shouted, loudly enough for the whole neighborhood to hear. "It worked!" He'd made a giant step forward. This was actually the right formula, after all these months of trying. Compost into crude oil? It could be the energy breakthrough of the 21st Century. He'd win the Nobel Prize. He'd be the savior of the problems between the U.S. and the Middle East. Josh punched a victorious fist in the air. The implications of this were endless!

Ah, nothing like the sweet smell of sulfur in the morning. He gathered his notes and logged on to the U.S. Patent website so he could start filling out his application immediately. No sense wasting time. Some other bio-tech dropout like him could be working out these very details in his own garage somewhere right now, and no way would that guy beat Josh to the punch.

***

Upstairs, she exhaled for the first time. She'd kissed him. The memory of his lips on hers still tingled. Morgan caught a glimpse of herself in the mirror. Whoa. She'd kissed him looking like this? Hair all disheveled, wearing nothing but a cami and her robe? No wonder the warmth of his hands felt so near on her back when he'd kissed her in return.

The water steamed as it filled the tub. He had kissed her back, hadn't he? It wasn't just a mercy kiss. Or a thanks-for-breakfast kiss. He was too breathless afterward for that to be the definition. But then he pushed her away with the correction, *fake husband*. Josh was right: she was, in truth, only his fake wife, and no way should she let herself get too serious about him when he clearly was still only in this for the business arrangement. She was letting her heart take control of her actions this morning, all because of being dumb enough to admit to herself that she really did want him, did want to fight for him.

But that experimental kiss she'd given him to check if his temperature was even close to hers in this relationship had felt so good, so right, every breath of it. Could he not feel how right they were together, too? In that moment, she'd seen in his eyes how he was feeling about her — looking at her like she was his angel. No man had given her that look before. She shut off the faucet and slid into the water, wanting to steam away everything but the feel of his lips on hers.

Truth kept washing up on her like the little waves of this tub lapping against the skin at her collarbone. She wanted Josh Hyatt, all of him, to be hers. She didn't want to be a Wife in Name Only with a Fake Husband. She wanted to be Mrs. Joshua Hyatt, regardless of the shifty foundation they'd started their relationship on. When she'd gushed like some crazed fangirl this morning that he was the smartest guy she'd ever known, she wasn't exaggerating. But that wasn't the only reason she might was falling in love with him. Josh was also endlessly kind to her, protecting her, making her feel like she mattered, all while extending caring gestures to her dog-obsessed mother and her rent-challenged sister. He was still contributing to Tory's rent with his weekly paycheck. What live-in guy would ever have the gallantry to do that? Josh was something more than anyone she'd ever known.

Best and most of all, she could talk to him, as herself, not some fake version or hollowed out deer-in-the-headlights mute. That alone drew a stark contrast between

222

Josh and any other decent guy she'd known. Being with Josh let Morgan be Morgan, not bottled up and afraid.

She gasped as she realized it. *She needed Josh.*

Her head was buzzing with him. *Josh, Joshua, Josher.* He was becoming much more now than her fake husband, which was why when he reminded her of their status, her blood had turned to ice, and she'd pulled away. But then, sitting beside him, she'd thawed so quickly.

Maybe that was what marriage was about. Even if a person hurts you, you love them enough to let things like that heal, love them enough to not hold a grudge.

How could she hold a grudge against Josh? He was so good to her, and to Tory, putting his relationship with his girlfriend at risk by helping Morgan get her grant, going along with the roller coaster demands of the Seagram Scholarship disaster without complaint, and a million other good things, not the least of which was simply being there for Morgan, coming home to her every day, just being someone she could talk to.

When this all ended, she was going to have a serious void in her life.

This couldn't end. She couldn't let it. It was just a beginning.

May Brielle Dupree stay in Germany forever.

***

"You feeling better yet after pulling that all-nighter?"

Josh blinked a few times. Morgan sat on the edge of his bed wearing a blue dress that matched her eyes. She had her hand on his shin, the warmth of it seeping through the blankets somehow.

"I'm leaving for church in a bit. Do you want to come? Afterward, I thought we could do something to celebrate your breakthrough—if you're rested enough, that is."

Josh had slept about twelve hours, and with the

223

pressure of Morgan's hand on his leg, he was more than rested. She'd better get away from him, or he'd be revved way past the rested zone. "Yeah. Sure. What did you have in mind?" He wouldn't say what he had in mind, not if he was planning on keeping this as a business arrangement and making it so the annulment could go through without a hitch when this was all over. Dang, that girl was attractive. Her future husband, the real one, was one lucky son of a gun—and Josh was a total priest for handing her over unscathed. A hot and bothered priest.

"Nothing too flashy. We're still poor students, remember?"

He wouldn't mind whatever she had planned. It was just cool that she thought of him, and thought so much of his breakthrough. Morgan was cool.

After church, they changed into jeans and Morgan had Josh load a big basket in the back of his Explorer. "I hope you like cold salmon."

Cold salmon? How did she know it was his favorite?

They headed down to the coastal highway. "It's low tide. You want to walk out to Haystack Rock for our picnic, since that would take less driving, or do you want to do what I had originally planned?"

Josh liked Haystack Rock, and he hadn't been there in years, not since his freshman bonfire party days, but he wouldn't mind a little ride in the car with Morgan today. The sun was out, and her hair had glinted in it when they were walking out of church together. "Whatever you had in mind sounds great."

They steered south on the coastal highway. "Is Manzanita Bay too far?"

Not if he was getting to sit beside Morgan all the way it wasn't.

On the drive she asked him questions about his research, and he tried to keep the details on the non-technical side so she could understand, but she seemed to get whatever he told her, and even asked some questions that proved she did and suggested a few things that he hadn't thought of. They wouldn't work, probably, but they did get him thinking in other directions about what he could do with the next round of process experiments.

They talked about growing up in Oregon, things they'd done as kids like pick wild blackberries. Morgan had made jam with them; Josh had used them to make dye and ruin three of his best shirts, much to his mother's displeasure. Morgan thought this was funny. She seemed to get his sense of humor. Nice.

"I guess that's why I wanted to take this trip today. When I was a kid, my grandparents took Tory and me for a weekend and we came to Manzanita Bay and saw the shipwreck. It was so creepy and so alluring at the same time. I loved it."

"You want to go see it again this afternoon?"

"Oh, we don't have to, but I do want to picnic where we can see it. Is that okay?"

Anything was fine. She could convince him to buy her the shipwreck at this point.

Morgan sighed and rested a hand on his arm like she understood. Then out of nowhere she dropped a bomb on him. "Hey, I know I was out of line yesterday, and I want to apologize."

What? He had no idea what she was talking about, unless she meant the kiss out of nowhere, for which he could not accept any apology. A sizzling kiss from a beautiful woman in a thigh-length robe never required apology. "Out of line?"

Morgan bit her lip, the lip that tasted better than berries. Finally she spoke. "I shouldn't have said that about your decision about your major, or implied that Brielle was telling you how to be, or whatever."

Oh, that. Josh exhaled. No, she shouldn't have. He swallowed hard. Josh was tired of everyone second-guessing his decisions. Sure, Morgan had a point that Josh did have a passion for the bio-tech world, and the more he'd dug into his classes in foreign policy, the more he'd struggled to keep his head above water and his grades above Cs. But it was a means to an end. It was the best and possibly only way for him to be together with Brielle long term, since she had her career already settled, and if Josh wanted to be part of her life, he needed a job that was as mobile as hers was. Nothing else would do, and Josh hadn't forgotten any of his resolve that had cemented inside him that day when he left her at the airport. That was the main point of all of this, including *this* this. He looked at Morgan. Wasn't it?

"So, yeah. I've gotten to know you well enough in the past few months to be sure that you know what you're doing, and that you're not in anyone's control but your own." Morgan put a hand on his. "I trust you."

She did? Suddenly the bristling in him from a moment before softened. She trusted him. The words were almost a foreign phrase, they'd been said to Josh so seldom in his life as the youngest of the brothers, as the son of Bronco Hyatt. Someone trusted him. Morgan did. She really was the angel she looked to be.

"Oh, look. We're at the bay already. This trip flew by."

Morgan changed the subject and started talking about what the shipwreck had been like when she saw it as a girl, but Josh was in a spin cycle comparing Morgan to Brielle. Brielle had never said those words to him, *I trust you.* Morgan's words were re-echoing inside him. Brielle might be fire, but Morgan was a drink of cool water. Brielle was energy, while Morgan was a reservoir of peace. Brielle had been through a lot with him, including when Bronco cut Josh off; Josh had expected her to break up with him soon afterward, but ultimately she hadn't. Josh and Morgan were enduring a series of storm systems, and they'd weathered them well without even a serious argument.

It wasn't wise to be drawing these contrasts. Not smart at all.

"Oh, look!" Morgan pointed at a perfect spot on the beach for their picnic, a place where the sand sloped just right so they could watch the waves and kind of lean back against the sand at the same time. Josh brushed Brielle out of his mind. She was gone, and Morgan was here, and this was a day he should focus on Morgan since she was doing this whole thing for him and in celebration of his success, something Brielle might never do—not over compost, anyway. He carried the basket over to the sand and decided to just enjoy the day with Morgan. She really did look great in jeans and a sweater, and she'd been amazing with his family, and she had a nice singing voice that he'd heard again today during the hymns at church. She could do more than just a mean Dean.

"I have a confession," she said through bites of grapes. "Here, catch." She tossed one and he caught it in his mouth. "Good! Wow."

"Don't look so surprised. I'm a champion grape-catcher. What's your confession?"

"I called Heather to find out your favorite food."

"You did?" *Morgan got Heather's number?* "Heather's cool. Sometimes she and Chip are the only cool people in the family."

"And you."

"Not by comparison to them. They stay calm through all Bronco's machinations. Hey, are you cold, or something?" He looked and noticed she was shivering. "Do you want me to get..." He was going to say his blanket from the truck, but they were using it as their picnic blanket. The weather in Oregon never got too cold, not even in late November like today, but a breeze had picked up, and Morgan looked like she was feeling it.

"I'm all right."

She wasn't.

"Come here. I'll warm you up." He didn't wait for her to move; he crawled over and sat behind her, a leg on either side of her hips, undoing his jacket and pulling it around both of them. His face was in her hair, which smelled like vanilla and mint today, and her back was up against his chest. Her torso quaked at intervals. "Wow, you really are cold." He rubbed his hands up and down her arms to warm them and tightened his legs up against hers.

"Thanks." She leaned back into him, her neck touching his neck, her soft cheek touching the side of his face. Their breathing started to match each other's as they watched the waves roll in, break, and recede, saying nothing. Josh breathed Morgan's honeysuckle hair and her essence, and soon he found himself turning his face a little toward her soft cheek, pressing his upper lip against her skin, breathing slowly but feeling his heart rate rising.

This woman fit well in his arms. She pulled her legs up and nestled against him even closer, her face turning slightly, their cheekbones now touching.

If she moved another millimeter toward him, he'd lose it and be kissing her.

Her soft breath rose and fell. The waves crashed. And then he couldn't hold back a second longer. She was too close, too sweet, too gorgeous. He kissed her cheek, stretched and nudged her face toward his with his nose. His lips were on hers, and they insisted she respond in kind—which they did, with surprising intensity, not to mention endurance.

A bit later, after he'd given her mouth nearly all the attention it deserved and was considering her neck and collarbone, some seabirds' cries brought them up for air, and Morgan hummed to him, "Oh, you are amazing, Mr. Hyatt."

"I am, am I?" Nice. He liked being told he was amazing. But maybe she made him amazing.

"I've never been kissed so well."

Josh couldn't remember being kissed better either. Truthfully, he couldn't remember much of anything right now. Just the sea and the woman whose lips made him ache for raspberries every meal. "You're a bit of amazing yourself, Mrs. Hyatt." When he said that, something happened inside him he couldn't pass off as pretense. *I wish it were her real name.*

Things had changed. The dinner at Bronco's had solidified their friend status, as had the moment she'd cheered for him when he made the breakthrough in his research. *She's basically my best friend right now.* Who else did he tell about his research? No one—he couldn't. It had to be secret from George at work because he was a bio-tech researcher, too, and he'd lost all his former bio-tech friends to graduation. He hadn't broken into the social hierarchy of his new major. Brielle was gone, and while dating her he'd pretty much cut himself off from other social interactions because they'd been so close-knit.

Morgan was it. She was his *person.*

He toyed with a curl that had fallen at her temple. She was all warm now, and he had no excuse for staying so close, other than he couldn't leave.

He half-laughed. Well, that was good—his wife was his friend. Anybody would hope that would be the case.

But that kiss yesterday in the kitchen didn't have friend written on it. Rearrange and drop some of the letters, and fire was what it spelled instead. The way her spine felt pliable under his hand, the way her hair intertwined in his fingers. The places her touch sent his mind shooting. And their serious togetherness here on the beach had girlfriend written all over it. Friends don't make out on the beach. Nuh-uh. Not hot, hypothermia-curing making out like this. He could take off his jacket in a Wyoming blizzard after a session like that.

His wife was becoming his girlfriend.

And Josh was getting confused.

Chapter Twenty-Four

I can't believe they are making us do this." Morgan shoved another wadded up piece of newspaper into her backpack so that it would look *fluffy* and *full.* As if it didn't look full enough with the metric ton of accounting books she had to carry every day. Television people were psychotic. Why did they have to do this shoot, anyway? Hadn't they just been on TV moving into Seagram's Campus House a few weeks ago? Everyone watching would be sick of them. "I have two tests this week. Wasn't the plan that they were giving us all this so that we would have time to study and be better students?"

"It sucks when testing weeks coincide with holiday TV specials." Josh had already fluffed up his own backpack. Well, not *his* backpack, actually; he had on the one Seagram's studio had given him. His own didn't pass muster, according to Darshelle. "Should we walk or drive?"

"Oh, I should've told you. They're sending a driver in some kind of golf cart to get us across campus without needing a parking pass. First we have to go to the ice cream shop, then to the top of Old Main, and then we are being filmed walking up that woodsy hill on the north side of campus."

"The one with the snake infestation?" Josh looked alarmed. And who wouldn't be? Already this semester three students had been treated at the hospital for snakebite after using the hill as a shortcut.

"That's the one." Morgan zipped her bag shut, deciding it looked sufficiently fluffy. "I hope they're passing out Kevlar socks so when we get bit the snakes need dental work."

"Stupid animal protection laws. Oh, sorry. I know, I sounded like Bronco for a second."

"You don't have to apologize to me for wishing all snakes extinct." Morgan looked longingly at the pile of books on the kitchen table, knowing it would be a few hours before she could hit them again, and they weren't hours she had to waste. She'd been up late every night plowing through assignments, writing research papers, and basically memorizing the U.S. tax code. "Does my hair look okay?" She knew it sounded weak, asking Josh this, but he'd been kind of distant ever since the kiss on the beach, or at least it had seemed like it since she wished every day had been as filled with kisses as that one, and there hadn't been any follow-up, just back to business as usual, so she was genuinely as insecure as she sounded.

It must be that he didn't think of her *that* way, and she knew it now, even though it stung deeper than any snakebite.

Josh gave her a short glance. "Yep. Looks great."

Exactly. Exactly her point. He might see her, but he didn't *see* her. Not the way she saw him.

At the ice cream shop, Darshelle seated them across from each other at a small iron table.

"Josh, spoon up some of the butter pecan and feed Morgan. Morgan, look like you enjoy it. That's it. Yeah, eyes closed like this is ecstasy. Perfect."

Morgan opened her eyes, and Josh was staring at her, his jaw a little slack. She couldn't help but pull a smile. "You jealous?" She meant that she was the one eating the ice cream and he wasn't.

"Of the ice cream? Yeah."

She pushed his shoulder.

"That's perfect!" Darshelle said. "So playful. Exactly what we want to see. Man, it's like you're not some comfortable married couple; it's more like you're just getting to know each other flirting. Love the chemistry. Now, let's go to Old Main. We're going up top."

A swift buzz across campus in the golf cart took them to Clarendon's oldest building, with its clock tower adorned by a weathercock. It was the defining structure of the university, the one they put on all their brochures, and Morgan and Josh were getting their first trip into the bell tower.

"Is there an elevator?" Ernie the cameraman said. "It's what? Six million stairs up?"

Morgan was glad for the first time that she only had the fluff-filled backpack instead of her books as she climbed all six million steps of the circular metal stairway up the tower. "Do you need a hand with any of the equipment?" she asked him.

At that, Josh reached down and grabbed one of the cameras. "Dude. No wonder you've got forearms like Popeye the Sailor Man. This thing is heavy." But Josh shouldered it and kept busting his way up the steps. Morgan raised a single eyebrow reflexively. Huh. Nice strength her husband had.

"Now, you two. I want you to lean a little out the window beneath the clock, reach out like you're waving down to us." Darshelle had them hooked up to walkie talkies, which were kind of old-fashioned, considering they could've just used phones, but whatever. She worked for Seagram, and chances were, the guy insisted on things being done a certain way. Morgan tried to obey, but she was a little short to be leaning out the window that was higher than her shoulder. Josh could do it fine, but Morgan was going to need to stand on something.

In despair she looked around. There was nothing up here on this narrow platform, not even an old two-by-four or tool box. It was bare floor. And her fluffy backpack wouldn't work.

Josh fiddled with the window and got it open. "We

have to lean out? Does she know how far down that is? Like a mile."

"Don't fall, Josh." Morgan teased him despite her worry.

"I won't. And don't worry, Morgan. I'll catch you if you fall."

"Chances are we'll go down together."

"Never were truer words spoken..." Josh gave her a knowing look, and Morgan understood exactly what he meant. They were on a tightrope over an alligator pond with this lie of a life they were leading.

"Morgan? I'm only seeing your hair here in the shot. Can you, uh—"

Before she could respond into the radio, Josh picked her up. "You need a boost." It suddenly sucked all the air out of her lungs, having his arms so tight around her. It'd been so long since that embrace on the beach, she'd almost forgotten. "There." He maneuvered her toward the window. She put her hands on his shoulders, he was holding her up so high.

"There. Now we got you." Darshelle's voice crackled and fizzed. "There. Now wave to us. And then give us a little kiss."

Kiss! Again? Morgan's throat went dry, and her lips tingled. If he wasn't into her that way, even though he'd seemed it a hundred percent at the shipwreck, it didn't change how much she wished he were and how much she ached for the possibility that her kiss could change all that.

A look down into Josh's eyes confused her. Did he want to obey the order? She couldn't tell what he was thinking, but there was definitely a hesitation there, and it stabbed at her.

Ernie, the cameraman who'd followed them up to get a secondary angle on the shot, was all set up now. "That's good. Good pose." He walked around them. "Darsh, we don't need the kiss. This will be perfect."

233

"Oh, okay." Darshelle sounded as disappointed as Morgan felt, or maybe only a fraction. When Morgan's arm's strength failed, she fell into Josh's arms. He kept her there a second, and then another second, and then he let her go.

"That's TV life, boys and girls. You climb six million stairs, get a shot in about ninety seconds, and then you head back down." Ernie sighed, resigned, as he shouldered his burden again. He already had it packed up. How much time had passed while she'd stayed in Josh's arms looking at him? Wasn't it just a second or two? She couldn't tell now. Time was weird.

They followed Ernie down to the golf cart.

Darshelle took them to the base of Snake Hill, as everyone these days was calling it, and said, "We'll have a long shot of the two of you climbing the hill while we recap your inspiring story. I'll be at the top. Walk in a leisurely fashion so we can get the shot. I'd like you to canoodle."

"Canoodle." Josh helped Morgan out of the golf cart, just like he got the door for her every time they rode in his car together. "And that is…?"

"You know. Look like you're in love."

Morgan shot him a look, but then she gauged herself. "No problem." She hoped she caught herself in time so Darshelle wouldn't see her worry. In place of worry she flashed Josh her best flirty smile. Not that she had practiced it much, but it might work. She hoped she didn't look like an ailing wildebeest as she did so.

Josh played along. "See you at the top." He said it to Darshelle, but he had both eyes on Morgan, and the look sent radiant heat through her chest. He really did have the most excellent teeth to go with his smile.

Walt, the other camera guy, went with Darshelle, and Ernie stayed with them again. He had the right camera for tight shots. But, to Morgan's relief, he walked off a distance so Morgan could say a word to Josh.

"What are you thinking?"

"About throwing a canoodling curve ball."

Morgan laughed. "How?"

"Isn't this the hill where all the snakes are? Now, don't freak out."

"I don't think the snakes are poisonous, so I wasn't freaking out."

"Stick with me." Josh took her by the hand, and she scooted beside him so their arms touched. It was nice. They walked hand in hand a few yards, taking their time, kicking through the mulch of fallen autumn leaves, looking up at each other occasionally and laughing, getting approving yells from Darshelle. After a bit, though, Josh whispered, "Fake a snake bite."

"Now?"

"Now."

"Ouch!" Morgan grabbed her ankle. "Ouch!"

"She's been bit!" Josh yelled. He scooped Morgan up in his arms. She had to turn her face to his chest to keep from showing that she was laughing. He ran the rest of the way up the hill, almost threw her on the ground and pulled off her shoe and sock, then said, "I'll get the venom out. One of you prepare the tourniquet."

"Tourniquet!" Morgan squeaked. "No tourniquets!"

"I'll call 9-1-1." Darshelle came running up. Morgan's heart leapt. No way should this ruse devolve into an ambulance ride.

"No, no. We've got time." Josh already was bent over her foot and rolling up her pant leg. "If I suck out the venom, we'll just drive her to the hospital. It's gonna be fine." At that, Josh leaned over and started giving her ankle a hickey. "Go with it," he whispered so only Morgan could hear. And then his lips were on her leg again, and she had to keep herself from going nuts.

"Get away, sir." Darshelle suddenly spoke with authority, and Morgan looked up. Some strange man with an outrageously large camera had come barreling in at high speed, and he was taking shot after shot of Josh and Morgan. "I'm sorry, sir. This is a closed shoot."

"I'm not *sir*. I'm Paulie Bumgartner."

Josh looked up, and clearly the game was done. "Oh, no."

***

Josh lugged his backpack of textbooks into the house. "Morgan?" No answer. She must still be at class, a thought that disappointed him a little, to his surprise. He'd come back early today, frustrated with the pile of dates and names he'd had to memorize for his Politics of Developing Countries test. Who even cared about a country with a name that had no vowels in it?

Oh, great. Now I'm sounding like Bronco. Josh slogged his way through the house into the room with all the books and slung the eighty pound backpack onto the wingback chair, making it slide a little across the wood floor with a rumble.

A gasp came from the other sofa, and Josh looked over to see Morgan, who he'd obviously awakened, rubbing her face and arms. "Sorry, Morg. I didn't know you were in here." Every time he'd seen her face ever since Bumgartner snapped their venom-sucking picture for the tabloids a couple of weeks ago, spears of guilt pierced him, even though Morgan had shrugged it off when Josh brought it up. He knew Paulie Bumgartner the Bum's M.O. He sat on incriminating photos until the victim's moment of weakness and then sprang them on the world, and any caption Paulie concocted would sting Morgan deeply when the pictures appeared. He also knew that every minute he continued to keep her as his wife, he endangered her future as a private citizen.

Josh had almost started avoiding her over it, even

236

though in his heart he knew he should be there to support her, protect her. It wasn't something he was proud of, and he wished he could make things better for her—for them. But the photos were coming, he knew.

She half-smiled. "I must've crashed. Tax Accounting is just *so* stimulating most of the time, but I stayed up too late studying for a test, and bam. Mr. Sandman." She scooted over, making room for him.

Josh came and plopped down beside her and let out a long exhale. "You have tests, too?"

Morgan stifled a pretty little yawn. "You want me to help you with flash cards or anything? I could quiz you if you need it."

She'd do that for him? "Uh, sure. Actually, that would be awesome." Getting all the names and dates and spellings had been his biggest challenge so far, and the only way to get them all was rote memorization. "I can name all the elements in the periodic table forward and backward, with all the atomic weights, but ask me when Laotian King Savang Vatthana had to abdicate his throne at the uprising led by Pathet Lao, backed by the Soviets, and my brain is soup."

Morgan raised both eyebrows. "I don't know how you could be expected to spell anything that happened in 1975 in Laos."

Josh snorted. "How did you know it was in 1975?"

"I heard you studying last night."

Oh, she had, had she? She was listening to him while he talked to himself in his room? Something about that struck him—but not as all bad. "I guess I'd better be quieter."

"I don't mind. Here. Hand me your cards."

Josh tugged them out of the outside pocket of his backpack and passed them to her, his fingers brushing against the skin on her palm as they made the handoff. She was warm, probably because she'd been sleeping. "I hope you can read my handwriting."

"I'm an expert." Morgan began quizzing him on every place from Cambodia to Bhutan to sub-Saharan Africa, leaders' names and dates of political control, border changes, alliances and war zones. So much of it hurt his brain, but Morgan's hints made it easier. She gave him a mnemonic clue now and then for names like *Zimbabwe rhymes with Mugabe* for remembering that country's president's name and *Burkina Faso had a revolt in 1984 from being named the Republic of Upper Volta.* It was surprisingly helpful.

Once Josh was pretty sure he'd exhausted her by going through his stack of flash cards three times, he sat back and closed his eyes. "Thanks, Morgan. I think I've got it. Is there anything I can help you with? Memorization, tax conundrums, shoulder massage?"

"Well, I'll never refuse a shoulder massage." She twisted around on the couch and moved her long hair to the side. "I fell asleep here and kinked my neck funny on the pillow."

Josh looked at the skin of her neck where it met the soft cotton of her sweater and hesitated a moment before reaching for it. It felt so intimate to be sitting near her warmth that he had to pause and make sure he wasn't crossing some line. A memory of her kiss in the kitchen a couple of weeks ago slammed him, making his heart rate speed up, and it sped even more when he recalled the beach. They hadn't been this physically close for a long time, since the camera shoot didn't count.

He'd been doing everything he could to put those growing feelings of closeness aside — maybe needlessly. She had given him that kitchen kiss as a congratulatory token only. The beach kissing was for the same reason, just a celebration that got carried a little too far. He'd done that kind of thing at beach bonfires a lot in the past, so it didn't count. And now he was giving her a *thanks for helping me with my Politics of Developing Countries flash cards* back rub, not a *hey, let's get closer, baby* back rub.

Josh pushed a stray lock of her hair to the side. This would be fine. No problem. He wouldn't even think about how his hand felt against her skin when she slid the neckline of her sweater to the side so he could get to where the muscle was tight, and he'd completely suppress the urge to put his face closer to smell the honeysuckle of her hair. None of that—he wouldn't think of any of it.

"Mmm. That is exactly—" Morgan exhaled. "You're very good at this."

"I'm a man of many skills."

"Now, *that* I believe." Morgan relaxed against the sofa, and Josh kept working on the knot in her shoulder until he could feel it go loose. "That's *so* much better. Don't tell me that while you were out of college for a couple of years you were busy at massage therapy school."

"Just a natural."

"Mmm." She hummed again, and Josh felt that hum go buzzing through him so strongly he realized he'd better let go now. He gave her shoulders one last press, and then he patted them and pulled her hair back into place. Morgan leaned backward, across his lap. "I haven't been this happy since...since I gave back my roller skates. Thanks for forcing me to do that, by the way. You're so wise. Mmmm. Can I just rest here a minute? I've been up so late so many nights..." She looked so peaceful.

"Sure," Josh whispered, adjusting a little so his feet were on the coffee table and his head rested against the cushions. "We'll just take a quick power nap and then get back to studying."

He closed his eyes, his whole torso warm with the radiant heat of Morgan on his lap, her chest rising and falling. Soon his own breathing matched hers, and he placed a hand on her stomach and dozed. *Just a power nap. Twenty minutes.*

239

Six hours later, the clock on the mantel above the fireplace chimed what seemed an endless number of times, and Josh's stomach growled, the combo rousing him from a very nice dream about Morgan laughing at every joke he told. He opened an eye to peer around and figure out where he was. The couch. Eleven p.m. Whoa. That was some power nap. He tried to sit up, but soon he realized he was all tangled up beside Morgan, her waves of hair on his same pillow, her head nestled against his chest, his arm around her shoulders. She'd curled up against him and looked so peaceful there, he hated to disturb her, but this was definitely not part of the definition of keeping a safe distance. All along he'd known that never consummating the marriage was sufficient cause for an annulment, and the lynchpin of their plan for obtaining one without any hitch. He could just hear the pointed questions at the annulment board *Did you sleep together?* Well, yes and no…

No. They hadn't. And Morgan was not that kind of girl. She'd probably freak out if she woke up and found that she'd even accidentally slept beside him for these few hours, so he had to do what he could to allay that.

"Morgan?" He rubbed her shoulder gently. "We should get back to the books. Can I bring you a drink or something?"

She gulped and nestled up against him again, like she was in a pretty dream and didn't want to leave.

"Morgan? It's late."

"Oh, Josh." She woke a little more and then opened her eyes and leaned up and kissed him softly. Josh's insides exploded like the Fourth of July. "I can't thank you enough for helping my shoulder kink. You're wonderful." This last word was more of a sigh than a word, and it sent an electric current through him at least as potent as her kiss.

"Morgan, I—" But she'd drifted again. *I think we'd better be a lot more cautious.*

240

Morgan fought her way out of the grogginess of the dark tunnel of sleep she'd been in for what felt like a million hours, the most recent dream of which she'd been kissing Josh until he looked like he'd never leave her. That was a happy dream of wishful thinking because that wasn't how things worked between men and women, but she wouldn't mind revisiting it again soon. Finally she could open an eye, and she didn't recognize where she was for a minute. Oh, yeah. The library. She was cold right now, without a blanket, but she hadn't noticed it in the night. Weird. She always noticed if she was cold in the night.

Wait a minute. She'd been warm for a reason.

"Hey, Morgan? You awake?" Josh's voice came from somewhere else in a hush, like he almost didn't want to wake her, but knew it was time. A glance at the clock — after six — told her it was. Oh, man. She *had* been asleep forever — nearly twelve hours! "Do you want to sample some of my gourmet cooking skills?"

Morgan sat up, straightening her sweater which had gotten all bunched up on her stomach, and saw that Josh was setting a bowl of Cheerios on the coffee table in front of her. He'd paid attention to what she liked for breakfast. Wow.

"Thanks. I love Cheerios."

"I know." Josh sat beside her with his own bowl of some kind of flake cereal. "It's the least I can do for all you helped me with last night."

"Uh —" Morgan had a vague memory of flash cards and a back rub, but a vivid memory of the kissing-Josh dream. Part of her couldn't recall what was real and what was sleep. "What all did I help you with, exactly?" She gulped a bite of cereal, but it stuck in her throat. She should not be sleeping by a man she wasn't married to.

Even though she was married to him.

My life is so warped.

"You know. Studying. Stuff."

"Stuff." Did she really kiss him? She didn't know. Was that the *stuff*?

"Uh, yeah. Stuff."

That answered her question, as did a dawning awareness of what had happened. She *did* kiss him, just once, and it wasn't really intentional—or at least it wasn't planned. It just… happened. And she'd liked it, and then she'd sunk back into dreaming of more of it. Her face was blazing red, and to cool it she took another quick bite of cereal with cold milk.

They had better be more careful. She knew she was falling for Josh, but she couldn't let herself get so comfortable with him that she ruined things for both of them—or that she let herself get tremendously, irreparably hurt.

"About that…" Morgan looked up at him with all the apology her face could muster.

"Don't worry. I'm human. We're human. We get sleepy and our guard goes down. Say, you wanna go pick up some coffee before your test?"

"Sure. But Josh? I'd better not get sleepy anymore."

***

Josh dropped Morgan off at her test and then walked to his own building across campus. Nine thousand facts dive-bombed his mind, and only a few of them had to do with African dictators. He'd just spent the night with Morgan in his arms, and when she woke up, the only thing she'd said was that it had better never happen again.

At that statement, two competing halves of him went to war. True, said the logical half of him, but the other more egotistical side of him shouted that she ought to want to wake up beside him every morning because he was so

242

worth having. Shah! A girl like Morgan could have anyone she cast a glance at. She wouldn't waste her time on him.

He yanked the door to the political science building open, nearly whacking an oblivious student engrossed in his headphones. "Sorry, dude." But dude didn't hear him, and Josh went back to eating his heart out.

Morgan had felt so amazing curled up next to him it was almost like a religious experience. He'd definitely glimpsed heaven, or at least a sleeping angel.

So when she said she'd better not get sleepy again—in essence that she'd better never repeat that divine moment for him—it kicked out all his pride, leaving him a heaving mess inside.

She didn't want him. And he *shouldn't* want her.

Those two mantras surfaced and resounded, taking over his entire brain for the duration of the test on Mugabe and Zimbabwe. Josh completely bombed it. All he could do was chew the yellow paint on the side of his pencil and remember how that honeysuckle smelled and how she said she never wanted him to smell it again.

Josh was going to have to make some kind of drastic change, or his ego was going to take more than a simple bruising. It was going to die.

Chapter Twenty-Five

It was morning, and Morgan got up early. "Josh?" She wanted to know how his political history test went, whether she'd ruined it for him by not letting him get a good night's rest. She'd hate herself a little for that, but she wouldn't have traded that feeling of waking up beside him for anything.

"Josh?" He'd had work after class, so she didn't see him last night. "Josh?" If he was still asleep she hated to wake him, but when she peeked in his room, she saw he hadn't slept in his bed. A sick worry formed in her stomach. She'd known it was a risk, even if it was partly a sleepy accident to kiss him and lazily fail to leave his side all night, but she didn't think it would make him abandon her.

She tried to not worry as she went to class. She'd have to focus, as it was. Finals were coming up soon, and she couldn't blow them — not after all the machinations she'd gone through to get this far in the semester. For the next few hours she'd put Josh Hyatt out of her mind, like he'd obviously done with Morgan.

Why didn't he at least text and tell her he was all right?

Ugh. It wasn't like she owned him. It wasn't like they were really married and he owed her that courtesy. Business partners didn't owe it to each other to tell where they were every waking or sleeping minute. A dark cloud settled over Morgan's mood, and the second hand of the clock on the wall in her Cost Accounting class slowed to a crawl. Was that real or perception? Was it because her mind had sped up so much with thoughts of self-doubt bombarding her so fast that she was in some kind of hyper-time? The biggest doubt attacked when she remembered Josh's description of Brielle: she was a woman on fire, ready to take on the world, organized, driven, exciting.

Morgan saw herself as anything but exciting. She was an accountant, for heaven's sake. Wait, not even that. She was a student aiming to become an accountant. When in the history of Earth had an accountant set the world on fire — in any manner? Never, that's when. Morgan had no interest in setting the world ablaze. It wasn't her way. She could barely talk to people, let alone inspire or incite a group to action of any kind. Her ambitions were so much more domestic, and the older she got, the more so they became, especially as she discovered cooking from the never-ending refrigerator. Contrasting herself to Josh's globe-trotting girlfriend with a short skirt and a long jacket who was out taking charge of every situation and slashing and burning her way through life's mundanity, Morgan looked like boredom with boobs.

Maybe pop culture said blondes had more fun, but Morgan was living proof of the opposite. Not that she knew what color Brielle's hair was. Maybe the girlfriend was blonde, too, and maybe Josh had picked Morgan for his scheme because she reminded him of Brielle and could keep him warm while the real girl was gone.

Morgan rolled her eyes at this self-immolation. Frankly, it wasn't necessary. She and Josh were friends, friends with some chemistry, but in the dreams after that kiss, she'd let her mind roll farther and illustrate a future for them, even though it couldn't happen. He didn't suddenly owe her any more attention or devotion just because she threw herself at him at the beach and in the kitchen with the waffles or made herself too available to kiss on the couch.

Oh, but that couch kiss warmed her, even the memory of it.

245

Her heart wrenched. Josh was the one guy she'd really wanted. Maybe ever. And he was hers — and not hers.

"Ms. Hyatt? Did you do the calculation?" It sounded like the professor was asking her for the second time, and she had been in a Josh spin cycle in her brain.

"I'm sorry, sir. Which problem?"

"Number sixteen."

Right. Sixteen. She looked down at her homework and finally responded, luckily with the right answer or she would have been embarrassed. As it was, everyone in class was looking at her, and she felt the weight of their stares.

Isabel caught up with her after class. "Tough homework, huh? You spend the whole weekend doing it?"

The question sent Morgan reviewing the roller coaster of events of the weekend. "Uh, yeah."

"You okay? You seemed a little...absent today." Isabel kept pace with Morgan as they crossed the Quad. "The luscious Josh Hyatt still treating you right? Because if you ever get tired of him, chuck him my direction."

"Uh, that's my husband you're talking about." Morgan rolled her eyes at her own hypocrisy, just as her phone started ringing Mom's tone — croaking frogs. "Everything's fine. But my mom's calling. Gotta take it."

As she picked up, though, Isabel inserted, "My boyfriend proposed to me on Thanksgiving. We're planning a quick Valentine's Day wedding so we can apply for the Seagram Scholarship." She smiled and dodged away.

"Mom?" Morgan waved Isabel goodbye, giving her a thumbs-up as Isabel blissfully gave a wave of the sparkly new diamond on her left ring finger back at Morgan. "How's Nixie? You guys have a good trip to see Aunt Jolene?"

"Oh, the dog's fine. And I got a lot of poetry done. Vancouver Island always inspires me."

Great. More sand, more frogs. Morgan rolled her eyes

and wished again there'd never been any poetry to begin with. Or frogs. She hated frogs.

"But the reason I'm calling is not about me. It's about you!"

"Really." Morgan didn't know how to respond to this. Mom was a good mom, but she was pretty self-absorbed a lot of the time. "I'm doing just fine. Getting ready for finals."

"Oh, good. How's Josher?"

Uh, lost? Gone forever? Never telling her where he was again? Morgan didn't know what to say. "He's doing great. We went to dinner with his family a few weeks ago. It was interesting."

"Oh, wonderful. I hope they were nice to you."

They weren't, but Josh kept her safe until they thawed. "I took your rice recipe. They thought it was amazing."

"The one with the caramelized onions? Everyone loves that. I haven't made it in years." Mom went on a nostalgia tangent for a few minutes until Morgan was nearly late for her next class. She stood at the door wishing Josh had called instead of Mom right now so she could breathe again. Just knowing whether or not she'd ruined everything would help unkink her neck.

"My class is about to start, so I'd better go."

"No, darling. I haven't even told you the news. It's so exciting I don't know how I didn't lead with it." Uh-huh. That would have been nice, as now the professor was setting her book on the dais and students were opening their laptops to take notes on her lecture. Morgan shifted her weight, impatient for the news. "I've got it all planned. It's late, of course, by several months, but it took me this long to get things all set, and the soonest I could book The Victorian was May twenty-fifth, two weeks after your graduation, which I thought you'd definitely like to have over with before you launched into wedding reception hoopla anyway. I mean, the final touches of flowers and

247

catering and bunting and guest lists will all be taken care of by then, but you'll want to have a dress fitting and things at the weight you are then — let's hope your dress from your actual wedding still fits. You did have a dress, didn't you? You're not going to be with child by then are you? Because it really won't fit then."

With child! "No, Mom."

"No, what? No, you won't be preg-o, or no you didn't have a dress?" She burst into a Mom-belly-laugh at that point, and Morgan tried again to sign off, to no avail. "Sorry, hon. I'm just so excited about all the details, everything coming together. Several gifts have already started to arrive in the mail, actually. I've invited everyone. Everyone! All my college friends, all the people from church, your great aunts and uncles from Maine and Wisconsin. They're all flying in, and I've got hotel space booked for them at the Red Lion, and it's going to be the biggest party this family has ever seen. I can't wait to see some of my long lost cousins. It's going to be absolutely amazing. I hope you're okay with lavender and green as your colors. I told The Victorian that's what we wanted."

Lavender and green. Morgan's mind went into a blender. She had to go to class. She said thanks and hung up, her arm falling helpless at her side. What had just happened? Morgan wandered into class, still reeling from the Mack truck that had hit her. Class was halfway through when she realized the first wave of implications of the call: all her family was coming to celebrate her wedding — they'd booked flights and hotels — for the exact week when she and Josh would be signing the annulment proceedings. Her insides lurched.

It was too much. She jumped up from her seat and booked it out the door into the hallway. She made a beeline for the trash can at the end of the hall where she emptied the contents of her stomach. A few minutes and a rinse of her mouth later, she slunk back into class. Her professor gave her a knowing but sympathetic smile.

"It's okay, Mrs. Hyatt. I was almost bedridden with my morning sickness. If you need to lie down, my office is in 252A. I have a sofa in there."

Humiliation burned Morgan's cheeks. "Thank you. That's really sweet of you." She sat through the rest of the lecture trying to calm her brewing nerves, and still not knowing where Josh had gone, or if he'd ever come back to her.

***

Josh pulled up at Chip's house. It was late, but he'd called ahead, letting Heather know he was coming. She had a bed ready for him, and they could talk in the morning. Josh didn't sleep much—again. Every time he closed his eyes, he was back in the sand or on the sofa with Morgan beside him, and it didn't end with merely kissing his wife. He woke up three times in a cold sweat.

Over a bowl of cold cereal, Josh and Chip had a man to man.

"So, Morgan." Chip got the ball rolling.

"Morgan." Josh stopped the ball. There was too much to say to get it all out before Chip had to leave for the veterinary clinic. And too much he shouldn't tell.

Chip tried again. "You guys doing all right?"

"Better than all right."

"And that's why you're looking like a dog who lost his favorite chew toy."

Josh had chewed on Morgan, all right. Her lip, her ear, her neck at the beach. At snake hill he'd sucked on her ankle. He'd held her in her nightgown in the kitchen and on the sofa, but she'd said he needed to keep his distance, and that she wanted no repeats of any of it. Just bury his chemistry and his ego and forget the moments where he was ready to chuck all his former plans and just go for

249

broke with Morgan. Apparently she was only in it for business, after all. How could he tell Chip his own wife wasn't in love with him? He'd sound pathetic.

Besides, Chip knew how Josh had felt about Brielle. In fact, Chip and Heather had been the only ones to tell him exactly once to drop her, and then they let it drop. He appreciated that discretion. Everyone else harped like an entire choir of harps on that same note. But Chip had respected Josh's decision to go after Brielle and do what it would take to move their relationship forward, and he was the only one Josh would trust with this conversation, which he knew he had to get off his chest. It was too much to process alone.

"I'm not sure where to start."

"Start at the beginning." Chip checked his watch. "I have an assistant running the office this morning, so my first extraction isn't until noon."

That relieved all of Josh's tension. "It's like this." His dam broke. Josh spilled the whole situation to Chip, from the inception of the idea of getting married for the grant application to the year delay for annulment, from the disaster of the huge scholarship to the coercion of moving in together, from Claire's threats about the paparazzi to Paulie Bumgartner's surprise attack at Snake Hill.

"Wow." Chip rubbed his chin. "You are in deep. I had no idea."

"I never in a million years thought it would spin this far out of control. The plan was never to do more than sign papers, collect a one-time government grant, and then say hello again a year later on annulment day. It was never to live together, to have any kind of physical contact, to let her meet the family…" *To see the ruby on her finger and think it looked right, to wake up in a cold sweat having forgotten Brielle's very existence.*

Chip got a wry smile. "She's who I'd pick for fake marriage, too. Well played, man." He raised an eyebrow.

"So, what's to worry about? It seems like it ended up with more bonus benefits than you ever expected."

Josh only felt the weight of the worry pressing down heavier now that he'd detailed it. He'd never get out from under it, not with his life's plans intact—whether Morgan was interested in him or not.

"Follow along with me. One, you got out of that hole you were living in, and two, you're seeing Morgan's gorgeous face every day. I bet she cooks you dinner, too. Does she make that rice stuff often?" Chip rolled his eyes up in his head like he was reliving the ecstasy of eating Morgan's rice from Friday night.

Exasperation welled in Josh. Chip had to understand, at least a little. "I'm worried about cheating."

"What? No. Do not cheat on Morgan. Don't be ridiculous." Chip leaned forward. "Do that and I'll drag you behind my speed boat with raw steaks tied to you during shark season."

"No, not on Morgan, on Brielle." Josh knew Chip didn't have a speed boat.

In his mind, Josh had committed to Brielle, and when she'd left, he swore to himself he'd do whatever it took to get to where they could make their promises officially.

"That's ridiculous. You're married. To *Morgan*." Chip let the words dangle.

Josh knew he'd put his brother at risk by explaining the full situation—because if the IRS or the Student Loan Police (if there were such a thing) ever questioned him, he'd either have to lie to protect Josh or turn him in, a terrible situation to put his only cool brother in.

"Listen, I swore to keep it a secret. You can't tell anyone."

"I have to tell Heather. We are the same person."

Josh had, of course, known that would be the case. "Just be sure Heather knows I'd never hurt Morgan on purpose."

251

"You're planning on hurting Morgan?" Heather sidled into the room and poured herself a bowl of Frosty Flakes. "Do, and I'll probably hurt you. That girl is the sweetest thing since Froot Loops, and they list sugar as their first ingredient. Plus, where did she get those light blue stones? Did you tell her that's my favorite color? I'm having them made into a necklace. And again, if you do anything to hurt her in any way, I'll use it to strangle you." Heather made a fist at him, and Chip gave her the Reader's Digest version of Josh's troubles: needed a grant, couldn't get it due to Bronco's jerkitude, got fake-married to Morgan, things spun out of control, and now he was confused, and the paparazzi are on his trail.

Hearing the struggle boiled down made it seem even worse.

"So you basically married for money. Big deal. It happens all the time in romance novels." Heather, however, shrugged it off. "Nothing all that wrong with it."

"Except that we're not planning on staying married. We got into it with an end date in mind."

"You're divorcing her? What, are you plumb loco?" Heather set her coffee cup down and the contents splashed over the side onto her hand. She licked the spill off it, speaking all through the incident. "She's definitely going to get hurt, but not as bad as you are."

"Enough with threatening to hurt me, Heather. You couldn't hurt a fly, or even a flea like me." Josh rolled his eyes. "We won't be divorcing. We'll get an annulment."

"You are a flea, but I didn't mean I'd hurt you. I meant you'd have a gaping hole in your chest for the rest of eternity if you let that girl go. She's infiltrated every part of you—it's plain as day. She's heart of your heart, flesh of your flesh, marrow of your bone—"

"Enough." If Heather had any idea how untrue that was, at least the joining of the flesh part, she wouldn't joke. "I get it. And it's not exactly where we're at, emotionally."

At least Morgan wasn't, from what Josh could tell. Sure, she'd planted a kiss on him last night on the couch, but it was a sleep kiss. She'd been in a dry spell, being married to him, no other dates to scratch her itch. There had been the kitchen kiss, but it was congratulatory. He'd kind of forced himself on her at the beach. Again, it was that whole congrats, you're a bio-tech winner make-out. He couldn't trust any of those displays of affection—especially after she explicitly told him to keep away from her from now on.

He probably had a hangdog expression on his face because Heather said, "It may not be where she's at emotionally, although I've got my own guess, but it's no doubt where you're at. Women can sense these things, Josh. Trust me." Heather sat back, picked up her cereal and took a big bite, satisfied with her assessment. "Besides," she said through her crunching, "annulments aren't just granted for any old reason. There has to be proof of fraud or something, doesn't there?"

"We'll be able to get one." Josh didn't think he'd need to explain, but they were being so dense about it that finally he said, "If the marriage has never been consummated, it's considered sufficient grounds if an annulment is sought."

Heather stifled a gasp and started to cough on her cereal and milk. It took her a second to calm down, and then she said, "Well, no wonder you're such a basket case. Josh, I have had moments where I thought you were brilliant. This is not one of them."

"Ditto, dude." Chip said through his Wheatabix then started to laugh, and it grew until it was annoying. Josh was sorry he'd told them anything, and his anger must have shown on his face because Chip calmed down and finally said, "Sorry, man, I can see this is serious to you. I'm just thrown off by how unexpected this all is. I mean, kapow! She is the hottest thing I've seen on your arm since you got that wicked sunburn in the summer after your freshman year of high school. And you're married. Come

253

on."

This was not making things any easier for Josh, and he pushed away from the table. His milk in his bowl was warm now and his cereal soggy anyway. He took his dishes to the kitchen and tried not to chuck them at the wall like he wanted to. "She's a good girl. She's saving herself for her *real* husband, not wasting herself on a fake one. I'm not going to disrespect that." Much as it was killing him to do so.

Besides. She doesn't want me. He now resigned himself to that fact.

Heather was at his side, and she pulled him into a hug. "Sorry for treating it lightly. I can see you're in serious doubt here." She pulled back and hopped up on the counter, taking an apple from the basket and tossing it to him. "Tell me what's really going on in your head."

"I don't know. That's the problem." Josh squeezed the apple so hard it would have crushed if it had been mealy, but it was fresh.

"Let me see if I can recap. Tell me if I'm right or wrong. You went into this planning to use it as a way to get your education so you could please Brielle and finish school, and then you and Brielle could move forward in your relationship. Right so far?"

Pretty much right. He didn't like the assessment that he was only back in school to please Brielle, but it was true. He gave a shallow nod.

"Okay, then things changed when you and Morgan had to move in together, against both of your wills, but still it complicated things because she's this sweet girl, and super attractive, and now you're not a hundred percent Team Brielle anymore, and you're feeling guilty."

Morgan was more than sweet and hot, like a description of Thai food—she was smart and funny and knew what made him tick—but Heather wasn't wrong. "Okay, that's close enough."

"So, what do you want?"

"I don't know." But suddenly he did know what he wanted. "I want to know if Morgan is interested or if she's just being nice to me. She's pretty nice to everyone." From the way she made older people feel important to how she called and found out Josh's favorite food, Morgan was a nice girl. But she was to everyone. In fact, she hadn't proposed this whole thing for her own benefit—wasn't this whole thing contrived so that Tory could start school and not have to wait another year? And she'd been so nice about her mom's sick dog, and she considered Mr. Seagram's feelings, and everyone else's. She was nice. How was Josh supposed to know where her niceness stopped and her true interest kicked in?

He might have a sudden wildfire blazing inside him for Morgan, one that was going to be almost unquenchable at this rate living together and seeing her daily, but his logical mind was strong enough to put out the conflagration of emotion and passion singeing him.

Logic told him these two women were like car payments. If he switched loyalties now from Brielle to Morgan, it would be like getting that incredible rush of buying a new sports car, one with a raspberry red paint job and a fantastic grille. However, for years Josh had been making payments on a daily driver he could count on: Brielle. Now and then he'd driven so-called sports cars before meeting Brielle and they all only had wanted him for his connection to the Hyatt money. Brielle had stood by him even after Bronco's big edict, and that made her the safe, right, solid, steady choice. He was committed to paying off that reliable sedan's car loan. In a similar way, now that he was a semester deep in his new major, he was determined to power through and get that foreign policy degree.

Josh ignored the part of his logic that hollered that Morgan took him when he was penniless and didn't even

255

know his name—because she only did it as a business arrangement, and despite the kissing, he had nothing to convince himself otherwise.

"Yeah, Morgan's probably just nice to everyone." Josh was a mere business associate.

"No one can find that out besides you. I mean, she might tell a friend, but it would be hearsay, and you'd never be convinced."

"That's probably true." The research scientist part of Josh would insist on getting his own results from his own experimentation, no matter what anyone else said—except Morgan. But she was so reticent about most things, he doubted she'd come out and say anything.

One thing was clear, though. Until he was sure about whether he planned to go All-Morgan, he'd better keep his distance when the sun went down. That kiss in the night was proof he'd be likely to repeat it any evening she sat on the sofa doing homework in front of the fire. Otherwise, the annulment plans were toast, and so was Brielle's trust.

"You have room on your couch for me for a few nights?"

"I guess so. Running away won't answer your question though, Josh." Heather took an apple for herself. "All I know is you'd better figure out what you want, or someone is going to get hurt."

Josh didn't admit it aloud, but it might be himself.

Chapter Twenty-Six

On Friday night late, Morgan woke to a noise rattling in the kitchen. The big, empty house didn't generally have quirks or creaks, so it had to be someone, a person, making that noise. Josh hadn't been around since Monday morning when they went to get coffee, and Morgan had almost given him up for dead. She tugged the covers tight over her head, glad for the first time that she never dared sleep in the master bedroom because an intruder wouldn't think to find her in a guest room.

A sound of metal on glass sounded again, shooting terror through her veins. Oh, her kingdom for a baseball bat! She had to know who it was — and she'd have to call the police if someone was here robbing Mr. Seagram of his property. Well, someone besides Morgan and Josh, that was. Much as she trembled, she had to see what was going on — just a peek.

With all the stealth she could manage she crept down the hall to the top of the stairs where she could see down into the kitchen. A light was on! Some burglar — what kind of idiot thief turned on a light? And it couldn't be a horror movie killer. They all knew the best way to attack was to keep the lights off.

Another dropped item's clamor was followed by a soft swear word. It was a man's voice. There was a man in her house! Her blood froze in her veins and her fingernails were digging against the grain of the wood floor's planks. *Please don't let him come upstairs. Please don't let him come up here.*

The grandfather clock's ticking had never sounded so

loud. Or maybe that was her heart and it had moved right up next to her ears. Please let him take what he wants and go away. Please. She sent a prayer heavenward.

Then, the guy stumbled into view. The brown hair and build were familiar.

"Joshua!" Morgan gasped, at which point, Josh's head snapped in her direction, and he dropped the stoneware plate he was holding, letting it clatter and break on the flagstone flooring. "What are you doing?"

In two seconds she was down the stairs and had thrown her arms around his neck. "Where have you been? I was convinced by Tuesday morning you'd up and died in some horrible bloody car wreck, and I would never see you again." Or that he'd jetted off to Germany to be with the woman he really loved, she'd thought but didn't say aloud. "I'm so glad you're all right." She pressed her head into the little indentation between his shoulder and chest, where it fit exactly. His arms at first didn't embrace her — he probably didn't expect to have a woman in a nightie throwing herself at him like this — but then he pressed her to him.

"Yeah, sorry about that. I, uh, went to see my brother for a day or two."

"Chip? Is he all right?" Suddenly she laughed. "Sorry, I'm all keyed up. I heard the noise and thought you were some kind of break-in. I'll calm down now." She was such an idiot. "Clearly, you're fine, and I'm overreacting to everything. I do that when suddenly awakened from a deep sleep." It had been more than a day or two that Josh had been at Chip's — or had been avoiding her.

"Sorry to wake you," he said again. "I was just grabbing dinner on my lunch break."

"Lunch." Morgan bent down and started picking up the broken pieces of plate and the scattered parts of his ham sandwich. He bent down to help. "Luckily stoneware doesn't shatter much."

258

"I've, uh—they put me on the night shift at the water treatment plant, so I had to couch surf at my manager's place, too." He tossed the debris in the trash. "I'm not going to be on the same schedule with you much for a while."

Morgan deflated as quickly as she'd floated into ecstatic relief at seeing him again. "That's too bad. I can leave your dinner on a plate if you want."

"It's obvious even a ham sandwich challenges me, huh?" His eyes crinkled at the sides. "I should tell you not to go to the trouble, but I'm too hungry to have pride."

Morgan went to the microwave and pulled out a plate of food covered with plastic wrap. "I've been leaving these in here for you. You never ate them, so I thought you hadn't been here at all." She tried again to keep it casual, but she had something more pressing to ask him. "Did you happen to see that picture?" It had been a trending topic, and it was just as stinging as Josh had warned her it would be. She winced at the thought of it.

"I should have punched that guy in the face and taken his camera and run over it with the golf cart."

"Aw, well. He has to make a living, I guess." Morgan tried to downplay it, but the captions of the photo still stung. *Disgraced and Disowned with the Disheveled Ditz.* Ditz! Where did the reporter get off calling her that? When she agreed to fake-marry Josh Hyatt, she didn't realize she'd signed up for public shaming. "But let's avoid him in the future, if possible."

"Amen to that. I'm sorrier than I can say that you have to go through this stupidity," Josh said through a bite of pulled pork. "This is really good. Thanks." He ate a few more bites, exhaling as if in relief. What had he been eating the past few days? Morgan's heart unspooled toward him like a thread. He was going to school in the day, working nights, eating…what? And prepping for finals, when? His schedule was worse than hers when she was unwillingly working full-time at Veg-Out. The urge to go and comfort

259

him with an embrace tugged at her, but something kept her back. He had a leery kind of look, like he was a little afraid of her, so she stepped away, only glancing at him as she went to the fridge and poured him a glass of juice.

His leeriness sent her nerves spiraling. If only they were dating at this point and could have what Tory called a DTR: a define the relationship talk. Morgan desperately needed to know if Josh was at all into her—even though the idea of finding out he wasn't terrified her. From the way he seemed last week he was, but then he went stealth, not even answering her texts. It killed her every day, especially when the photo hit the tabloids and she was left to deal with the fallout alone. It was the first truly insensitive thing Josh had done since they got married, and it cut deep.

But he'd warned her it could happen, and that it would be bad. She did tell him she could handle it. Maybe he took her at her word. Ugh. If only she knew where he stood, what he felt, what he was thinking.

Then it dawned on her: their DTR had already occurred. The two of them had made it crystal clear months ago exactly what this relationship consisted of before they even set foot in the county building. The rules of this relationship were set, and Morgan had violated them by showing she'd evolved. In response, Josh had dialed it back, taken himself away from her igniting flames, and let her cool off instead of calling her on her misconduct. In a way, it was pretty good of him, even if it left her with a gaping hole in her chest where her heart used to be.

"I got a bit of bad news and a bit of good news while you were gone." She sat up on the counter, the quartz cold against the backs of her bare legs. She didn't even remember her robe over her cami and boy shorts tonight, coming down in just her pajamas to check on her alleged home invader. "Can you stand to hear either?"

"Lay it on me." He swigged the last of his juice and sat himself down on a barstool, what looked like a safe distance away. Yeah, he was definitely avoiding her.

"Up front, I want to say I know that I have it handled. I can manage it." She glanced at the ceramic frog centerpiece on the table for an injection of anger-courage. "My mother thinks she's throwing us a wedding reception. She's inviting *everyone*, she says."

"Whoa. Talk her out of that."

"That's a little like talking a salmon out of swimming upstream."

"Still, talk her out of it. That can't be good."

"I know." Morgan took a cleansing breath. "I'll handle it." This was a lie, but maybe with Tory's help…

"What's the bad news, then?"

"That was the bad news."

"Oh, good. You had me worried. I generally go with the good news first."

Ah. Interesting insight into Josh Hyatt's personality. Morgan filed that one away. "I guess I don't know if you'll define this as good news. Siggy invited us for dinner again. He wants us to show up the night finals are done." Then Morgan remembered some more bad news, but she wasn't sure she wanted to lay it all on him at lunch-slash-midnight.

"I'm not sure I know if that's good or bad news, either." Josh frowned and took his glass to the dishwasher. Morgan hopped down and trailed after him.

"There's something else." She bit her thumbnail and looked up at him, trying not to let the fear show, but knowing that was impossible. "He's sending the cameras again. Here. Christmas morning. They're going to film our first married Christmas together. We, uh, need to be in love."

Josh's head snapped up and he looked into Morgan's face. "Didn't they get enough at the snake bite event? I thought that would at least make them back off for a while."

261

"Apparently not." She gnawed at her nail even harder. "It was one thing to meet us at the ice cream shop, but it's another to have them here at the house. It can't look like roommates live here. It has to look legit." And by legit, she meant that it had to look like they were a married couple in every way.

Josh nodded like he was soaking in her meaning, and she wasn't sure what he was thinking about it. He didn't say, and her stomach twisted with the nerves of it.

"I'm sorry, Josh. If it wasn't contractual, I would have told them no. I—" She didn't know how to combat the emotion in Josh's face, which she couldn't read at all. Reading whether he was worried or angry or annoyed—impossible.

Josh reached for his lab coat. "If we have to, we'll make it work." He went toward the door to the garage. "Thanks for dinner. I don't know when I'll see you. I'll try to be quieter next time I come home in the night."

Morgan watched him go. It was like they were strangers again, just having met in the parking lot at Estrella Court. Her eyes and sinuses stung, and she had to swallow hard when the door to the garage shut tight.

She never should have tried to push herself on him. It'd only served to push him away.

***

Josh pulled back into the parking lot of the water treatment plant and had to sit, letting his Explorer idle a minute to get himself together. Curses dripped from his lips. Morgan had been wearing her barely-theres and giving him sustenance and looking up at him with those deep blue eyes while biting that thumb. He was going eighty miles an hour inside, and it had taken all he had to not wreck the casual moment by throwing her on the sofa and kissing her blind. How did she make bed-head look so

262

good? It had even looked amazing in the paparazzi picture, her blue eyes alluringly half-closed. Sure, he knew that was a trick of Bumgartner's camera that took sixty shots a second, but geez. Morgan made the mundane seem sexy.

And then, Josh was stuck listening to all the mundane business details of their arrangement, trying not to think about how sexy they were coming from Morgan. The threat of a wedding reception scared him most, but going to Seagram's place didn't seem like a picnic, either. It seemed more like a tightrope walk over a vat of steaming acid. Seagram could ferret out a fake relationship, or tension between him and Morgan, for sure. Josh had better take charge of his lingering self-doubt, at least for that day.

Oh, and when the cameras showed up on Christmas morning — that was going to be a killer. Right now he was a hundred percent anti-camera, but like Morgan pointed out, it was contractual. He cursed the contract again. They could just give back the hundred thou' right now and move out. Maybe they should — before anyone got any deeper. Like Josh.

Meanwhile, it was a genius move that he'd demanded the night shift. It was the only thing keeping him from taking steps too far with Morgan. Honestly, he'd been avoiding her for more reasons than that, though — he also hadn't wanted to face the truth about whether Morgan was into him, if she wasn't. It was the big question Heather agreed he needed to find out. However, tonight's conversation proved conclusively if he hadn't known it already — she was just being nice to her business partner. She asked nothing about him, other than saying she'd been worried when he didn't call. But that was only human kindness. Nothing more.

This realization shouldn't have dejected him so much.

In the meantime, his pile of letters to Brielle hadn't grown while he worked nights. When was she coming home, anyway? The original plan was a full year, but would they let her off for good behavior at some point? What about holidays? All these weeks of not hearing from her had started to wear on him. His letters to her were pretty vapid except the three a couple of months ago where he'd come completely clean and detailed the whole thing going on with Morgan. Something told him he'd need to be able to explain things to her about this someday. Otherwise, they were getting shorter, especially considering how little time he spent doing anything but school, which he didn't have the enthusiasm to write about. Then there was his compost bio-tech research, which Brielle didn't have the enthusiasm to hear, and work, which — water treatment facility, so yeah. Of course there was his main activity, spending evenings studying with Morgan, which no one needed to hear about but Josh and Morgan. Since taking the new shift, Josh did miss playing the piano and singing with her.

Focus. No, *focus*. Josh pictured himself on Brielle's return day. He could see their reunion and his handing over this big stack for her. Look, the world's most boring letters. Did you miss me? She'd take one look at them and declare him the dullest man on the planet.

Maybe he shouldn't focus on that.

Even when his official letter came yesterday from the U.S. Patent Office, declaring that the application he filed last year had taken another giant step forward, he hadn't included it in the letter he wrote yesterday. Brielle would probably consider it a lack of attention to what was *really* going on in the world, and she was right, but he could twist it into incrementally combating the global energy crisis; not that she'd agree. Although, maybe he wasn't giving her enough credit. Just because she'd been anxious for Josh to start back to Clarendon College, it didn't mean she wouldn't want him to be well-rounded. This stuff would look good on a résumé. She'd definitely get that.

He dug through his wallet and found an old picture of

him and Brielle together from that time they went to Mazatlán with his family. He looked happy in it, and Brielle looked like a girl in love. They were pretty young then, only twenty, the summer before Bronco's big slash and burn tactics on Josh's life. It seemed like a long time ago. Brielle had excited him then, too. Even the wild curl to her hair proved what an exciting woman she was, every strand wound tightly, ready to spring at any moment. Josh was always a little breathless around her, and a thousand times he'd wondered what she saw in him.

Potential. At least that's what she'd said. It was a little like her hair, the potential energy of the coiled spring, and she'd said she saw it in Josh. He remembered a warmth growing in him when she told him that— because he extrapolated from the statement that she was going to be around to see that potential energy come to fruition. He'd pinned his hopes then and there, and in his mind he'd made a commitment to be there for Brielle when he became what she expected him to be.

Guilt slammed Josh like a high speed train. What was he doing screwing around, possibly messing up his future plans, getting his head and heart so out of whack living with Morgan? Even when he avoided her by changing his schedule, she still threw off his focus, as Brielle would say, by racing into his arms in the dead of night, and saving a plate of dinner for him.

He shouldn't even be here. How had he let himself get cajoled into this? The truth was, when the grant came in, Josh had had enough money for his schooling—and rent if he kept working, which he had. He didn't need to be perpetuating this lie with Morgan in this giant mansion for his own sake, for hers, or for Mr. Seagram's. They could have turned Seagram down, said keep the money, keep the mansion, forget it. He kicked himself a hundred times for not just manning up in the moment, for getting carried down the current by fear of what someone else would think.

In point of fact, Josh didn't need to be here. He could live in a tent on the beach.

When that dinner with Mr. Seagram hit, Josh was going to have to look for a way out.

**

Josh straightened his tie in the mirror. "Morgan, you ready to go?" he hollered over the radio playing in the master bathroom. She was singing Christmas songs.

Brielle could sing, too. She might not appreciate Dean Martin, but she did sing the national anthem at an Oregon Ducks game once. Uh, not that he should be making comparisons.

He and Morgan had both finished their last finals today, after which Josh took a power nap to refresh from working the night shift. When he finally crawled out of his sleep cave, Morgan hinted that they should start planning their Christmas morning strategy for the film crew, and he'd let her quiz him on different outfits she might wear. She honestly looked good in all of them. He didn't know what she was worrying about. Now they were going to be five minutes late for dinner at Seagram's unless they hit all the lights just right.

Josh grabbed his sport coat and snagged the gift for Seagram off the bed. Morgan had wrapped it without telling Josh what it was. "Do you want me to warm up the Explor—" Josh's voice cut out, like someone had pulled the plug to a radio, which was basically what happened to his brain when he saw Morgan in her red party dress. He probably would need to have his eyes surgically reinserted into his head later. "You look—"

Morgan smoothed the fabric at the curve of her waist. "Is it too...?"

"Nuh-uh. It's just right." Josh couldn't move his legs,

but somehow he floated over beside her, encircled her waist with his arms and pulled her to him. "It's so right." Without brain activity, he was kissing her neck, her jaw, her collar bone, behind her ear. "You smell right, too." Some kind of pheromone was coming off her in undulant waves. He was drugged by it, completely under its spell, and going for broke.

"Josh." She was pliable in his arms. "I—I'm going to have to redo my makeup if you keep that up."

He didn't care. She'd have to get dressed again, too...

He snapped to attention. "You're right. We're going to be late." He let her go, his brain coming back into focus, and silently berating himself. Geez. He'd been so controlled these past three whole weeks since their sleep together on the sofa, and now, five seconds in her presence during evening hours and he became some kind of animal? What a dope.

But she did look incredible in that dress.

Josh had intended to talk to Morgan during their drive to Seagram's about the fact he was planning to bring up the truth with the guy, but now that he'd gone berserk with that out of body experience just now, how could he even broach the subject? He'd look like a freaking hypocrite wanting to have his cake and eat it too.

Morgan had gone back in the bathroom and was fixing the damage he'd done to her hair and lipstick and was still singing to the radio. When "Let it Snow" came on, she danced over and whisper-sang in his ear the *when we finally kiss good-night* line. His juices went all crazy on him again. Yeah, there was no way he was up for a confessional with Seagram tonight, even though he was sure he needed it more than ever before. This was getting too deep, but it turned out maybe Josh preferred swimming in deep waters.

"I hope it's okay I brought some food," Morgan said to Seagram as he greeted them with the holiday kiss-hello at the door. Morgan managed the awkward salutation fine, but Josh just shook Seagram's hand.

Seagram let them into the house, and Morgan kept talking about the bread she'd made with things from the fridge. "I used this bag of cranberries and made a cranberry citrus thing. It might be good—I mean, I hope it is."

"When did you have time? I thought you had finals today." Mr. Seagram led them into his dining room, where Morgan set her dish on the table. Josh then handed him the gift Morgan had wrapped. He graciously accepted it.

"I did. But Josh took a nap this afternoon, since he's been working nights. I had some time. In fact, thanks to your generosity, I don't have to work, and I've had some free time all semester, which I've never had in my life. I've loved having time to learn to cook—and you gave that to me. Thank you." She graced Seagram with a beatific smile that no doubt warmed his heart.

Josh did a double take. Morgan was *learning* to cook? Was there anything she wasn't a natural at?

"You look very nice tonight, Morgan," Seagram said. "Those pictures online didn't do you justice." So Seagram had seen them. Great. At least he wasn't making a big deal about them. Well, with as much money as the guy had himself, he'd probably done his share of dealing with the nuisance of the press at some point or other.

Seagram led them to a seating area deeper in the mansion, choosing a spot for himself on the long sofa first, leaving Josh and Morgan the narrow love seat. Josh wedged in beside her, and Morgan's thigh pressed up against his. He wasn't sure he was going to be able to make intelligent conversation with all that contact with her red dress.

"So. Josh. I've heard about Morgan's free time now. What about yours? How is progress on your composting-into-crude-oil going?"

Josh's chest took this like a bullet to the lung. How did Seagram—or anyone—know about that? Had Morgan told him? After Josh had been so careful all these years to keep it secret? The glance he shot her must have looked wounded because Seagram laughed.

"You're probably wondering how I knew. I wear a lot of hats, Josh, and one of them is being on a patent approval board at the U.S. Patent Office. Don't blame Morgan. I sleuthed it out myself when I heard you had a work station set up in the shop at the back of the Campus House property." He smiled, which did a little to soothe Josh's roiling emotions. "Now, tell me. Progress?"

"Good progress, sir." He might as well report, since nothing he did could ever be kept private, apparently.

"Good! That's what I want to hear. That was half the reason for this whole scholarship experiment, you know — getting you to a position where you had a chance to complete your research. Your mother would have wanted that." Seagram looked self-satisfied, like a frog with a gallon Ziploc full of flies, but Josh couldn't help feeling invaded. What business was it of Seagram's what Josh's research amounted to? Oh, yeah. Josh took the cash and the house, and in exchange handed over all rights to his private life.

Seagram rattled on about different things — local politics, the state of academics at Clarendon College, the likelihood of a super volcano — until he hit on something that reeled Josh's attention back in. "We're looking forward to a little Hyatt, aren't we?" Seagram chuckled. "Now that first semester finals are over, you can get started on first trimester baby-making."

Now, that was an invasion of privacy, if ever — The heat around Josh's collar spiked.

Morgan took that volley, though. "Oh, Mr. Seagram. You want to pry into our little secrets. Don't you know, a man and wife are the only ones allowed to have those kinds of discussions?" She gave a tittering, flirty laugh that defused the situation.

She never uses that laugh on me. Why not?

Seagram chuckled. "Point taken. But if you're not going to have a babe in arms the moment of graduation, do you already have an accounting job lined up, Morgan? I've got an opening at my corporation with your name on it, whenever you like. And Josh, if you're not averse, I'd rather hire you in the research biology lab at my Starry Point facility right out of the gate than wait around for you to take a bunch of classes you've already obviously surpassed with your own research efforts. You'd have your own lab setup, your own team. This work you're doing is not only important to science, it's got implications for national security. Now, don't go protesting. I've had an eye on you for the past three years and kept tabs on all the progress you've been making. Clarendon is all fine and good, but it's only a means to an end, the end being a steady, well-paying job. What's the harm in leap-frogging straight to where you're meant to be?"

Josh and Morgan exchanged glances. Her eyes registered pure fear, which mirrored the panic in Josh's own heart. But a second look at Seagram showed nothing but beatific warmth.

A bell sounded from the kitchen area, and Seagram stood. "I believe that's our dinner. I'll go see to the final details and then call you as soon as everything is ready. Just get cozy on the couch there, kids."

Josh gave Seagram a wan smile and, coerced, snaked an arm around Morgan's shoulders. As soon as Seagram was out of earshot, Morgan wrenched toward Josh.

"We have to tell him. We have to, Josh. This is going too far."

Josh's mouth was a desert, and his mind reeled with the offer spinning in front of him like a Christmas ornament on the tree, sparkling, alluring. If he reached out and took the pretty present, he could abandon school classes and tests and Laos and Mali and Burkina Faso, get

270

back to bio-tech research full time, have his own lab...

"Are you even listening?" The love seat was so narrow, Morgan's leg had pressed halfway on top of his, and he glanced down at it now. No, he wasn't listening. He was looking. And liking it. So, so many reasons to stay in this farce and make it real. Two of them were long and lean and ended with open toe, sling-back shoes.

"Come on, Josh. This is serious. I can't let things get worse. Siggy is going to be hurt."

Just then, Seagram reappeared. "Did I tell you? I've had eleven couples contact me and say they got married just to apply for the scholarship. You're both doing a bang-up job. I can't thank you enough."

This reality check hit Josh. They were not doing their job. They were total frauds, and Josh knew it. Morgan was right. They needed to face facts and tell the truth. Telling the truth about everything would have consequences: it would mean more years at Clarendon studying the history of Qatar, no job with his own lab, and a different path in life altogether; but it was what he'd been planning in the first place. Just because someone offers you a steak dinner doesn't mean you won't like the peanut butter sandwich in your sack lunch as much as you would have in the first place. Well, almost as much.

Besides, Brielle was part of his sack lunch, the one he'd packed for himself. Not that she'd appreciate being defined as a peanut butter sandwich compared to a future with Morgan and Seagram's facility as steak dinner. He silently cursed. Josh's decision-making process swung wider than the two-story high pendulum at the Portland Science Center.

Seagram was still chuckling, as he boomed back into the room and dropped his next bombshell, proceeding with making Josh's life even more complex. "In fact, I've decided to reward you. Can I give you your Christmas presents early? Oh, look how cozy you are, sitting on the couch.

271

Everyone should get such a good start in marriage and in life." He sighed, and then came over and handed Josh a box, and another to Morgan.

"Go ahead. Open them right now." The old man's eyes sparkled from behind his wire-rimmed glasses and Josh could see the smile from behind the beard.

Josh was worried. The job offer was one thing, the house another, and the money they could pay back. But what was in the box?

Morgan had lifted her box's lid. "Car keys?" The words hit Josh like a slap. Morgan stuttered, "I don't know what to say." She sounded like she really didn't know what to do. He looked over and saw that they belonged to an Italian sports car. Morgan would look so hot in that.

"Say you'll take that old truck of yours to Junque for Jesus and drive this until you can afford something that runs when the temperature dips below seventy degrees. It's not new. It's something from my collection I've had for a while but don't have enough time to drive. It's reliable, though."

Josh was the goldfish in the water of the unplugged blender. The tension was killing him. He lifted the lid of his box. There, too, sat car keys. "Oh, hey. Sorry, but my Explorer is doing fine. I can't accept this. It's too much." And from the brand of car that decorated the keychain, it *really* was too much.

"This, my son, was your mother's favorite make of car." What Mr. Seagram said was true. Josh's mom wasn't much for material things, but she had a soft spot for car design and followed the evolution of the Land Rover style over the years but had died before Bronco got around to buying her one—probably based on the fact it was British-made, not American. "You'll be driving it for her sake."

What could Josh say to that? His arguments died in his throat. Instead, he spluttered, "Thank you, Mr. Seagram. Thank you so much."

"Look, kids. My wife and I weren't blessed with children. I know you're not nearly invested in me as I am in you, but over the past few months, I have come to regard you as my own. And when I brought up future children of yours, I guess I was kind of fishing. I'm sorry. What I should have asked directly is whether you'd consider allowing me to be the godparent to your children." A tear had sprung to his eye and slid down his cheek, making Josh feel like the dirt he was.

Then they went into the dining room where the weight of the chains of obligation weighed a thousand pounds heavier on Josh. They endured a gourmet dinner of epic proportions and eked out responses to Seagram's further conversation until they finally escaped — in their new cars from Seagram's fleet.

Chapter Twenty-Seven

organ couldn't have been more confused by Josh's reaction to her in her red dress on the night of Seagram's party. After weeks of fully ignoring her, he'd suddenly plugged in and come at her with a full-on attack, after which, someone somewhere unplugged him again, because she hadn't seen but a shadow of him as he trailed up to bed in the mornings after his shift at the water treatment plant.

Meanwhile, the preparation of the house for the camera crew's arrival on Christmas was left up to Morgan—with a little help here and there from Svetlana. Okay, a lot of help. For a woman who obviously was raised in an impoverished country, she knew how to create sheer opulence with Christmas decorations. She ordered a tree from the department store twice as tall as the one Morgan had picked out at WalMart—and it came pre-decorated, pre-lit, and it could play a series of lovely, chiming holiday tunes when activated with a remote control. The white and gold ornaments sparkled, giving a warm glow to the whole room, which was draped with garland, bedecked with white and gold bows. The mantel had six different nativity sets from all over the world, as well as nutcrackers in several heights and enough angel hair that if she covered it in paper and stuffed it against the wall, it could insulate the whole ground floor of the house.

"Svetlana, it's amazing. You've outdone yourself." Morgan gave her a hug and went over to the tree and pulled out a small gift for the woman. It wasn't much, but Morgan had handmade a necklace out of more agates she'd collected on Cannon Bay beach. Svetlana looked good in black, and the agates would set that off.

"Thank you so much, Mrs. Hyatt," Svetlana gushed through her strong accent. "I didn't get you anything."

"Are you kidding? You've given me everything, every day since I moved in here. From the full refrigerator to the clean linens to the mopped floor. You've been the reason I could focus on school and restore my GPA to health."

"I don't know what is GPA, but I am glad it is healthy. You should be healthy, Mrs. Hyatt. I have never worked for someone who always does her own dishes. You are very special woman. I am very sorry that I have not kept your secret." Svetlana pulled a sorry frown.

Secret? But before Morgan could ask, a buzzer went off in the kitchen. Her pies were done, and if she left them too long, they'd crack right down the top. She dashed in there, and by the time she came back to the living room, Svetlana had left for the day.

Ah, this room. It was gorgeous. It was the most gorgeous, appealing Christmas display Morgan could imagine. She'd wanted to double check it with Josh, to make sure he agreed it was just right, but he was avoiding her again.

It stung.

How could he switch from boiling hot to below-Kelvin-zero cold toward her in the blink of an eye? Her heart was taking a beating from it. When he'd gone all beast on her before Siggy's party, she'd let herself think this is it, he's finally coming around. That evening, she'd felt so close to him, despite the jolt of being given cars by Seagram. She'd known Josh would be able to help her figure out what to do about that, and she'd planned to talk to him about it at length while they relaxed in front of the fire when he was done with work. But then, just as instantly, he reverted to his cave, leaving Morgan with emotional whiplash.

It was time she had a talk with him. Now that finals were over and the pressure of schoolwork was off, she was going to have to address the situation. If that meant telling him how she really felt, so be it. And then, at least, she'd know whether he was in this or not. Because she couldn't really bear this back and forth. Life had taught her she had to be flexible when things didn't go her way, and Morgan had learned to be elastic, but even elastics could snap.

***

Josh finished the last line of his letter to Brielle. *Love, Josh.* It always looked so strange on the page. Still, he folded it and put it in the drawer. This was his shortest letter ever, and the hardest to write. Somewhere in this stack he'd come clean with Brielle about the truth of his marriage. However, telling her where he was at emotionally at this point still remained up for debate.

This particular missive turned out to be nothing but a miss. *I miss you. I hope there's Schnitzel for your Christmas Eve this year. Those Germans had better be treating you right.* It seemed hollow. But months without seeing her made what they'd had feel far away, much farther than just a continent and an ocean's span.

He'd tried to sleep after his night shift, but it was no use. The smells of pumpkin pie kept waking up his stomach, which growled. He hadn't eaten pumpkin pie since Mom died, at least not home-baked. Finally, he'd gotten up, showered, and written this letter. He gave a last fleeting glance at his bed, and then he realized he ought to go downstairs and see if Morgan needed any help. The cameras were coming in a couple of hours, and he'd left all the work to her. Why'd they decide to move it up to Christmas Eve instead? The plan all along had been Christmas morning. Oh, well. Josh was at the mercy. He'd sold his soul to these people. It would be dark anytime now, and they could show up.

"Hey, Morgan. Need a hand?" Josh didn't mean to startle her, but she jumped, bobbling the pie plate she was pulling out of the oven. It nearly dropped, but Josh reached in and steadied it. Fool. He burned his fingertips something fierce. "Ow!" He pulled it back, jamming them in his mouth to cool them.

"I do need a hand, but you don't need to fully sacrifice yours. Thanks for saving the pie." She set it down on the stove. "Quick. Let's run it under cold water." Morgan pulled him toward the sink, turned the faucet to cold, and placed his hand under the running water. It instantly felt better. "You only had it on the heat for a split second. If we cool it now, it will heal fast."

She was stroking his palm, moving his burned fingers one by one under the cool stream. Her touch soothed him even more than the water did. Her gentle caress made him forget all the pain, and all he could feel was her hand, her fingers, Morgan.

"Morgan."

She looked up at him, worry in her deep blue eyes.

"Thanks. They feel much better."

"You need to keep them under cool water. Don't take them out too soon." Her eyes never left his, but her hand strayed from the faucet's stream. She was losing concentration, and he liked the effect he was having on her. Yeah, he liked it a lot.

Josh took Morgan's hand, and he led it from the sink and placed it on his shoulder. He took her other hand and placed it on his other shoulder. He planted his own hands firmly on Morgan's hips and looked down into her fathomless blues.

"You really are beautiful, you know."

Her eyelashes dipped, and she shook her head.

"I'm so lucky." He wasn't sure how else to express all the reasons why that were warring inside him for

277

prominence. "Why are you so good to me?" A thousand memories of their days together flashed through him, from her laughter at his jokes, to the way she bravely came sneaking down the stairs a few weeks ago in the night to defend Seagram's house from intruders, thinking nothing of her own safety. And looking so good as she did it. Just like now. He liked this girl, and even though she was probably the most attractive woman he'd seen in his life, his attraction to her was a lot more than just to her pretty face or slamming body. She was goodness—and like putting his burned fingers under cool water, she'd healed him, every day, with her touch.

She looked up at him again, hope alight in her eyes, and he had to admit, it was contagious. He'd gone the rounds in his mind, written the boring letters to Brielle about classes and avoiding the things he really cared about like his research—and Morgan.

There. He admitted it. He cared about her—whether she was just going along to get along, whether she was only being kind, he didn't care about that. He wanted to make her care about him for real. Looking at her this way, he realized why all his attempts to keep things on a slow burn with her, or off the burner completely, were useless. She had lit his fire.

"Morgan, you're amazing." Ugh. It sounded so hollow compared to the pithy reasons he ought to be able to express.

Something clouded her face. She visibly gulped. "Josh? We should talk."

Heat shot from Josh's scalp down to his toes in a quick wave. She was going to tell him that he shouldn't look at her like that, that she wasn't interested in being anything but business acquaintances, that he was pushing things too far. He should have known this would be coming, but now that it was hitting, he wasn't sure how he was going to handle it.

278

Or would she admit feelings for him, too? And if so, what was he going to do?

They were at a crossroads.

"You're right." He took her to the living room, and had a brief moment of indecision about whether to sit beside her with his arm around her shoulder, or whether they should sit across from one another where he could see into her eyes. He wasn't sure which was more distracting or dangerous to his logical reasoning.

Morgan sat on the couch, and then she decided for him by taking his hand and pulling him down beside her. She rested her head on his shoulder and bent her long legs over his lap. This was cozy.

"Like this? Is this how we should sit for the camera?"

Oh. Business. She meant they needed to talk business. Cold water splashed on the heat that had crept into Josh's torso. "Uh, sure. Whatever you think." He was such a fool. She wasn't past the professional relationship stage, and here he was thinking long term. Fool.

"And how do you think we should act for the camera? What are we going to say?"

Josh gathered his wits. "It depends on what they ask us. Is it going to be Darshelle again? And the same two cameramen?"

"Ernesto and Walt, yes. I got a message from Darshelle with a list of the interview questions."

"Interview." Josh's mind said this with an exclamation point. How was he going to answer this time? Before, they'd gotten lucky.

"I'm nervous about some of them, and you know I'm not very good about talking to people."

What was she saying? She'd charmed the frost off his whole bizarre family with her conversation. "What kinds of questions?"

"I'm fine with the *How did you do this semester in school?* and *What are you doing in your spare time?* questions. It's this one that has me worried." She lifted the list so Josh could see. She was really close to him, and that vanilla mint was wafting off her hair and permeating his sinuses until he had to swallow hard and blink twice to refocus. Just when he'd gotten used to the honeysuckle and could start to ignore it, today she smelled like white Tic Tacs tasted. How could she do that?

"Let me see." He took the list and tilted it toward the tree, which was giving off quite a glow. "What? When's the baby? Where did that come from? Is this more of Seagram's godparent insistence? Because if it will throw him off track, we should just tell him yes."

Morgan winced on one side of her face and looked at the ceiling. "It's beyond that." She winced again. "There might have been an, uh, incident. At school."

"An incident?" Josh let his mind go a really dangerous direction—like that Morgan had a boyfriend on the side, and the two of them had…

"I'd been talking with my mother right before my Advanced Accounting class, and it was when she told me about the reception, and it made me so upset that—oh, this is really embarrassing."

"What?" Josh asked, his mind already taking relief. If it involved her mother, it didn't involve a boyfriend and a pregnancy scare. Of course he should have known Morgan wasn't that girl.

"The whole thing just made me run down the hall and throw up. The professor drew conclusions and announced them to the class, including the words *morning sickness*." She rolled her eyes. "It's pretty hard to be pregnant when you've never given yourself to a man. That phenomenon has only ever happened once in all history, and I guess that's what Christmas centers on. But still."

Josh laughed a little at this, mostly propelled by relief. "People." He shook his head, reaching up and stroking Morgan's hair to shake loose more of that intoxicating scent. "The rest of the questions seem all right. We'll do fine."

"I'm afraid the cameras are going to want to see newlywed lovebirds in their nest. It was one thing to be doing silly dating things all over campus, but this is life at *home*."

"Why are you afraid of that?"

"Uh…" Her eyes closed a second.

"Can't you act like that? Is it too hard?" He tried asking this with a light tone, but he knew it was transparent. At least it was to him. "I'm not going to have any problem."

"You're not?" She looked relieved. "Okay. Me, neither." She nestled up even closer to him, and he reflexively put his arms around her. It didn't seem to matter what way he embraced her—like this, or like they'd been together when her arms gave out in the bell tower, or with him carrying her through the waves like in that picture over the king-sized bed upstairs, or any other way—she fit, like a body meld. Properties of atomic chemistry came to his mind. Some chemicals formed ionic bonds, and others were covalent, naturally bonding with other chemicals. When he was with Morgan, he felt like the sulfur to her oxygen, each of them giving equally, sharing two electrons, forming a strong, natural bond, putting each of them in the chemically noble state.

Great. Now he was making chemistry analogies about her. The chemistry coming off her was doing weird things to his mind.

"So, there's got to be a perfect kiss for the camera." She said this, and it came out timidly, like she'd been contemplating it and barely dared say it, but it hit him like the pheromones did the other night when she wore red— rocking his world. "It can't be too…you know."

"Too what?" Too short? Definitely not that. He was looking at her lips now.

281

"Too…gross."

"What? Like this?" Josh knew how to walk right through an open door. In a slice of a second his mouth was on hers, kissing it with intense passion, sucking off all her raspberry lip gloss and giving her neck a beard burn the editing people were going to have a rollicking time blurring out. And, to his supreme satisfaction, Morgan was giving back as good as she got. Soon she was sitting full on his lap and turning his hair into what had to be a tousled mess. "Or were you thinking more like this?" he asked through ragged breaths, and then continued his assault, trying new nuances to his kissing, and learning a few from her as well.

The doorbell rang.

Morgan nearly fell off the sofa, trying to scramble to her feet. Her hands went to her hair, tugging it back into place. He'd never seen it look so good. Then she reached out and smoothed his hair, looking a little dazed, her chest rising and falling faster and more distractingly than ever.

"I'll get it." Josh said. "You put on more of that raspberry lip gloss. It's my favorite."

"Your —?"

He zipped away before she could finish, and the cameras rolled into the living room, led by Darshelle, who looked festive in a green sweater and black velvet pants, but not nearly as festive as Morgan looked with that natural red blush going on. She had more glow on her than the golden-lighted tree.

"Mr. and Mrs. Hyatt. How is your Christmas Eve? Mmm. Do I smell pumpkin pie?" Darshelle inhaled deeply.

"I made some for everyone, for after the shoot. I hope no one is allergic." Morgan was at Josh's side, pressing her body up against him, and he snaked his arm over her shoulder. She fit well here, too. He'd like to explore the other possibilities of where she fit.

"Let's get this over with fast, then, so we can get to the pie." Darshelle clapped her hands and led them to the reading room, where the tree and the fire were all so cozy and a few of the sofa cushions were now askew. She straightened them as Josh pulled a grin at Morgan who looked mortified. Josh repositioned himself on the sofa, with Morgan across his lap like they practiced. With any luck, they could resume this seating arrangement later, after the annoying intruders left. Josh had some unfinished business with Morgan Elise Clark Hyatt, and something he'd maybe like to give her for Christmas she'd never had before, if she was as into him as he hoped and as she'd seemed a minute ago.

Stupid camera contract, interrupting what might have been quite a pleasant Christmas Eve.

Darshelle looked over the setup. "Perfect. Great job getting this all exactly right. It's just what Siggy will love. Especially this." She waved her hands toward Josh and Morgan. "You two are striking just the right note. Now, let's roll film." She pointed at Ernesto, or Walt, to begin. "Josh, tell me how school went for you this semester."

The questioning went exactly as outlined, including a few questions about the new Christmas presents from Seagram, which Josh had to bite the bullet and gush about, and thankfully Darshelle left off the pregnancy question. Josh had heard Morgan whisper something to the interviewer back in the entryway. It was probably to deflect that line of inquiry. Just as well. He didn't think Morgan would like to talk about throwing up. Who would? It saved everyone holiday embarrassment. The taping eventually stopped, and Darshelle came over and sat on the coffee table in front of them to give them both a hug.

"It was perfect. You two are the perfect couple. I can't believe how well Mr. Seagram chose when he picked the two of you. This next installment we'll put on air tomorrow as part of a larger Christmas special detailing all of Mr. Seagram's philanthropic efforts in hopes of inspiring other wealthy people to make a difference in individual lives."

She patted Josh's knee and Morgan's arm. "Your contribution to this effort is much larger than you know. Mr. Seagram has a broad agenda, and what you're doing will make a difference in the lives of many people. You're doing what Christmas is really about—dispelling fear of doing what's right."

Josh didn't know what that meant. He glanced at Morgan. She looked as puzzled as he felt.

Darshelle and the men took their pie to go. It was Christmas Eve, after all. The sooner they finished the cut for air tomorrow, the sooner they could get home to their families.

"What do you think she meant? All that hokum about dispelling fear?" Josh asked as he came back to where Morgan was still curled up on the couch. "I'm not sure I'm ready for that kind of responsibility."

Morgan didn't look as troubled by it as Josh felt. She looked like a sleepy cat, her knees at her chest, her head on the cushion of the couch. In an absent voice she said, "Oh, probably his agenda to get college couples to marry. You heard him at dinner the other night."

Josh probably hadn't heard. He was too much in his head to retain anything at that point. "Why does he want to do that?"

"Oh, Siggy thinks college kids put off marriage and then end up postponing starting families, and it's going to result in demographic winter, and he's taking up his own battle against it. He's probably right. But I guess we're probably the epically worst choice, not the perfect choice, to be his poster children." All this spilled lazily from Morgan's lips. She was tired. She'd been up working all day, getting this place to look amazing for tonight. She'd even made pie.

No question, she was right about Seagram's choice of the two of them being unfortunate. Josh let a pang of guilt pass through him, but he let it sail right out. Tonight's

284

interview wasn't half as stressful as the first one, possibly because, at least for Josh, there was much more reality to their reality programming this time.

"You want me to go pick something up for dinner?"

"Oh, it's Christmas Eve. I should have made a turkey or something." Morgan looked sleepy, not hungry. "If you're hungry, I can cook something."

"No, I'll order pizza. I worked at Pizza Town one summer in high school, and believe it or not, Christmas Eve was probably our biggest night of the year."

"That's kind of sad." Morgan pulled half a smile, her eyes shutting.

I'll take care of it. Josh pulled out his phone and sat down near her on the couch. *I'll take care of you.*

***

Morgan only barely noticed when the pizza came, sinking back into blissful sleep after seeing Josh tip the guy. She'd hugged his neck as Josh carried her up to her room, set her gently on her bed and brought an extra blanket to place over her so she wouldn't have to wake up enough to climb between the sheets. She'd snuggled in and dropped off in no time. Nothing wore her out like a good kissing match. He gave her delight-filled dreams.

She awoke when the sun's rays hit her eyes through the white lace curtains. When she looked around, she realized she wasn't in her room. She was in the master bedroom. Above the bed loomed the picture of her and Josh in the waves, lips locking, and she blushed, remembering their most recent encounter and the intensity of it.

"You finally waking up?" Josh's voice sounded from the master bathroom. "Merry Christmas."

Morgan pulled the blanket up around herself, happy all the way through for the first time since moving in here. "Merry Christmas."

Josh came and sat down on the bed beside her. "I made you some breakfast. When you're ready, come downstairs." He had on an ugly Christmas sweater, red with a white deer and snowflakes. Morgan smiled, not expecting either the breakfast or the sweater. He came and kissed her hair before heading out the door, but taking one glance over his shoulder at her as the door swung shut. What did she see there in his face? It was new. She hoped it wouldn't fade.

Lightning fast, she bathed, dressed in the cutest sweater and jeans she could find, and padded downstairs in her bare feet to find a toasted bagel and three kinds of cream cheese waiting for her.

"If I were a betting man, I'd put my money on your favorite being triple berry. But you might go for cinnamon honey. Or you might be a purist. I don't know."

"This is so sweet, Josh. Triple berry. You win." She sat on a barstool while he slathered the bagel with pinkish-purple schmear for her.

"I can cook if only the toaster is involved, see?"

"I bow to your prowess." She took a big bite, her soul relieved at getting food at last, after being too busy and then too tired to eat much yesterday. "Mmm." She licked her lips, and noted that he watched that action. Then she remembered. "Oh, I have a present for you, too, but there's something else."

"Something else?" He got a wicked grin.

She rolled her eyes. "Not that. I mean something came in the mail for you yesterday, and you were asleep so I set it aside, then we were, uh, busy." Making out. And she forgot. "Sorry." She slid off the chair and went to the cupboard where she organized all their mail and bills and things.

"I'm not sorry." He came over and put his arms around her. "Never apologize for that."

"For keeping your important letter from the U.S. Patent Office?" She looked up into his eyes, and watched

286

them catch fire.

"The letter came?" He dropped his arms and took it from her hand. He said nothing while he ripped it open and perused the text. Morgan held her breath until the smile spread over his face. "It worked! It's been approved! I got it!" He threw his arms around her waist and swung her in a circle until her hair flew back and she started to get giddy, laughing along with him. "Best Christmas ever!" He kissed her, and then she kissed him back, and then they were kissing and moving toward the staircase where they sat down and kissed until they were breathless.

"I got you something," Josh said at last. "It's not much, but can I bring it to you?" He got up and disappeared for a minute. Morgan heard rustling from the room with the Christmas tree, and then Josh reappeared. "I wish it could be more. You've done a lot for me these past few months, Morgan." He gave her a small box, wrapped in silver paper with a red bow. He looked nervous.

"I'm sure I'll love it." She removed the paper and peeked inside. "Oh, Josh!" she gasped even before she even saw the full contents of the box. "It's exquisite!" There, on a little bed of cotton was a necklace and pair of earrings that exactly matched the style of the ring he'd given her when he proposed. Deep gold setting, antique-looking solitaires, none as large as the ring on her finger, but just as red and fabulous. "You didn't have to do this."

Josh looked sheepish. "To be honest, I didn't plan this. I had something else, more cheesy, in mind, but Heather and Chip insisted. After they met you, they got this out of my mom's stuff in their attic and wouldn't take no for an answer until I agreed they should be yours." He rubbed the back of his neck. "I wasn't sure how you'd feel about them."

How she would feel about them! She felt like they were the highest class jewelry she'd ever seen, let alone been given. She felt like they were incredible. She felt like she was a queen. Her mouth was dry. "You were right—I do feel a little twinge at accepting them, but thank you. They are absolutely gorgeous. And the fact they were your mother's makes them even more precious to me. I'll cherish them."

"Cherish them? I want you to wear them. We'll go out on the town, New Year's Eve, make a night of it. You can wear that red dress." He put the chain on her neck, and the earrings through the piercings in her ears, in an act so intimate she felt even closer to him than when he was kissing her. The brush of his hand at her neck, gently tugging at her earlobe, pushing aside her hair. She had to clench her stomach muscles so they wouldn't quiver.

"I might look ridiculous in my casual aqua sweater with this incredible, timeless jewelry."

"You look stunning. As always." Josh pressed a kiss to her ear. "And Morgan?" he whispered, sending the tremors through her again. "I heard from my job. They're changing my shift back to days, so starting with New Year's Eve, my nights are yours."

Her innards screamed. What all did he mean by that? Was Josh actually getting more serious about her? Could it possibly mean as much as she hoped?

"It's a date," Morgan would have said, but Josh was kissing her again, and her heart was racing. The whole process they were going through was so backward. Marriage, kissing, then dating. Shouldn't it be the opposite? Probably, but for them, it seemed to be working. The ring on her finger felt so right. Everything felt so right. How could it be wrong? They were right. This was right. It was time to let him know.

"Josh?" she nuzzled his ear. "I'm getting..."

She was going to say *serious about you*, but he wouldn't let her get the words out, and she wasn't sure how to put them because her mind wanted to say *serious about you* and everything else wanted to say other things. But what could be wrong about being attracted to her husband and admitting it? Nothing. It was right. And every bit of her knew it except her conscience.

Josh worked his way all over her face with his lips, tugging her hair and tilting her head back so he could more easily kiss her throat. She put up no resistance. Finally, she was so thoroughly kissed she fell back in a heap on the carpeted steps. "Josh," she whispered. "I'm getting serious about you."

"If this is how you do serious, I'm all for it." He didn't miss a beat, leaning over her to kiss her some more. "I'll take serious all day every day." And he went back to his work, this time on her ear, until her stomach growled, and he stopped for a moment. She'd only had a single bite of her bagel before their distraction. "You didn't get to eat yet, though. I'm being selfish."

The truth was, she probably couldn't eat a bite, not with all her chemistry mixing the way it was right this moment, but she took the breather to say, "I have a present for you, too."

This present would take courage—much more courage than she ever planned on mustering before she'd gone on that Tuesday afternoon's shopping trip to the bridal section of the department store with Tory—who'd pressured her and pressured her until Morgan finally snapped and bought the daring thing. She'd told herself she'd only give it to him if she was statistically confident he would accept. Morgan wasn't statistically sure he would, but she was sure he was more likely at this moment than he may ever be. She heard herself emitting a high, nervous laugh, even as she went upstairs to retrieve the present. She'd bought him some cologne, a kind she knew he would smell amazing in, but she'd give that to him later, and from the deepest recesses of the walk-in closet in the master bedroom, she extracted the small gift that said *Josh* on the tag in her best handwriting. Her skin was buzzing. Would he understand

289

the implications? Would he accept them? Or would he take her aside, apologize, and let her down easy?

Whatever the outcome, she knew she had to take the risk. She glanced up at the huge portrait of the two of them hanging over the bed. *We're right together. We have been all along.* And it steeled her nerves. Bring on the rejection, if need be, but she had to know. She peeked inside the lid of the box and saw the lace of the bridal garter. Would he even get what she was giving him? What if she had to explain it to him? Nah, he'd get it. Her breathing was shallow. If he rejected her, he rejected her. *But he might take what I'm giving.* And then her whole life would change. One more cleansing breath for courage and she turned on her heel to go make her present and face her fate.

But the doorbell rang. Dang it! Horrid timing! She hung back, courage draining away, clarity coming back to her that this was too risky, that she was jeopardizing their whole friendship, everything they'd built. And then she heard Josh's voice float up the stairwell as it exclaimed—

"Brielle?"

Chapter Twenty-Eight

Josh stood rooted to the spot, cold wind blowing into the house, chilling his face, his body, and his chemistry. He reflexively wiped the side of his mouth where he knew raspberry lip gloss probably lingered like a petroleum spill. He could still taste Morgan on his tongue, feel the ghost of her in his arms. And yet, this other ghost he'd almost forgotten now stood before him.

"Joshua! Merry Christmas! I'm here! Home!" She smiled wide and stepped into the foyer in her tall boots and her suede jacket, curls jutting out from beneath her winter hat. Her arms were laden with packages, and Josh took a few as they toppled from her arms, catching them before they fell. "Thanks, Josh. Good catch! Man, I'm so glad I finally tracked you down. Weren't you living in that place closer to the beach when I left?" She craned her head back to gape at the ceilings, the walls, the large kitchen. "What'd you do, win the lottery? This place reminds me of one of the palaces of the Bavarian prince I met while I was in Germany. You must be doing very well for yourself. You get a new job or something?"

In no time, her jacket was off and draped over a chair. Brielle set her bags down on the long table with Morgan's frog on it as decoration, narrowly missing the half-eaten bagel spread with purple cream cheese that he hadn't let hungry Morgan finish because he was too hungry for her. Now he thought he might never eat again, his throat and stomach were so tight.

"Uh, no. I'm, uh, still working at the water treatment

291

plant." He took a nervous glance up the stairs to where he figured Morgan was still getting his present, possibly hearing this whole conversation, and set the remainder of Brielle's things on the kitchen counter.

"You took a second job, then? Like, as a bookie? Because this place is beyond, way beyond." Brielle was walking to the china cabinet, opening it and fingering the gold-rimmed dishes. "I mean. Wow, Josh. When you said you were going to prepare for when I came back, I had no idea you'd go so lavish for me."

Every word from her mouth was a harder punch in his gut.

He pulled an anemic smile when she sauntered toward him. "I'm impressed," she said, lifting an eyebrow. "Now, be serious about how this happened. I saw the word Hyatt over the front door, so I know I'm in the right place. What happened, did Bronco not only write you back into the will and give you a lump sum up front to buy this mansion? Like two million dollars? Because this palace didn't come cheap."

Was that how much this real estate was worth? He'd never dared try to put a value on Seagram's Campus House, but leave it to Brielle to appraise its price immediately. He shook his head. "No, Bronco and I are still barely on speaking terms."

Brielle laughed. "Oh, it's moved to *barely* now, has it? Well, that's a giant step forward."

Yeah, all thanks to Morgan and her magic. Josh felt himself turning into a wet rag being twisted, twisted, and twisted dry.

Brielle came and draped her arms around his neck. "I have to know. This is killing me. You were crazy rich all along and holding out on me, weren't you?" She pressed her nose against his chin, then against his cheek, the way she always used to for signaling she was ready to kiss him.

Josh needed at least a minute before he was ready to

292

kiss Brielle, though. He cleared his throat, backing away a little and letting his arms drop. "This place belongs to a friend of my mother's. He's letting me—" Josh almost said *us* "—live here for this semester and next."

Brielle's eyes did a double-pop. "Wow, generous." She looked around some more, apparently not daunted in the least by his casual snub of her affections, but that was true to type for Brielle. "Too bad it's not permanent. A girl could get used to digs like this. Super generous."

"Right? I was shocked when he offered." At least that part was true. He went to the table and took a bite of the bagel, which lodged in his throat. Josh wasn't sure where in the house was safe to go with her—so many touches of Morgan were everywhere. Confusion had him on the rack, at high-speed stretch.

Brielle's phone rang in her jacket pocket. She checked the face of it. "Sorry. Gotta get this." She spoke into it, saying, "*Fröhliche Weinachten, mein schatz,*" and she made kissy sounds in German. It gave Josh a chance to think.

What he wanted to do was run upstairs, tell Morgan everything was going to be okay, to not worry, and he would take care of everything. But then his head said, *Dude. This is everything you've been waiting for.* Brielle was here, affectionate, happy, bringing presents. She came to him for the holiday, sought him out even when he knew he was hard to find. She finally, definitely wanted him. He'd waited three long years for this moment and had jumped through more flaming hoops than a circus dog did in a year.

Well, he assumed that was why Brielle had come—to make things right with him.

It was such crappy timing. Just when yesterday happened, just when he finally knew what he was going to do about (and with) Morgan, which direction he'd take at the crossroads, *kaboom*, Brielle came and exploded the whole intersection, giving him a concussion and a ringing in his ears. Maybe a little vertigo.

Over by the kitchen counter, Brielle spoke in animated German into the phone. Her curls bounced as she nodded, her tiny frame wiry and strong against the stone countertop, her fingers drumming. Always in motion, always on high. Brielle. She was intensity incarnate.

And she had come back to him.

It shouldn't surprise him so much, he guessed. The day she'd left him in the airport, she'd been a little evasive, but she'd never been vague about her long term plans with Josh—she'd wanted him, the grown-up version of him that she saw through her periscope to the future. The lens of her life was always a hundred percent in focus, and Josh's had been, too, when he'd looked through hers. It was only when he started living with Morgan that he'd picked up a wide-angle lens and started seeing other things come into view.

Josh could tell Brielle's phone conversation was winding down, even though it was in German and he didn't know anything but *ja* and *nein*. She was pacing back and forth, and suddenly he noticed she didn't return to the kitchen but took a beeline for the library, where the Christmas tree and all the filming setup was still in place. When she saw it, she about dropped her phone and had to bobble it against her ear. She signed off the call fast.

"Josh! Look at this place. It looks professionally decorated. What the heck? It's gorgeous. It looks like a woman's touch has been here."

"The housekeeper helped." Helped Morgan, his wife, he should say. But he wasn't sure even whether it needed to be brought up, let alone how to broach the topic. This whole scenario with Brielle dropping in unannounced wasn't in the plan. The plan was Brielle would reappear exactly when Josh and Morgan were ready to annul the marriage at the end of the school year and no harm would be done, and Brielle either wouldn't need to know, or else she'd admire him for his scheming ingenuity, especially when she found out he'd been faithful to her throughout the sham marriage. That was how it was supposed to play out. Not Brielle showing up just after Josh had gotten all hot and bothered over Morgan in that tight blue sweater and put his mouth all over her skin and smeared his whole face with her raspberry lips to the point he was ready to chuck the whole idea of the sham marriage, of the foreign diplomat life with Brielle, of even remembering Brielle's name, and make the fake marriage a real one.

Either this woman had the worst or the best timing ever, depending on how things turned out in the end. Either this was a crisis averted between him and the woman he'd always envisioned for himself, or a crisis created between him and the woman he might be discovering he was really falling for. *Getting serious about,* Morgan had said.

The fight or flight instinct ratcheted to ten now. "What do you say we go for a drive? I have a new car."

"That, too? Nice upgrade. Bronco Hyatt's son shouldn't be driving a junker." Brielle followed him out through the kitchen's door to the garage where she had a series of spasms over the Land Rover and Morgan's vintage De Tomaso Mangusa.

"Housekeeper, mansion, two car garage of luxury vehicles? Josh! You've been holding out on me. Why didn't you write and tell me all this good news?"

Josh let her in, and then he went around and slid into the driver's side of the Land Rover, even though she clearly was salivating over the Italian sports car.

"You told me not to," was all he could say. He would have said, *I did write — about thirty times. The letters are upstairs in my desk,* but he wasn't sure about them at this precise moment. Also upstairs was Morgan, and she had prepared a thoughtful gift for him, and he had been waiting for it with almost held breath. He gave a last glance at the door to the house as he pulled out of the garage, signing a silent apology to Morgan, not sure what was going to happen next.

"Oh, pish. You should have found a way. At least an email, man." She pushed his arm, and they rolled out of the driveway, away from the house where he could breathe again, and off to where he hoped a drive down the coast would reset his vision. What was he going to do?

***

Morgan chucked the box at the back of her closet, tempted to go and stomp it just to make sure it would die — just like her self-confidence and her dream of finally being something real to Josh Hyatt. Tears burned her eyes, and a stinging hit every nerve in her sinuses. She had to swallow hard not to hiccup as she inhaled against the impending crying.

Where had that woman come from? Worst Christmas surprise of all time. Far worse than the Christmas surprise when Mom had told them Dad had left. Even at six, Morgan had seen that coming and almost felt relieved by it, knowing she wouldn't miss Mom's crying because he was so inconsistent in his support of them.

Morgan stepped into the bathroom and splashed cool water on her face, hoping to lower the chance of tears, but it was useless. They were coming, and her eyes were rimmed red, making the blue of them all glossy.

Ugh. And she'd even put on raspberry lip gloss for him this morning because he said he liked it. The tube still sat on the countertop, and she tossed it in the trash, where she hoped he'd see it, accusing him.

She paced the room in her bare feet, wishing she'd hear him slam the door and yell through the front window at that girl, "And don't come back, you hear?" Then Josh would come loping up the steps, take her in his arms and

296

say, "Darling, I was only waiting until I'd told that wench where to go, so I could finally give you all of me."

But it didn't happen. Instead, after a few minutes, she heard the door to the garage open and shut, and then she heard a car pull out. A glance out the window of her own bedroom showed Josh driving away in his new jeep thing with Brielle Dupree at his side (what Morgan could see of her), the girl all animated and making happy hand gestures as they went.

She knew if she threw up, it would only be dry heaves, since she hadn't eaten. Nothing was worse than dry heaves. She couldn't let herself get that upset—even though the emotion of this eclipsed the time her mother informed her about the reception and Morgan hurled at Dr. Carol's class.

The prof had accused her of being pregnant. *Ha.* The single syllable laugh came out bitter, reflecting how instantly her own husband had rejected her the very second his old flame came waltzing in. He'd left Morgan so much colder and more alone than he'd found her, since now she knew the meaning of heat and having someone in her life. Someone real.

Or someone she'd thought was real.

From somewhere in the house, she heard her phone chime a text. Dragging herself to find it, Morgan exhaled. It was from Tory.

What happened when you gave him the surprise? Come on, tell me. It changes everything, right?

Morgan sighed one of those shuddering, post-crying sighs. Everything had changed, all right, but not in the way Tory meant.

Morgan could feel her tongue tying in a knot, her soul hollowing out, her mind sinking into the Conversation Coma. Even if Josh came right back, she knew she'd never be able to talk to him, to tell him the things she was thinking.

Writing something down might help her sort things

out in her mind. She couldn't write well, but at this point she could write better than she could speak. She knew the kitchen pretty well by now, and that there was nothing to write on there other than the backs of envelopes in the cupboard for bills. She began a search of the master bedroom for something tucked away. Nothing was in any of the dresser drawers or the cabinet. She checked her own bedroom and found a small pad of sticky notes in the desk, but those wouldn't work. The next two bedrooms had nothing useful, either. It felt awkward, but Josh's room had the biggest desk in the whole upstairs, so she sneaked in and tugged at the center drawer. Nice pen. She snagged that. The right side drawer had a good stack of stationery, and she slipped a leaf of it out of the sheaf. Then her eye landed on another stack of papers just behind it, bundled with a string.

Morgan knew she should tear her eyes away from the top page. Nothing on earth sanctioned the reading of someone else's private letters, especially when they were tucked at the back of a drawer. Her hand trembled and her fingers dropped the pen, while her other hand gripped the stationery too tightly, crinkling it.

My love.

That's how the letter started.

I think of so many things we've experienced together, from laughter and kisses to heartache and stress, and I can't think of anyone I'd rather go through them with than you.

Sledgehammers slammed Morgan right between her eyes and square in her gut simultaneously. This was exactly what she deserved for prying into private documents— pain, excruciating pain. Tears she thought she'd cried out, sprang anew, like a geyser, pouring down her cheeks. She slammed the door shut and fled to her room, put on her shoes and grabbed her car keys. For the first time since Siggy offered her the car, she was grateful it was something with incredible power because she needed to slam that gas pedal to the floor and scream down the coastal highway, away from here, away from all this pain.

***

"It's so pretty here in winter." Brielle threw her arms wide, as if embracing the whole landscape of the ocean and forest. "Stuff is still green and blue and pretty and—ugh. The snow in Germany fell and basically turned sooty immediately, at least in the part of the city I was in."

"What city were you in?" Josh didn't even know that much. He had them touring down the coastal highway, heading south through the small towns. He might stop somewhere, but for now it felt safer for him to keep driving past the several scenic overlooks of the Pacific.

"Oh, didn't I tell you? The East Berlin office. Huh, I could have sworn I read you in on all of that."

"No."

"Well, never mind. It's just so great to be here. It's a feast for the eyes. Want a granola bar?" She fished in her purse for a bit and pulled out two packages, offering Josh one. He shook his head. "It's great to see the scenery, but it's even better to see you. You can't possibly guess how much I've missed you." She rested her hand on his arm. Her fingers were cold and their temperature radiated into his skin, to his bones.

Josh kept his eyes on the road. "That's good to hear." Her statement didn't exactly quantify how much she'd missed him, but he didn't press her. She was acting like he could have contacted her, and vice versa, had the occasion arisen. "Tell me about Germany."

This was like unscrewing the valve on a fire hydrant, and Brielle gave description after description of the German countryside, the buildings, the train system, the food, the castles she'd been to, the gelato she'd eaten, the kayaking trips in the Spreewald, whatever that was, on the

299

weekends.

"It sounds like you had more time to see the country than you'd originally planned." Josh had expected her to talk more about work, but then that was classified, wasn't it?

"Lots more." Brielle didn't miss a beat. "I can't wait for my next assignment. You're how many credits closer to your degree? Because we're going to have incredible experiences together—seeing the world, making tough decisions along the way, but charting the course of a safe global future." She set a hand on Josh's leg. "You and me, Josh. Mr. and Mrs. Hyatt, just like Mr. and Mrs. Smith." She loved that movie, and they'd watched it together a few times over the years.

"We're going to be assassins, huh?"

Brielle gave a hearty laugh. She had a great laugh. "We're going to storm the world!"

Josh knew he'd bombed his Cold War Relations final. Working the night shift at the plant left him dragging when it came to test time, especially after skipping sleep the previous day to   cram details of Russian names like Khrushchev, Brezhnev, Gorbachev and a bunch of other -evs he couldn't pronounce. He knew they were important, and when he'd studied them earlier in the semester he'd been able to distinguish them perfectly; but when the final hit, he ended up scribbling something illegible and adding -ev to the end of where a name should be, hoping to fool the professor into thinking Josh knew what he was talking about. The professor was not amused.

All that work, and he wasn't many credits closer to world-storming. It wasn't something he wanted to tell Brielle while she was reveling in his company. He squirmed in his seat. A voice at the back of his head echoed Siggy Seagram's offer for Josh to come work in his research facility for alternative energy. He shushed it and concentrated on Brielle's words, because she'd turned serious.

"Josh, I missed you. Yes, Germany was a whirlwind experience, but without you, I realized especially this last three weeks, I felt like a part of me was missing. I loved all that, but none of it was a fraction as good as it would have been if I'd experienced it all with you."

A quick glance showed Brielle's eyes earnest and real. She meant it. She'd wanted him there. "I missed you, Josh," she whispered.

"I missed you, too." Truly he had. She was vibrancy and life. But it didn't penetrate him with that buzzing he usually felt around her, and he had a suspicion of why. *He'd fallen for Morgan.*

Brielle inhaled sharply and said, "Whew. Okay, but you were pretty swamped with school and work and stuff, too, and getting into that house, so that must be why you weren't thinking about me even enough to write me at all for the last few weeks. Man! What a coup that house was, though! Good on ya." She went on again about Seagram's house, and Josh finally responded, but he was testing the waters as he did.

"The best thing about the house is the workshop out back."

"Ooh. A workshop. You always wanted a workshop." Brielle shook his elbow a little, sharing his excitement. "Did you work on your chemical stuff?"

Wow. She was taking an interest in his passion at last, and with renewed excitement of his own he told her about the patent approval. "I opened it just before you arrived this morning."

"Well, no wonder you were all glowing and red-cheeked when I got there. I thought maybe you'd just come back from a Christmas morning run or something, although *you're* much more likely to spend it in church, ha ha. But I can see why you'd be excited for that approval. Way to go, man. I never knew you had it in you. A patent! That'll look good on your résumé when you apply for diplomatic jobs."

"Yeah." He heard himself say this from down a long tube. "Résumé."

A wolf was eating him from the inside out. He hadn't been rosy-cheeked this morning from patent excitement; he'd been with Morgan. He might still have raspberry lip gloss on his neck, for all he knew. When Brielle expressed that Josh had been busy with school and work and stuff, she had no idea what all the *and stuff* entailed. Like getting married to a super hot blonde who would never say, *I never knew you had it in you.* Instead she'd say, *You're the smartest guy I've ever met.*

He cursed at himself under his breath. He was drawing comparisons. He swore he'd never do that to either woman. Was it possible for a man to love two wildly different women at the same time and not be a colossal jerk?

"So," Brielle was going on. "I've got a lot of family commitments this evening, and a couple of appointments tomorrow, and basically I'm jammed this whole week, which is why I had to hunt you down this Christmas morning, but since you were all alone and probably missing me, I'm sure you don't mind, right?" She patted his arm. He didn't respond. "Did you know Claire is getting married? She asked me to be her maid of honor, which is partly why I came back for the holiday. Her wedding is this coming weekend, and preparing for that will keep me totally tied up, but would you be my date for the wedding? It's on New Year's Eve."

New Year's Eve. That rang a bell. His date with Morgan. She'd wear the rubies.

Brielle went on, almost nervously, which was really not her style. A sudden vulnerability surfaced that Josh hadn't expected. "We can go to the wedding for a while, and then there's a rocking party I thought we could attend, and then afterward, maybe we could spend some time, just the two of us. We haven't been together, just the two of us, for a long time, Josh." Her hand pressed his shoulder, and then she reached up and ran her fingers across his neck. Again he prayed the lip gloss wasn't there in a slick.

The two of them. Together again. He had waited so long for her to take him seriously, to hear her express clearly that she wanted him, to be with him, that she was proud of him for his research and accomplishments. It was the music he'd been waiting to hear for a long time.

That exploded crossroads from earlier reappeared in front of him again. Down one road lay Brielle and the intensity of her rip-roaring life. Down the other lay quitting school, settling for a job without a degree, working for Seagram who was generous to a fault but who also might turn his favor away from Josh at any minute, leaving him without a chance of getting another job, but also with Morgan, the gorgeous blonde who wanted a steady home life and taught herself to cook and play the piano. She was incredible. That road looked really enticing, the steak dinner road.

But Brielle was no peanut butter sack lunch. Being around her again reminded him that she had substance and grit and verve that energized him. He knew he was being an idiot, letting his soul tear in two like this when he'd been a hundred percent sure just an hour earlier. Self-loathing racked him for his sudden indecision.

But suddenly he was being presented with everything he thought he'd wanted.

Maybe Morgan's close proximity every day and every night was the reason she'd ended up infiltrating his brain — and nearly his bed, if Brielle hadn't shown up right when she did. Close call, maybe? Sure, Morgan was sweeter than honey. He loved honey, even when presented with that drug Brielle's grandiose descriptions of a larger life injected into his veins. The drug was a rush. He'd been an addict to it for years.

But now he'd gotten clean, free of it for months, and

he'd tasted the sweetness of a different kind of life, a life where he was the smartest man a good woman knew.

So why did the drug even tempt him now?

It wasn't fair to Brielle to keep her in the dark, or to Morgan to not tell Brielle the whole truth, whatever that may entail. Anguish twisted at his insides again. He would tell her about Morgan, about his feelings and how they'd changed—he had to. He just didn't know how.

Josh opened his mouth to say something, hoping divine inspiration would fill its emptiness. But before he could speak, a loud roar came up behind them, and Josh glanced in the rear view long enough to see a dark green flash before it peeled around them, going at least eighty-five miles an hour in this forty zone. The Doppler effect as the sports car tore past growled in their ears, and then all they saw was tail lights, and Josh jolted. Only one De Tomaso Mangusa in dark green existed around here.

"What was that?" Brielle half-laughed. "It was almost like an Autobahn moment. I remember this one time, in Germany when we were driving and as you know the Autobahn has no speed limit, and…"

That? That was his wife.

Chapter Twenty-Nine

I'm not at Mom's." Tory's voice through Morgan's phone sounded like she was eating. "And wow, are you playing one of those pole position video games? Or are you somewhere watching NASCAR? I didn't realize they did stock car racing on Christmas day." She crunched some more. "I'm with Rosencrantz. Luckily Guildenstern croaked, so Rozer and I could finally hit it off. I'm meeting his family, you know."

"That's great." Morgan knew her response's enthusiasm probably rang hollow as she downshifted on a hill, but even through her supreme distress, she still recoiled at the shock of what Tory'd said. Meeting his family? That had happened fast. Well, not as fast as Josh and Morgan's, *Nice to meet you now let's go get married* debacle, but still. "He's the *third* guy you were making costumes for."

"Bingo. But he's only a part-time actor. He's not even equity — unless you count that he deals in equities down at Manwaring and Tyne. He's a banker by day who likes Shakespeare, so he tried out for the part and got it. First play of his life. I showed him the theater ropes." Laughter splattered in the background.

"You're at a big family gathering?"

"This guy has eleven brothers. Can you believe that? And they all have kids. It's one of those mega-families. I love it. And the little kids keep having me paint their faces with snowflakes and Santas and stuff. I bet their moms want to kill me."

"I bet they love you for letting them have a break." The

road opened up again, and she really hit the gas. The speedometer was all in metrics, and she didn't have the focus to do even that simple conversion to miles per hour.

"You didn't text me back." The sound of a shutting door came, and then the background noise hushed. "I was worried. Everything okay?"

Uh, no. It was definitely not. Morgan's throat tightened and she let off the gas a little since she couldn't see through her tears.

"I'm glad you like this Rozen dude. Does he have a non-stage name?" Morgan strained to keep her voice even and the vibrato of crying steady.

"Richard Young, Junior."

"Ooh, and if you had a son, he could be Richard the Third."

"I already thought of that. But Rich and I are afraid of jinxing the kid into having severe back problems."

Morgan remembered that Richard III was allegedly a hunchback. "You're already talking about what to name kids, huh? Sounds kind of serious."

"It is kind of serious. I never thought I'd fall this fast for someone, especially someone with a solid career and a 401K." Tory sounded happy, and Morgan wanted to share in it, but her own anguish put up a wall. "Hey," Tory said, "you're not driving somewhere, are you? You guys should come up and meet this family. The more the merrier. They couldn't have more food here if this were a Costco, so there's definitely enough for both you and Josh. I bet he and Rich would like each other."

"I bet they would, but—" Her voice broke here, and a catch in her throat revealed that she'd been sobbing just before the call.

"Oh, hey, sis. You don't sound okay. Are you all right?"

"I almost told him. I almost did."

"What happened?" The noise behind Tory went quiet.

She must have left the loud party to listen better. Concern filled her voice.

"His real girlfriend came back just as I was about to throw all caution to the wind."

"What? Where did she come from? Did he know she was going to show up?"

"I don't think so. He sounded really surprised."

"What? So you were standing there and saw it all happen? What did she say when she saw you? Because there's no way in the universe she's hotter than you. I bet all her claws came out."

Morgan shook her head and told Tory about being upstairs. She didn't tell her about the present she threw at the back of the closet. "He's been writing her letters all this time."

"Uh, okay. That's not all that strange, is it? Why would you even know that?"

"I might have accidentally read one."

"And?"

"And there was a whole stack of them."

"You read a whole stack of love letters from the man you love to another woman? That's like drinking arsenic. Stupid move, Morg."

"Duh, no. I just saw the top one. I didn't even necessarily read it. Scanned. There's a difference."

"Whatever. Okay. So why were they sitting there? He didn't send them?"

Morgan hadn't asked herself that question. But it was beside the point. "I don't know."

"So what happened when she showed up? Was he ecstatic? Did they run off together?"

"Left me standing there like I never existed. He took off with her in his car after about two minutes."

"Probably so they could have a private conversation. You'd do the same thing. Maybe he's dumping her right now. That's a merciful thing to do—dump her privately. It shows character."

"That girl doesn't seem like the type he'd dump." Her eyes cleared a little and she went back up to speed when picturing this Brielle person together with Josh. It wasn't right. How could they be right when Josh and Morgan were so right?

"Why? He'd be certifiably insane to want whatever it is she's offering when he's got you in the palm of his hand—no, make that with his ring on your hand."

"He said she's smart, organized, has all her ducks in a row."

"So do you."

She did? Morgan never thought of herself as that type. She skirted around a stray deer in the road, barely tapping the brakes before hitting the gas again.

"Don't sound so stunned. You're totally organized and have all your ducks in a row. You attack life like a maniac, doing whatever it takes to get your degree. You've worked a horrible job to put yourself through one of the most expensive schools in the country, and then you're graduating and will no doubt get a job at one of the best accounting firms out there. Clarendon's job placement is basically a hundred percent, or it would be exactly a hundred percent except it had to tick down once for the guy who got in the waterskiing accident a day after graduation and couldn't work for a year. But otherwise, it's pretty much guaranteed you've got a blindingly bright future. Did this girlfriend go to Clarendon?"

"I don't think so. I think she was at State of Oregon Collegiate." Hadn't Josh told her that?

"Uh, see?"

"I don't care about that. All it means is I did better on a test for high school students and had a good day."

"Whatever. It means you are organized, smart, and have all your ducks in a row. Probably more than she does. I mean, wasn't she supposed to be gone for a year? What's she doing back? Did she get fired? Was it a real job or just one of those unpaid internships like I keep getting offered?"

"Tory, you know you're worthy of your hire. Besides, I don't want to start judging Brielle." Comparisons just injected pride into the equation, and that wouldn't fix anything. "If Josh was or is in love with her, I'm sure she's got to be a top notch person."

"Whatever. Men fall for the wrong woman all the time before they find the right one, which you most definitely are. Does his family like her?"

No. They didn't. Especially not Bronco, but that was definitely not a great gauge of a person's worth, or of Brielle's rightness for Josh.

"Because, after today with Rich's family, I can see for the first time something I never saw before."

"What's that?" Morgan didn't necessarily want to hear about perfect, fresh, uncomplicated love right now, especially when her own hopes were crumbling around her like the walls of Jericho at Brielle's single trumpet. "That family matters?"

"It's more than that. When a person gets married, it sets off a reaction."

Yeah, a chain reaction of never-ending complications and heartaches.

"It has a beginning, but if the elements really combine, then it's possible that what they've done by making that choice is create something that doesn't have an end. It's like that old saying. Anyone can count the seeds in a single apple, but only God can count the apples in a single seed."

Morgan did not need this pressure. She was already a pot on the stove with a lid about to explode with steam. "Don't lecture me on the sanctity of marriage, Tory. This day has been trauma, through and through, and I can't even imagine how it could get worse." She pressed the gas to the floor. Trees blurred past. She skidded around a slow car, a Land Rover like Josh's, and then sped until her tachometer was in the red before she upshifted. "You're the one who got me into this."

"I didn't sign your marriage certificate, Morgan."

"You talked me into moving in with him, after being the one who signed us up for the Seagram Scholarship."

"You never would have agreed to it if some part of you didn't know it was the right thing for you to do. And don't go telling me you are doing all this for me, anyway. I know you said you had to go to work at VeggieVictims so I could start school, and that you had to finish this year, do or die, so that I could go, but I told you a hundred times I never wanted to go. I'm perfectly content with doing hair and working at the theater. I'm happy. I like my life. I get to help people like Mrs. Reeves, giving her perms in my free time. If I'd been in school, I never would have met Rich, and he is quickly becoming the best part of my life. That's what I've been pushing you to realize—that Josh Hyatt is the best part of your life. Wake up and look around you. See the truth before you miss out on the biggest happiness ever handed to you on a silver platter. You kept your feelings so secret, and you're so shy and modest there's no way he could have guessed you're panting after him. You moved so slowly getting him to see how much you're in love with him, that now, if you're not careful, he's going to think you don't even care." Tory's voice dripped with exasperation, and she huffed. "Now, quit watching Formula One on TV and go get the man you love."

Tory never wanted to go to college? Morgan slowed a little. "You never wanted me to support you while you were in school?"

"No. And I don't even know why you had that idea. I'm a hairdresser. A dang good one. Books aren't my thing. Give up on that fantasy right now."

"He's already chosen. He picked Brielle." She slowed a little more. Trees stopped blurring.

"You don't know that."

"Oh, yes I—" The words clipped off in Morgan's throat when lights came flashing in her rear view mirror red and blue. A siren became audible as she pressed the brake. Wow, how long had that guy been following her? "Sorry, Tory. I have to, uh. I might be going to jail."

"We'll talk later, then."

"Bye."

***

"Your wife? What do you mean, your wife?"

Josh wanted to punch something. "A lot happened while you were gone."

"It sounds like it." Brielle removed her hand from his shoulder and crossed her arms over her chest. Josh decided now was not a good time to stop driving, so he kept on going down the coast. "What's she like? Is it her money that bought the mansion on the hill and this posh car and your china closet with the gilt-edge dishes? Did you find yourself a sugar-mama? Is she older? Some cougar who made it big and wanted a boy toy?"

"No. No, now stop that. It's nothing like that. She's a student. And like I told you, the house is being loaned to us by a friend of my mother's."

"Your mother is dead."

"My late mother's."

Brielle drummed her fingers on the dashboard of the car, clearly not appeased. "She's a student. And you're living together in that house. I see. When were you thinking of telling me this? It seems like something you should have led with, Josh. *Hi, Brielle, I'm glad to see you, but I'm married.* It's pretty big news. I would have appreciated a little heads up on that right when I arrived at your house on Christmas morning. And oh, nice. You left your wifey and came with me for a drive—on Christmas morning. No

311

wonder she was driving like a Formula One racer on meth when she passed us. Did you even tell her I came by? Did you even tell her about me? About our plans? What were you thinking was going to happen next?"

Brielle's voice was rising in pitch with each successive question she posed, each accusation creating a more pinching tone.

"Look, Brie. There's a very long explanation. And when you hear it, I'm pretty sure you're going to laugh..."

Brielle at this point didn't look like she'd find anything funny ever again as long as she lived. "Ha, ha. Amuse me."

"As for telling you, I was pretty sure your good friend Claire already had."

"Claire is getting married this week. Do you think she can talk about anything other than herself?" Brielle had a point, but still, in a way, Josh was relieved and bothered at the same time. "Josh, I thought we'd worked all this out before I went to Germany. I'm here now, just as we always planned."

"You never indicated to me that you were coming back at Christmas."

"You never indicated to me that you were going to marry a reckless driver as soon as I was out of sight. Which one is worse, Josh? Which?"

"You're getting really upset, and I think you should take a deep breath and let me explain." If she knew that there really was a good explanation, and that he'd done all this for her in the first place, she'd see. He was sure. "It's going to take some patience on your part."

"Patience! Patience! Josh, I have been nothing if not patient with you. Long years I have waited for you to get to this point, to where you're almost done with school, and we are almost able to finally be together. And you're what? Telling me you jumped the gun and jumped in bed with some woman? This is beyond patience you're asking of me right now."

312

Josh's stomach did several flips in succession. He'd seen Brielle get upset before—over small things, like not getting the table they'd reserved at the restaurant, or being seated in coach when they thought they'd upgraded to business class—but she'd never been agitated like this. He didn't know what to make of it—whether he should be flattered that she cared this much about her future with him, or whether she was just being unreasonable.

"Please, Brielle. Hear me out."

"Oh, I'm all ears," she said, but the way her knees pointed toward the door and her face looked out the window at the trees, she didn't seem like she'd care what he said next.

Josh took a deep breath as they came around a bend. "It all started when my grant got denied, and—"

He had to stop talking because what he saw next prevented words. He slowed way down to watch the unfolding horror.

Luckily, Brielle supplied them. "It looks like your wife won't be driving recklessly anywhere else on this festive day."

Josh watched with stomach clenched as a police officer clipped handcuffs on Morgan and pushed her head down to guide her into the back seat of his squad car, leaving her De Tomasa Mangusa stranded on the side of the road, its tires still smoking in the cold winter air.

Chapter Thirty

An hour and a half later, Josh pulled up at the police station. He'd made Brielle drive the Land Rover home while he took the Mangusa with his own key for it back to their garage. It was still Seagram's car, after all, and he couldn't leave it abandoned on the side of the road to let the police tow and impound it. Who knew Morgan had such a lead foot? Probably not even Morgan. Man, he must have really upset her to make her engine go that fast. A thousand apologies perched on his tongue, and he wasn't going to be able to utter a single one, not as long as he was still with Brielle.

A woman who drove like that might have serious rev in her own engines, he thought absently, and then forced himself back to the gravity of the situation.

"Hello, officer. I'm Josh Hyatt. I'm here about my wife Morgan Hyatt."

"Oh, the fast chick. I booked her."

"Has bail been set?"

"It's pretty high. Ten thousand."

"Dollars?" Josh's throat collapsed.

"Yes, but you only have to post ten percent of it and she goes free. If she doesn't show up for court, you forfeit the bond." The officer then explained the procedure for posting bond, a fact of life Josh never expected to have to learn, especially through bailing out Morgan, of all people.

After Josh had pulled out his wallet and noticed only twelve dollars decorated its folds, he made a desperate call to Chip. He hated asking, after everything his brother had already done for him lately. He started the call with a sheepish, "Merry Christmas," and then told him, "Morgan's in a bind. And so am I."

Unfortunately, Chip couldn't help him. He was maxed out credit-wise from opening his veterinary practice.

"Why don't you call Bronco?" Chip said.

"Bronco. Ha."

"It's Christmas. Even Ebenezer Scrooge softened up on Christmas."

"Ebenezer Scrooge had ten times the charm and heart and wit of Bronco Hyatt."

"Amen to that," muttered Brielle, who was sitting beside Josh in the orange plastic chairs of the police station waiting room. She understood Bronco's shortcomings better than anyone, having been the target of his vitriol more than once. Not that she wasn't equal to his attacks. She'd put him right back in his place, which was one of the reasons Josh had stuck up for her when Bronco went ballistic about Josh's plans to propose to her a couple of years ago. Bronco needed someone who could go toe to toe with him, not another person to just roll over and do what he said. Didn't he? Wasn't that what Bronco needed? Someone to put him in his place?

Morgan hadn't put him in his place; she'd let him be himself and not let it get under her skin.

"I'm not calling Bronco."

"I wish I could help you, man. I just haven't got it. Not even for Morgan. And I'd sell my kidney for that one."

Josh shot a sideways glance at Brielle, but it didn't seem like she'd heard the endorsement from Chip.

"Well, Merry Christmas, anyway. Thanks, brother."

Josh made a fist. This was ridiculous. What was Morgan thinking, going that fast? The officer put it this way: *Criminal speeding is eighty-five miles an hour. We clocked your wife at a hundred and six.* Brielle had choked a little.

Twenty minutes later, Josh still didn't know what to do. He mentally listed every person he dared ask, and it amounted to Sigmund Seagram and Bronco Hyatt. Seagram had already done far too much, and the debt they owed him was beyond ridiculous.

He broke down and dialed Bronco.

Ten minutes later, the money had been wired, and Morgan was presented at the double-paned Plexiglas door in a detainee jumpsuit. Dang, that woman made even that stupid orange thing look good. The officer had her sign some things, and then she received a plastic bag with her clothing, after which she left Josh's view, presumably to change back into her sweater and jeans.

"So, this is your wife." Brielle's voice was terse, her body a tight wire when Morgan returned.

"Morgan," was all Josh could say. He was having a hard time meeting either of their eyes. "The Mangusa is home already," was the only thing he dared say to her. Her eyes stared wide at him, all blue yet sorry. Flecks of black smattered the edge of her temple. She'd been crying.

I never meant to make her cry.

"Hi, Brielle," said Morgan, softly. "Thanks, Josh. I'm sorry for interrupting your day."

"Don't worry about it. Bronco posted the bail, anyway." He wasn't sure what to do. She looked so drained and helpless, like a lost baby deer. Instinct told him to put an arm around her, support her as they left the station, but logic told him that could both embarrass Morgan and tick off Brielle. He'd already seen Brielle ticked off today, and he'd rather not go through that again. "Let's just get you home." He said this low, trying to be comforting. "Did you have any personal effects still to pick up?"

Morgan just nodded, even more worried than before. "My phone and keys. Your mother's necklace and earrings."

At this, Brielle sighed heavily and took Josh's arm. "What? You're letting her wear your mother's jewelry? I am sorry, Josh, but this might be too much for me right now. I'll be waiting out in the car. No, never mind. I'll call a cab." She let go of his arm and curled up a little, her arms hugging herself. "Maybe I'll call you later, not sure. We're still on for New Year's Eve. I'll see you then." Her parting shot nailed him right in his heart, and probably Morgan's, too, even though Brielle fired it ignorantly.

Morgan looked up at him. "New Year's?" she whispered. He gave a slight nod, and Morgan spoke up, calling after Brielle's departing figure. "Brielle? It's really not fair you should be the one to take the cab. I'll call my sister. This was all my fault."

She pulled her phone from the bag the officer handed her and looked up at Josh. "Go." She was already dialing her sister, he could see.

Josh stood blinking for a second. Really? Morgan was telling him to go after Brielle? It was either the most callous thing or the most self-sacrificing thing she'd done for him so far in all the time he'd known her. He'd have to find out later which it was, although the black smear near her eye made him think it was the latter. Hope it was the latter. If so, how could any woman be so good?

"Brielle?" he hustled after her. "I'll give you that ride." Josh jogged out of the police station and bumped hard into the shoulder of none other than Paulie Bumgartner.

"Whoa, Josh Hyatt. What are you doing at the police station?" He snapped a quick succession of shots. "And who is this little firecracker you're chasing? Is it the fiancée you exiled to Europe so you could have the fiancée and the wife, too? Where's the blonde? Get too many women and you end up with problems, boy. Problems that end with the po-po."

"Brielle," Josh called, ignoring Paulie. "Let's get out of here."

"So! You're taking your old chicky in your new chicky's car. What class, Hyatt. All class all the time with your family." Clearly the Bum thought the Land Rover was

Morgan's, but Josh wasn't going to explain.

"Don't you have a family, Bumgartner? It's Christmas. Be there for them." Josh shuffled Brielle into the Land Rover and then hopped in the driver's side and roared away, grateful the lout hadn't seen Morgan come out of the station.

"What was that?"

"Paparazzi."

"Paparazzi! I thought you shook them." Brielle seemed more upset, even, by old Paulie's presence than by the whole meeting Morgan incident. "I'm really not in a position where I can have my photo posted anywhere." She looked anguished.

"Me, neither," Josh said, thinking about Morgan's feelings, her family's feelings, and Seagram's feelings—the angry and upset ones where Seagram felt like kicking him out of the Campus House and demanding repayment on the back rent, which Josh could obviously not pay.

Josh shot Morgan a quick text: *Paprazzi alert. Stay put until Paulie vacates the premises.*

"No, I mean seriously. This could get me in real trouble. If you see that Paulie person again, promise me you'll give him a fake name for me. Tell him I'm your cousin from Canada. Anything." Suddenly her hurt from earlier had morphed into this strange panic. She'd turned like the weather on an island.

She was being extra paranoid about this, and Josh noticed a growing irritation inside himself. Possibly her panic about Paulie Bumgartner had something to do with her embassy job and going deep cover over the past semester while she was in Germany, but Josh wouldn't know since she never *read him in* on any of what was going on in her life.

"What exactly went on with you over the past several months? Were you being stalked by terrorists, or what?"

"No! Hardly. And I really don't know how you have

any business asking me for the intricate details of how I spent my time, when you kept a *marriage* from me." So she was still furious. Not that he could blame her.

However, this was a little thick. "Look, you're the one who laid down the law. You were explicit, telling me not to contact you."

"I never said anything so cut and dried as that."

"That's how I remember it."

"You didn't even email me." She looked up at him with hurt in her eyes.

"Because you said not to." He hadn't meant to hurt her, obviously.

"I was sure you'd see through something like that. I wouldn't ever want to be completely separated from you, Josh. We're each other's better half. I'm yin to your yang. We are the push and pull. I didn't want you to cut me out of your life completely, certainly not like this." She hiccupped, and curled up a little, pulling her knees up onto her seat and hugging them to her chest as she looked out the window. She looked smaller.

"I never cut you out of my life." Part of him wanted to reach for her, but his arms wouldn't move. "I married her for you."

"You do know how wrong that sounds." She looked over at him at last.

"Of course I do. I'm not a fool." He exhaled deeply. "What happened is I lost my student funding. Bronco makes way too much money, and whether or not he claims me as his son, the IRS claims me as his dependent." He turned off the highway back into Starry Point.

"Not if he doesn't claim you on his taxes."

"Oh, yes. Even then. Believe me, I did the research, made every legal appeal, took the case to the limit. It was a dead end."

"So get a loan. People get loans." The practical Brielle resurfaced and she released her knees.

"Not me. Bronco knows too many people, blocks too many roads."

"That's persecution."

"That's what I said."

"So get a job. Pay for college."

Josh chuckled mirthlessly. "At Clarendon's per-semester costs? It's a first class education, but it comes at first class ticket pricing. I was already admitted, and I couldn't let that go to waste. You said so yourself."

"They do have the top foreign policy program in the nation." Brielle brightened a little. "Are you just loving your professors? Are you genuflecting when they walk into the room? Because once, at a seminar at State of Oregon Collegiate, I went to a lecture by Clarendon's Dr. Hammerhill, and afterward I went up to him and he invited me and three other students for coffee, and I think that little trip to Starbucks might have changed my course of career forever. Is he one of your professors? I've been wanting to ask how you're loving your classes."

How he was loving them? It was hard to measure something that small, except maybe micrograms. Enduring them, yes. Mostly. But loving them, not so much. "We can discuss that later. What you need to know right now is that you have Morgan to thank for my being able to attend class at all."

At the mention of Morgan's name, Brielle's face blanked out again. "I can't imagine."

"The only way to get free of that noose of being claimed as a dependent by Bronco was to get married."

"So you proposed to Morgan and are living happily ever after in a mansion."

"So Morgan—" He was trying to remember whether he'd suggested the marriage or she had. It was Morgan, right?

Brielle's ire rose again. "Morgan heard your Hyatt name and figured you were the path to riches, and since she looks like *super* Barbie, even in an orange jumpsuit, you thought, why the heck not, and hooked up with her before she knew what good she was to you, or that you were the disenfranchised son of a millionaire."

This was pretty sour, even for the situation. "I wish you'd just listen instead of jumping to conclusions, but fine. I know this is a bitter pill to swallow so believe what you want, but Morgan is a nice person, and she gave up a lot to help me out. Frankly, she was in a similar situation herself, and had ended up losing all funding with just one year to go. It was mutually beneficial."

"Oh, I can just imagine the *mutual* benefits."

"Let your imagination stop right there, Brielle. The plan was," he hesitated before correcting himself, " —*is* to annul." But even as it came out it felt strange, foreign.

"Well, what's taking you so long?"

Yeah, what? The hurt in Brielle's voice made him wince. He had to think a moment of how to phrase it, and he had to get the image of Morgan sitting at the piano singing Dean Martin songs out of his head, of her laughing as he sucked imaginary snake venom out of her ankle, of her falling asleep after he worked the kink out of her neck. Finally he answered, "There's a rule if the marriage is annulled, any grant has to be repaid immediately and in full, so we were forced to wait out the school year."

"And forced to just move in together to wait it out. In your mom's buddy's mansion." Now she'd gone from hurt to a little angry, and he couldn't really blame her.

Truthfully it *was* kind of special since his mom's legacy was involved, but there was no real way to explain the quicksand that created the living arrangements. "Believe me, Brielle." He was pulling up at the front of the house, and Brielle sat for a second in her seat, just breathing.

"I want to believe you, Josh. Really, I do. I would have wanted to a lot more before I caught a glimpse of her." Brielle rolled her eyes and muttered something about peroxide. "I just wish you had trusted me with this information. You could have told me all of it as it was happening."

He had written it all, but he couldn't send the letters. "That's just it, Brie. I'm telling you now. I'm trusting you. Even telling you this much is a huge measure of trust. Can you see how much trouble I could be in if this got back to the powers that be? We'd be in up to our eyes for what's been going on. If I didn't trust you with my whole reputation and my whole future, I'd never be telling you any of this. It's you who's got to trust me."

Brielle sighed and looked out at the road. "I do trust you, Josh." Finally she turned to him, more vulnerable than she'd been even when she mentioned New Year's earlier. "Look, I'm sorry. I'm sorry for getting all upset about this. Frankly, this whole day isn't going how I envisioned it. This whole month has been a lot harder than I can express, so this reaction isn't *all* about you or today or this thing between us. I'm just—yeah. I wanted things to be so happy for us."

"Me, too." Josh meant that.

"Really? Because, if that's true, I want to believe everything you told me is the way you said, and that I *can* trust you, and that things really will work out for us." Her eyes pleaded with him. "They will, won't they, Josh? Just like we'd planned forever and ever?" This slightly broken side of Brielle caught him by the throat. She had folded her arms around her knees again, and she was hugging herself like she had to keep herself together, to keep from falling apart.

"How long are you planning to be in town?"

She looked at her feet. "My return ticket to Germany is open-ended."

Open. So she didn't have an exact date of leaving. What did she want from him? What could he say right now that was true to her, as well as to himself, and to Morgan? It

322

wrapped ropes on each quarter of him, and each pulled a different direction at full horsepower, threatening to tear him apart. "I didn't mean to hurt you, I swear."

Her cheek tugged to the side, a smirk of despair. "I'm going to think about this for a couple of days. I was trying to think of ways to get out of the wedding preparation so you and I could spend this week together, but now, I'm thinking distance would be better—for me." She bit both her lips together. "I know you've always said you wanted to be with me, and I've pretty much kept that on my back burner for years, assuming there would be a time. I really thought this would be our time."

Really? What about school? This was a curve ball she was throwing him. He still had another full year after this one—plus retaking Cold War Relations—before he'd be at the point where he thought Brielle expected him to be for things to move forward. "Really? Even without my finishing my degree?"

"Well, I—" Brielle's voice cracked a little, but she collected herself. "I just need you right now, Josh. Germany was beautiful, but not every aspect of it was as hunky dory as I may have intimated." She swallowed hard and blinked a lot of times fast. She'd never been emotional like this. He reached to her, putting a hand on her shoulder.

"Brielle. I swear, it was all for you. Every choice."

Brielle nodded, saying nothing and put her hand on the door. "I'll just dive into Claire's wedding appointments until New Year's. Meet me at the reception. Oh, and I left your gifts on the table in there. You can open them if you want to. Or just...whatever." Hurt and confusion marred her face. Even her springy curls looked a little wilted. They tugged at him. She got out quickly and headed to her rental car.

"Wait!" he said. "Give me thirty seconds. There's something I need you to have." He dashed up the stairs and was back down in a few seconds, panting. It might be

323

the wrong move, but he had to prove to her that despite the appearance of everything, he hadn't been disloyal, he hadn't forsaken her, no matter which way things ended up between them from here on out.

"Here." Through the window of her car, he handed her the stack of letters he'd been keeping. "It's proof. You deserve to at least know what my intentions were. Read them."

She glanced at them and then set them on the seat beside her. Staring at the road ahead she said, "I'll see you Friday." And she drove off.

This was not how he imagined their first reunion after Brielle's return from Germany.

A text came in, an apology from Brielle, he hoped.

Morgan: *Paulie Whoever is still outside the station. I'm staying put like you said, but...*

Josh restarted his car and went back to the station to pick up his wife.

***

Morgan knew she would have to treat this in a businesslike manner. No more pretending this was her real marriage or that she and Josh could make this work. Not with Super-girlfriend back in the picture and dropping in and whisking Josh off for long drives down the coast.

After a full hour of waiting for the paparazzo to take off and go find some Christmas cheer elsewhere so she could call Tory and get her ride home, Morgan finally decided to text Josh. While he was coming, she figured out what to say, and (luckily) Paulie melted away into the afternoon fog.

"Josh, this is serious." As soon as they were out in his car, she launched into the planned words, only then realizing they mirrored the last words she'd spoken to him — *I'm getting serious about you* — before the juggernaut of

324

Brielle's German blitzkrieg hit. It made her stutter a second, tripped suddenly by the nerves that suddenly resurged, the old familiar fright accompanied by the Conversation Coma, just as she'd feared.

"I know. And I'm sorry." Josh put the car in gear and handed her a pair of sunglasses to wear, apparently to go incognito, as if that would prevent damage that was already done, but which at least gave her enough irritation to get over the hurdle of being tongue-tied.

"Not about Brielle. I'm happy she came back to you, if she's what you want. But putting that aside, we've got a much, much bigger problem. That Paulie fellow got pictures of you and Brielle together. He will publish them, and am I wrong to think it could cause us some problems? I don't mean *us* us." Morgan waved her hand between herself and Josh. This conversation felt like tightening screws in her soul. "I mean between us and Seagram."

Josh's shoulders slumped. He slowly shook his head from side to side. "I told Brielle about our setup."

"You what?" Morgan sat up straight. "I thought we agreed—"

"I know. I know." Josh looked genuinely miserable. He should be. This whole house of cards was coming tumbling down all around them. "It was a weak moment."

"Couldn't you have just waited until after the annulment? Is she that impatient?" Morgan suspected Brielle might be a very impatient person, from how she looked so high strung during the two minutes they'd been in the same room at the police station. "What's left of this whole scheme? Six months? We're almost halfway through this nightmare."

She didn't mean to imply that being around Josh was a nightmare, but it came out, and truthfully, most of this day fit that description. He wasn't making it any easier with this revelation. Morgan had had to tell Tory—and Josh had agreed to that up front. They'd needed her help with the

325

photos, the move to Josh's apartment for the filming, all that. But now he'd told his brother, his sister-in-law, his girlfriend. "Who are you going to inform next—that Bum person with the camera? Go ahead. Hand him a fifty-page story about our misdeeds."

For the first time since she'd become friends with Josh, Morgan was really, truly mad at him. It didn't matter that the anger was fueled by the hurt of his abandoning her at the first second his old girlfriend came into view. Seriously, how could he endanger her like this? Especially right after she'd been stuck at the police station, where she was probably getting a preview of her future if the police found out about their fraud.

Josh hadn't spoken for a full mile. Finally he said, "It's been a nightmare?"

This question touched a chord in her, plucking at the string of her heart, and she exhaled. "No. No, that's not what I meant." They were close to campus now, nearly home. Morgan didn't know what she'd find there—maybe Brielle had moved in. She'd left enough junk on their kitchen table to be luggage. Maybe Brielle was setting up house in the kitchen, making Josh's Christmas dinner, or worse, waiting for him upstairs in the master. Ooh, what would she think of the photo above the bed? Morgan only spared a fraction of a second picturing the girl's face when she first caught sight of that picture. Yikes.

But while there was photo evidence of their relationship, Morgan knew it was all faked. And she knew what had to happen next.

"Josh, Mr. Seagram will see the photos of you and Brielle. I know because he saw the last photos of you and me with that mean-spirited caption. We are basically employed by him, and we've breached his trust. He's a church-going man, and he has all kinds of high ideals and standards, and we are supposed to be his shining examples. While it's obviously not fair to us for him to expect our

326

perfection, we are being handsomely paid for it, and living a lie. Frankly, this is not the woman I want to be." Saying it aloud gave Morgan a sense of empowerment, and she finally said what had been on her mind since the police station. Well, since before she got pulled over, actually. "Can we please not go home?" Morgan didn't want to see what was waiting there, anyway. "Can we please just go straight to Mr. Seagram's?"

Josh gripped the steering wheel tighter and then loosened his fingers a few times. Finally he gave a slight nod and made a turn at the next corner.

It was time to come clean.

Chapter Thirty-One

It was with heavy steps that Josh walked around to the passenger side of the Land Rover to let Morgan out at Sigmund Seagram's circular driveway. He pulled the one personal key he had off the key chain, ready to return the vehicle and house key, and then call his water treatment coworker George to see if he could couch surf at his place tonight. Christmas night, geez. Mrs. George, whoever she was, would love that, no doubt. At least Morgan had a place to crash at her sister's. She could go back to life as before, probably even with roller skates involved.

It had all been a nice glimpse into ease and luxury, but he wouldn't want it for too long. He may turn into Bronco.

"You okay? Do you want to tell him, or should I?" He helped Morgan out of the car. Her mouth pressed into a grim line.

"We should each tell our version of the story — the truth, of course. But before we go in, I have to give you something." She looked up at him with the blue eyes wide that got him every time. Soon, her warm hand had touched his, and she pressed something into his palm. He looked down and opened his hand.

"The ring?" An arrow shot through his heart. He hadn't expected this as a consequence.

"Brielle was right. I can't be wearing your mother's jewelry. It's almost as big a breach to dishonor your mother this way than it is for us to be play-acting and defiling the sanctity of marriage by what we've done."

"Wait a minute. We never once defiled the sanctity of

marriage." He had to put his foot down here. "We were trapped into this by government regulations, and you know it."

"We made a mockery of its sacred meaning, Josh, and *you* know that." She was reaching up and unlatching the necklace, and then she removed the earrings and pressed them into his hand. "I did really love these. They were beautiful. Thank you. They meant the world to me."

Maybe it was just Josh's wishful listening, but he was sure she put emphasis on *the world*. He should ask her what she meant by that, whether she meant she loved him. He opened his mouth to do so, but the front door swung open and there stood Sigmund Seagram in his full bulk of glory in a red business suit. It must be his idea of festive clothes. Eccentric millionaires had eccentricity in several facets of their lives, apparently.

"Well, I'm honored! Thank you so much for thinking of a lonely old man on a Christmas Day evening. Come in, come in!"

Guilt almost buckled Josh's knees, but Morgan pulled him forward, obviously doing the trudge of shame herself.

"I'm sorry, Mr. Seagram, but we are not here on a joyous errand," she said. "I'm afraid we have some very bad news."

Seagram ushered them into his living room, where a fire crackled and the tree from last week was decked with even more ornaments than before, if possible. "Whatever it is, it can wait until after hot cocoa."

Josh knew that to be impossible. "I'm afraid not, sir." It wasn't going to result in a friendly cup of anything, if Josh's prediction held.

"Well, then. This sounds serious."

There was that word again. Morgan had used it twice already today—first, in a way that made his stomach drop into his jeans, and then in a way that'd made his blood run cold. Yes, this was a serious day. Seagram directed them to sit on that blasted narrow love seat, where they couldn't help but touch legs. Josh did not need that distraction right now. Apparently, neither did Morgan. She perched at the edge of the couch and shot Josh a worried look— the lost baby deer face he knew too well and was a sucker for every time. He rose to protect her.

"Sir, we have not been what we've seemed."

"A happily married couple of college students? You've been unhappy? Or you're not married?"

"Uh, not that sir." Because they'd been married, and they'd been happy—at least Josh had. Josh didn't know how to frame it, so he finally plunged in. Man, how many times was he going to have to recount his sins today? Maybe Morgan was right and he should just hand Paulie Bumgartner a typed version so the whole world could read it for themselves. *Joshua Hyatt Lives a Lie*. That could be his headline, although he was sure Paulie would conjure up something more salacious than that, like *Loser Son of Hyatt Holdings Defrauds American Taxpayers*. Yeah, that was more like it.

Josh sank onto the sofa as he explained the whole saga of the fraud, seeing hurt grow in Seagram's eyes as the story unfolded.

Seagram said nothing for a long time, just nodded.

Morgan, Josh saw when he finally finished and dared look at her, was crying silently, tears wetting her whole face. He reached for a Kleenex from the box on the end table and handed it to her. She only twisted it between her hands.

I really never meant to make her cry.

Finally, Seagram heaved a sigh. "As I've said before, marriage is something so dear to my heart that I'll go to extraordinary lengths using my time, energy and a lot of resources to promote it in any way I can. This seemed like a far better use of money than some TV ad about it or a billboard. And it would have been."

The guilt punched Josh's gut again, while Seagram went on.

"And I do think it still could be. I'm not a CEO of a large company for nothing. I ask the right questions." He looked straight in Josh's eye, which took some doing, since for Josh meeting Seagram's eye right now was acid pouring on him in the chemistry lab. "And the right question is, *do you love each other?*"

Morgan spoke for the first time since they sat down, and it came out a strained whisper. "Josh has someone. She was in his life before—"

"I know all that," Seagram said.

Seagram knew all that? What was that supposed to mean? Had he vetted them so thoroughly? If so, how—? The turmoil in Josh's insides spun donuts.

"But," Seagram went on, "that doesn't answer the question. *Do you love each other?*"

Josh sat silent. Maybe it was his male ego, but he didn't want to be the first to answer. If she was going to say no, he didn't want to be the loser saying yes. He glanced at her glistening face and saw she was searching his eyes. That twang in his heart plucked again. He swallowed, but there might still be some of that bagel somewhere lodged in his throat.

"Morgan?" Seagram turned to her, and Josh fought the instinct to jump between her and her accuser. "Do you want to field this one?"

Before today's massive meltdown, he would have put odds at fifty-fifty that she'd answer yes, especially after how sweetly she slept after he tucked her in bed last night, or how thoroughly she kissed him on the stairs. But now—well, she'd been pretty furious with him outside a few minutes ago. A glance told him her chin visibly trembled, and really, that woman had been through a lot today. He'd put her through some of it. Most of it.

Sometimes we get mad at people we love. Josh brushed the

331

thought away. *People we care nothing for do not merit emotional response.* The thought persisted and expanded, and he shoved that one aside, too, but not before he allowed a fraction of it to lodge and tell him he still had some odds better than a long shot that Morgan had a bit of love for him.

Love! That couldn't be the case, could it? What kind of an inquisition was this, anyway? Sure, she'd been friendly, kissed him, even when she woke up beside him on the couch, kissed him back when he went all *gross* on her yesterday before the cameras came, got him a present, kept dinners in the microwave for him, sang with him, messed around, acted happy when she saw him again after he'd gone AWOL for a few days. Evidence pointed to the possibility that she liked him, certainly cared for him, and could let her blood rise for him when he pushed her into it. But *love?*

He had to remind himself to exhale while he waited for her to answer Seagram.

Which she didn't.

Seagram cleared his throat. "Neither of you is answering." He slapped both his legs with his palms and stood up. "Well, then it seems we have come to a point where a decision must be made."

Josh almost opened his mouth to protest that it was too soon. They had some discussing to do first, but Seagram was off and running.

"If you're not in love and are intent on getting that annulment you're planning on, I will not prosecute you for fraud—because you came to me first."

Josh exhaled in relief. He'd been sure that Seagram would send them to court, possibly on criminal charges. It looked like Morgan had seen this possibility, as she crumpled against the sofa and pushed the back of her hand against her mouth. Shah—she'd already been to jail once today and probably had no interest in going back.

"I'm going to give you the benefit of the doubt—meaning I assume you're being silent because you sincerely don't know the answer to the question." Seagram paced the length of the small room, wringing his hands. "I'm not a monster, but I don't like it when someone abuses my good will. For that reason, I'll give you a time limit—say, a week—to come up with a definite answer to my question. Once you've made your choice, though, I want you to see it through: meaning, you stop pretending one way or another; either be man and wife for real or else don't spend another night under my roof, or my reputation, as liars."

The edict hit Josh with a thud. A week?

"Oh, I'll just be lenient. Make that until the end of the year." Seagram swung around and looked them in the face. Normally that would sound like a long time, but this was Christmas Day. "I'll need your answer by the morning of January first."

Morgan let out a little hiccupping sob and said, "Thank you, Mr. Seagram. You're too good to us."

"Yes, I am." He frowned. "Now, get out of here before I change my mind."

Josh palmed the car keys he'd intended to hand over, but Seagram eyed them. "Don't think about making some kind of a scene of returning my gifts unless you're sure, a hundred percent sure, you want to dissolve this family unit under the law and in the eyes of God."

Dissolve a family unit? Josh's mouth went dry. He'd never considered what he and Morgan shared that way. He shot Morgan a look to see what her reaction was to this phrase, but she only looked exhausted. He should take her home.

"Thank you, Mr. Seagram. So much." She went to Seagram and gave him a hug. Josh heard her whisper in a tiny, tired voice, "I'm so sorry."

"Me, too," Seagram whispered back.

Well, that made three of them.

Chapter Thirty-Two

Morgan chewed her thumbnail as Josh drove her toward home. "Thanks. I couldn't speak." The anger at him from earlier had drained, along with all her other emotional energy. Today had taken a serious toll on her. A Christmas to remember. She sighed.

"That's okay." He seemed more somber than even before. She wanted to rest a hand on his arm to reassure him that she wouldn't let him be prosecuted, she'd do whatever it took, but she didn't dare, not after his deafening silence at the question of whether he loved her. Couldn't he have even said *sure, maybe a little* and let her exhale?

But he hadn't. "I guess you can drop me off somewhere and then you can go wherever Brielle is." *Please say she's not at our house.* There she went, thinking of it as their own house together, which it wasn't, and may not be after another week unless she could help him see the light about her. What good would it do now to tell him how she really felt? Maybe some, so maybe she would—after she found out where Brielle was staying.

"She went to Claire's."

"Oh." Morgan had full recollection of Claire. "Claire. With the fangs."

"That's the one."

Wonderful. Morgan's stomach growled audibly. She hadn't eaten in so long that starvation sapped her energy and ability to deal with everything that had been hitting her in wave after wave.

"You need food."

"Everything's closed. It's Christmas."

"Not everything. Didn't you ever watch that movie about the BB gun? You'll shoot your eye out, kid? If so, then you know we can get a nice dinner of Chinese food even today."

It was too thoughtful, and she pulled a smile as he pulled around a corner and headed into Starry Point's business district to the Golden Dragon Palace, where they were playing "Here Comes Santa Claus" on a loop the entire time she ate her crispy fried duck.

"This is so great. Thanks for dinner."

"I guess this is our first date."

"Oh, is that what this is?" Morgan asked, lifting her stir-fried button mushrooms with chopsticks.

"It has to be." Josh shrugged. "You heard the man. We have one week to experience a whirlwind courtship and decide whether we are going to stay in the mansion or go to jail."

"He said he wouldn't send us to jail."

"We didn't get it in writing."

"Oh." Morgan's appetite vanished as her blood drained to her feet.

"Oh, I'm not saying he will prosecute. But I think the only reason he let us off so easily is he held out hope."

"What about you, Josh?" Morgan ratcheted up her courage. "Do you have any hope?" Morgan couldn't believe the question had escaped her mouth, even though it had been poised there in some form or other for the past several weeks, if not months. "I mean, uh—" She started to backtrack. "I mean, you're saying we should try?"

"Well, I'm saying dating you is better than jail and a criminal record for fraud."

"Thanks a lot."

"I'm sure you feel the same about me."

He had no idea how she felt about him—mostly

335

because she'd never done a blooming thing to let him know. Sure, she'd kissed him, but guys could detach physical affection and deeper emotion more easily than women could, or at least more easily than Morgan could.

"Let's just say I'm game. Let's give this a whirl." She twirled her chopsticks to inject fun, but it felt hollow. Then the brick wall loomed between them again, and Morgan had to ask. "But what about Brielle? She's here. You're here. There's no way you can just, you know—"

"Brielle is booked for the week, until New Year's Eve, actually. She's part of Claire's wedding party, and she won't be a factor."

What? Not even a factor? "Uh, I don't know if I can believe that. Of course she'll be a factor."

Josh was quiet for a moment, and finally he said, "I'll do everything I can to keep her from being a factor, Morgan. There's a lot on the line—for all of us."

That was for sure. "And what am I supposed to do?"

"You're supposed to ask me to call the water treatment plant and get the week off, and then I'll tell you it's not a problem because someone else claimed all the shifts to get holiday pay of overtime, so I'm scheduled off from now until New Year's."

"Really?" This news made Morgan brighten for the first time in hours. "Well, what do you want to do?"

"Sky dive."

"No."

"Water ski?"

"In this weather? Where? Ensenada? I hear Mexico isn't very safe right now." Morgan could just picture the drug cartels kidnapping them both and leaving them in a Mexican prison for no reason other than Josh was the son of a millionaire and demanding ransom. *Bronco might pay for mine and not Josh's. Ha.* "If you could have your heart's desire, how would you spend five free days?" Morgan knew how she'd spend hers: stretched out on the sofa, watching a few movies, ordering take-out, reading a book she chose herself, going for a few walks on the beach with someone who could make good conversation.

Josh rubbed his chin. He'd cleared his whole plate of General Tso's Chicken. "My heart's desire, huh?" He pulled a little smile. "Much as I like the idea of Ensenada with you, you're probably right."

He liked the idea of Ensenada with her. That was a good sign.

"So?"

"So, I'm afraid I'll sound boring." He opened his fortune cookie but didn't read the paper, just crumpled it onto his plate.

"Say it anyway. Honestly, I swear I won't think anything sounds boring. I'm too exhausted from the stress of finals and school and getting the house ready for those cameras and—" She'd better not say wondering whether Josh would finally take her as his wife.

"That's exactly where I'm at. My heart of hearts needs a complete veg out."

"Oh, not like that awful diner that tried to beat me into beet borscht."

"Oh, no. No, not at all. I mean like become a vegetable, a couch potato. Although, is a potato a vegetable at all? Or is it a starch?"

"Root vegetable." She knew that one. "And nothing sounds better to me. We could, say, get a really nice vacation home— hey, we happen to have one— with a lovely housekeeper— got one of those, too— and a stocked pantry— check, check, check— and just sit by the fire, watch some movies...talk..." Was she being too forward by saying the talk part when she knew she meant make out on the couch?

Josh apparently didn't think so. "I'd like to talk. Maybe we could hit the beach. You could show me about the agates."

His mention of the beach reminded her: this was a special week of the year on the Oregon coast. "Winter is the best time to find agates," she said absently while searching her mind for whether or not she'd seen a pair of binoculars somewhere in Siggy's Campus House.

Yeah, this might end up working out just fine.

***

"What I can't believe is that they didn't impound my car." Morgan forged ahead of him on the trail, and Josh got a full view of her rear view as they went. It made his backpack a little lighter but not much.

"What I can't believe is that you're asking me to hike up this steep outcropping when you promised me a week of doing absolutely nothing. Bait and switch, girl!" To be fair, she'd let him sprawl on the sofa watching cop dramas for the past twenty-four hours, bringing him little snacks and playing with his hair. He'd almost kissed her once, but he didn't want to let things get murky. He had an important decision to make and he didn't want to get kiss-drunk. Morgan's kisses weren't just intoxicating, they were inebriating. "What's in this thing, anyway? An anvil?"

"Two. But I'm sure you're manly enough for it. I've seen your triceps and your pectorals."

"You have?" She had? "When?"

Morgan laughed—and it shocked Josh, because it was that high, lilting flirt-laugh he'd heard once or twice before, but never for something he'd said. It penetrated him. He'd have to see if he could elicit it again.

"If you don't remember, then I'm not telling."

He reached out and smacked the back of her leg. "When have you ever seen me with my shirt off?"

"I have photo-documented evidence of them—right over our bed."

Then he remembered the whole swimsuit photo shoot.

338

She called it our bed.

"And there was that other time."

"What other time?" Had she been spying on him?

"Uh, the closet?"

Oh. The closet. That first morning they slept at Seagram's, when he'd caught her in just her towel, back when he'd been willing to flirt with her, thinking no harm could come of it, and he'd given her the eye while he took his time flexing as he put on his shirt. He was such a dork.

But she'd noticed. Heh-heh. And remembered. So it'd worked. Yeah, he was a dork. A dork who had a ruby ring in his pocket, still burning a circle in the skin of his hip. She'd given it back when she thought it meant nothing, he understood, but it had pained him more than he wanted to admit even to himself. Every morning he slipped it into his jeans pocket for some unknown reason. For a second, he'd considered arguing with her when she'd returned the necklace and earrings — those weren't part of a sham; they were a gift freely given for all he'd put her through the past few months, and for how good of a sport she'd been through it all. But he hadn't had the heart to delineate the two gifts so starkly at the time, and now, a few days had gone by. Fun days, but they'd stretched long as the hours had been filled with random conversations about childhood and favorite foods and dream vacations and arguing about whether the fifth or the seventh *Star Wars* movie was better. Morgan Elise Clark Hyatt was a *Star Wars* junkie. Who'd have guessed?

And they shared a birthday — in about a week. She'd probably bake him a cake, but he'd have to think of something big to do for her in return. *Would they be together to celebrate it?*

"Okay, so you're right. I'm manly enough for two anvils." Luckily, they reached the summit she was aiming for just then, before he started really huffing and puffing. He set down the bag, right on his toe. "Ow."

"Oh, are you okay?" Instantly she swung around to check on him, concern in her eyes. Those blue eyes. They got him every time. Dang.

"Fine. I'll be fine." He did a fake manly shoulder straightening. "But I'm going to need sustenance. Is there food in here?" He started zipping open the bag. He'd been the recipient of Morgan's planned outings before.

"Yes, but we need to catch the sight before the sun sets." Morgan scooted him away from the bag with a swing of her hip. It bumped his shoulder, and he toppled into sitting position. "Here they are." She produced a pair of binoculars. "For whale watching. I haven't done this since I was a kid—my mom used to bring us out here sometimes, and I'd always argue with Tory about which of us saw more mama whales and which saw more baby whales. Now I know neither of us did—at least not in the December watch."

"Why not?"

"Because the mamas go to the Gulf of California to give birth in the warm waters. The whales going by are pregnant mother whales and, er, non-pregnant male whales."

She was so cute sometimes. It seemed like the very word pregnant made her blush. Some people could make the whole idea of pregnancy sound clinical; others made it sound coarse or undesirable; Morgan somehow made it seem holy.

There he went again with his angel imagery for her. Morgan wasn't an angel. She was a human, definitely. She had her faults and weaknesses. But she was probably the closest thing he'd met to an angel in this life.

The question was, did he want an angel? Or did he want a girl on fire? Not to say Brielle was some kind of devil—she wasn't, by any means, but she had a flame of serious intensity, one that could burn the unsuspecting moth's wings. He brushed Brielle from his mind. He'd promised to not let her be a factor, as if that were possible, but he at least would try.

He helped Morgan spread out a blanket and then he sat beside her, when he noticed she was shivering. He unzipped his jacket and stretched it around her shoulders in hopes of warming her. "Oh! Look!" She'd been adjusting the binoculars, aiming them out at the water. Now, with them still on the strap around her neck, she held them out for him to look through. "Can you see them?"

Josh leaned over to peer through the lenses. Her hair was sweet in his nostrils, the vanilla mint of the white Tic Tacs again. "Uh, I don't—oh! Wow. Yeah, I see them!" There, some distance off, he could see the dark skiffs of their backs just above the water's surface. One, two, five, nine. "There are dozens."

Morgan's voice sounded happy. "Every year during this week, thousands migrate past here. We caught them just right. And the water is calm, so they're easy to spot. It's the perfect day."

It did kind of feel like the perfect day. No work. It was unseasonably warm. He had a pretty girl with great-smelling hair at his side, the sun was shining, and he was watching whales. How many guys out there could say they were having as good a day as that?

Josh gave her back the binoculars so she could look, too. "That's amazing. Thanks for showing me this. I've never seen them before."

"Never?"

"My mom did blackberry picking, but not whale-watching. We were in Portland, so it's farther inland."

Morgan offered him the binoculars. "Then you should look again. It's something to let seep into your soul." Her eyes were bright, and she was smiling. For a long moment he stared at it, letting her smile seep into his soul. It felt good.

***

On the drive back, Morgan knew she had to bring up a topic with Josh, to thank him for something. It was going to be a little rocky, getting it to come out right, if at all, but she wanted him to know how much she appreciated something.

"Josh?" Her voice might have trembled. "I have to thank you."

"For being manly and carrying the anvils? Sure. Anytime, Morgan. I'm your circus strong man."

"Yes, you are." She pictured him in one of those wrestling onesies with a handlebar mustache and one of her stupid-laughs escaped, the high-pitched kind that made her embarrassed.

He reached over and put a hand on her leg, a smile in his eyes. It was a good thing he hadn't smiled with his teeth, too, because they were her weakness. She had to keep focused—and keep him focused.

"Actually, I wanted to thank you for being a gentleman, and for respecting me enough to let us figure out the answer to Seagram's question a real way."

"What do you mean?"

"I mean, a lot of people say the only way to find out if you love someone is to sleep with them. And when Seagram asked his pointed question the other day, my mind jumped to that immediately."

"It did?" Josh simultaneously gulped and brightened, shooting her a look she couldn't misread. He soon collected himself again, though. "Right. I mean, that's the way people think these days."

"And since we're technically married, it would probably be a logical thing."

"It would." He agreed almost too readily.

But Morgan wasn't done. "I guess I appreciate your willingness to get to know me—the real me—before

342

insisting on the other way of, you know, getting closer."

Josh nodded, and Morgan silently exhaled in relief. She'd done it. She'd said what she meant to say, and it came out pretty much the way she'd hoped it would.

"I'm not against that way, Morgan. But you're right. In our case it would complicate things too much. We still have to make a major decision, and one choice would require staying away from each other's beds so our annulment could go through. Otherwise, messy divorce, Seagram looking even worse, losing other people's trust, you not being the woman you want to be for the man you'll ultimately love." Josh kept his eyes on the road through all this, and what he said made perfect sense. All the reasons.

Why did they come accompanied by a poison dart?

"You're so right," was all she could say. And then her mouth was talking before her head was thinking. "But the other choice might be all right, too. I mean, we *are* legally wedded."

Josh's head whipped toward her, and the wheel jerked a bit on the car. Dishes from the picnic lunch clinked in the bag on the back seat of the Mangusa. "Trust me, I've given that some careful thought as well."

He had?

***

Two entire seasons of a classic cop drama on streaming video later, on a TV they found in the attic and dragged to the library, and sixty-three rounds of poker in which Morgan beat him fifty times, Morgan and Josh emerged from their television and snack food coma into the light of the beach on Thursday afternoon.

"You really are the poker player you claimed you were."

Morgan blushed at the memory of her flirtatious challenge on the day they paid their tuition. "You

343

remember that?"

"I remember a lot of things." Josh raised an eyebrow. "Like how irritated I got when other guys gave you the once-over."

"I recall *you* giving me the once-over more than once."

"Maybe so, but it was my right." He helped her over a boulder and they headed down onto Cannon Bay's beach. Morgan got a warm rush thinking he'd been possessive of her right out of the gate.

"You're going to teach me to hunt agates, right?"

"Right." Morgan was wearing her down jacket, as the weather had gone cold again. Josh looked freezing in his plain hoodie sweatshirt, but he was an Oregon boy. He knew what the weather was like out here. "Now, we're going to look for them up here near the edge where the driftwood collects."

"Why here?" He seemed genuinely interested. That was something she'd come to really appreciate about Josh the past few days. When he wanted to know something new, he had a curious mind, and even better, he didn't mind letting her be the one to tell him about something she was already up on. He didn't have to be a know-it-all. That was the thing she'd noticed about really smart people: the ones who seemed to know the most, like Josh, were almost never the ones who acted like it all the time.

"Because agates come from erosion of cliffs along beaches and rivers. They wash out to the ocean and get polished in the surf over time. Then they come back in the tides and get caught here at the edge of the waves by the driftwood. Winter is the best time to collect them."

"But the ones you gave my sister?"

"I found those over the summer. They were nice. I got lucky. The better agates get exposed when winter storms remove the sand and expose the agates underneath."

"Amazing."

"I know, right? God thought of everything."

"Well, that, too, but I meant you." Josh's words sucked the breath out of her lungs.

"You did?"

He just smiled. "Mm-hmm." His eyes crinkled at the edges. "Now, where's my bucket? I'm getting some agates."

"Only a gallon a day. Oregon State Beach rules."

"A gallon!"

"I know. Probably impossible."

"Girl, I am far lazier than that. The only gallon bucket I'm thinking of filling is one from Kentucky Fried Chicken. Hey. Do you think they'd take agates as barter payment?"

They set to work, finding large and small specimens of the smooth, transparent stones. Mostly they found white, but then Morgan found a light blue one and a yellow, and then Josh came up with a rare pink. They had about a cup and a half at this point—nowhere near a gallon.

"Those waves look too cold to take pictures in." She stood with her hands in her jacket pockets to keep warm.

Josh came and stood beside her, and they looked out at the gray, winter curves breaking on the water, side by side, so close she could hear his breathing. "Much. But don't tempt me to throw you in, because I'm easily tempted."

"Is that right?" Morgan laughed. Ugh! That stupid little twittering laugh again. She stopped it short. "I just die every time I see those pictures over that bed. If I were doing home decorating, I'd choose something so much more tasteful than that."

"You would? I think it's hot."

"Exactly."

Then he laughed and pushed her upper arm. She pushed back, and then—no dummy— she ran away from the direction of the waves, up the embankment toward the car, while he chased her. Not until nearly the top did he tackle her.

"You made me spill my agates!" she squealed.

"You're going to make me—" He stopped short, and Morgan looked up to see a big black camera lens in their faces. Josh jumped to his feet and pulled Morgan up. "Paulie, get a life. Don't you have a life? Why do you want to follow around a happily married pair of students with nothing to their name?"

"That's not what I hear, Joshie boy."

"Which part isn't what you hear?" Morgan challenged, surprised at her own impetuousness.

"The happily married couple part. I caught you coming out of the police station with another woman on Christmas Day, Josh. You know that part. What's wrong in your fairy tale marriage to this walking, talking cover model that you'd need another girl on the side? Or are you just a glutton for women?"

"Please, Paulie. Be a man. Look, I'll introduce you. This is Morgan, my wife."

"Pleased to meet you," Morgan said, extending her hand. "How's your family? Are you enjoying your stay in Starry Point?"

Paulie gave a momentary stare at the extended hand, paused, wiped his palm on the front of his plaid shirt, and then shook it. "Charmed, Mrs. Hyatt. You come from around here?"

"Don't answer that, Morgan." Josh's voice came out wary.

"I'm just here for school. I'm nearly finished."

"What, in fashion merchandising?"

"What's that? Does Clarendon College even have a department like that?"

"You just look like the type." Paulie had a perpetual sneer, and Morgan felt a twinge of pity for him.

Josh didn't like the guy, clearly. "Morgan is not a type. She's a real woman, with a real brain, and real feelings. She's a good person, and she's someone I care about a lot, and someone you'd really like if you weren't so busy trying

346

to make a buck off her. Can't you get a job doing something that doesn't destroy people's peace, man?" Josh's words ricocheted around in Morgan's mind and heart. *He cared about her a lot.* He didn't say loved, but he would have been reticent with this vulture. *Morgan is not a type. She's a good person.* Josh's assessment of her tumbled through her, giving her warmth and peace.

"Nothing that pays as well." Paulie laughed without mirth, and Morgan felt even sorrier for him — until he spoke again, that was. "And you said you cared a lot about her. Not loved. So I'm taking that as proof positive for my article." He had a laugh like Skeletor's this time. "See you later, sucker. Despite the frolicking in the sand dunes pics in this batch here," he patted his camera, "I know this girl isn't the woman you love. Your real girlfriend's best friend put me onto that weeks ago. I've just hit pay dirt." Again with the Skeletor laugh. It bored a hole in Morgan's soul, letting her peace drain out.

"It's not true, Paulie. I do love her. Now take that to the bank."

Paulie dashed away, as Josh chased after him, but Morgan stood paralyzed by what she'd just heard. *He loved her!* Josh had said it at last. Morgan's knees went a little weak, and she had to catch her breath against the thousand tingling points of her skin and mind and soul. *He loved her.* Did he mean it? Or did he just say it to get Paulie off his back? He had to mean it. Everything he'd done this past while served as evidence.

Morgan collected herself, bent and began picking up the spilled agates one by one, until Josh had chased Paulie out to the parking lot and had come back for her.

"You do?"

"Do what?" He was breathless, himself, from the obvious exertion. Maybe he punched the guy. Morgan didn't want to know. "Do think Paulie Bumgartner is a total bum? Yes. Yes, I do."

Morgan sighed. He wasn't going to read her meaning, and she was still left in suspense, too frightened of the real answer to press him. "Thanks for getting rid of him. I tried my best to be polite."

"I know you did. And your charm works on every living soul."

"Not Paulie Bumgartner's."

"His soul isn't living. It's been dead and gone to Hades for decades."

"Gotcha." Morgan took Josh's offered hand as they crossed the parking lot with their buckets of agates and went home.

***

Josh was shaving when his phone chimed a text in the other room.

Brielle: *It's New Year's Eve, Josh. I will be watching for you tonight. Wear something red. Well, a red tie. Claire's colors are red and green to be festive. See you. XoXo*

Josh dropped the phone like it was a hot potato. Was it New Year's Eve already? Where had this week gone? Oh, yeah. The beach, whale watching, and the way of all the world: deep into a TV-induced vegetative state. Josh felt more rested than he had in months, years. Being around Morgan was so relaxing. She was easygoing and went with whatever. She liked the TV show he picked, and then he hadn't minded the one she chose—it was pretty funny. They'd thrown popcorn in each other's mouths, and she'd only been uptight about making sure not to leave anything extra for Svetlana to clean up.

And he'd been a very good boy—even when she came down last night in her little, short pajamas to watch the last episode of the legal drama they were both really into. He hadn't touched her leg, even when it was just inches away, taunting him, basically. Man, his wife was something hotter

348

than fire. But he didn't dare get burned. Not until he was sure.

And now, the day was here when he had to be sure—and declare it one way or another.

If he knew what was going on in Morgan's mind, it would make it a little clearer to decide. If she wasn't at all serious about him anymore it would make it a lot easier for him to walk away—maybe. The truth was, every day with her, he'd dug in a little deeper. Or maybe she'd dug a little deeper, burrowing into his soul. Walking away at this point was going to require some pain. He'd only be able to do it if...

"Hey, Josh." Morgan bounced in. Her hair was in a ponytail and she wore her workout clothes. He hadn't seen her in them since that day they went to the bank to put their names on the joint checking account—the same bank where their hundred thousand dollar scholarship lay untouched.

He could have Morgan and the hundred grand, too, if he chose them.

"Hey, Morgan." He tore his eyes back up to her face.

"What'cha looking at?"

"I can look at my wife."

"Good point." She pulled a little smile at him, and her voice did that little flirty laugh he couldn't resist. "I'm back from my run. Did you want to tell me what's going on tonight, so I know how to dress?"

Josh stared at her, not sure how to answer. He had to see Brielle. And that was extremely inconvenient, especially considering the deadline. The clock on the wall ticked audibly.

"Uh, didn't you say tonight was our night on the town?" She did finger quotes. He vaguely remembered that phrase, and he definitely remembered now that he had two dates for New Year's Eve. "If you don't mind loaning them back to me—just until you're sure—I'd be honored if I could wear your mother's ruby necklace. After all, that was part of the original plan, right?" Morgan suddenly pulled a nervous smile. "Uh, maybe I could put them with the red dress. You liked that dress when I wore it to Mr. Seagram's house that night for dinner, I think."

Oh, yeah. He liked it. Probably way too much. Oh, his head might be starting to hurt. He rubbed his hand up and down the cheek he hadn't shaved yet. "Red will be perfect."

Chapter Thirty-Three

Morgan fidgeted with the zipper on her red dress. She could get it before, but today the top few inches wouldn't quite go up. "Josh, can you help me with this part?" She had to ask him. She didn't have any choice. It was either get some help or go out on their night together partially unzipped.

Josh came up behind her. While she lifted her hair he slowly raised the zipper, his fingertips caressing the back of her neck. When he finished, she turned her head to see if he had that wicked grin he got whenever he was thinking about kissing her.

But instead she saw pain.

"Are you all right, Josh?" She turned around and took his hands in hers. With her heels on, she was just a few inches shorter than he was, and she could look him almost right in the eye. He seemed far away.

"Morgan, I'm really sorry."

"Sorry about what?"

"Sorry about what I've done to us."

Morgan laughed a little. "What have you done to us, Josh? Made us lazy couch-dwellers for the entirety of our Christmas vacation? Because I can't think of anything I needed more after months of being under the academic gun." She slid her arms around his waist. "You gave me exactly what I needed. Like always."

Josh's face got even more clouded.

"Okay, so what is it? You're not happy. Don't you want to go out tonight? Because if you'd rather, I can dial back my New Year's Eve excitement and we can just stay home. But, I mean, this is our last night — before we have to report back to Mr. Seagram in the morning. I just thought — " She'd thought she'd like to go out with a blaze of glory before the pretty dream had to end, when he went back to Brielle and she went back to Estrella Court and roller skating and quitting school and groveling before Carl's feet, just so she could begin paying back all the grants she'd be forced to repay.

Josh took Morgan's hands from his waist and pulled her over to sit down beside him on the bed. He looked more serious than she'd ever seen him look, and a sinking heat flared in her stomach.

"We've needed to have a frank discussion for a long time, Morgan. And since we've been given an ultimatum, I don't know how I can let us put it off any longer."

Frank discussion sounded like a blessed relief, but with the look on Josh's face, Morgan thought she dreaded it more than a final she hadn't studied for, which was kind of what this was. She had no experience with this level of a relationship before in her life. She was unstudied and unready and unbraced for it. But like a scheduled train it was coming anyway, and Morgan panicked.

"Josh! Before you say anything, I want to tell you — thank you. You've made my life blessed. For the first time, I had someone to wake up to, someone to sit by in church, someone to talk to at night when my studies were done. You gave me a glimpse of how good life could be."

Josh's face twisted, but she didn't want to stop until she'd told him.

"I'm not sorry one bit — about any of it, except maybe the sin of omission."

Josh cocked his head. "What does that mean?"

"I mean when Mr. Seagram asked whether we loved each other and I didn't answer. My silence was a lie." Her voice caught in her throat, and she had to collect herself before going on. "If he'd asked it months ago, it would have been a lie to stay silent then, too. You've been in my heart ever since you helped rescue my mother's dog from certain death. Then you saved me time and time again, even if it meant we dragged each other into the mess we're in now. I wouldn't trade a single minute of it."

Josh closed his eyes, and he looked like he'd stopped breathing. Morgan had done it. She'd ripped her heart out of her chest and thrown it palpitating at his feet, to either pick up and cherish or stomp on and walk away. He wasn't moving—physically or otherwise. Morgan bated her own breath, terrified of what he might choose next. But it had been too long coming, and she'd never dared do it before. She had to now. The moment was upon them. And she refused to let him slip away simply because she wasn't brave enough to admit how much she wanted him.

"I want you, Josh. I want us. Together. I'm in love with you, and even if I didn't start out intending for this to happen, it's what my secret heart has wished for all along." Every tendril of her soul stretched out to him. He had to feel her aching for him. With courage, she lifted her hand and reached over and intertwined her pinkie finger among his fingers. "I love you." This last came in a longing whisper.

Josh's eyes popped open and met hers at last. A hopeless smile pulled at the side of his mouth. "Oh, Morgan." The words were almost inaudible.

"What, Josh? What? Say it. Tell me what you feel. Don't leave me suspended in agony here." Tears were welling hot in her eyes, and they'd mar her makeup soon for their date on the town, which Morgan swiftly began to understand was not going to happen. From the look on Josh's anguished face, it was over.

"Please, Josh. Please." The first hot tear spilled, and she felt it burn a trail down her cheek.

Josh flopped back on the bed, kicking off his shoes. Morgan lay down beside him, reaching out and pressing her hand to his upper arm. She kissed his forehead, which he'd done to her so many times before. With tenderness filling her heart as she did so, she recognized the sincere emotion that accompanied a kiss such as that. She'd always received that kind of kiss from Josh with mild disappointment, but now she saw how filled with true feeling it could be.

Josh breathed in and out for several long seconds, and then he said, "You've slain me, Morgan."

"Slain you?" Was this some kind of play-dead? She waited another long moment for his response.

He opened his eyes and looked up at her through his lashes. "It's like this." He huffed out a breath. "We came into this with a clear purpose: get the grant and get through school—you, so Tory could get started; me, so I could graduate and join Brielle in the international policy career."

Hearing that other girl's name was a knife in Morgan's heart. "I know, which is what made it so wrong of me to be pining for you all that time."

"Pining? You were pining?"

"Why do you think I made you dinner every night?"

"You're nice? Like to cook? Can't see food go to waste?"

"Those were excuses I made out loud, but it was really because I wanted to show you how much I was in love with you—but without telling you in so many words, fearing it would drive you off." Here she went, spilling all her secrets to him, even the worst, most closely kept secrets of her soul. "I've never cooked for anyone else in my life. I thought I could win you by *playing wife*." Speaking of driving him off, these words were going to send him shooting away—sure as anything. But it was time. He was right—this discussion and truth couldn't wait another day. She had to come completely clean. So she pressed on, biting her lip until a little blood drew. Being honest was easy—just like opening a vein.

"On that one morning, after we went to see your family, I couldn't stand it anymore that you didn't know how I felt, and I threw myself at you in the kitchen. You kissed back, and for a minute, I let myself hope you felt something for me, too. It's so desperate-sounding now, I know, but you'd become something to me—something huge."

"I had?"

"Josh, do you know that before I met you, I could never speak to a man I was remotely interested in? I would go into what Tory called the Conversation Coma, and I'd just be a blank. Guys would take an interest in me, ask me out, and then I was the most boring girl they'd ever met, and no one ever called me twice. I was an empty shell, as far as any guy worth knowing could tell. It was only the jerks who didn't care, so I was stuck with them for years, getting the worst of their treatment, and feeling the worst about myself. Then...you."

"Me?" Josh's eyes were open. "I never saw that in you. You were always just yourself."

"Right? I did have that first blackout when I was with you, and I was sure it was happening all over again. But then, somehow, no." Her tears dried a little as she explained, but her heart was warm, and his cologne was spicy. "You just put me at ease. Maybe because of Brielle—because if I knew you weren't even available, I didn't have to think of you as a *possibility*. I could always talk to *non-possibilities*, like that old caretaker at Estrella Court, for instance, or professors, or people at Veg-Out."

"So I was like a customer. Just a business deal."

"Maybe I saw you as safe." She laughed, and it again came out that high-pitched giggle she hated herself for. But when she did it, Josh put a hand on her waist, pressing her body deeper against the softness of the bedding. Why hadn't she been sleeping on this cloud all this time? What a waste of a perfect mattress.

"Oh, I am most definitely not safe." Josh suddenly got that devilish grin she craved, showing those excellent teeth. "Not when it comes to you. I had to beg George to give me the night shift so I wouldn't throw you down on this bed and complicate everything."

Morgan bit her lip. "But, in a way, wouldn't it have uncomplicated everything?"

Josh's eyes closed again, and he rolled onto his back, his hands under his head and looking up at the ceiling. Morgan nestled up against him, her head in the nook of his shoulder and chest.

"Morgan, these past few days have been incredible. You have been incredible. The whale watching, finding agates, the time we've just spent together. I'm going to go out on a limb and say it has been the best week of my life."

Morgan gulped. It was how she felt exactly, but she didn't interrupt.

"If—"

"If, what?"

"If I hadn't met Brielle first, made those commitments to her, I'd have been all over you the first time I saw you in that gravel parking lot climbing out of your junked truck. I'd have gotten your number and taken you to all the finest student-affordable dinners in a ten-mile radius. I wouldn't have taken no for an answer. I would have possibly even proposed for real by now."

Morgan gulped. This could have all been hers, if she had just gone about things in the right order, instead of screwing up so massively by trying to go through the back door.

"Are you saying…?"

"That I'm in love with you?" Josh reached over and stroked her hair. "It's not something I've felt very often in my life. But I know when I'm with you, I don't want to be with anyone else. And I know when I'm with you, I want to be a far better version of myself, and make everything in your life the best it can be."

"It sounds like how I define love, Josh." She was so close to him, she could hear his heart's pattern, and as he'd spoken it had sped up, and now it was thudding low and quick against her ear. He rubbed his hand down her arm, letting it come to a rest at the narrow part of her waist before her hip curved up. Her own heart had a race of its own going on, as her mind fought what her body wanted to do.

Josh finally nodded. "If only."

The words hit Morgan like a bucket of cold water. He was lamenting losing her, but implying its inevitability.

With the most supreme sacrifice she'd ever made, she swallowed hard. "I know you promised her you'd give her New Year's Eve. It was after we'd planned to go out, but I can see now what you need to do." She sat up, almost feeling like a surgery had to separate herself from him. "Go to her. Give her the best of you. I can't be your second choice, Josh. It hurts far too much as it is." Now the tears sprang back and came coursing out of her eyes. "I'll be packing up the house, so don't look for me tonight, but just meet me at Seagram's in the morning. We can tell him then what we've decided." She was on her feet, sliding back into her heels, smoothing her hair and the folds of her dress over her curves. Man, the guy was giving her up—and she was insisting on it. Tory would call her an idiot, and Morgan wouldn't argue. "I hope, someday, someone will be as loyal to me as you are to what you know is right. Brielle is so lucky."

Morgan was a wretched fool.

She shut the door behind her.

***

Josh sat stunned when the door gently closed behind her, his heart dying as she left him, insisting that he go to a

357

fate he didn't want, all based on a duty he didn't think he was wise now to have been keeping, even mentally.

Morgan loves me. The words ricocheted in his mind, paralyzing him, not letting him jump off the bed and go after her, which he should. All the kindnesses she'd shown him were for *him.* They weren't just some kind of generalized niceness—they were expressions of love all along, and he'd cheapened them by not recognizing them for what they really were. The innermost parts of him had always held a tiny spark of hope that this was the case, but he'd covered those sparks, sure that it couldn't be.

The way she'd looked in his eyes as she admitted to never being able to speak to another man besides him was like she'd opened a door to her soul and let him look inside. When she did, he realized he'd seen her soul a few times before, and it was beautiful. She was allowing only Josh alone to see it. *No other man had been granted access to those precious sights.* The thought made his shoulders straighten and broaden. *I'm her man. That's basically what she just told me.*

The power of that realization shot adrenaline through him.

All this time he'd mentally compared the differences between Brielle and Morgan, sometimes thinking what he wanted was the never-ending Spy-Versus-Spy exhilaration that the idea of Brielle provided. But the truth was, Brielle had never let him into her world. She told him it existed, said it was exciting, but he'd never participated in it, and certainly never got a sense that she would give him a part of herself. *Wasn't that the essence of marriage? A unification?*

He needed to think this out. He let his science mind take over and make a comparison based on chemical formulas—somewhere he felt comfortable.

Say, for instance, that he and Morgan were sulfur monoxide—Josh the sulfur and Morgan the oxygen, the two of them sharing a covalent bond, each giving two

358

electrons, completing each other's outer shell. Equal sharing, equal sacrifice, something different and rare — and that in certain circumstances that had even been known to glow — created when combined.

Compare that to the bond he always imagined he and Brielle shared: carbon sulfide, with Josh still the sulfur, but Brielle the carbon. In fact, his chemistry mind had always thought of her as carbon, the building block of organic life. As carbon sulfide their bond was a triple bond, where they'd shared so many more electrons to complete each other. But now that he considered it more closely, that sharing hadn't been equal.

All along, he'd thought of the carbon giving, giving, giving to his sulfur, just like Brielle had to give and give while she waited for Josh to become what she needed him to be.

Suddenly, though, the thought occurred to him Brielle hadn't been the giving one in their covalent bond. Instead, Brielle's carbon had *taken* more of his sulfur's electrons, demanding them to fill her shell. And despite the triple bonding to complete their electron shells, it wasn't as natural a covalence as the equal sharing between him and Morgan's sulfur monoxide, and it was easily broken down.

Brielle insisted that *if* she was going to accept Josh as her partner, he'd have to be the exact person she dictated, do the job she did, have the same interests she had, make the same hobby choices, even. He'd have to set aside all his passion for energy research, snuff out the candle of his inventiveness, and focus on the history of political relations between countries whose names he couldn't pronounce — *and* live in those countries, where he couldn't even get access to the chemicals and equipment that let him do the research that really turned him into a thinking, creating, world-changing man.

Josh had to do what he had to do — it was time to go to Brielle and let her know that things were over and done.

359

He'd wasted too much of Morgan's time already by not being honest with himself and not opening up to her when she was giving so much of herself to him. It was time.

With a rush of excitement, he dialed Morgan's number. She didn't pick up, but he couldn't leave something this huge on a message. He needed to be face to face with her, or at least speak to her on the phone.

Yes. This was right. This was so right.

He dialed her again. Surely she'd pick up now.

No. Well, he'd take care of things and go to her as soon as he was free.

He pulled out of the driveway and headed through town to the coast. He needed to steel his nerves, figure out his line of argument for when he met Brielle. He'd have to bring years of expectation to an end, and he knew it would be tough for him, despite the fact he was the one breaking up, not the one getting dumped, maybe even tougher, especially if Brielle was the new Brielle with the vulnerable side she'd shown him last week.

Gazing out in the waves, he imagined the whales' passing, the agates roiling and being polished, and the way Morgan looked when she taught him about them.

Echoes of something Morgan said weeks ago came wafting back to him. Making a man in his own image was *God's* job, not a girlfriend's.

Morgan was right.

She might be soft-spoken, she might not be setting the world ablaze with her so-called big plans for change, or defending the world against terrorist threats, but Morgan was wise. She had good counsel for him. She didn't throw it in his face or argue about it. She said it once, and then she let it drop, allowing him to eventually (and in this case after far too long) come to her very wise conclusion in his own time.

Morgan would never force him to be what *she* insisted he be. She'd take him as he was and encourage him to be the best version of himself, jumping for joy when he succeeded, wrapping him in her loving arms when he fell short of his goal.

And feeding him, body and soul, every single day he was in her presence.

Morgan. Morgan Clark. Her gentleness didn't shout at the world, it whispered.

How would I like my own children to be raised? What kind of life do I want to live?

He glanced out at the ocean and an earth-shattering realization hit him—why Bronco couldn't stand Brielle, and why Brielle fought so hard against Bronco: *they had the same personality.* One came in a much cuter package with freckles and spiral curls in her hair, and for the time being her energy was focused solely on her career and the larger global threats—but life evolved. Time would come where their world would be within the walls of their home, and *then* how would Brielle's blazing temperament flare out? Josh pictured char and ashes.

If Brielle did ever intend to focus on home and hearth. Did she? Josh didn't actually know. Every conversation about the future with her had centered on living in Pakistan and rooting out the threats there, or on their lives in some Sub-Saharan African outpost, fortifying the U.S.-installed government against warlords and insurgents. Children didn't pop up in that picture ever, unlike the many times he and Morgan had talked about their own childhoods, and her plans to make her own kids' childhoods happy.

The old crossroads loomed in front of him, but this time there was a blinding neon sign pointing the way Josh ought to go. No, the way he *wanted* to go. Forget about duty and previous commitments and who saw whom first. For the first time he could see beyond the horizon to the end of the road with Morgan, and at it stood a vast green valley of happiness. All he had to do was take his first step down it, and then never look back.

But he'd have to tell Brielle.

He called Chip instead.

"Hey, man. Happy New Year." Chip must be watching a movie. It was loud in the background. "I'm really glad you called. You and Morgan going to come up tomorrow morning and watch the Rose Parade with us? And then the game? Tell her to bring some of that rice stuff, and we'll all try to play it cool, not gush all over her about it."

"She makes some other good things."

"Oh, tell her to bring those, too."

"Can't, man. Sorry." They had to go see Seagram. And he had to do a lot before that.

"Dang. That's a bummer. I mean, we like you, but we love Morgan. How did *you* get so lucky? She's amazing."

"I know." For the first time, Josh said this with conviction. He wanted to go on and on about it, but he'd called Chip with a question, and he'd better ask it. "But I've got girl trouble."

"What? You do? I can't imagine in what universe Morgan could be trouble."

"She's not. Brielle came back."

Chip groaned. Josh was taken aback. He hadn't known Brielle was groan-worthy.

"Not her again. I swear, we all thought you made a slick escape. Heather and I have talked it over a thousand times, how close that was. She's the worst."

She was? Josh didn't necessarily want to hear that. "I have to see her. She's here from Germany."

"Send her back!" Chip hollered this. "Okay, okay, sorry. I can tell you're really into Morgan, and that's… just, thank goodness you're finally seeing light and truth. But you have to cut that other hernia of a girl loose."

"I promised her I'd spend New Year's Eve with her at her friend's wedding. Morgan told me I should go to her."

"Morgan did? What is she smoking?"

"Nothing but barbecue brisket. But she is right, Chip. I

did make commitments to Brielle. Morgan deserves a man who keeps commitments he makes."

"That's for darn sure." The background noise around Chip dampened. He must be finally taking this seriously. Josh relaxed. Chip had his back. He'd know what to do. "Morgan is by *far* the best thing you've ever done, man. Do *not* endanger that, no matter what she says."

"I know she is. I love her. She's amazing. But Brielle—"

"Brielle is mean." Chip didn't let him finish explaining the situation.

"She is?"

"She doesn't care about you. That's the whole reason all of us hated her, Bronco most of all." Chip sounded exasperated. "You might think Bronco is your worst enemy, and he's no stellar paragon of virtue, but he did the best thing he knew how to do to get that woman out of your life. He's just not a very creative manipulator. I told him he should just tell you he didn't like her and why—that she was trying to turn you into her Mini-Me, the male version, and steer the vehicle of your life in every way—but he said you'd never listen, and he would do whatever it took to keep you away from her. That's why he cut you off. He figured she was a gold digger. That's why he kept you from getting jobs to pay for your school in her ridiculous life-plan for you which you *obviously* hated, and why he was bent on getting her away by lining up that job in Germany for her. He figured you'd find someone else while she was gone."

"What?" All the air sucked out of Josh's lungs. "Bronco lined that up?" No.

"Duh. How else would *she* get that job? At an embassy? Please. No one is going to hire anyone as irritating as Brielle Dupree without being leveraged. Bronco spent nearly all his political capital getting rid of her. *Saving you.*"

Josh's mouth went dry. "I had no idea."

"I know. Bronco, believe it or not, was too nervous about losing his relationship with you to tell you any of this."

"Well, it would have made me hate him. He was right about that." But Josh had hated him anyway for the past three years while all this stewed. Somehow, though, the knowledge that Bronco would go to such incredible lengths to protect Josh lit a candle in his heart, the first light of respect for his father he'd felt in a long time. "But I can at least see his motives."

"Josh." Chip sounded serious. "I know you think you loved that girl, but we could all see it was some kind of warped infatuation." He cleared his throat while Josh sat stinging at the accusation, wishing it wasn't true but still knowing the accuracy of it cut like a knife. "But back to your question. You called with the conundrum that you'd made a commitment to Brielle, and Morgan insisted you keep it."

"That's right," Josh whispered, wishing for any way out of it now. "I can't disappoint Morgan."

"Answer me this, pal. What commitment *did* you make to Brielle Dupree? And, more to the point, what promise did Brielle ever make to you?"

The time machine of Josh's mind dialed back over the months to when he was standing in the airport with Brielle, begging her in his mind to promise him, to allow him to promise her —

Do you want me to wait for you? he'd asked. She'd purposely misunderstood him. He could see that now. *And she'd said no!* Besides that, she'd evaded him when he'd tried to pin her down in any way.

After nearly a full two blocks of driving while Chip waited silently on the other end of the line, Josh said, "None. She didn't promise anything."

"And you?"

Josh knew he'd committed to her in his heart, and that

he was a guy who didn't take things like that lightly. At least he wanted to think of himself that way. Obviously Morgan thought of him that way, and that was probably the thing that had made it so difficult for him to let go of what obviously had died and embrace the living breathing relationship between himself and the woman he truly loved.

Morgan. All along he'd said for Brielle he wanted to be the best version of himself; Morgan *made* him the best version of himself.

"Nothing. I didn't actually make any concrete promises." Brielle wouldn't let him. He would have—he knew that, if she had, but she hadn't. Wow. Stating that aloud made bells chime in his head, the Liberty Bell, actually. Nothing was said between them, not in so many words, although he'd assumed it was understood, and apparently Brielle had come back to him on Christmas acting like it was understood for her as well. But there was no bargain made, no real commitment. *He was free. Always had been.*

Chip didn't say anything for a bit, but then when he did, it nearly made Josh swerve from the road and into a parking meter. "So, then, what commitments did you make to Morgan—whether either of you intended to keep them or not?"

Josh swallowed hard. Whether the vows were made with real intent or not, they were made. Legal proof of them existed, and everything (well, almost everything) Josh and Morgan had done in their lives since that day was evidence that the two of them were committed, husband and wife, legally and lawfully wedded. Neither had dated someone else, neither had abandoned the other, they'd lived together, eaten meals together, gone to church every Sunday together. Everything but the final act of *making* her his wife indeed, and that was no one's business but their own. In the eyes of the law and before God and man, Josh had vowed to be Morgan's husband.

"I've had it all backward." He tugged a smile, knowing how much this conversation enabled him to fully embrace at last the feelings that had tugged at him for months. He could have her. He *should* have her. His wife.

"You can say that again." Chip's background noise ramped up again. He was done with this conversation. "Now, go give that other girl the boot, and quit breaking Morgan's heart. Because if you don't, I'm scared of what Heather will do to you. It won't be pretty." Through the phone, the sound of Chip giving Heather a peck on the lips sounded. "Oh, by the way—we have some good news. We're not telling the rest of the family just yet, but since you're Heather's favorite brother-in-law, she insists."

"What?"

"You're going to be an uncle. In June."

"That's great, Chip. Congratulations. Good things come to those who wait."

"Good things come to those who sleep with their wives."

"Hey," Josh warned, but the happiness that lurched in Josh's chest for Chip and Heather's long-awaited blessing confirmed everything he'd decided about Morgan and family and the cycle of life. He wanted Morgan and everything she offered—providing he could get Brielle out of his life, now that she'd finally expressed that she wanted a life with him.

***

Josh rounded the corner and sped toward the church. He pulled out his phone again and dialed Morgan. She didn't pick up. He had to tell her he was doing what she asked, but not in the way she insisted. He wanted her, not Brielle, and Morgan deserved to know that.

He dialed again, no luck. And texting this kind of life-changing information was just too impersonal, even for this day and age.

He pulled up in front of the church where Claire's wedding had taken place earlier in the afternoon. It was a small, traditional building of white clapboard with a cross atop the steeple and Christmas lights on a wreath at the door. Josh was surprised Claire hadn't wanted to be married in some fancy hotel. The harpy who'd made his life a tabloid festival for the past month really seemed the flashy type, not the tiny church type.

The stack of letters he'd written Brielle weighed heavily on his mind. How had she reacted when she'd read them—if she'd read them? Giving them to her had been a huge risk, he knew. They were proof of more than just his intent toward Brielle; they proved his and Morgan's intent to defraud the system. He'd been playing with fire by writing them, and then he'd doused himself with gasoline by handing them over.

However, he also knew he wouldn't be able to look her in the eye and say he'd fallen out of love with her without showing her proof that he'd never forgotten her. Maybe that would soften the blow. Brielle deserved at least the knowledge that he'd never been untrue to her, even though at the final moment of choosing, he couldn't choose life with her.

It was pretty low to be doing this to her at her best friend's wedding, but Josh had a deadline with Seagram and no way around it. Besides, Morgan deserved this as well, not to be kept waiting another day for him to quit his wishy-washy show of commitment, when in truth he was a hundred percent Team Morgan. This conversation had to happen tonight. His heart quailed, but he steeled it.

Josh parked the Land Rover and pushed himself through the double doors of the chapel.

Suddenly, a girl in a white dress stopped him in his tracks before he could set foot beyond the vestibule of the church.

"Joshua Hyatt, as I live and breathe." Claire looked a lot more normal with natural auburn hair than with what Morgan had termed the cherry Kool-Aid red she'd been sporting last time they crossed swords.

"Sorry, Claire. I know how you must feel about me," and he knew how he felt about *her*, "but Brielle asked me to come, so I hope it's not too much of an imposition on your most important day."

Claire rolled her eyes. "Oh, please. I just can't believe you'd show up here." She looked ready to launch shoulder-mounted missiles—but, strangely, not at Josh. She looked at him with an air of conspiracy. "And that you'd forgive her, after what Brielle put you through these last few months? Wow. Just wow."

Josh cocked his head to the side, looking around to see if anyone was listening. They were alone. He proceeded with caution. "She was pretty incommunicado."

Claire threw her head back. "Ha! I'll bet she was—with you, at least. I mean, I was glued to her posts until everything hit the fan in the news, which, by the way, was all after I sent that loser-face reporter after you. Sorry about that. Hope you can forgive me. I should've kept my temper better, but you know what they say about redheads."

Josh just nodded dumbly. He had no idea what kind of things had hit the fan with Brielle. Or that Brielle had been making posts of any kind. Wasn't she *going dark*? Below the radar? He'd never done an online search for her, since she'd been so bent on secrecy when she left, and why would he waste his time?

"I mean, that whole whirlwind between her and the director of the diplomatic mission—their big trysts in the Bavarian hotels, the embassy cars they took on the Autobahn all the way to Bremen, the castles on the Rhine—it would have been a fairy tale if they hadn't been caught."

"Caught. Right." Josh's stomach spiraled.

"I mean, glory! What a wreck she made of his career and his marriage and his family. I told her sixty-five million times she was far better off waiting for you to finish school—or to just hurry up and get married to you without the school stipulation—and not go after that slimy diplomat. I mean, I was always sure your dad would forgive you and give your money back if she was patient enough, but she wouldn't listen to me. She just had to chase him through Europe, acting like nothing else existed. Yeah, I'd been mad at you for getting married the second she left—and to that girl who was so much prettier than Brielle. But when I met your wife she was so nice I couldn't stand that you'd upgraded—and I was furious."

"So you sent Paulie Bumgartner after us." Josh gritted his teeth. This whole conversation was pummeling him.

"Hey, I just apologized for that. Didn't you hear me? I was wrong. It was well-meant. I thought it would hit the Portland news through some other publishing company than my own, and Brielle would see what she was doing was wrong and come back and fight for you. Which, I guess, ultimately she did. But not until after her whole world crumbled like the Berlin Wall in 1989."

Josh's mouth was as dry as the one pot roast Brielle had ever cooked for him. "So, the diplomat chucked her?" He hated tipping his hand, showing how much he didn't know.

"Weeks ago. She's been drifting jobless through Europe for a month, probably trying to scrape together airfare home. I mean, I wanted to kick her out of my wedding, after all the disgrace she was to herself and basically the whole United States diplomacy effort, but geez, she's been my best friend for two decades, and I couldn't just tell her to forget it. But she's pretty busted, you know. No one here is giving her much of the time of day. Not after what she did to that man's family, to you, to herself, to her own family. No one has much respect for her

369

at this point. I'm just glad you got out more or less unscathed, frankly, and scored with that incredible, super-sweet wife. You're a really nice guy, Josh. Do, please, forgive me for the reporter stunt. It was ill-conceived but well-intentioned as her friend who didn't know how low she'd really sunk at the time. You have to see that." Claire put a hand on his shoulder, and planted a kiss on his cheek. "Thanks for coming to my reception."

Josh watched her flounce away in her dress that looked like an upside down white cupcake and realized that Claire had, after all, launched her shoulder-mounted missile at him, whether she meant to or not.

The clock chimed eight, and a band started playing smooth jazz from the depths of the church's hallways. Josh stood letting the music muffle out, and he backed against the wall of the vestibule. A few wedding guests filed past him, chatting and holding large gifts, probably toasters and crock pots and blenders. Things people needed to start their lives off right together.

Josh let them blur past him while the enormity of Brielle's lies sank in. Well, not lies, exactly, other than claiming she had an open-ended return ticket to Germany. Otherwise, they were sins of omission, Morgan had called them. Confessional oversights.

Morgan lied by not telling me she did love me; Brielle lied by not telling me she didn't.

Josh made a fist, his mind filling with the sight of Morgan walking out and shutting the door behind her, her steps hollow on the wood floor as she walked down the hall to the other bedroom. He could almost taste the astringent salt of her tears on his tongue if he thought about it, in stark contrast to all the sweet she'd given him with her raspberry lip gloss. He'd only given her bitterness.

Morgan was his first choice. So what was he doing here, feeling guilty about explaining things to a woman who'd made him her second choice? Or maybe her third, or

370

farther down the hierarchy, for all he knew. Josh was Brielle's *last* resort. She'd even admitted to keeping his commitment on her back burner all the time for *someday. Maybe.*

And even more, what Claire had said about Brielle's whole motivation for sticking with him had muddied the waters even more. When Brielle left for Germany, her words at the airport had puzzled him. *Eventually things will calm down. They will smooth out.* He'd replayed them a hundred times, no, a thousand times in his mind since that day, but he'd never assigned much meaning to them other than the idea that they'd both be done with school, ready to take on the world together. That would be the smooth, calm time to come. But no.

She meant Bronco would relent and bring Josh back into his good graces – and his finances. She'd gone to Germany to wait that out, or postponed committing to him until she was sure all her ducks were in a row, meaning Josh's money. She'd had her blaze of fun in Germany, burning up that diplomat like Nero fiddled while Rome went up in flames.

Sick tides of realization roiled through him. Had she actually ever cared about him for himself? When she'd accused Morgan of being a gold digger earlier this week, it had been telling of her own intentions, not Morgan's.

His chest got tight. Brielle had been stringing him along, waiting for a better situation to come up, a more sure thing. But then, after everything else in her life imploded, Brielle had come waltzing back to him, her place of last resort, the guy she thought would be her backup plan after she'd sown her wild oats. What did she think? That he'd never find out? Didn't she realize just how public everyone's lives were these days? And that becoming the wife of a Hyatt, a son of Hyatt Holdings, was nothing but an invitation for the press to completely rip to shreds her background? She was a family scandal waiting to happen— a legitimate one.

Then the most humbling and horrifying thought of all weaseled its way into Josh's mind:

Bronco had been right.

It buckled his knees, and Josh collapsed against the wall, using it to hold himself upright, or he would have fallen to the floor, right beside the lighted garland and faux marble pillar wedding decorations.

Josh pulled out his phone. He dialed Morgan as fast as he could. She had better pick up this time. He needed her, just to hear her voice. That would steady him, remind him that everything was going to be all right.

"Morgan! Morgan?"

"This is Tory. She doesn't want to talk to you, but I'm not letting her or you off that easily."

"Tory, thank goodness. Tell her not to do anything." He scrambled upright again, energized by the fact he was finally almost speaking to Morgan.

"What. Did your ex dump you, or something? Because Morgan isn't exactly the type of girl who deserves sloppy seconds. I have a few choice words for you right now, Mr. Hyatt—"

"Stop, Tory. You can save them and say them to me from now until forever. But just tell Morgan I'm coming. I've been trying to get a hold of her for hours." Josh gathered himself, strength coming back into his knees as he said the words that suddenly felt more right than anything he'd said to anyone ever in his life.

"She's not going to see you. And right after *I* see you, I'm probably going to get arrested for assault, so don't even bother coming to Estrella Court." Tory let it slip where they were, and he headed for his car to get there fast. Josh wondered if it was on purpose. Tory had always been on his side—he knew that from what Morgan had mentioned over the past few months. But she did sound mad. *Morgan just had to relent.*

"Please, Tory. I swear I only came down here at

Morgan's insistence, and the whole time I knew it was wrong to even waste the time, and that I love Morgan and only Morgan. Honestly, I haven't even seen Brielle. And —"
He had his hand on his car door, ready to climb in, when a hand on his shoulder stopped him.

"And you're dying to?" Brielle's voice came like liquid lava into his ear. She placed fiery lips on his neck, and her voice flooded him. "Because you've finally gotten rid of that ball and chain bimbo you were shackled to, and you're ready to light your life on fire with the woman you've loved forever?"

"Bimbo! You're with her now, Josh. Get lost." Tory's side of the phone hung up.

"No! Tory! Wait!"

"Oh, Josh. I'm so glad you came. You always look irresistible in red. I can't keep my hands off you. We'd better go in for the reception before I do something that will make us miss when they cut the cake."

Chapter Thirty-Four

Josh's insides hollowed, like they'd been flash burned in the hydrogen fire of the Hindenburg. He stared at the dead call on the phone, knowing Tory would never pick up. He went to open the door of the car again, but Brielle snatched the key fob from his hand and locked it.

"Sorry about that little display. I just had to, you know, defend my territory." She smiled at him, a broad, toothy smile, like the cat who got the canary. Then she mellowed a little and took his arm, leading him onto the sidewalk. "You came to see me, and we have a lot to talk about." She squeezed his arm, and Josh had to grit his teeth at her acting like she'd done nothing wrong.

"Yes, we do."

"Right? Because those letters you wrote made me realize you're as true to me as I am to you. We've been through a lot together, Josh, and I'm ready to make it permanent, just like you are." She came around in front of him and looked right up at him. Her hair was done, and her makeup was perfect. She would've looked radiant if he didn't know better.

"Brielle, there's something important—"

"Do you have any idea how much I've been longing for this moment, Josh? Just you and me together? I've missed you like a hurricane." She threw herself into his arms, assaulting his face with her kisses. "Your letters were the greatest aphrodisiac ever. We shouldn't wait another minute to make it all official between us. It's been years coming to this point. I'm yours. All yours." The words came through breathy breaks in the kisses she covered him with.

He pressed her back. He'd been too familiar with these kisses in the past, and he wasn't about to let them sway him, not with all he knew, and with how he felt about both the women in his life. "Brielle. Please. I'm really sorry. It's not happening." He was here to make things right. "The letters were just to prove something that has passed and gone."

"Nothing has passed. It's all future for us." She backed him up against the door of the Land Rover and draped her arms around his neck. Josh looked into her face and saw an aching desperation in her eyes. "I see now that what you did was for me, and I am ecstatic. We're going to make it, Josh, just like you always promised we would. I know I had my doubts, and I might have been afraid, but you showed me your heart. It's true, just like mine."

Her clear anxiety raised a sense of pity in him, but not guilt. He was doing the right thing, and his resolve had cemented. "No. It isn't happening. I'm sorry." The letters were figments of the past—a dead past. A past she'd killed, and one he'd allowed to die a natural death, even as his own present and future with Morgan had come alive.

"Of course it's happening. We're Josh and Brielle." She sniffled now and brushed at a cluster of tears. "Say it five times fast. It's so right. We've come too far to turn back. You and I both know that. We had a rocky patch, but I'm ready to rebuild and go forward." From her purse she pulled the stack of letters. "These prove you're ready, too." Her voice cracked. She almost sounded crazed. He had to calm her, but still be firm.

"Brielle." He softened his voice. "I'm not."

Tiki torches lining the walkway to the church flickered in the evening breeze. There were dozens of them putting off a glow bright enough to see Brielle's face. Tears drew black mascara trails down her face, and her eyes were rimmed with red. She'd been through a lot, and she wasn't handling it well. Pathos racked him.

She refused to let go, like a bulldog with its quarry. "It won't be easy, I know that, after what we've had to work through, but I like a challenge, and I know you do, too. You rose to every occasion, Josh." Her voice sped up now, with the worry clearly tormenting her. "You threw your career overboard for me. You let your family know I was more important to you than them or their so-called approval. *You chose me.* You even told your controlling, manipulative horse's behind of a father where he could go with his inheritance when I told you it was the right thing to do. You pass. You *pass*, Josh. You're in. I'm totally ready to let you have me. Finally. I know I've been putting you off all these years. And telling you good-bye at the airport when I left for Germany was one of the toughest things I ever did because I didn't know if you'd be true to me while I was gone. But from what you wrote here—" she thumbed through the letters "—you were always loyal to me. Do you know how much I respect that? And do you know how hot that is? You are going to make the best foreign agent. We'll use my contacts, get you the ultimate job. We'll live on the Amalfi Coast together, gathering intel, eating in Italian cafés, getting tan."

Her mention of the Amalfi Coast only served to send an image of the blue waters to his mind, the same blue as Morgan's eyes.

"Brielle." He said her name softly, almost apologetically. "I know."

"Of course you know. Our future is so bright we don't need shades. We need welding helmets!" The hitch in her voice betrayed these confident words as the last ditch effort they were.

"No, Brielle, I know what happened in Germany, and why you're back now. And if you're honest with yourself, you know it's over between us. You never wanted me

376

most." He almost didn't want to let the guillotine drop. But she'd cut the rope of it herself. "But it's more than that. I came here tonight with only one woman in my heart."

"Of course you did." The content of the words wore more confidence than their delivery. "I'm the one girl you've thought of since you became a man. I made you the man you are, Josh. We're going to change the world. Together."

There were so many things wrong with that statement, he couldn't begin to address them, so he let it slide. He thought of his parents, of his family members, of his professors, of George at the water treatment plant who took a chance on him when no one else in all of Starry Point would hire him. They'd contributed to the man he was. He thought of the things about himself he'd had to bury because of Brielle's non-approval of them, particularly his gift for bio-tech engineering and research. The truth was, Josh *was* going to change the world — just not with Brielle.

Brielle had already changed someone's world, destroying a family, if Claire's gossip was to be believed. That wasn't the kind of change any world needed, and Josh hated to say what he had to say next.

"Brie. I'm pretty sure you'd better spend time working on changing your own world before you go stirring up things in the larger global aspect."

The last light of forlorn hope in her eyes faded completely now and her eyebrows fell. At last she must have realized that he knew all the details of her shame. For a second she looked horrified, then terrified, then broken.

"Joshua." She stepped toward him, her chin trembling. "I'm coming to you. You asked me if you should wait for me, and I said yes."

"You didn't. That's not how it happened."

"It is. It's how I remember it. We were standing at the airport, I was on the cusp of a new adventure, but desperately wanting to hold onto you. I had a foot in each world."

"You left, you didn't look back. I moved on, and I know you did, too."

"No, I was distracted. You were distracted. And now we've both seen the light. It's time, Josh. Our time." Her voice quavered on the last word, and it shot a pain through Josh's heart. He had loved her, but so much was different now, and everything Claire had said was killing any last remnant of that love.

"I'm sorry, Brielle."

"How can you say that? How can you just chuck everything that we built over the last several years together?" Tears leaked down her cheeks, wetting the freckles.

"I should ask you the same thing. You chucked it all, while I sacrificed."

"On the surface, Josh, you realize *none* of what you did looks like sacrifice, but I believe you." She stepped forward, holding the papers to her heart for a moment and then extending them to him. "And these letters? I bet if you just look through them, it will rekindle all those feelings. We don't have to look backward. We could look only forward." She had always been laser-focused on what she wanted, and clearly, what she wanted right now was for Josh to relent.

But it was too late, and he could see that she wouldn't surrender until he dealt her a death blow. "According to Claire, you made some real mistakes in Germany. Is that why you came back to me?"

"No!" Brielle pounced at this, nearly dropping the letters, but she clutched them to her chest. "I came back because Germany made me realize I wanted what I already had."

But what she didn't realize was that she didn't have him. "The reason you're holding those letters right now is you told me to never contact you." He watched as her eyes

378

dropped again, making it obvious that her protests on Christmas that she'd never told him not to write had been faked. "Your choice to put my affection for you on a starvation diet is what killed it." Meanwhile, Morgan had been feeding his soul daily, nurturing a love that he now recognized as a real love, not a demanding, forcing kind of love.

"Look at me, Josh. Look at what I'm offering you. It's the *world*, my love." Her eyes pled with him. But it was no use. The fire he'd always felt for her had gone out. "Please, you can't ask me to step aside."

"I'm not asking you to step aside. I'm asking you to look inside. Be the woman we all know you can be. She's a good one. But she's not ready to be anyone's somebody. Not yet."

With that, he made a play for his keys, attempting to grab them from her hand. The keys clattered onto the asphalt of the parking lot. Claire and her groom came out of the church just then, but when they saw the dying embers winking between Josh and Brielle, Claire put out a hand to hold her husband back.

Josh went to his car, while Brielle stood stunned for a moment, just staring at him. But then her face glazed into a mask of hurt, and the tears flowed freely.

"This is completely unfair. It's a bait and switch. You gave me these letters, and I accepted them, I *believed* them. How can you do this to me? I won't let you."

Josh let the car door slam against his leg. It hurt like crazy.

"I didn't do this to you; you did it to yourself. Be honest with yourself for just a moment." He had to be harsh now, and it pained him more than the car door on his shin. But she wouldn't see reason or believe he was cutting her loose. He'd have to be more than clear.

Her mouth hardened into a straight line. "Honesty gets people into trouble, Josh. If there's one thing a study of foreign policy teaches you, it's that." She glanced down at the letters in her hand. "For instance, you have handed me concrete proof that you're living a sham, and in two seconds I could call up your old buddy Paulie Bumgartner or even your eccentric benefactor Sigmund Seagram and tell either of them about the fraud you've been living."

"You wouldn't."

"No, but if I do, I'm sure it will be about seven a.m. tomorrow morning when you'll be getting a knock on the door of the mansion you share with that fraud. The IRS will be coming to take you down to their offices for questioning, and your precious *Morgan* will spend more than an hour in orange this time. She'll have to give up all that slathering lip gloss and you'll never get any conjugal visits, and who will feel sorry for you?"

"Not you, apparently." Every word she said was making the rightness of his choice all the clearer.

"Not me." She sniffled. "Not me." She broke into tears again, full on crying. "I can't—Josh. I can't." She was cracking now. "I'm not going to ever be your wife, am I?"

Pressing his lips together grimly, he shook his head.

The hurt in her face suddenly metamorphosed into something else: anger, with a hint of psychotic break. It almost looked clinical. With a low growl rising up from her chest, Brielle wailed, "Well, if I can't be Mrs. Hyatt, neither can she!" Brielle brandished the stack of letters like a loaded gun. "Claire has Paulie Bumgartner's number. I'm calling it. I'm calling it right now!" She'd crossed over from hurt to mad to vindictive fast—and had come totally unhinged. Josh could understand why—her career and relationships and hopes had all crumbled in the last few weeks, and this must have been the final straw. However, the crazed look in her eye made it seem like she might inflict some self-harm—right after she fired the weapon of the letters at Josh by calling the paparazzi and wrecking his and Morgan's life.

"Don't think I won't, Josh. I've got nothing to lose. There's nothing more dangerous than someone with nothing to lose."

"Brielle—" Josh shook his head, putting up a hand to stop her.

In a flash of black and white, two figures slipped up behind Brielle, snatching from her hand the stack of letters. Claire's husband restrained Brielle, pinning her arms to the disturbed woman's side, while Claire made a break for the tiki torches.

"Here, Josh. Help me burn them. Your sweet wife does not deserve to have a single word of these hit the press."

Josh shot an apologetic look at Brielle, and then hurried over to help Claire, knowing the letters contained damning evidence against himself, but that more than anything they contained waning interest in the woman, showing less and less ardor with each letter. It was why he'd decided to give them to Brielle—so that she could see hard evidence of the evolution of his feelings while Brielle froze him out from abroad. Something inside him also hoped the letters would soften the blow when he broke up with her, so that she could say she should have seen it coming.

Unfortunately, she was a woman pushed beyond her limit, and she'd threatened to take the low road with them, even if it would mean publishing to all the tabloid-reading public her own humiliation as a woman rejected.

Wow, she really had reached rock bottom. Josh winced, and his heart lurched one final time for Brielle, who stood shaking either with rage or sorrow in the torchlight.

Claire's groom took Brielle by the shoulders, and he hustled her away.

"Come on, Brie. It seems like you've either had too much or not enough to drink tonight. Let's get you back to the reception line so you can greet my parents' friends and make excuses for the bride while she cleans up your mess.

It's the least you can do as her maid of honor." The church door swung shut behind them with a thud.

Brielle was gone. Forever.

Claire held another letter to the flame, and glowing ashes of the previous letter floated with an orange rim up to the eaves of the church where the cold air extinguished it. Josh took another leaf, not sad to let them go.

"She's been through a lot. I tried to be as gentle as possible."

"I know you did. She'll bounce back—eventually. I know her better than anyone. Trust me."

Josh nodded as the blackened leaves curled and glowed in his hand.

Claire said, "I've already called Paulie Bumgartner to inform him what I told him last month was in error—that you and Morgan are legitimately married, and that this was all a vindictive ploy from a spurned ex-girlfriend. He said he had pictures of Brielle and you coming out of a police station and he's waiting to use them for just the right moment. I told him I'd buy them from him, but I wanted an exclusive."

Josh looked up in abject shock as Claire put another letter to the flame. "What do you mean, you'd buy them?"

"I told you I had a publishing company, right? It's celebrity news, and Paulie is one of my best suppliers. I know I should have told you this, and it's lower than dirt of me, but there's big money in it." She named a company Josh had heard of. He about choked on his own tongue to find out Claire ran it.

"You don't have to do that for me, Claire. I wouldn't want you to go to so much trouble."

"It's not all for you. Even though I have been completely furious with Brielle for months, she's still my friend of twenty years. I don't want to see Paulie sell them to the highest bidder and wreck her life even further any more than you do."

"I'll pay you back."

"No, you won't. Besides, I'm the one who caused this whole mess anyway. And another besides—your pictures aren't exactly high dollar. As a disowned son of a little-known local millionaire, you're not just small potatoes, you're bits of leftover fries at the bottom of the carton."

"Uh, thanks."

"Ah, I don't mean it that way. I mean, I can get them cheap, and I can bury them. It's the least I can do after what I put you through."

She was right, of course, but Josh didn't need her to rub it in. Besides, the truth was, Paulie Bumgartner had inadvertently done Josh a favor: those pictures he took of Josh and Brielle at the police station had forced him and Morgan to go to Seagram and spill their whole story, which prompted Seagram to give him and Morgan a deadline for making a decision about their relationship—something they might have never done. They might have gone on in the agony of suspense for the remainder of the spring semester, and their feelings for one another might simply have died on the vine. Josh might have let them—and missed out on the best thing he'd ever had anywhere close to his fool grasp.

Bumgartner wasn't the enemy here.

Josh was.

His weak moment of indecision had caused this mess. By not telling Brielle the second she stepped through the door of the Campus House all about Morgan, he was now standing in the cold night at a wedding burning his own anemic love letters, while the real woman he loved was somewhere thinking he had abandoned her.

Even with Brielle's manipulations now under complete control, there were consequences Josh would have to face.

"Thanks for your help, Claire. I can take it from here. Congratulations on your marriage. I hope it's happier than mine would have been to Brielle."

"I love Brielle. She'll grow up. She'll be somebody's wife someday, and she will be fine."

Josh was just glad it wasn't going to be him.

Claire left and went back inside to her guests after this ten minute interruption from her reception. What a champ she was—on the biggest day of her life. She wasn't all bad.

He got in his Land Rover and laid his head on the steering wheel for a second to think about how to patch things up with Morgan. Now more than ever he could see what a jerk he was for not chasing her down this afternoon, and for not shouting what he felt immediately and with full clarity to her and to the whole world.

What could he do to convince her? Did he have any evidence?

There were, of course, the remaining letters that he never dared address to her or give her, but that he'd written to Morgan each time he'd tried (and sometimes failed) to write one to Brielle. When he grabbed the letters for Brielle, he'd thrown the stack for Morgan in the back seat of the Land Rover, not knowing quite what he'd end up doing with them. They were vague, cryptic almost, but he'd told himself that he had to write them to get the complexities of his confused emotions toward her out of his system. They weren't much hope of showing Morgan proof, but they were all he had.

He prayed they'd be enough.

***

"Morgan? Morgan. Please, can I come in? We've got to talk." Josh's voice came through the hollow wooden door like the winter wind coming off the ocean: insistent and unwelcome.

Morgan sat on the sofa, hugging her legs. She still wore the red dress he'd zipped up, but on her legs she had a pair of Tory's old blue sweatpants, and instead of her incredible, empowering spiked red heels she'd planned to wear for her New Year's Eve night on the town with Joshua Hyatt, man of her dreams, she was in a pair of fuzzy slippers with the face of Cookie Monster on the toes.

What she wasn't wearing was mascara. That was gone almost sooner than Josh had left the Campus House to go after the woman he really loved.

Tory came into the living room and handed Morgan a big cup of cocoa. "You want me to get rid of him?"

"Morgan." Josh's voice came through the door again, pleading. "I'm not giving up. I will stand here all night if I have to."

Tory shot Morgan a look. "All night, he said. It's only eight-thirty. He sure wasn't at that wedding reception very long."

"Morgan, please?" His rapping accompanied the calling. "It's cold, but I don't care. I'll wait until they have to remove me with ice-melting salt."

At this Morgan pulled a smile. It released some kind of endorphin in her that gave the first iota of relief from her dark fog of misery of the past two hours since she walked away from Josh. She'd told him she loved him, had lain bare her whole heart to him, and he'd said those dreaded words, *if only*.

It turned her soul into a giant cavern, with the re-echoing words bouncing back and forth inside her ever since.

If only. If only. If only.

She couldn't agree with them more. If only she hadn't talked to him from her truck. If only she'd ignored his little problem at the mailbox. If only she'd never gone to him for help with Nixie. If only she'd never said anything about her own financial aid problems. If only she'd been stronger against the gleam of his teeth. If only she hadn't thought every word he said was charming. If only she hadn't let his kiss pierce her. If only she hadn't let him cure her incurable

Conversation Coma. If only he hadn't become her best friend.

If only.

The tears were welling again, and she needed to blow her nose.

"Morgan, I've got to talk to you." He sounded cold, desperate now. Morgan's heart trailed out to him. He wasn't a monster or anything. She'd just told him she loved him, and he'd said he loved her, too, but that he'd loved someone else first. It was like that awful Jane Austen book *Sense and Sensibility* where Mr. Ferrars can't be with Elinor because he promised that awful, scheming shrew his heart first.

Not that Brielle Dupree was an awful, scheming shrew. She was probably a very nice person or Josh wouldn't have ever fallen in love with her. She had a mean friend in Claire, but that didn't automatically prove she was mean herself. Just because Chip and Heather didn't think much of Brielle didn't mean she was wrong for Josh. *Only Josh knew who was right for Josh.*

Wincing, Morgan sipped the cocoa Tory brought her, but it burned her tongue.

Tory came and sat down beside Morgan, bringing a blanket against the cold. "It's dark. It's New Year's Eve. This apartment complex gets patrolled regularly by the local cops looking for drunk and disorderlies. Josh could get in trouble, and you two would be in the paper again in the police blotter."

"Again?" Morgan's heart jolted. "We were in there?"

"Your little speeding charade on Christmas did make the news. Luckily, almost no one takes the paper anymore."

Morgan sank lower into the couch. She held the side of the hot stoneware mug up against her cheek, letting the warmth seep into her skin. It was probably making her face red.

"The paper also said the county attorney's office was

386

not pressing charges, due to extenuating circumstances."
Tory raised a brow. "You must have told them about the
ex-girlfriend showing up on Christmas morning of your
newlywed Christmas and going all ape and stealing your
husband."

Morgan just nodded. That was pretty much the story
she'd told through sobs. The prosecutor had been a woman,
and she was extremely sympathetic. She'd said she had a
lead foot herself, especially when provoked, and she
couldn't imagine anything more provoking.

The knocking on the door stopped. Now there was a
scraping sound.

"Is he trying to dig through the door like that raccoon
that came in last spring?" Tory went to the window and
lifted the curtain. "Oh, no. He's just got out a pencil and
paper and is writing something."

Morgan's head lifted. "What's he writing?"

"I don't know. It's on a piece of yellow stationery."

Oh, that yellow stationery. How she loathed it, every
sheet of its eye-searing text. "Tell him to go away."

Tory slid the window open, and cold air blew in,
freezing Morgan to the bone. "Josh? Morgan's just not up
for it tonight."

"Can you just give these to her, then?" Josh came over
and handed Tory a stack of yellow stationery through the
slice in the broken window screen of the ever-luxurious
Estrella Court. "I'm going to be in the car. After she reads
them, she'll want to talk to me, I'm pretty sure. They'll
require some explanation. I'll be in the parking lot."

Morgan heard his unmuffled voice, and her traitorous
heart leapt.

Tory slid the window and the curtain shut, and came
and dropped them on Morgan's lap. "I'm going back to
Rich's house. We're ringing in the New Year together, and
then I'll be home."

Tory had someone. And soon, she'd probably have

someone permanently, and Morgan would be all alone. Even Mom had Nixie. Morgan sucked in a shuddering breath. Her future gaped its dark maw before her.

"Go on. Have a good New Year's. Sorry I interrupted it."

Tory closed her eyes then looked at the cracked ceiling. "Don't be a fool, Morgan. No matter what happened today, marrying him is the best thing you've ever done. Don't flush that down the drain."

Cold air blasted through the door as Tory went out. The door shut with an extra slam of the wind. Morgan held the big mug of cocoa with both hands, wishing the warmth could radiate through all of her, thaw the block of ice that was left in the cavity of her chest, where her heart should be.

Slowly, she let her eyes drift toward the pile of letters.

Chapter Thirty-Five

With a fight against both the fear build-up around her icy heart and the logic that kept shouting, *He left you, and he would have loved you IF ONLY*, Morgan let herself lift a sheet of the cream-colored stationery. The top letter began,

Morgan,

Even if I couldn't tell you out loud all these months, my feelings for you have been real, and they've grown like a living thing. I'm no poet and not even much of a writer. The notes may all be short, but they're the realest thing I've ever told you—without telling you. I hope you'll read them—and give me another chance.

Love,

Josher

He'd called himself Josher. Memories of their first day spent together leapt to her mind when she'd called him that. Morgan smiled in spite of herself. Just because he'd hurt her, it didn't mean her love for him was dead. It had grown too slowly, too strong-rooted to be completely killed by his rejection this afternoon.

He'd signed it, *Love, Josher*. The first word of that phrase hit her next. The ice in her chest cavity crackled, like a cube being dropped in a drink. It was still there, but it wasn't as strong as it was before.

I can't look at these. These are the letters he wrote Brielle—aren't they? Morgan's throat was dry. She picked up the cocoa and sipped it, holding the hot cup again for a while as she fought against herself.

Finally, curiosity won. Her hand trembled as she slid

the recently scribbled letter off the top of the stack and saw the date at the top of the first letter: August. But—Josh and she had only just met then, and married. He didn't know her at all.

You're not what I was planning on, but I so scored.

That was all there was to it. No argument—he wasn't a poet. Something else was written and then scribbled out, so it looked like he'd attempted to write more but lost his nerve. He hadn't put her name at the top or signed it. It wasn't exactly everything Morgan would ever wish for in a love letter, but maybe it was better than nothing. In a way, it was shallow but sweet. That pretty well described their beginning together. A few innocent, meaningless kisses to go along with their scheme to help one another get through school against great odds. Shallow, but sweet.

Morgan lifted that page and looked at the next.

Never saw that coming, the way you fit in my arms when your sister made me hold you for the pictures. After that, more was blotted out. What else did he mean to say? Morgan remembered that fit and that it had surprised her. Huh. He'd noticed, too.

The next few were just sentence fragments.

Those blue eyes, I can't —

The ring isn't what I would've chosen, but on you —

We never should have done this, but you're a good sport and —

Where did you learn to— Morgan assumed he was talking about her cooking, from the date at the top. But it could have been about her kiss.

You made Bronco smile. Who can do that?

After that, they started to focus less on her appearance, or little things she could do, but more on what he felt.

I'm with you and I'm free.

You actually cheered when I told you about the breakthrough —

It's a different world than I expected opening up —

None of the letters could ever be considered a love letter. They didn't express love, or praise, exactly. However, they did chronicle some of the things they'd faced—together. They were just a line here and there, incomplete fragments of thought, stillborn ideas almost. Why did he even keep them? Morgan would have crumpled them up and thrown them away. Oh, but she was so glad he hadn't. Each line gave her a tiny glimpse into his mind and the metamorphosis of his attitude toward her. From a pretty-eyed object who could cook and be a good sport when the chips were down, to someone who made him look at the world in a new way—these proved he'd changed how he viewed her.

But why give them to her now—when he'd gone to Brielle as Morgan insisted, gone to his duty with his prior commitment and made good on it? Brielle had come for him, and Josh was bound. Then why bring her these notes? It was either to torture her or to beg for her forgiveness.

Or to ask for her back?

The question burned in her, almost hotter than this cocoa, almost hot enough to melt the ice around her heart, but not quite.

The final letter from the stack lay on the couch next. With trepidation at what it might say, and with disappointment that they ended too soon, Morgan waited with her hand poised over it. At last she slid the paper aside and revealed the note.

My love.

That's how the letter started, and suddenly, Morgan's eyes burned with the salt tears that were her near-constant friend this evening.

I think of so many things we've experienced together, from laughter and kisses to heartache and stress, and I can't think of anyone I'd rather go through them with than you.

Her heart crashed from side to side in her chest, a roaring in her ears sounding as the blood raced through her veins, and that ice went into insta-vapor.

That letter she'd read inadvertently on Christmas hadn't been for Brielle. *It had been for me.* Her breath caught in her throat as she tried to inhale, and she hiccupped instead.

"Josh?" She jumped up from the couch, threw open the door and went tearing out into the cold night in her Cookie Monster slippers and red dress over her sister's sweats. "Josh!" She made a run for the parking lot, to the gravel spot where he had always parked, expecting to see the old Ford Explorer there, and being confused when something else was parked there instead. "Josh!" she called, and the lights of the interior of that interloping car came on, and Morgan realized he was there in the Land Rover. Past and present collided, and in a second, Josh was out of the driver's side and running toward her.

Morgan threw herself into his arms.

"I'm your love?" She echoed the words from the final letter.

"You are." He smothered her mouth with kisses. "You most definitely are."

"But what about—"

"Never mind her. She's not you. You, Morgan Clark Hyatt, are my love. I want you. I choose you. I choose the life that lies ahead of us together."

Morgan kissed him back, ignoring the cold wind off the coast, pressing herself up against Josh as if doing so could make the two of them one entity. "I have waited so long to hear you tell me this. I can't wait to let Mr. Seagram know tomorrow."

"I can. Because there's a lot to do before that." Josh put her in the car.

"I left Tory's door open!" Morgan hopped out of the car and dashed back to Tory's apartment. In a flash, she gathered up the letters from Josh, pressing them to her heart. She slipped off Tory's sweats and slippers, and slid her feet back into her amazing heels. The necklace from Josh still hung at her collarbone, and she ran her fingers across it. A note scrawled to Tory on a post-it on the table said, *You were right. As always. I love you, sister—almost as much as I love Josh Hyatt.*

***

The living room glowed with nothing but the lights of the Christmas tree still lit and the fire, which made a warm spot just the right place for Josh to say what he needed to say to Morgan, as soon as the moment arrived.

Tomorrow they had the big assignment of going to see Seagram, apologizing, taking him a printout of the bank statement showing that they had held his hundred thousand dollars in trust, and hoping he would be understanding and not treat them with the full brunt of how the two of them deserved to be treated. At least of how Josh deserved to be treated; he didn't figure even Seagram in his most volatile eccentricity could enforce dire consequences on Morgan. Seagram, just like that county prosecutor over her ridiculous speeding ticket, was totally charmed by Morgan and taken in by her sweetness. Just like Josh.

Tonight, however, he had other plans.

What was taking her so long? He went to the kitchen island and watched from a barstool while she finished making them a snack. She'd insisted, since neither of them had eaten dinner. She wouldn't take his help even though he offered because she said she loved doing something for him. He wouldn't put the brakes on that. Besides, his nerves had started to ramp up, and he would probably get clumsy or get in the way.

"Cold ham sandwich okay?" she asked over her shoulder, her hair falling down her back in blonde curls and waves, over where he'd helped zip up her red dress earlier.

Anything. Anything was fine. Josh couldn't sit on the barstool anymore. He came around and stood next to her, handing her the bread from the bread box.

She's mine.

Almost.

They sat at the table, where he ate his sandwich in three bites, washing it down with a Coke, aching for her to eat faster. But she paused to look up at him with those eyes blue as the sea.

"Josh, was that last letter really for me?" Morgan's voice had a hint of trepidation as she looked up from her sandwich.

"Yeah." He couldn't believe she was still thinking about them. "But I don't know what possessed me to give them to you, when they're nothing but worthless, one-line mess-ups." They were so embarrassing.

Morgan's eyes dipped and she set her glass of water down. "They're worth something to me. More than you know."

Really? They even made sense? At the moment, Josh had been desperate. She wasn't answering his calls or coming to the door at Tory's place. The letters on the back seat of the truck hit his eye, and in a fit of recklessness he thought of giving them to her. As soon as he'd made that decision, peace had come over him, and for the moment it seemed like the right thing to do. Then, the moment they landed in her hand, he'd been sick, realizing she'd know — one, that he was a sucky writer of love letters; two, that he had been keeping notes all the time they were together, and that he'd been pretty surface-focused for a long time about her; and three, that he was a goner and had been so for a long time, all while keeping her at a distance and being untrue to both Brielle and Morgan at the same time. And himself.

"Really? How much?" He hadn't known how she'd

react to them. However, his instinct, or maybe his prompting guardian angel, had been right. They'd been the thing that brought her running to find him. He glanced toward the kitchen and caught sight of the sink. Memories of the day he'd burned his hand and she'd healed it with the cold running water flashed to his mind. He stood and lifted her to her feet, pulling him close to her. She was amazing.

"Everything." She placed her arms around his neck and twirled the back of his hair with her fingers. It was heaven. She kissed his chin, along his jaw, up to his ear, where she whispered, "Absolutely everything."

Shards of electricity shot through every part of his body. "Come with me." He took her by the hand and led her to the living room. First, he placed her on a chair beside the glow of the tree, which made her hair look like spun gold. "There's something I need to ask you."

Morgan laughed softly, that flirty, feminine laugh that went straight to his heart. She was looking up at him, her blue eyes deep and wide and expectant. At the dip of her collarbone lay the jewel he'd given her on Christmas Day, glinting a dark red against the twinkle of the tree's lights. Perfect.

Josh, heart pounding in his chest and his ears, slipped to one knee and pulled from his shirt pocket the thing he'd been holding onto for just this moment.

"Morgan. Everything we've done has been out of order. Marriage, then love, then dating. And I'm sure I made you suffer to some degree. Like Oscar Wilde said, if we men married the women we deserved, we'd have a very bad time of it. I'll never deserve you, but I'll live the rest of my life trying to. And I'll do everything in my power to make your life blissful." These were big promises, but looking up at the calm strength of her face, its beauty and goodness, for the moment, he actually believed he could deliver on them. He was invincible with the power of this woman's love. "Morgan. Will you be my wife?"

Josh knew Morgan understood all he meant by this. It was more than just a living arrangement, a joining of their legal affairs, or a promise to support or be there for one another. It was a request to be one with him, from now on and forever. The thought of forever with Morgan gave him a vast vision that he'd felt when the two of them stood together looking out over the waves and broad horizon of the Pacific Ocean—a never ending expanse to explore. Together. Come what may.

Morgan took a second and inhaled sharply. She licked her lips and bit them. A smile broke out over her face, and she nodded slightly. "I love you."

"I love you." The words came so easily off his tongue. Why had he waited to say them? With tenderness, he reached for Morgan's hand. "I kept this warm for you." He slid the ring back onto her ring finger. It sparkled against the lights, just like the necklace and earrings did. "But I got this as well. The ruby was only an engagement ring. I thought we needed this." From his pocket he pulled a second ring, a simple gold band, and slid it onto her finger beside the ruby solitaire. "It's more than a promise—it's a vow."

Morgan slid off the chair and onto her knees beside him. He went onto both his knees, and then he kissed her with the tenderness and passion he'd reserved for his someday wife—who happened to be here in his arms, as his present day wife, at this very moment.

"Your wedding band?" Morgan whispered as she ran her hands up and down his arms and down to his fingers.

"I never took it off."

At that, she seemed to return the affection he'd felt for her but with exponential passion. Her breathing sped and she seemed to ache for him like he wanted her as his wedded wife.

"Josh, I never was able to give you your Christmas

gift." Morgan's face reddened, and Josh wondered what she was so worried about. "It's under the tree."

Josh leaned over and dug around beneath the branches until he found a small box tagged with his name on it in Morgan's handwriting. The box looked dented on one side, but he'd ask about that later. For now, Morgan inhaled sharply as he lifted the lid. She was pretty cute when she was nervous.

The moment Josh laid eyes on it, he laughed out loud. "Yeah, baby." He pulled out the elastic, satin, and lace and swung it on his index finger. "That's my signal. It's time I did something else, Morgan."

She pulled back in alarm. "What?"

He laughed, realizing she thought he might be pulling away and leaving her. Not a chance. He stood up and scooped her in his arms just like in the photo of them in the waves that had hung above their unused bed all these months.

"Carry you over the threshold."

Chapter Thirty-Six

"Josh and Morgan, I need the two of you to come for the pictures." Mom clapped her hands at where Morgan and Josh were standing near the six-tiered white cake piled with spring lilacs and sugared purple pansies. It had turned out quite well, if Morgan did say so herself. "We have to get everyone together, and it's like herding cats."

"Don't you mean frogs, Mrs. Clark?" Josh teased, and Mom paused for a second to realize he was doing so. Mom was always caught off guard by his teasing, but she'd get it someday. They had a lot of years ahead of them.

"Oh, Josh. You're being the frog. Now, come on. Quit ogling the cake. Morgan did a masterpiece, I know, but you're not going to get a single bite of the chocolate caramel fudge layer until after the pictures are done. Bride and groom in the center, party of the bride on this side, party of the groom on that."

Mom had transformed the back yard of the Campus House from the most beautifully landscaped back yard in Starry Point into the most beautiful wedding reception venue on the Oregon Coast, in spite of the frog motifs thrown in here and there. It took Morgan's breath away to look at it—and to look around at all these people she had come to know and love, from Rich and Tory, to Siggy and Mom, to Chip and Heather who were representing the Bronco Hyatt contingency today.

"Oh, Mr. Seagram. You're going to go right here, next to the bride." Mom placed Siggy in the line, and then she spoke to him confidentially on a theme she'd echoed a hundred times. "It was just so, so good of you to walk my daughter down the aisle at the church this morning. It would have made her father proud." Mom always got choked up when she talked about Dad, even though he'd done so little for her in life. She must have really, really loved him.

Siggy smiled. "It was my pleasure. I've grown to love Tory like a daughter these past several months. In fact, I probably like her about as much as I love your other daughter. And your poetry."

Mom blushed and bustled to fit absolutely everyone in the wedding party into the line. "Too bad you couldn't be in your wedding dress, too, Morgan, since I originally planned this as a reception for you and Josh. But that belly of yours won't permit it." Mom patted Morgan's growing baby. Why did people think a pregnancy automatically granted them permission to touch a woman's stomach— something they'd never do otherwise? Besides, she was only four months along, barely showing. Then Mom whispered, "It's almost like a honeymoon baby, isn't it? How romantic for you and Josh." Little did her mother know. "Just five months left and you'll be a mother, and you'll have a faint idea of how much I love you."

Then Tory gripped Morgan's hand hard. "I'm so glad you're my maid of honor."

"Matron." Morgan laughed. It sounded old. But no question, she was a married woman, and therefore a matron. "I'm so glad you and Rich could be so happy together, and that you didn't mind putting a rush order on your own wedding."

"Mom made people buy plane tickets. What choice did we have? But I was glad for the rush." She looked up at Rich with a lovelight in her face. Morgan squeezed her sister's hand hard. Tory and Rich's three-month engagement (from Valentine's Day to Memorial Day weekend) smoothed over all the non-refundable plane ticket problems, as well as taking the heat off Josh and Morgan. She'd never wanted a big party, even one as nice as this.

"And isn't it nice that I also like lavender and green?" Tory rolled her eyes.

"Tory, you're the soul of good-heartedness."

"No, you are, Morgan. Thanks for putting up with me all the time when I was pushing you in your relationship with Josh. I should have trusted you to figure it out in your own timing."

"Actually, I needed that push from you. Thanks."

"And I needed that push from you about school. I'm not enrolling at Clarendon like we planned, but I'm going to go to Astoria's community college and get my office management degree so I can be Rich's right hand man. Er, girl."

"Until the little Richards come along. Don't wait too long. I don't want all our baby's cousins to be on the Hyatt side." She glanced over at Heather, who was looking nearly ready to crack open, stomach first.

Tory laughed and patted Morgan's belly. See? Everyone did it.

The photographer snapped a picture just then, which made the bride and her matron of honor laugh as Paulie's shutter snapped in fast succession. He'd gone legit, quit his paparazzi gig, and his first big wedding shots would go on his online portfolio later this afternoon—thanks to Morgan and Josh. They'd recommended him to Tory and Rich for their wedding shoot when he said he needed some beautiful people for his first clients. That, and he'd be the baby's photographer when Baby Hyatt came along in October. Morgan smiled at the thought. A year ago, she could never have dreamed she'd be standing here, between her own husband and her married sister, and expecting her first baby.

When the photos finished, the guests began filing in,

and Morgan and Josh found a wrought iron table beneath the white silk tent. When they thought no one was looking, she tossed a grape for him to catch in his mouth. When he did, expertly, he leaned over and caught her up in a kiss.

"Ah, newlywed bliss." Mr. Seagram strolled up and sat down beside them at their table. "I see it hasn't worn off yet."

"Not yet." Josh shook Siggy's hand. Morgan still couldn't believe he hadn't prosecuted them—but instead had insisted they keep living in the house until Morgan graduated, which she did last week, her growing belly hiding under her long black gown. Moreover, he'd insisted they both come and start working for him at his various enterprises starting next week. Josh was going to be the head of a research lab Seagram owned in Starry Point, and Morgan would be part of his accounting team, at least until the baby was born.

Most shocking of all, he'd refused to accept their return of the scholarship money. Instead, he insisted they use it for a down payment on a house, since they'd be moving out of this beautiful mansion in the next few days to make way for some other young married couple Seagram had decided to bless—and put on Darshelle's interview radar. Josh and Morgan only had one more contractual filming: after the baby was born. Morgan couldn't wait to see how Josh would be as a father. Just thinking of it made her heart warm.

"I'm sure you've considered my request to name the baby Sigmund."

"Only if it's a girl." Josh joked, knowing Siggy was joking, too. "And if she's as pretty as you are."

Seagram just laughed. "I've never been so excited for a baby's birth."

"You're still planning on being his—or her—godparent, I assume," Morgan said, reaching her hand across the table and resting it on Mr. Seagram's. He turned his hand over to press Morgan's.

"Of course."

Morgan really ought to stop apologizing for the trouble she'd caused him, for the stress they created with their deception, but it felt like she could never quite say it often enough. "Siggy, I wish there were a way to thank you enough for all you've done for us, especially after all we put you through on Christmas Day."

Seagram threw back his head and laughed. "Oh, never mind that. I knew all along there was something going on. Or not going on, as the case was. Svetlana told me first thing. She's too loyal to keep a secret like that. I was just waiting it out, hoping the two of you would figure out for yourselves how in love you were. It was obvious to me the electricity snapping between you. You'd get it, I knew."

Morgan's mouth hung open, and she had to force it shut. He'd known all along? Suddenly, a conversation with Svetlana came back to her and made a lot more sense—that the housekeeper apologized for not keeping their secret. Slowly, Morgan nodded. Then her eyes met Josh's. "Yeah, it was always there. How could I resist him? He's the smartest, best man I ever met."

Josh put his arm around Morgan's waist and pulled her to him, yanking her onto his lap where he kissed her, clearly not caring who saw what at this point.

"I think I'll just go over and see what Desiree Clark is doing." Seagram stood. "The mother of the bride could probably use a cold drink right now."

"Mr. Seagram." Morgan tugged herself away from Josh's insistence. "Thank you for making my mom feel special, especially about her new book coming out. It's so important to her, and it's nice she has a kind fan."

"I'm not simply being kind. *Toads in the Sand* is going to shake up the poetry world, guaranteed. It's a worthy sequel to her debut."

Right. Morgan resisted the urge to roll her eyes, and let

him wander off to his fandom. Absently she wondered whether Mom would eventually see how much Siggy was in love with her.

Just then, up walked the last person Morgan expected to ever see. "Mr. Hyatt." She edged her chair back and got to her feet. But Josh was already on his, telling her to stay sitting down.

"Dad. What are you doing here?" Josh's teeth sounded clenched when he talked. Clearly, the tension toward his father hadn't subsided, even now. Morgan wished there was something she could do to facilitate it.

"Please, Mr. Hyatt, sit down."

"Call me Bronco," he said in his gruff bellow as he pulled out the chair and joined them, Josh not looking too pleased. "I'm not going to blister up your day for long. I'm on my way to Astoria and wanted to see my grandbaby. It's looking like a lump right now, isn't it." Bronco craned his neck to eye Morgan's stomach. Morgan shouldn't have expected anything more tactful from him, and she decided to let it slide, but she was glad Josh obviously inherited a bigger dose of his mother's personality than his father's.

"Now you've seen him. Or her. Thanks for dropping by." The resentment palpitated off Josh. "See you at the christening, okay?" Well, at least he was consenting to that. Morgan exhaled a little.

"Now, son. Don't be so hasty. I'm actually here offering an olive branch."

"I don't need your olive branch, or even the whole tree, if that was what you were offering. I'm making my own way, and I'm providing for my family, and we're doing just fine. Sigmund Seagram has put us on our feet, and we're not going to disappoint him."

Morgan swallowed hard. She knew Seagram couldn't be anything but a prickly topic for Bronco. "He's been very kind to us, Bronco. We owe him a lot. Our whole marriage, even."

Bronco harrumphed. "You're reading too much into this, son. As always. I'm just here to apologize for the way things went down, what with that harpy of an old girlfriend you had, but as you can see, things always work out for the best when you accept that father knows best."

"Dad, your olive branch isn't much of a branch. It's not even much of a twig. The last thing I care about is an old girlfriend at this point."

"Well, that's at least a relief. Your wife *far* outshines that one. And every other one, frankly. Good choice." Bronco almost looked at Morgan with some love. It was new, and suddenly, she could see something in him that gave her hope for a real friendship somewhere down the line. She'd play the long game with him. After all, he was to be her children's grandpa.

Bronco leaned in. "I just want you to know that I never meant to hurt you. I only did it all for your good." And then in a halting whisper he said, "I'm sorry, son." And he got up and left.

Josh stared after him for a long moment. Finally, he blinked a few times, pulling his head backward in surprise and shrugged a shoulder. "Never thought I'd hear those three words. Not from him."

Morgan rested a hand on Josh's. Time could heal a lot of things. Maybe even this.

The reception sailed on, and when it wound down and the bride and groom drove off in Rich's highly decorated *Just Married* car, Morgan took a deep breath of the cool spring air. With relief, she grabbed Josh's hand. "I could use a little toes in the sand time." The stress of finals and then the wedding, all while being pregnant, had taken a toll.

"What took you so long?" Josh sped her to the garage and placed her in the passenger side of her car. He liked driving the Mangusa more than the Land Rover, and she'd been a little leery of it ever since she tested the limits of its handling and speed a few months ago. In no time, Josh had them down at the beach, and Morgan kicked off her heels. They walked through the sand, God's pedicure.

They walked a while, Morgan's eyes alert for agates, even though it wasn't the season, her soul content to just be at Josh's side. The foamy edges of the waves lapped against their toes on this unseasonably warm spring day. Morgan inhaled deeply. "I love the smell of the salt."

Josh strolled along beside her, looking good in his white shirt, open at the collar, sleeves rolled up, pant legs rolled up, too. She knew she was probably getting the hem of her lilac-colored dress wet, but she didn't care. Just being with him made everything else okay. How did she get this blessed?

"It's good we get to stay in Starry Point. You can have the beach anytime." Josh stopped and took Morgan by the shoulders. She looked up into his face. He was smiling the smile that got her from the very first. It still penetrated her heart. But then it morphed into the wicked grin and he said, "I know why I like it so much."

"Oh? Why's that? Because it reminds you of family outings at the beach as a kid?"

"No. Because it reminds me of family outings at the beach as an adult. The engagement photos, the shipwreck..."

The word conjured the memory of when she'd made him the picnic and then skipped eating it to show him how she was starting to feel about him last fall. "There was sand on my scalp for a week."

"I've always liked the way you make me feel at the beach."

"Is that right? You liked those family outings?" She felt heat rise to her cheeks as she remembered how she'd had to bury her shyness for him.

Josh pulled her close, kneeling down and kissing the rounding of her belly. He could do that all he wanted.

"Yeah, that shipwreck was when I knew I'd like to be the one to bring your babies to play in the waves."

"Really?" Morgan giggled that dumb laugh again. "It's the first time I knew I'd never want anyone else to."

"Are you ready to let your baby play in the waves right now?" Josh scooped Morgan up, as effortlessly as if she hadn't gained a single pound with the pregnancy, and took her laughing into the waves, where he reenacted the kiss that Tory had captured last fall, and Morgan thanked her lucky stars that her mother ever wrote that book. Sand might not be such a bad thing after all.

Books in the Legally in Love Series

Legally Wedded (A Marriage of Convenience Romance)
Attractive Nuisance (A Courtroom Mystery Romance)
Mergers & Acquisitions (A Lawyer Romance)
Wills & Trust (A Courtroom Mystery Romance)
Asked & Answered (A Lawyer Romance)
Illegally Wedded (A Marriage for Citizenship Romance)

Other Books by Jennifer Griffith

The Lost Art (A Millionaire Makeover Romance)
Immersed (A Millionaire Makeover Romance)
My Fair Aussie (A Millionaire Makeover Romance)
Big in Japan: Accidental Sumo
Chocolate & Conversation: A Jane Austen Culinary Romance

Author's Note

I've got five kids, and the oldest was in the process of applying for college as I began writing Legally Wedded. I had to write this book to channel my nervous energy somewhere productive because the whole process freaked me out entirely — especially the paying-for-college part. Holy smokes! How do people even manage those enormous sums? The scarier part is that four more of my kids are coming up through the ranks. Who is going to pay their tuition? Maybe a bazillion people will fall in love with this book and buy it.

That said, I must point out emphatically that I don't advocate fraudulent behavior. If my kids tried this stunt to pay for college, I'd probably be the first to march them to jail. However, I'm hoping that the consequences Josh and Morgan have to face in this book are enough of a cautionary tale to prove to any reader in a similar financial bind that faking a marriage to get free money is not a good idea.

The fact that things worked out for their happily ever after, both for their finances and for their love? Fiction! Pure and simple! Girls, do not try to snare a husband this way. It won't work. Love ya, but it's true.

Also, there's a three-day waiting period to get married once a marriage license is obtained in Oregon. Josh and Morgan would have probably chickened out in real life.

Meanwhile, I hope you enjoyed this bit of reading fluff. I'm always the first to admit my writing will not change your life. It's just meant to be a little escape with a cup of cocoa on a chilly afternoon curled up on the sofa. We all need a little escape from life's pressures, so escapist fiction is my goal, and I hope *Legally Wedded* was a fun escape for you. If it was, please write a review on Amazon and/or Goodreads! Books need reviews!

Acknowledgements

I need to thank, first of all, Gary, my husband for being my content adviser as well as the person I bounced all my ideas off for this book. He was the first pair of eyes on all the text, and he helped me see how to make things work. Plus, if I know anything about romantic love, it's because of him.

Next, I need to thank some men who have no idea they were involved in the process of this book. Some high school friends of mine made a recording of their *a capella* repertoire, and I found an old tape of it just as I commenced writing this text. Luckily, I also traded my old Suburban in for an even older one—*with* a cassette player. Then, as I did my writing, I had some of these great songs going through my head. Many thanks to Brad Ransom, Tyler Castleton, Greg Chandler, Jason Rich, Tim Rawlings, Troy Hobbs, and whoever else was part of The Music Men for the great tunes that drove this book.

Oregon Coast 101's website provided great websites for the research for the setting, which is a fictional town and college, but which is based on a beautiful area I'd love to really visit not just virtually someday.

My friends on Facebook were a hilarious and excellent resource when it came to thinking up names for the vegan diner. The FB Brain Trust rules! Thank you!

Another huge thank you to my critique partners and editors, Donna Hatch and Cynthia Anaya (C.J. Anaya), for their great feedback and expertise. They are also amazing writers, and I'm sure you'd enjoy their books. Check them out!

To my kind and generous line editors, Brittany Gardner and Paula Bothwell, my undying gratitude. They caught errors and glitches my brain never could see. I also thank my ANWA writers group for their constant support and encouragement. Every book I ever start would likely die on the vine without their reminders that it's okay to keep going.

Finally, a giant thank you to all the readers of my kind of escapist fiction, who like to take an afternoon and just go worry about someone else's romantic problems for a while, get a laugh or two, and melt into a silly book. I can't thank you enough for being so kind as to read this and my other books. You make it fun and fulfilling to have this hobby.

About the Author

Jennifer Griffith lives in Arizona with her husband who is a judge and her muse. They are raising their five *brilliant* children in the desert and feeding them too many Otter Pops. Jennifer writes light, sweet romances she calls Cotton Candy for the Soul. Her Legally in Love Collection stems from the fact she fell in love with a handsome law school student who now serves as a judge—as well as her muse. She also writes the Millionaire Makeover Romances, millionaires and makeovers being some things with which she has less experience.

Jennifer loves old cars, landscape paintings, fresh bread with raspberry jam, and reading. She lived in Japan during college, where she once ate a cricket on a dare. She also traveled through Europe, where she slept a night in a castle on the Rhine. Jennifer worked summers in a cookie factory, and she spent a few years working for the U.S. Congress before becoming a wife, a mom and an author.

If you would like notice of when the next books in the series become available, as well as occasional sales, please sign up for Jennifer's newsletter via authorjennifergriffith.com, or by downloading the exclusive short story "The Cheerleader and the Ghost" from BookFunnel. You can unsubscribe at any time, and your email will never be shared.

Made in the USA
Coppell, TX
01 September 2020

36079668R00233